MALIBU

Elite 8 Studios Book 2

Emmy Sanders

Beta Reading by C.J. Banks, Georgia Johnson, and Lauren

Editing by LesCourt Author Services

Proofreading by Ky

Cover Design by Natasha Snow Designs

ISBN: 9781967130016

Content Warning: This book covers mental health topics of anxiety, panic attacks (on-page occurrence), panic disorder, and PTSD. There is also mention of homophobia and the brief detailing of past "conversion therapy," child abduction, and assault. Please take caution if this subject matter may be triggering for you.

A special thank you to Jen, not only for your invaluable insight into the mental health topics covered in this book, but also for your friendship and support.

Contents

Chapter 1

MAL

"I don't know about this, Jerome."

"Don't know about what?" the man asks, raising one arched eyebrow my way.

I look down at myself. At the neoprene wetsuit hanging dangerously low on my hips. So low, in fact, I can see where my pubes would start if I had any. The material clings uncomfortably to my hips and legs, and I vaguely wonder if I'll even be able to get hard in this thing, it's so tight.

A spritz of cold water jerks me from my ponderings, and I reel back a step, blinking in surprise. The production assistant, not missing a beat, steps forward and peppers a fine mist over my naked torso.

Warn a guy, geez.

"I don't see the problem," Jerome continues on as the assistant walks around me, making my chest and back glisten.

"The sand?" I hedge. I realize I'm grasping at straws, but I don't know what else to say.

Jerome's eyebrow waits, judging me. With his leather jacket, crossed arms, and no-nonsense stare, my boss cuts an imposing figure. Although not a threatening one.

"Where'd you even get it all?" I ask, stretching my toes down into the soft, tawny granules underneath my feet as I stall. I wonder if real beach sand would be this clean.

Jerome waves me off. "We live in a desert."

"I just..."

"Spit it out, Malibu," my boss says.

Jerome runs a tight ship. He may be blunt at times, and he has a propensity for yelling on set, but he's a good manager underneath it all. As executive producer, he's always treated his performers at Elite 8 Studios well, so I know if I tell him I don't want to do this scene, he'll listen. The problem is I don't have a valid excuse to give him. I've done worse things, *weirder* things, than lean into the surfer-dude persona that's become my brand.

Sure, I have long, blonde hair that runs in loose, wavy curls to my shoulders. My eyes are clear blue like the ocean. And my body is lean and toned. But I'm not actually from California, and I've never been surfing a day in my life.

No one here knows that, though.

It wasn't my intention to lie, but on my first day at the studio, someone mentioned how I looked like a Cali boy, and I didn't correct them. That's why Jerome gave me the moniker Malibu, and that's why everyone here thinks I really am this laidback former surfer, when that's so far from the truth it's laughable.

I mean, I've never been to the coast or even stepped foot in a body of water. And with my never-ending anxiety and panic attacks, I don't know the meaning of the word "chill," not when it feels like I'm a rat in a wheel, constantly trying to stay far enough ahead that I don't spin out and land on my ass.

Spoiler alert: I already have.

In the grand scheme of things, maybe it's harmless—letting my coworkers and friends think this Malibu façade has some basis in reality. We're all performers, after all. But there's a difference between acting on set and in real life. And my real life lies keep piling up.

Same as my debts.

I know it shouldn't be a big deal, playing the role of an actual fake surfer. I've certainly had enough practice pretending to be *Malibu*.

Yet, as I stand here on set with my toes dipped in sand, skin warm from the artificial lights overhead, I've never felt like more of a fraud. I've let the ruse go on too long, and now, it feels as if by enacting this scene, I'll be hammering the proverbial nail in my coffin. Sealing my fate. Trapping myself inside this impenetrable box of lies stamped "Malibu." A box I built for myself.

Melodramatic, I know. But I'm starting to feel like I'll never be able to crawl out of the mess I've buried myself in and just be...me.

I want that so badly I ache with it. I'm tired of lying to my friends, even by omission. I'm tired of the constant battle against my anxiety. And I'm tired of feeling like, no matter what I do, I can't escape the demons from my past.

No matter how fast I run around the spinning wheel, I'm stuck in the same loop, over and over again. Another lie. Another bill. Another panic attack.

I want a moment of peace. Of clarity.

If only I knew how to find that.

A long, internal sigh is all the pity I allow myself. What would I even say to Jerome? *Sorry, boss, I don't want to play surfer fuck-boy today because I'm having an existential crisis at twenty-seven.*

There's no reason I can give that would allow me to back out of this scene without arousing suspicion. And that's not something I can afford—quite literally. It's bad enough that my friends found out about my financial troubles when I got evicted from my apartment a few months back. If my boss gets wind of the secrets I'm hiding, I may very well end up out of a job, as well. I can't let that happen.

So instead of whining, I buck the eff up and shrug off my previous comments. "It's fine. Just seems like the surfer thing is a little on the nose."

"It's the number-one request from your fans," Jerome replies dryly.

"To get sand in uncomfortable places?"

"To play yourself for once," he says. "To be *Malibu*."

The sentiment makes me cringe.

"Look, is there something I need to know?" Jerome asks, fixing me with an assessing gaze.

I shake my head quickly.

"Then let's get started. You can fuck on the surfboard if you don't want sand up your ass."

"Considerate," I mumble, turning away and walking toward my partner for the afternoon.

Trevor looks me over as I approach, and I give him a beaming smile.

"Everything all right?" he asks.

Damn it. Perceptive bastard.

You'd never know it by looking at his hulking frame and numerous tats, but Trevor is surprisingly sensitive. His moniker here is Bruiser, and while he does fuck like a freight train, Trevor doesn't have a mean bone in his six-and-a-half-foot tall body.

"Yeah, just fine," I say with a flick of my hand, dismissing his concern.

"Seems like this would be right up your alley," he notes.

I cringe again.

"C'mon," I say, patting Trevor's bulky arm, ready to get this over with. "Let's do this."

Trevor nods, and we take our places in front of the large green screen in Studio 2. Several props are set up around the room, including a beach umbrella and a surfboard wedged in the sand, and when they superimpose the water behind us, it'll look realistic. Although two men fucking in broad daylight in the middle of a beach is a little less believable, but hey, this is porn. Sometimes the fantasy is better than reality.

"Ready?" Jerome yells out from behind the cameras.

I take a quick, sweeping glance of the room. Two cameramen flank Trevor and me. Jerome is standing at the ready, tablet in hand so that he can guide our scene as needed. Marco, the boom operator, towers above me just out of frame, his strong arms holding up the heavy weight of his equipment.

Each and every crew member is staring right at us, waiting to get to work.

And me? I nod my head, resigned to play the role I've perfected.

As I'm washing sand out of every-damn-where, debating all of my life choices, Alex's lilting voice rings throughout the locker room.

"Did you have fun in your natural habitat, boo?"

I roll my eyes. "You know it. I love the sand."

He titters. "I bet."

"What are you doing here?" I ask.

He stops outside of my shower stall, flicking the curtain to announce his presence. "You know I practically live here."

I chuckle, shutting the water off. Steam continues to billow around me as I quickly pat myself dry and squeeze out my hair. Before stepping out of the shower, I wrap the towel around my waist, and when I fling the curtain back, Alex gives me a wide grin.

"Are you stalking me?" I ask, amused as Alex trails after me toward my locker. "Malibu" is stenciled across the front in gold lettering.

"Can't a bestie stalk their other bestie?" he asks, tone suspiciously sweet.

I drop the towel and tug on my briefs before looking over at my friend-slash-coworker, who's still smiling a little too widely. "I'm okay," I tell him with a sigh.

He deflates a little. "I know that, boo."

"Do you? Because you're hovering." I squeeze more water out of my hair before tipping my head down and shaking out the curls. When I fling upright, Alex snickers at me.

"I love when you do that head flip. It's very *Baywatch*," he says.

I shake my head, recognizing his deflection for what it is. "As I'm sure Dixon has already told you during your weekly Malibu meeting—"

"We don't have those."

"—I'm *fine*. I'm back on my feet, and I'm not spiraling anymore."

Alex's face softens, and he squeezes my bare arm. I almost can't stand it, the sympathetic looks. Alex, Dixon, and Niko are the only ones who know a fraction of what I'm dealing with, and even though he claims they don't have meetings about me,

I know they *do* get together to check in, like friendship parole officers.

I can't say I blame them for treating me like glass. Especially Alex and Dixon, since they've known me for years. Dixon started working at Elite 8 Studios—one of the biggest producers of gay porn in the country—before me, and Alex joined shortly after. The two are as different as people can be.

Alex, who goes by the moniker Tink—like the fairy—is short and feisty, with floofy blonde hair and hazel eyes. He's slender and boyish—he looks like a twink; let's call it like it is—and he nearly always has a smile on his face.

Dixon, on the other hand, also known as Dix, is over six feet tall, has dark hair and skin, brown eyes, and sports a perpetual scowl. The man isn't nearly as tough as he comes across, though. I know from experience.

Niko is the newest performer here—and the newest member of the *Malibu Watch*—and he and Dixon are dating. Nicknamed Adonis, he's Greek with curly brown hair, a rather stunning face, and a disposition completely opposite from that of his boyfriend's. The man could charm the pants off just about anyone with his charisma.

They've been good friends to me, looking out for me despite my attempts to slip under the radar as of late, and I appreciate it. I do. I can see that they care. But it makes me feel like crap because I'm still lying to them.

They know I've been having money troubles ever since I started paying for my mom's palliative care. And they saw me hit rock bottom: getting evicted, living off the complimentary snacks from the break room, and making bad decision after bad decision in an attempt to fix my life. They saw me floundering, and they stepped in.

But what I told Alex is true. I'm not on a downward trajectory anymore. I've been staying with Dixon rent-free, even though it scrapes at my dignity to do so. Niko helped me reorganize my finances so I can be smart about how I'm paying off debt. And Alex has been my relentless cheerleader, coaxing me on with peppy zeal.

I'm lucky to have them, I know that. But I'm still keeping secrets—like the truth about my past—and I'm afraid of what will happen if I come clean. Will I lose these men?

I wish I would have been honest about myself from the get-go. If I could go back—if I'd known how much I'd come to appreciate this place and these people four years ago when I first accepted a job in the adult entertainment industry—I'd do things differently. I'd have trusted them from the start because now, I know I could have.

But I can't change my past choices, and the lying and the hiding is slowly eating at me. I'm not sure how much longer I can keep it up. But do I have a choice?

"I know you're fine," Alex reiterates. "But I still care about you, so you're going to have to suck it the hell up and let me mother hen."

"Yes, Mommy," I quip, tugging on my shirt swiftly enough to displace my prior thoughts.

Alex grins. "I'd make a *great* Daddy."

"Really?" I ask, looking over at my five-foot-nothing waif of a friend. "You wouldn't rather be someone's boy?"

Alex narrows his gaze my way and clicks his tongue. "Watch it, Curly. I'm not afraid to spank you."

I laugh, but when I think about it, I wouldn't mind having someone to take care of me. Not as a boy, exactly, but it'd be nice to have fewer worries. Less weight on my shoulders. A knight to swoop in and pull me atop his great, white steed, holding me tight as we outran my troubles. Doesn't everyone wish for that just a little? Someone to sweep us off our feet?

Too bad fairytales are just like porn. Not real.

I tug my pants on. "No punishments today, thank you. Trevor's cock was enough."

Alex hums happily. "That beast is a reward, not a punishment."

"If you say so."

Many of us here treat sex as the job, but Alex enjoys it on a whole other level. And Trevor, who just so happens to have one massive dick, exceeding Elite 8's reputation for eight-inchers, is one of his favorite partners to work with. I, on the other hand, prefer my poundings not to leave me sitting gingerly for the rest of the day.

"Are you heading home?" Alex asks once I close my locker.

"To Dixon's," I correct him.

He does that soft look again. "Still home."

I shrug. "I'll see you in a couple days." I'm not scheduled for another scene until Friday.

Alex hops in close and gives me a tight hug before stepping back. "Take it easy, Mal."

I'm not exactly sure how to take it easy, but nevertheless, I nod before walking off. When I get to Dixon's, it's easy to hear that he and Niko are occupied in his bedroom, so I grab my headphones and plop onto the couch, keeping myself busy by scouring my new requests.

Since Jerome is already giving me as much time on set as he can, I've had to supplement my income in other ways—my side hustles, as I think of them. Genevieve, my second employer, only calls when she has a job for me, and since I haven't heard from her in a week, that leaves me with my webcam for the night.

I don't show my face in my videos; I can't. It's in the contract I signed for Jerome that I'm not allowed to perform for any competing sites while I'm employed at Elite 8 Studios. Technically, I'm in breach of that contract—a fireable offense. But I keep my face out of the frame for my private shows, so it'd be almost impossible for Jerome to catch me.

Dixon is the only person I've told about my arrangement with Genevieve—and he promised he wouldn't tell Jerome—but even he doesn't know about the camming. Yet another way I'm keeping secrets from my friends.

I grimace as I look through one particular request that involves my toes. Twenty bucks isn't enough to have me doing that. But there is an offer for a couple hundred dollars for a private half hour. That's worth it. I message the guy back, setting up a time later to jerk off for him.

I barely hear it when Dixon approaches, but luckily, I'm able to snap my laptop closed before he has a chance to see what's onscreen.

"Hey, Mal," he greets me when I remove my headphones.

"Have fun?" I ask, smirking when Niko comes sauntering down the hall, his long, brown hair a rat's nest around his face.

Niko ticks up his chin, walking past to grab water from the kitchen.

Dixon simply chuckles. "Niki and I are going to order Thai. What do you want?"

"I'll just make something later," I reply, not about to spend money I can't afford and unwilling to ask Dixon for more than he's already given me, which is plenty.

Dixon sees right through me, though, leveling me with a glare. "I'm buying whether or not you want me to, Mal. So you might as well tell me your order, or I'm getting you shrimp and watching you eat every goddamn piece."

I shudder. "God, no. *Fine*. The green curry with tofu."

"And the papaya salad?" he checks.

"Yes, thank you," I mumble.

"Was that so hard?" he asks, joining Niko in the kitchen. The two lean into one another's space, grinning like lovesick fools.

Yes, I think to myself. That *was* hard.

I hate this. Being indebted to other people, feeling like I can't keep myself afloat in life. I'm working three jobs, and it's still barely enough. I don't know what it'll take to turn things around, but I'm desperate to find a solution.

And, maybe one day, I'll be able to find *that*. Someone to look at me the same way Niko stares at Dixon. Someone whose face melts when I'm near, like how Dixon's does every time Niko is around.

But it's not going to happen anytime soon. I can barely take care of myself, let alone a boyfriend.

And no one, not even a knight, deserves to be saddled with a hot mess like me.

Chapter 2

Henrik

"Mr. Larsen—"

"I am done with this conversation, George. This is the second job these contractors have botched. You need to replace them."

"It's not as easy as that," my head of property development whines over our phone call.

I heave a sigh—not bothering to hide my exasperation—and pinch the bridge of my nose, welcoming the blackness for once as my world goes utterly dark. "Make it that easy. We are not working with them again. Find someone else to finish this project."

I hang up before George can attempt to make any more allowances for a company who clearly doesn't have their shit together. I'm not about to accept shoddy construction work when we can afford better.

My blood pressure comes down as I end the call, but my mood, unfortunately, does not improve with the silence that greets my ears. Neither does my impending migraine.

"Gloria," I call, ringing my administrative assistant. "Would you bring me a cup of tea, please?"

Her voice pipes through the intercom. "Of course, Mr. Larsen."

"Thank you," I reply before letting go of the button and sinking back in my chair, eyes shut tight, as if that would make a difference.

Gloria comes in a moment later, her heels clacking against the marble floor. She sets the cup of tea on my desk, the china rattling briefly, and then takes a step back.

"Anything else I can do for you?" she asks.

"No, thank you," I answer, leaning forward and grabbing the cup. I release a sigh, pure relief this time, as the first sip of Pickwick Earl Grey hits my tastebuds. It's almost too hot to drink, but I welcome the scald down the back of my tongue. The bitter, bergamot flavor settles me like few other things have the ability to do.

Gloria's steps fade with her departure, and a moment later, my office door closes with a soft thud. I'm getting ready to dive back into my never-ending workload when my sister's ringtone pierces the air, disturbing my brief stint of silence.

I accept her call, as I always do. "Yes?"

"That's no way to greet your favorite sister," Alma says.

"My only sister," I point out.

"Well yes, but still your favorite. Right?"

"Yes, dove," I reply dutifully.

Alma hums, clearly pleased, and I roll my eyes, grateful she can't see it.

"To what do I owe the pleasure of your sparkling conversation?" I ask dryly.

"Our parents are worried."

I sigh. "This again?"

"This *always*," she says. "You know they can't help it."

"I am not a teenager anymore, Alma."

"No, I know—"

"I'm forty-two goddamn years old. *Forty-two*. They have no say over my life," I grit out a little harsher than I intended. It's not Alma's fault our parents don't know the meaning of the word *independence*.

"I know," she says calmly. "They just love you."

"And I'm fine."

"Then maybe you should return their calls once in a while to let them know," she presses. "Or, even better, come home with me next weekend and show them yourself."

"I'm busy next weekend." I'm pretty sure.

"Then another time," Alma practically pleads.

"You don't have to be our go-between, Alma."

"You don't leave me any other choice," she says. "When they can't get through to you, they start blowing up my phone." She sounds more resigned than put out by that fact, and I hate that she's caught in the middle, but it's not my fault Diederik and Sigrid take the meaning of *helicopter parenting* to new heights.

"You could ignore them," I point out.

She sighs. "You know it's not easy for me to do."

"Tender heart," I say fondly.

"So are you," she says. "Even though you don't let anyone see it."

I huff an incredulous breath. No one, apart from my own sister, would describe me as tender. "I'll call them back," I concede.

"Thank you, brother of mine. I'll let you get back to your tea."

Alma clicks off the call before I can ask her how she knew I was drinking it. I guess I'm nothing if not predictable. With a shake of my head, I return to my considerably cooler cup, able to drink down a healthy swallow before my phone alerts me of the time.

I press the intercom again. "Gloria, I'm going to stay another hour or so. You're welcome to head home."

"Are you sure, Mr. Larsen?"

"Yes. Have a good evening."

"You, too, Mr. Larsen," she replies.

I finish up the acquisition paperwork Benjamin, my personal assistant, forwarded me earlier, and that's as far as I get before the throbbing in my head demands I call it a night. I didn't get as much done today as I'd hoped—when do I ever?—but I need a pain-reliever and a dark room, or this migraine will follow me into the morning.

Admitting defeat, I shut down my computer and call for the car. Less than twenty minutes later, my chauffeur, Charles, is dropping me in front of my building, and after a quick hello to Delroy, my doorman, I take the elevator up to the top floor. The moment the doors swish open, I let out a deep breath, the soft light and calming scents of home providing some measure of comfort.

The respite is short-lived, however, seeing as one step inside the foyer, I trip over an obstacle and nearly go sprawling to the floor. Luckily, or maybe unluckily, I catch myself against the sharp edge of the entryway table before I can fall.

"*Fuck*. Denny!" I call out, rubbing my arm and then reaching for the shoes lying haphazardly on the floor. I place them to the side of the door as Denny comes shuffling around the corner.

"Shit! I'm sorry. I forgot," he says, voice apologetic.

"This is the third time," I say flatly.

"It won't happen again," he claims.

Yeah, well, that's what he said last time and the time before that.

Denny steps close, and his hands slip beneath my suit jacket. He brushes his fingers up the sides of my dress shirt, the touch coy yet suggestive. "Can I make it up to you?"

I try to muster up even an ounce of interest, but it's no use.

"Maybe later," I say, side-stepping him and walking into the kitchen. I fill a glass with water and chug it down before grabbing my migraine medicine from inside the cupboard, shaking out two pills and swallowing them.

"Anything I can do to help?" Denny asks, rubbing lightly over my back. He gives my jacket a little tug, and I let him maneuver me out of the material.

"I just need to lie down."

Denny follows as I make my way into my bedroom. He stays near the doorway while I close the blinds and black out the Vegas lights. It's not until I'm unbuttoning my dress shirt that his footsteps draw near, but he doesn't say anything.

"What is it?" I ask, trying and failing to keep the ire out of my voice. Denny has only been living here for a month, but I'm already sensing this isn't going to work. He's been enthusiastic about the sex, but if I'm not fucking him, Denny is bored. And vocal about it. It's not my job to keep him entertained, something he's well aware of yet chooses to ignore, and no matter how much patience I try to will into my being, I can't seem to call up enough to deal with Denny.

I should end it now, but I keep hoping it'll get better. It won't.

"I just missed you," Denny says, the pout evident in his tone.

I finish undressing, leaving my Tom Ford briefs in place, before I swing back the sheets and climb between the cool layers. Denny sighs, and I finally answer him. "Why don't you go out with some friends?" I suggest.

He harrumphs. I found that cute the first couple times. Now I'm over it.

"Fine," he says, turning on his heel and stomping out the door. I wince as it slams shut, wondering if it's time to call Genevieve again.

It'll have to wait. Right this minute, my head is throbbing, and I can barely string two thoughts together, let alone deal with a long-overdue phone call. Instead, I close my eyes and let myself drift uneasily into sleep.

I don't know how much time has passed when a series of loud bangs wakes me some time later. With a groan, I roll over and tap my phone, discovering it's not even nine o'clock yet. The two hours of sleep I managed did nothing to quell the storm inside my head.

The noise outside the bedroom ramps up in volume: a few hoots, some laughter, music kicking on in the living room.

"Fucking hell. You've got to be kidding me," I groan, swinging my legs over and rolling out of bed. The rhythmic tattoo inside my head is just as loud as the one blaring over the speakers, and for a moment, I have to hold onto the side of my mattress to regain my equilibrium.

Once I'm stable, I tug on a pair of lounge pants. Too damn irritated to bother with a shirt, I head for the door and pull it open angrily. I'm halfway down the hall when my foot catches on one of Denny's shirts, and I curse yet again.

"Denny," I call over the music, stopping at the entrance to the living room.

"Oh, hot *damn*," one of his friends says.

"Your daddy looks pissed," another whispers loudly.

"I am not his daddy," I grit out. "Turn off the goddamn music."

It takes a second, but the sound cuts off, leaving my ears ringing as Denny's indignant "Yes?" pierces the air.

"What the fuck are you doing?" I growl, in no mood to temper my temper.

"You said to hang out with my friends," he replies like a petulant child.

"I also said I had a headache, so what made you think *this* was a smart decision?" I retort, my hand on the wall for balance as my head swims and spots dance across my vision. *Shit*, this is a bad one.

There's a beat of silence, and then Denny says, "Sorry." He doesn't even sound it.

I rub my eyes, heaving a sigh. "I think you should go, Denny."

"What?" he squawks.

"This isn't working. You should go," I reiterate.

"You can't just kick me out!"

"Actually, I can. That was part of the agreement."

He gasps before rushing up and pushing my chest, barely swaying me an inch. "You're such a dick!"

I sigh again, grabbing Denny's wrists and lowering them slowly. "I'll give you an extra ten grand if you make this as painless as possible."

The fight leaves him in an instant, as I knew it would.

"I'll have Benjamin deliver your things," I add.

"Fine," he says, just short of a whine. "You're a cold-hearted bastard, but you have a nice cock. I'll miss it. Not you."

Charming.

He sniffs before breezing past me, sending a waft of cold air over my skin. I wait at the entrance to the living room, the awkward silence stifling as Denny's friends whisper to one another in his absence. Ignoring them, I count down the three minutes it takes for Denny to grab a bag of his things and whiz back past me.

"Come on," he says, prompting his friends to follow him to the elevator. He pauses at the threshold. "Bye, Henrik."

"Goodbye, Denny."

He steps through, and the door whooshes closed, dinging with a finality I can feel in my bones.

I slump immediately.

I'm so tired of this, going round and round with these boys, but the alternative—being alone, truly alone here—is the less appealing choice. It's borderline terrifying, if I'm being honest. Of course, my parents would have a field day with that knowledge. I'm sure they'd insist on me moving home immediately, telling me how they knew it all along and that *it's okay to need a little help, honey.*

I clench my hands into tight fists at the prospect, my fingers aching with the tension.

That's not something I'll ever allow to happen. I've come too far, worked too hard, and if all it takes to keep the empty void at bay is to have some shallow twenty-something occupy my sanctuary, so be it.

Hopefully, the next one lasts longer than a month.

When I get back to my bedroom, I pick up my phone. "Call Genevieve."

It rings three times before the call goes through, and Genevieve's smooth, dulcet voice greets my ear. "I was hoping I wouldn't hear from you quite this soon, love."

"I need another one."

"Tsk, tsk, tsk," she says lightly. "I take it you already sent poor Denny to the curb?"

"He'll be fine," I grumble out, flopping back on my bed and closing my eyes.

"Yes, he will. He's a handsome young man. He'll be snatched right back up. It's you I'm worried about, Henrik."

"I'll be fine, too," I say, softening my tone. It'll do no good to gripe at Genevieve when all she's ever done is try to help me in her own way.

"Will you?"

I sigh. "Yes. I simply need another one."

Genevieve hums. "I'll see what I can do."

"Tomorrow," I tell her.

She makes a noise of surprise. "That's a tall ask, Henrik."

"I'll pay handsomely."

"I'm not worried about that," she says, her nails tapping against the surface of her desk. "Let me see what I can do."

"Thank you," I reply around an exhale.

Genevieve makes a quiet noise of acquiescence before clicking off the call.

I rub my face, my hand catching on the short stubble along my jaw. I need to shave. "Text Benjamin."

My phone chimes, announcing speech-to-text is rolling.

"I need an early cleanup and delivery to Denny's prior address on file *period*. Bring a bottle of my favorite Malbec *period*." I pause. "Thank you *period*."

My phone reads the message back to me, and I send it, knowing Benji won't mind the late-hour text. Feeling utterly drained, I drop the device onto my nightstand and roll onto my stomach, sinking my face into the pillow. The cool fabric does little to abate the jackhammering inside my skull.

Tomorrow. Maybe tomorrow will be better.

Chapter 3
MAL

My phone wakes me up much too early, and it takes me a moment of fumbling confusion to realize it's my ringtone making noise, not my alarm.

"Hello?" I ask groggily.

"Mr. Jones?"

"Uh, yes?" I force myself upright, rubbing my eyes as I try to kick my brain into gear. I'm not exactly a morning person.

"This is Melinda Barnes from Great Oak Home Living. I'm calling about your mother, Dorothy."

Shit.

"Uh, right. Yes. What is it?" I ask, my stomach sinking in dread as it does whenever the subject of my mother comes up.

"I'm calling to inform you that she had a small fall yesterday afternoon. Everything is all right," the woman rushes to assure me, "but she got a few bumps and bruises and was asking about you."

I clamp my eyes shut and hold the phone away from my mouth so Melinda from Great Oak won't be able to hear my labored breathing. I can't get my heart rate to come down, but once I'm fairly confident I can speak without a hitch in my voice, I say, "Thank you for informing me."

"Of course, Mr. Jones. Is there anything you'd like me to pass along? Perhaps a time you might visit?"

"No, thank you," I croak out.

I hang up before the woman hears me either scream or cry, but it doesn't make a difference. As soon as the phone falls from my hand, clattering dully against the floor an inch from my foot, I'm pulled under by the rushing in my ears.

No, no, no.

I slip off the bed, rolling to the ground and cradling my head in my hands as I remind myself I'm *fine*, I'm safe. But it's no use. I'm sucked under the swell—drowning, it feels like—as my lungs clamp shut and my vision goes spotty.

It never gets easier, the panic. The conviction that *this is it*. That there's no way I'll ever be able to resurface and find air this time. That this panic attack will be my last.

But through my disjointed thoughts and the near crushing weight of my anxiety, I remember the tips from my psychiatrist and stop fighting the undertow. I let it pull me down and out to sea, even as my lungs burn, even as my muscles tremble violently, even as every one of my instincts tells me to *flee*. And then I sink my fingers into the carpet to remind myself of what's real.

Carpet. I'm in Dixon's apartment. I squeeze it tight to ground myself.

A faint whirring sound. The fan overhead. I'm in the guest room.

Sharp inhalations cause the scent of detergent to filter through the haze. Clean laundry scent. Not my mother's preferred lavender brand.

The hairband around my wrist. I fumble for it. A quick snap of pain reminds me I'm in the present.

And slowly, slowly, I surface.

It takes herculean effort to get my bone-tired, shaky body off the floor, but after dragging myself into a nice, hot shower, I'm stable enough to handle the teapot. I fill it with probably twice as much water as I need for my cup and then set the pot to boil, taking a moment to practice my muscle relaxation techniques while I wait for it to whistle.

It says in my mother's file to contact me for emergencies only, yet no matter how many times I remind the employees at Great Oak of that fact, they still end up calling at least twice a month. And not once has it been a true emergency. Not that I need a reason for my anxiety to spike, but hearing about that woman sure doesn't help.

I get that it's hard to paint a seemingly ordinary, inoffensive woman with dementia as a villain, but that's exactly what she is to me. I shouldn't have to justify my lack of visits. I shouldn't have to explain myself. I shouldn't have to tell them over and over again that I don't want to talk to the monster that lived outside my closet. I pay for her to be there. To be taken care of. Isn't that enough?

It's more than she deserves.

When the teapot whistles, I grab it off the stove and pour piping-hot water over the bag in my mug. Steam swirls up, bringing with it the scent of lemon, and I inhale deeply as I make myself comfortable in Dixon's living room, attempting to shake off this morning's funk. Dixon himself isn't home from his workout and coffee run, so I have the place to myself.

I'm just finishing up my first cup of tea when my phone rings for the second time today. My pulse skyrockets, but when I see who's calling, I exhale in relief, even as my eyebrows pop up in surprise.

My work schedule—and thus my checking account—was sorely lacking for the next two days, but perhaps my luck is about to change.

"Hello?"

"Hello, Malibu dear. I hope I haven't caught you at a bad time."

"Not at all. What can I do for you?" I ask Genevieve, my boss. My *other* boss. The one only Dixon knows about.

"It's more what I may be able to do for you," she says.

I sit forward. "I'm listening."

"Can you come into the office? This isn't a conversation to have over the phone."

"Sure. I can be there in half an hour?"

"Perfect. I'll see you then," she replies breezily.

When Genevieve hangs up, I finish my tea quickly and head to the guest room to change. You don't show up at Genevieve's in sweatpants.

As I get ready, I can't help but wonder what she has for me. Another boring business dinner? A charity event? A straight-up house call? I'm not picky; I need the cash. But apart from my first interview with Genevieve, she's never called me to her office to give me an assignment. Most of our transactions are handled over the phone. Discretion is the name of the game.

So why now?

I arrive at Genevieve's a half hour later, as I promised, and am buzzed in by her receptionist. The young woman gives me a clipped nod from behind her desk, and when she indicates Genevieve is waiting for me, I walk past the small, plush waiting area to the boss's cracked-open door. I give it a quick knock, and Genevieve calls me in immediately.

"Malibu."

She says my name like I'm her favorite person, a talent I suspect she's perfected over time. Genevieve gets out of her chair, rounding her big mahogany desk to give me a kiss on the cheek. Her floral scent tickles my nose before she leans back and perches against her desk, her pencil skirt pulling tight around her thighs.

"Have a seat," she tells me gently.

I do as she says, waiting patiently as Genevieve taps her fingers on the sleeve of her semi-sheer blouse.

"I have a client for you to meet," she voices at last.

"Okay?"

I'm desperate for the work, but what's with all the cloak-and-dagger?

Genevieve walks back around her desk, sitting in her cushy chair and looking effortlessly at ease as she pulls out a folder, not even glancing at the contents, just tapping it with her long, polished nails. "It's an unusual case. He requires his escort to be live-in."

"Live-in?" I repeat. "As in literally living with him?"

She chuckles lightly. "Yes, and it's a six-month Gold contract."

My eyes widen.

Every job I've worked for Genevieve has been one night only. As an escort service, Genevieve's provides men and women to accompany paying clients to whatever public or private event they may have. Strictly speaking, *company* is all we provide. You won't find any sort of record or payment received for activities of a sexual nature, but that doesn't stop them from happening. Genevieve has a color-coded system, and anyone in the know knows exactly how to order the type of *activity* they're looking for. But it's all hearsay. No one could ever pin it on her because the system is word-of-mouth only.

Gold means full benefits.

But that's not what's shocking to me. It's the *six months* part.

"I don't understand," I admit.

She nods, like it's no more than she expected. "The client would require you to live in his penthouse for the next six months. To be at his beck and call if and when he needs you. To be *fully* available in all the ways that count. To be discreet and to follow his rules."

"Rules," I repeat, starting to feel like a parrot. "Like, BDSM stuff?" I was pretty sure that was code Gray.

Genevieve laughs, her straight, white teeth shining. "No, dear. No BDSM. His house rules. The man is strict."

"Anal," I supply.

Genevieve shrugs. "I suppose. The thing is they're not un-reasonable requests, but that doesn't mean he's the easiest to live with. Or so I've heard. He's gone through most everyone I have to offer him."

"Okay," I say slowly, nodding as I work through that infor-mation. How bad could he be? I know Genevieve wouldn't keep him on as a client if he were truly horrible. "What are the rules?"

"He'll tell you himself. You'll meet with him tonight."

"I'd start tonight?" I ask in surprise.

She nods. "If you're both amenable after your little meet-and-greet, you'll sign on for six months of service effec-tive immediately. Of course, you know he can't legally hold you there. You can, at any time, break the contract if you feel the need to do so. And he can do the same. For any reason."

I nod slowly, trying to internalize everything she's saying. Six months of continuous work would be a huge asset. Doing this job on top of my career in porn could be enough to help dig me out of my financial hole sooner than I'd anticipated. I might not even have to bother with camming for a while.

"Does he live close?" I ask. "I'll need to be able to get to the studio easily enough."

Genevieve's face falls briefly. "About that. There is a bit of a catch." She pauses a moment before revealing, "He has an exclusivity clause."

The shock of her words hits me like a blunt object, and I slump with the force of it. "Genevieve, I can't do that. You *know* how important my other job is."

I can't quit porn. It's the only thing keeping my bills from swallowing me whole.

"Now hear me out, love," Genevieve says, her tone soothing. "It pays $300,000."

I blink several times.

"Plus an extra $200,000 if you can reach the end of the contract."

Good grief.

"Half a million dollars?" I squeak out.

She nods, her expression softening at the look of wonder on my face. "Half a million for half a year, yes. What do you say, dear?"

Half a million dollars would be worth taking a sabbatical from porn for. Hell, even $300,000 would be well worth it.

"I'll meet him," I say.

She nods, crossing her legs. "I had a feeling that'd be the case. Grab his file on your way out, but keep in mind, it's very bare bones. The client prefers for most of his information to remain confidential prior to your meeting."

"Okay," I say with a nod, still stuck on mentally calculating what half a million dollars could do for me.

"He'll have a car pick you up at seven to bring you to his place."

I huff an incredulous laugh, and Genevieve smiles.

"This guy is really loaded, huh?" I ask.

"Quite."

"All right. Guess I'm doing this," I reply, getting out of my seat.

"Malibu," Genevieve calls out before I can make it out of her office. "There's one thing you should know."

"Yeah?" I ask, turning. Whatever it is, I can't imagine it would sway me away from a half-a-million-dollar contract.

Genevieve blinks, face carefully blank as she folds her hands together atop her desk.

"He's blind."

When a black Mercedes pulls up outside the curb of Dixon's apartment building at exactly seven o'clock, I straighten my jacket and head out the door.

Genevieve's receptionist instructed me to dress nice but casual. I wish I had a manual because I stood in front of my closet for a good half hour trying to decide exactly what that meant. In the end, I chose a deep-v shirt in a blue that brings out my eyes and paired it with an open, charcoal-colored blazer. It wasn't until I'd finished getting dressed that it occurred to me the color might not even matter to a man who may or may not be able to see it, depending on the extent of his blindness. Doesn't mean I shouldn't still try to look nice for him, though.

The late winter chill nips at my exposed skin as I step outside and approach the waiting vehicle, but the driver appears in an instant, rounding the Mercedes in a pressed black suit that matches the exterior of his car.

"Mr. Jones?"

"Yeah. That's me," I confirm.

He nods, opening the rear passenger door deftly. "Please, come with me."

I chuckle nervously as I get into the vehicle, feeling a little bit like I'm about to be whisked away to some sort of mafia man's headquarters.

Oh God, I probably should have confirmed that's not actually the case.

The drive is smooth, at least, the car blocking out most traffic noise and the tinted windows reducing the glare from the city lights, and within fifteen minutes, we're pulling into the underground parking garage of one of the swankiest residences I've ever seen up close. The building towers above the rest of Las Vegas, all gleaming blue glass that reflects the colorful lights pinging off every surface of its massive frame. I swallow as we descend into the garage.

Once the driver eases us into a private, marked spot, he comes around and opens my door. "Mr. Larsen lives on the penthouse floor," he explains, ushering me into the building. "Delroy will call the elevator for you."

I nod as if I understand what he's talking about, and then the man is gone, leaving me inside an entryway that screams wealth. The floors are gleaming white marble, not a single shoe scuff in sight, and fresh flowers flank both sides of the doors that lead outside. Gold accents cover almost every surface, including the elevator panel and mailboxes, and a massive chandelier hangs overhead, casting the space in an intimate glow.

Immediately, an immaculately dressed man I assume is Delroy steps forward with a welcoming smile on his face. "You must be Mr. Jones," he says, calling the elevator.

"That's me," I reply, wondering if I'm in some sort of alternate reality where this kind of service is normal. I feel widely out of my comfort zone.

"Mr. Larsen is on the top floor. I'll send you right up."

I simply nod. When the elevator arrives, he holds the door for me, keys in a code, and then presses the button labeled "P."

"Welcome to the building," he says before the doors close on his face, leaving me without a chance to correct him that I haven't yet agreed to stay.

The elevator starts to rise, but my gut stays on the ground floor, and my pulse pounds all the way down into my sky-blue Converse—the one comfort addition I allowed myself when picking out my wardrobe earlier. Blowing out a breath, I collect my hair behind my head, attempting to relieve some of the heat crawling up my neck.

I've never lived like this, surrounded by so much opulence. I have no clue how to act, no clue what to *think*, and I can't help but feel like this Mr. Larsen is going to take one look at me and send me on my way.

Except, *crap*, the man can't see. God, I'm going to make an absolute mess of this. It's not even a question.

When the elevator pings its arrival, I jump, releasing my hair. The doors whoosh open, and after one more brief internal freak-out, I step into the penthouse.

It's absolutely massive; that's the first thing I notice. The place spans the entire top floor of the building, of course, and as if that wasn't enough, it's surrounded by glass-paned, world-class views of a lit-up, glittering Las Vegas. The neon lights are familiar, but up here, it's like I'm in an entirely different world. Perhaps I am.

The ambient light inside is set lower than I'm used to, but it's not unpleasant. And as I take another step into the foyer, the distinct aroma of fall washes over me, like cranberry and crisp leaves. It's nice.

I'm so caught up taking everything in—the sprawling open-concept living space separated in only a few spots by brief segments of wall, the windows in every direction, the high-end furnishings and fancy black-and-white furniture, and the abundance of colorful art on the walls—that I miss one very crucial detail.

"Mr. Jones, I presume."

I nearly jump out of my skin at the sound of the client's voice, and when my head snaps his way, his lips quirk like he knows it.

"Yeah, that's me," I manage, my pulse jackhammering like a rabbit's.

He nods, hands placed casually in his pockets as he strolls toward me with surprising ease. When he stops only two feet in front of me, a small gasp sneaks past my lips.

His file said forty-two, and while his dark brown hair *is* threaded with a few strands of silver, he certainly doesn't look old. He looks damn *fine*.

His broad form is dressed in an impeccable silver button-down and smart black slacks that fit him beautifully. Short stubble graces his strong jaw, framing smooth lips. And his cheeks cut a sharp figure along the sides of his face. But it's his eyes I can't seem to look away from. Vibrant green, like fresh moss. Bright and clever. He's looking toward me, but he's not looking *at* me, and that's the only indication I have that this man truly is, as Genevieve told me, blind.

I don't know what I was expecting when I accepted the chance at this half-mil contract, but it certainly wasn't this man in front of me who, quite honestly, is so handsome I'm having trouble finding my tongue. I'm not sure if my continued elevated heart rate is because I'm nervous or because of *him*.

I want to lean closer and pick out the impressions of color in his vibrant irises. I want to count the specks and variation of tone. Want to trace my fingers over his cheekbones and down his chest so I can find out what lies under that pressed exterior. Want to hear more of the rich, deep tones of his voice. Want...

Christ.

I cut those thoughts off at the head and push them firmly away.

Attraction in my line of work is a dangerous thing. It can easily lead to blurred lines and heartbreak.

Everyone knows you don't fall for the client.

But I'm not that careless. I can't be.

I need this job. My wallet needs it. I'm here for one thing, and it has nothing to do with what lies beyond the allure of my body. As long as I remember that, I'll be fine.

This is a once-in-a-lifetime chance.

I won't mess it up.

Chapter 4

HENRIK

He smells like coconut.

That's the first thought that runs through my head, however inconsequential it is. It's not the least bit off-putting, either. Not like I'd expect it to be. Tropical is not in my usual wheelhouse of preferred scents.

I dismiss the boy's aroma and cant my head toward the white couch in the center of the living room behind me. Time to get down to business.

"Come, have a seat," I tell him, leading the way.

"Yeah, okay," he says, kicking off his shoes and, if I'm not mistaken, placing them on the mat near the door. I keep my appreciation for that bit of cleanliness to myself as I take a seat on the far side of the couch, crossing my ankle over my knee and waiting as the boy approaches. He sinks down gently beside me, his quick, quiet breaths the only detectable indication that he's nervous. I wonder if my reputation has preceded me.

"Your name?" I ask.

He jumps slightly, as if my speaking surprised him. "Genevieve didn't tell you?"

"Hm. I'd prefer hearing it from you."

Normally, I would have vetted my potential companion well before meeting them, but this time around, I was in a rush, not wanting to wait days or even weeks for a suitable match to be arranged. All I got from my brief call with Genevieve a few hours ago was the name Mr. Jones. Everything else worth knowing, I'll find out when Genevieve sends over his file, but for now, I want to hear the details from his own lips.

Not only because it'll give me a chance to learn more about the boy who'll be living in my home for the foreseeable future, but because paper only reveals so much. Voices give a lot more away.

"Mal," he answers after a brief pause. I can't help but wonder why he hesitated.

"Mal," I acknowledge with a nod. "I'm Henrik."

"Okay."

I huff in amusement, not all that surprised by his informal attitude. Most of the boys Genevieve sends are young, the type who'd prefer partying to serious endeavors. "How old are you, Mal?"

"Twenty-seven."

I nod again. Older than Denny, then, which ought to work in my favor. Hopefully, he'll be more mature. Although, at twenty-seven, he's probably too old for me to continue thinking of as a boy.

Honestly, his age doesn't much matter to me, so long as he can follow the rules. I'm particular about my space, but I have good reason to be.

"Have you done this before?" I ask.

"Escorting?" When I nod, he goes on. "Yeah, but never like this."

"You mean because you'll be living here," I fill in.

"For six months, yeah."

I hum. We'll see if he makes it that far. "Does that bother you?"

"I wouldn't be here if it did," he answers, although I get the sense there's something about the arrangement that doesn't suit him. I'll have to pry into that at a later time.

"How much did Genevieve tell you?" I ask.

"Not much," he admits, shifting around a little on his cushion. Yeah, he's nervous. "She said you'd have rules."

"That's true," I allow before standing up. "But first, would you care for a drink? Water? Coffee? Wine?"

"Actually, yeah," he replies quietly. "I think I could use a glass of wine right about now."

Nodding, I round the couch and make my way into the kitchen. The wine Benjamin delivered, a top-notch Malbec, is decanting on the island countertop, and I pour two glasses from the carafe. When I get back to the living room, I hold out Mal's drink. His fingers brush mine lightly as he clasps the stem, his coconut scent wafting close yet again.

Taking a step back, I reclaim my seat a cushion away. The smell dissipates slightly. "Rule one is exclusivity," I say, notching my ankle over my knee and getting right into it. "That's important, and if I find out you're fucking someone else, you're gone."

He coughs a little into his drink. "Right," he says. "That's fair."

"Goes both ways," I point out. "I won't be fucking anyone else."

"Okay," he replies. "Good to know."

"Rule two is cleanliness. No rearranging anything in my penthouse. If you use something, put it back where you found it. And no leaving shoes or clothes or any of your things strewn about."

"Easy enough," he says.

"Is it? Because that seems to be a difficult fucking rule to follow," I all but bark, immediately regretting the harshness of my tone. It's not Mal's fault that Denny and so many of the others seemed incapable of keeping their shit off the floor.

"Promise. I can be clean."

I relax my shoulders—knowing I need to give Mal the benefit of the doubt—and take a sip of my wine to regroup, enjoying the full-bodied, dry flavor as it coats my tongue. It's more than likely Mal will go the way of the rest of these escorts and be out the door within the next month, but perhaps he'll surprise me. I shouldn't draw any conclusions this early in the game.

Besides, I'm tired of having to adjust to new companions. The endless loop is exhausting, a headache in and of itself. I wish one of these boys would stick, at least for a little while.

Maybe this one will.

"The third rule is no bright lights or loud noises," I go on, softening my tone. "It fucks with my head."

There's an extended pause, and then Mal says, "Sorry, I was nodding. *Shit.*"

I quirk my brows but don't call attention to the slip. He seems jumpy enough as is. "Questions so far?"

I wait for the usual inquisition into my blindness following my comment about bright lights and sound. To be frank, I'm surprised it hasn't come up yet. It's usually the first question lobbed my way. But much to my surprise, Mal asks something entirely different.

"Is swearing in the rules? I would've thought so, but you didn't seem to care that I said 'shit,' and you're saying 'fuck' a lot, so now I'm not so sure."

I bite my tongue, amused despite my attempt to remain professional. "You can swear," I answer.

No matter what these boys—or men—seem to think, I am *not* their daddy, and I have no desire to be. That's not what this is about.

"I have headphones," he answers belatedly. "To keep noise down."

I nod, getting back to business. "Good. Rule four then. You sleep in the guest bedroom, no exceptions."

"Okay."

"Rule five—" I stop when Mal makes a gentle noise at the back of his throat. "Question?"

"I, uh...was just wondering if I'll get a list."

My eyebrows pop up. Maybe this one is going to take things seriously.

"Benjamin will draw one up with your contract," I tell him. "But there's only one more."

"Benjamin?"

"My personal assistant." When Mal doesn't say anything else, I go on. "Rule five—and pay attention because breaking this one will land you on the curb just as quickly as breaking exclusivity."

"I'm listening," he says gently.

"No sex if you do not want it." I pause a second so the words can sink in. "I mean that. I know I'm paying you to be here, but consent is important to me. Do not lie to me about wanting sex because you think you *need* to. If you lie, I will know, and you'll be gone. But I will never kick you out for saying no."

There's a lengthy pause, and I take another sip of my wine, letting Mal work through whatever he's thinking.

Yes, part of the purpose of these rules is to make boundaries and set clear expectations. I don't want any of these boys—men—developing feelings or making my life harder than it needs to be. They're here to keep me company, simple as that. Having rules, a guideline, sets the tone for our arrangement.

Simple. Transactional.

But the other part, rule five in particular, is because I need these escorts to know they don't have to *perform* to keep me satisfied. It's not about sex for me. That's just a perk, and *only* if my partner is amenable.

"I don't understand," Mal finally says, the confusion clear in his voice. "Genevieve said this is a Gold contract, which I thought means—"

"Fucking, yes."

"But only if *I* want to?" he asks.

"Only when and if you want to, yes. So if you don't find me attractive, we don't ever need to—"

He barks a laugh, his first unguarded show of emotion since arriving. The sound is light and joyous, and I like it more than I should. "That's not a problem, believe me."

I nod, trying to curtail my smile. I'm more than a little pleased to hear he, at the very least, finds me physically appealing. To be honest, that will make this easier. An arrangement on terms he understands.

Because why else would I hire an escort if not for sex? I'm not willing to share the real reason—that it's simply his presence I require.

Leaning back against the couch, I twirl my wine glass idly between my fingertips. "Then it really is pretty simple. I enjoy sex, but only when my partner is willing. Do you understand?"

"Yes, I understand," he says.

I finish off my wine and set the empty glass on the coffee table before opening my hands. "That's it."

"So, my clothes..."

"Yes?" I ask flatly, my chest souring in disappointment. It's not uncommon for these boys to ask for an extra allowance, but I'd hoped Mal might be different. Better.

Perhaps he's not.

"I mean," he says tentatively, "do you have any rules about how I dress or what I eat or, I don't know...how you want me to groom? I'm already *smooth* for my job—" He cuts off, silence falling for half a second. "Which is more information than you needed to know, even though you'll see for yourself soon enough. Not that—" He makes a sort of strangled sound before clearing his throat. "You know what? I'll just stop talking now."

The tightness in my chest abates, fleeing like shadows from the sun.

How...refreshing.

"No, Mal," I say lightly. "You can dress, eat, or groom in whatever way suits you."

There's another pause. "And I can leave, or like...go out? If I wanted to see my friends or—"

"Mal." I halt him, a chuckle breaking free. "You wouldn't be my prisoner. Just my company."

"Okay." The word whooshes out like a puff of air.

"Okay?" I check.

"Yeah, I'm on board."

I smile, the tension bleeding from my shoulders. "All right, then. I'll have Benjamin bring over a contract for us to sign." He's quiet, and I cock my head. "Is that a problem?"

"No, I guess not. I just don't have any of my things and…"

When he doesn't continue, I say, "I'll have Charles drive you to pick up your belongings tomorrow. For tonight, I'm sure I will have everything you could need."

He curses under his breath. "Yeah. Okay."

"If that's a problem—"

"It's not," he assures me. "I'm just trying to catch up. This isn't how I thought my day was going to go."

"I understand," I tell him. And I do. I'm asking him to pick up and rearrange his life on a dime. To make the decision to come live with me for days, weeks, months, without a chance to think it over at any great length. I need someone—him—here now, and I'm just demanding enough not to regret the sacrifice he's making.

I'm certain the promise of money smooths the way, but maybe I can also set him further at ease.

I drop my leg and shift forward, touching the spot between us. "Would you come here?"

After a quick exhale, Mal does as I ask, sliding close enough that his knee bumps my thigh. The smell of his shampoo, or at least I assume that's where the coconut scent is coming from, blows gently my way, making me think of sandy beaches, endless blue water, and bright, golden sun.

It's been quite some time since I've been to a beach.

"Can I touch you?" I ask.

I have a feeling he nods again, but then he covers with a quick, "Yeah. Yes."

With a hum, I gently place my palm on his knee and slide my hand upwards, skimming up his thigh, his side, and then down his arm until I find the wine glass still clutched in his grasp. He lets it go when I give a tug, and I set it beside mine on the coffee table. The next pass of my hand travels back up his arm, over the soft material of his shirt.

"You'll have everything you need here," I repeat. He shivers slightly as my hand drags over his bare neck. "I am particular about my home, that's true, but I want you to be comfortable during your stay, so please tell me if you are not."

Mal nods, and when I brush my fingers along the short stubble at his jaw, his breath hitches. His lips, as I discover, dragging the pad of my thumb over each arch, are smooth to the touch. And his hair... I'm surprised to learn there's quite a *lot* of it. The strands are thick and wavy, brushing the tops of his shoulders. I twine my fingers through the locks and tug gently, unable to resist.

"What color?" I ask, my curiosity getting the better of me. I might not be able to see anymore, but I can visualize just fine.

"Dark blonde," he answers a little breathily, making me hyper aware of just how close I've leaned into his space.

"Mm." I slowly pull my hands free and glide them from his temples to the sides of his eyes. "And these?"

One word. "Blue."

I nod, trailing my fingers lower, back over his stubble, down his neck, pausing at his collarbones. "May I?"

He nods again, and my lips quirk slightly.

I map his chest, feeling his breath pick up as I work my hands lower, simply trying to get a feel for him. He's not slight, not like several of the boys who've come here, but he's not made of pure muscle, either. A perfect middle ground. His stomach is lean and defined, abdominals tensed slightly under my feather-light touch, and he's warm beneath the soft material of his shirt.

Somewhat reluctantly, I let my hands fall away and sit back. "Thank you."

He makes a curious, quiet sound. "Sure."

Standing up, I pull my phone from my pocket. "I'm going to call Benjamin. Make yourself at home."

"Yeah. I'll, um, tell my roommate I won't be back tonight."

I nod before walking toward the windows, unsurprised when Benji picks up after the first ring.

"Yo."

I refrain from commenting on his unprofessional greeting. "Benjamin, I require your services."

I can practically hear his eye roll. "One of these days, my husband is going to revolt. And then you'll be down an assistant."

"Tell Gary I'll gladly fund his next golfing trip," I reply, running my hand absent-mindedly over the large pane of glass in front of me.

There's a pause, and then Benjamin is back. "Gary says you're excused."

"Thank you, Gary," I reply dutifully.

"What can I do for you, boss?"

"I need a new contract printed up."

"A new boy already?" he asks in surprise. "Moving fast."

"Yes, well, no time like the present," I reply. Benjamin doesn't say anything to that, but he knows me better than most. Maybe even better than my own sister. He knows how unsettling the blankness of my penthouse can be without someone to add dimension to the space.

"I'll be there shortly."

"Good man," I reply, hanging up without further ado.

Mal is still near the couch when I end my call, talking to someone on the phone and saying he'll explain everything tomorrow. I can't help but wonder what he truly thinks of all this. Bunking up with some lonely forty-something. Giving away part of his life to accommodate mine.

He didn't have to agree, of course, but if it's money he's after, that's something I can provide. I may not be able to give myself, but no one seems to want that anyway. And I'm okay with that. This suits me just fine.

Mal will stay here starting tonight. And who knows? Maybe he'll last a little longer than the rest.

Chapter 5

MAL

Henrik—holy cow, is that a sexy name or what?—takes care of some business while I wait for his personal assistant, Benjamin, to show up with the contract that will bind me here for the next six months. I can't believe I'm doing this.

Actually, I can. I'm desperate.

But when I stop to think about it, it's almost unreal. I'm signing on to move in with a guy I don't even know in order to be available for ongoing sex. All in exchange for a crapload of money. It's like a relationship, except not. I'm like...

Oh, my god.

I'm... I'm his sugar baby, aren't I?

I groan as I realize how much shit Alex is going to give me over this. And I have to tell him. Him, Dixon, and Niko.

Plus Jerome because I need to beg my boss to allow me an extended leave and pray I don't get fired. I can't tell him the specifics, of course, but I'll have to give him some reason as to why, out of the blue, I need to take half a year off. And I do intend to make it to the end of the contract for that bonus 200 grand. I don't care how much of an asshole this guy is. I'm sticking.

Although, to be completely honest, he doesn't seem like an asshole at all. Sure, he's a little serious, a little gruff almost, but that's not a bad thing. He seems to like order, he's more formal than most people I interact with, and I have no doubt he wouldn't hesitate to send me on my way if I broke his rules. But none of that makes him an asshole.

I mean, all he's really asking for is an exclusive, respectful sexual arrangement and an awareness of the accommodations he requires for his loss of sight. That's...more than reasonable.

It does make me slightly nervous, however, waiting for the other shoe to drop. Surely there's a reason he goes through so many escorts. Maybe he has a temper I'll discover soon enough. But since I'm free to leave the penthouse any time I want, I don't see that being a problem. If he gets too intense, I can always take a break.

The sound of the elevator arriving draws me away from my musings, and a moment later, a slim man wearing a bright magenta suit comes strolling through the doors. His blonde hair, lighter than mine, is styled neatly atop his head, and his face sports an expression equal parts clever and wry. His eyes find me immediately, and a smile reveals itself as he makes a beeline my way.

"You must be the new one," he says, holding out his palm. "I'm Benji."

"Mal," I say, standing up and shaking his hand.

"Mal," Benji repeats, whistling once. "If I weren't married, I'd be tempted to steal you away from Henrik myself."

"Back off, Benjamin," Henrik calls from down the hall.

Benji grins at me, eyes bouncing wide. "Possessive already," he whispers. "That bodes well."

"Does it?" I ask. I have no frame of reference for what Henrik is typically like. Is possessiveness a good thing? I can't say I have much—or any—experience in the dating department.

Not that that's what this is. We're not dating.

Benji nods several times. "For sure. Usually, he's disinterested at best."

Huh.

Henrik emerges from down the hall, somehow knowing exactly where his assistant is and stopping a few feet in front of him with his hand held out. Benji slaps a folder into his palm and follows his boss over to the large, sandy pine table in the dining room. Henrik pulls out a plush, black chair and sits down, holding out his hand again. Benji passes him a pen, and I wander over, watching as Benji places his finger in front of each signature line for Henrik to use as a guide.

I know I shouldn't stare, but it's fascinating watching Henrik navigate the basics of everyday living without sight. I can't help but wonder if he's always been blind or if it's a recent thing. Not my place to pry, however.

It only takes a couple of minutes for Henrik to sign his portion of the contract, which is more symbolic than anything and certainly not legal, and then he stands up and turns his head toward me.

Not for the first time, the weight of his verdant gaze hits me like a ton of bricks, stealing my breath away.

"Have a seat, Mal. Benjamin will walk you through the contract." Henrik doesn't wait for a reply before retreating to the kitchen to refill his glass of wine.

Once seated, Benji scoots in next to me. "I'll give you a minute to read through everything," he says.

I nod, surprised when Henrik swings back around, sliding a new glass of red wine my way. The contents of the glass swirl once before settling.

"Thank you," I tell him, appreciating the gesture even though I won't drink it. I never allow myself more than one.

Well, almost never. Dixon, I'm sure, has fond memories of me imbibing too much at the club this past fall. Back when I was about to be evicted and was desperate to forget my troubles, at least for one night. Didn't work out quite like I'd planned. All I got for my effort was a two-day hangover and concerned friends. I was grateful Dixon was there to pick me up off the floor. Not so grateful for the hangover.

Truth be told, I'm lucky that's all I got. I don't drink because loss of control escalates my anxiety and leads to more frequent panic attacks. At the encouragement of my psychiatrist, I cut out excess alcohol, caffeine, sugar—anything likely to make me feel off-balance. I have one drink now and again. I enjoy decaffeinated tea because it soothes me. And I try to maintain a healthy diet.

For a while, that routine was working. But then my mom's health declined, and I ran out of cash, meds, therapy appointments, and the stability I'd worked so hard to achieve. And now...well, hopefully things are turning around.

Henrik, my potential savior, despite not knowing that's what he is, nods at my thanks before returning to the kitchen and pulling out a few pans. I watch, transfixed, as he begins cooking what I presume to be his dinner.

Benji chuckles next to me, startling me somewhat. "Pretty sight, isn't he?"

"Goddamn beautiful," I admit.

Benji grins at me knowingly before he glances back at his boss. "He's a good guy," he says slowly. I wait, sensing there's more. "Don't take it personally if he's short with you."

"You know, you're the second person to warn me about that," I say, returning my eyes to the contract in front of me. Genevieve said something similar. "But I'm not worried."

Benji makes a soft noise next to me, waiting while I go through the fine print of my escorting contract. Once I sign half a dozen times, Benji packs the papers back into his folder.

"I'll be back with a copy," he says, walking off down the hall.

I return to watching Henrik, the man I'll be living with, having *sex* with, for the next several months. I can't say that will be a hardship at all. The man is fine; I can easily admit that. I've never had a preference for older men, but the fifteen-year age difference seems insignificant in the grand scheme of things.

What does give me pause is rule number five and the importance placed upon it.

I've had sex for money more times than I can count. Not only with this recent escorting gig, but for my career in porn. Several times a week, I get off for the cameras or with my client for the night—something I'm only able to do because of the extensive health screenings both employers require. I wouldn't dare risk my coworkers' health otherwise. But I've never thought too much about it—having sex for others—and it's never made me uncomfortable. It's basically routine.

Yet I can't help but wonder about Henrik's warning and how much honesty he'll require of me. Is there a reason I *wouldn't* want to have sex with him?

I can't imagine why, but then again, maybe I'm not the best judge of that. Sex, for me, has never been about what I want.

Is Henrik simply asking me not to fake it? Or does he need me to want it as much as he does? Would that even be an issue?

I want him right now; that's for sure. The way he touched me earlier, slowly mapping my features—I can't remember the last time someone touched me like that. Like they had no problem taking their time. Like they wanted to explore.

I want more of that.

Surely, that qualifies as being *willing*, right?

Benji reappears next to me, slipping a stapled copy of the contract under my nose. "Rules are on the last page," he tells me with a wink. Henrik must have mentioned I asked for a list.

"Thanks."

"You know, you look really familiar, but I can't place it," Benji says, scrutinizing me.

Well, crap.

If Henrik hasn't told his assistant I work in porn, I don't want to be the one to spill the beans. It's in my file, of course, since Genevieve insists on transparency when it comes to any and all sex work that her employees are involved in. But Henrik must not have shared that information with Benji—although it's pretty clear the man knows, even if he doesn't quite re-member.

Regardless, I go into damage-control mode. Pretending to think about it, I give him a cheeky once-over. "I don't think we've hooked up. I would've remembered you."

Benji laughs. "Oh, angel. I *definitely* would have remem-bered you."

"Must just have that kind of face, then," I reply, sending him a wink and a smile.

"Oh, yes, we'll get along just fine. Here," Benji says, amuse-ment dancing in his eyes as he hands me his business card. "My number in case you need anything."

"Like what? An escape plan?"

Benji snickers, leaning close. "You're the best one yet," he says, slapping my shoulder lightly.

The implication of his *yet* pings around my chest with a force I don't expect. For some reason, I don't like thinking about who comes after. I don't want to give Henrik a reason to kick me out. At least, not until our time is up.

Benji makes his way toward the exit, calling out, "Bye, boss," before stepping into the elevator.

Henrik nods in his direction as the door closes, and then his head swings my way. "Do you have any allergies?"

"Uh, no. But I don't like seafood," I admit, abandoning my seat and walking closer. Henrik tracks me until I stop on the other side of the stovetop island from where he's preparing food.

"Shame," he says simply.

I glance at what he's cooking, pasta with Italian sausage and red sauce, and even though it looks like quite a lot, I don't want to assume he's feeding me. He made it clear I'll be left to my own devices, and I assume that includes making my meals. Although it'd be nice to have someone to share dinner with on a regular basis.

"What is it?" he asks.

My eyebrow pops up at how adept Henrik seems to be at reading silences. I'm about to dismiss his concern, but then I think about his rules, and I realize the man probably prefers honesty. Well, honesty and cleanliness.

"I wasn't sure if I was invited for dinner or if I should make my own plans," I say.

Henrik's lips purse together, a furrow appearing in his brow as he turns off the burner. "If I'm home in time to cook dinner, I will always cook for two."

Oh, wow. Okay. That's nice.

I nod, belatedly realizing, once again, that he can't see it. "Um, thank you."

He hums, reaching into a cupboard for two plates, which he passes to me over the counter. A moment later, he hands me two sets of silverware, and I take the items to the table, setting one at the head where I assume Henrik will sit. There's a holder with cloth napkins nearby, so I grab two and situate them beside our plates. Henrik brings the pan of pasta over, cradling it in an oven mitt, and he feels out the trivet on the table before setting the hot dish down. I smile a little when he takes his seat and reaches forward, finding his place setting in the correct spot. I guess I did it right.

He dishes up his food with practiced ease before holding the tongs out my way. For a few minutes, we eat in silence.

"This is really good," I finally say. And it is. Better than anything I can cook.

He hums a little around his bite of food. He does that a lot, I notice—hum. As if he prefers the efficiency of the sound over voicing a full response. When Henrik's fork leaves his mouth, a little red speck stays behind on his full bottom lip. I look at that speck, overcome with the urge to lean across the table and lick it off. What would Henrik taste like under the sauce?

Henrik's chewing slows, and I bring my gaze up his face, just in time to catch his raised eyebrow. "Are you staring at me?"

Shit. Busted.

I clear my throat. "Yes."

"Surprised I can feed myself?" he asks, his wry tone a clear sign of displeasure.

Jesus, what?

"No," I rush out, not wanting him to think for even a second that I'm watching him like some sort of freak show. I lean forward and swipe the speck of sauce from his lip, licking it off my finger after. He doesn't even flinch. "My eyes were on your lips."

"My lips," he repeats, frowning.

"There was a little sauce, and, well, you know. You have nice lips." *Smooth, Mal.*

Henrik is silent for a moment, watching me in his own way. He makes a sound, almost like a grunt, and then he twists more pasta onto his fork and continues eating.

I follow his cue, even as my gut squirms. Did I say something wrong?

This situation is so far outside of what I'm used to. I'm not sure how to approach it. With all of my other escorting gigs, there was never any question of where the night would end. They order my services; I provide.

But this is different. I'm here for the long haul, and if I have any hope of lasting, I need to learn Henrik's unspoken rules as well as his direct ones. And so far, I can't quite get a grasp on this man or what he's expecting of me.

"Are you finished?" Henrik asks, breaking our silence.

"Yeah," I reply, grabbing my empty plate.

Henrik nods, and the pair of us clear the table. In the kitchen, he opens the dishwasher, and I set our plates and silverware inside. He washes our wine glasses, and after drying his hands, he goes to walk past me, out of the room.

"Henrik," I say before he can get too far. When he stops, I go on. "Do you need me tonight?"

"No, Mal," he replies, head turned slightly. "Get some sleep."

With that, he walks off down the hall, leaving me to my own devices, more than a little confused.

"I'm sorry, hold up," Alex says, waving his hand in the air. "You're working as an escort?"

Alex's wide, hazel eyes watch me in impressed incredulity as Dixon and Niko silently observe Alex's line of questioning from atop the massive couches we're sitting on in our break room at Elite 8 Studios. Although it won't be *my* break room after I have a word with Jerome.

Niko and Dixon don't seem to have any problem letting Alex perform the role of lead inquisitor, a position he's more than comfortable in. Nosy, but well-intentioned; that's Alex.

"Shh," I remind him, even though a quick glance confirms no one else has wandered into the break room. "Yes, I've been escorting," I say around a sigh. "Don't tell Jerome."

Alex's brows furrow. "I don't think that's against the rules, assuming you're following safe sex practices."

"I am, but I still don't think he'd like it. Just, please? Don't tell him," I plead. I'm already worried enough about losing my job when I tell the boss-man I need time off. I don't want him finding out about the rest. It's a slippery slope that could lead to the truth about camming and my money problems. My past. All of my lies.

"Fine," Alex says softly. "I won't. And you know I'm not judging you, right?"

"Yeah, I know," I tell him. I never expected any of them would. We all have sex for money.

And honestly, it feels kind of good to get this off my chest. One less lie I'm hiding behind.

"Okay, so what's so different about this new client?" Alex asks.

Dixon raises an eyebrow, waiting for me to explain what he already knows from our brief conversation on the phone.

I let out a long sigh. "I'll be living in his penthouse for the next six months, and I can't do porn while I'm there."

Alex blinks a few times. "His penthouse."

"Yes."

"So this guy is loaded. And you'll be his exclusive plaything," Alex correctly observes.

"Yes."

Alex bites his lip before an impish grin takes over his face. "He's your sugar daddy."

I groan, falling back against the couch as both Alex and Niko laugh their heads off. I knew they were going to give me crap about this arrangement. Dixon just stares at me with a shit-eating grin.

"It's okay, boo," Alex says around his laughter, leaning forward to pat my knee. "Everyone needs some sugar."

"Alex," I moan.

He holds up his hands and stands, leading me to believe he's done razzing me. That is, until the chorus of "Pour Some Sugar on Me" comes out of that smartass mouth of his. *Good grief.*

I ignore my friend's back as he walks toward the kitchenette, focusing my attention on Dixon instead. "Thank you for letting me live with you for the past few months," I tell him seriously.

He shakes his head. "No thanks necessary, Mal. And you're welcome back any time."

Hopefully, I'll be able to afford my own place after this, unless Henrik fires me before I can finish out our contract.

"Still. Thank you. And Niko, I'm sorry for being in the way. You'll have your boyfriend all to yourself now."

Niko wraps his arms over Dixon's shoulders from his place on the armrest, but he, too, shakes his head at me. "You were never in the way, Mal. You feel good about this guy?"

"Yeah," I breathe out. "I don't get any creeper vibes, if that's what you're asking."

Alex walks back over, cups in one hand and a bottle of apple juice in the other. "If you do, you let us know right away, Mal. I don't care how much this guy is paying you. Your safety comes first."

I nod, swallowing around the lump in my throat. I have some pretty great friends.

"Now," Alex says, lining up four plastic cups on the coffee table and filling each with a shot of juice. "Here's to Mal and his new, rich beau."

I roll my eyes but pick up a drink.

"To open minds," Dixon says, raising his cup in the air and exchanging a small smile with his boyfriend.

"To open hearts," Niko adds, bouncing his eyebrows at Dixon.

"To open legs," I mutter.

Alex titters at me, and we all say a cheer, downing our symbolic shots.

"Yum, you know what this tastes like?" Alex pops up onto his knees, shimmying in his chair as he starts to sing the lyrics to "Sugar, Sugar."

I bow my head as Niko and Dixon renew their laughter. With a small smile on my face, I pour another round of apple juice.

This may not be how I saw my life progressing—and I'm definitely going to miss working alongside my coworkers at Elite 8 Studios—but maybe this new job will be the turning point that allows me to claw my way to some semblance of control. Being a sugar baby, even though that's never what

Henrik referred to me as, won't be so bad. It's barely even different from what I'm used to.

Who knows? Maybe it'll be just what I need.

"To new opportunities." I down my juice.

Chapter 6

HENRIK

"Mal?" I call out, stepping into my penthouse slowly. Luckily, there are no shoes strewn on the floor, so I'm able to walk inside without incident.

I set my collapsible cane on the table and make my way into the living room, stopping to listen. There's some rustling coming from down the hall, so I follow the sound to the guest bedroom, pausing in the open doorway. Mal is clearly inside, but he must not notice me because he continues unpacking something into the dresser.

"*Jesus*," he gasps after a moment. "I didn't see you."

I'm tempted to make a joke—*funny, I didn't see you either*—but I refrain.

"You're unpacking?" I ask, even though it's obvious.

"Yeah. Charles helped me move everything, which wasn't much," he mutters.

"He said you didn't make it back until an hour ago," I point out, curious why it would've taken him all day if he didn't have much to pack. It wasn't that I was trying to keep tabs on him, but I'd asked Charles to inform me when he was available so

I'd know whether or not to schedule a different driver to bring me home.

Mal hesitates. "Yeah, I swung by to see a few of my friends. And, uh...then I kinda quit my job."

That brings me up short. "You quit your job?"

"Well, yeah..." he says slowly. "Because of the exclusivity thing."

Ah. I didn't realize Mal had been actively seeing another long-term escort client. That explains it. Maybe I should feel bad about monopolizing his company, and yet, I don't.

"Right. Well, I'll be in the kitchen making dinner."

His voice follows as I turn from the door. "Okay."

Mal continues unloading the contents of his bags as I pull ingredients out of the fridge and cupboards, all stocked and labeled meticulously in braille by Benji. The man has been managing the minutiae of my business and personal life seamlessly for the better part of a decade, ever since my vision became a real problem, and I honestly don't know what I'd do without him. I'd get by, I'm sure, but he makes my life multitudes easier by labeling my dry cleaning so I know I'm not stepping outside the house in a ridiculously uncoordinated outfit, doing the same with my groceries and meds so I'm aware of what I'm grabbing, handling correspondences outside of the office, and even transcribing important business files or contracts to speech or braille so that I can read them.

The man earns every one of the exorbitant dollars I pay him.

Even when he's being a pain in my ass.

"Yes, Benjamin?" I say, accepting his incoming call. I pop my Bluetooth earbud in so I can continue cooking.

"I need the deets."

"Details," I correct him. I mean, really, Benjamin isn't much younger than me. Yet he acts like a child.

"I'm rolling my eyes," he informs me. "That boy is a *snack*."

"Don't call him that," I grit out, chopping the bell peppers with a little more force than necessary before throwing them in the pot of sautéing butter and garlic.

I don't know which part I'm more bothered by: Benji calling him a boy when, for whatever reason, I've already dismissed him as such, or the implication of him being a *snack*.

"Was that a growl? Oh my."

"Benjamin," I bark.

"Boss," he barks back without nearly as much bite. "You can cut the stuffy bullshit. We both know you're not all that proper underneath the buttoned-up suit."

I look down the hall before remembering I can't *see* down the hall. Some habits die hard. Mal shuts what sounds like his closet door, so I continue on in a low voice. "I am not talking about this with you."

Benji sighs. "*Fine*. Then I guess I won't tell you what I saw when I stopped by last night."

That gives me pause. "What do you mean?"

"Now you're curious? Well, well, look at that."

"Benjamin, spill it."

The smartass loves riling me up.

"It was his eyes," he says cryptically.

I frown. "What about them? He told me they're blue."

Benji chuckles, the sound throaty and low. "Not that. They were glued to you the entire time I was there. Took the kid three times as long to get through the contract because he kept looking up and watching you."

"I..." My heart beats a little more staccato inside my chest. "So what?"

"So what?" Benji repeats. "The others were always checking out your place like they were calculating your net worth. He *likes* you."

I turn off the burner, straining the gnocchi carefully. "You sound juvenile," I tell him, even though his words have me going back through my interactions with Mal, wondering if what he's saying is true. It'd be an unfortunate complication. I'm not looking for attachments.

"Whatever. Do with that information what you will. *I* think you should plow him into your—"

"*Ben.*"

Benjamin laughs. "Right. I'll see you Monday for that meeting with the charitable board."

Silence greets my ear before I have a chance to hang up on him. "Pain in my ass," I mutter.

"Was that Benji?" Mal asks, just about giving me a heart attack.

"*Fuck.*" I grip the counter as my racing pulse returns to normal.

"Sorry," Mal says, sounding contrite. "Turnabout is fair play?"

I release the counter and snort. Grabbing the colander of gnocchi, I dump it into the vegetables, stirring the whole thing together. "Would you grab the parmesan from the cheese drawer on the left?"

Mal opens the fridge, making a curious sound. "Everything is labeled," he notes.

"Benjamin does that," I explain. "And yes, that was him on the phone."

I bring the dish over to the table while Mal grabs the plates and silverware, giving me a wide berth as he follows me into the adjoining dining room. We're still learning our way around one another, but I can't deny I'm glad he's here.

Although there's still time for him to disappoint me.

As we take our seats, Mal asks, "Does he ever punk you?"

"*Punk* me?" I repeat, eyebrows flying up.

Mal laughs. "Yeah, like mislabel something if you're being a dick. Not that you *are* a dick to him or anything." He mutters something that sounds like, "Christ, Mal, shut it."

I chuckle, shaking my head. "As far as I am aware, he hasn't mislabeled anything on purpose before."

Mal picks up his fork, and then he makes a sound, like a hum, in the back of his throat. "This is really good."

I nod my head once. "Thank you."

"I have a feeling I'm going to get spoiled here," he says, letting out a soft puff of air.

"Are you not accustomed to that?" I ask, starting in on my own food. I would've assumed as an escort, Mal gets treated to luxury often.

Mal finishes chewing, and it sounds as if he's shaking his head. "No, not at all."

"When did you start escorting?" I ask, making a mental note to read the file Genevieve sent over. It may give me some insight into this man and his life.

"About six months ago?" he replies. "Give or take."

I hum. "And the men you've been with...they haven't spoiled you?"

Mal scoffs. "No," he says plainly. "I mean, don't get me wrong. No one's treated me badly. Well, Dixon might argue against that one guy who left a few bruises, but it was *fine*."

My body tenses, and Mal cuts off suddenly, like he realizes he said too much.

"Bruises?" I ask, my voice coming out at a low register.

"It was nothing. I shouldn't have even said anything," he says, his fork scraping against his plate.

I shouldn't care, not really. I barely know Mal. But I can't let it go as easily as he wants me to. "Are we talking a few fingerprints on your hip or a busted cheek?" I ask slowly.

"Neither?"

"Mal," I say sternly.

He sets his fork down. "Just some marks around my neck," he answers quietly.

His *neck?*

"The fuck?" I bark.

"It was *fine*," he says again. "I don't know why everyone keeps making such a big deal out of it. The guy asked, I agreed, he paid me for it, easy as that."

"Why would you let him—" I cut myself off, realizing my fingers are clutched tightly around my silverware and I'm leaning forward like I'm about to jump across the table. Fuck, I need to cool it.

"I needed the cash," he practically whispers, deflating my sails.

The idea of Mal needing money badly enough to let some guy *strangle* him, probably during sex, has me seeing red. Consensual breath-play is one thing, but choking someone so hard they're left with bruises? *Fuck.* No wonder this Dixon, whoever he is, had a problem with it.

I set down my silverware, skirting my hand across the table until I encounter Mal's arm. I squeeze it lightly. "I would never, *ever* hurt you in that way. And I would never expect you to let me."

He swallows loudly.

"Okay?" I press.

"Yeah, okay," he replies softly.

I nod before removing my hand and flexing out the tension under the table. I'm undeniably keyed up, but I keep my mouth shut for the rest of dinner and through clean-up, trying not to let my frustrations bleed out. Mal doesn't need me biting off his head when it's the asshole who hurt him that I want to dismember.

It was for money; that's what Mal said. It's the reason he's here with me now. Because of the hefty payment. Even though it's asinine, for once, I'd almost wished Benjamin was right. Almost.

But that's not why I hire these boys. Men. Whatever.

Shit, now I sound like the one trying to act younger than my years.

I wouldn't be able to trust it, anyhow. That someone I pay to be here could possibly see me as more. People will go to ridiculous lengths for money, as evidenced by what Mal told me himself.

I'll never have more than this, and that's something I accepted long ago. I know how the world views me. First and foremost, they see someone disabled. Weak. Add to that the fact that I'm well-off, and the only people knocking down my door are those who wish to take advantage of me.

I'm not about to give them the chance.

Furthermore, as if that's not enough, I'm not an easy person to like. Or love. I'm admittedly prickly, I'm particular, and I have no inclination to change. Why would I bother? This lifestyle suits me just fine.

I may not have chosen the Retinitis Pigmentosa that slowly stole my vision. I couldn't do anything to change my fate. But I chose not to let it define me back then. And I can choose how to live my life now.

I don't need someone to take care of me. Apart from Benji, that is—I don't want to give him up. But he doesn't wipe my ass or shave my face or hold my hand to cross the street. I'm fully capable of living on my own. I don't need a partner. I don't need my parents breathing down my back like I'm still a scared nineteen-year-old learning about his genetic disorder for the first time. I don't need some great love to feel like I'm a complete human being.

All I need is a little company. Someone I can enjoy. Someone who reminds me that life is still flourishing around me. Someone to give my space shape and dimension. That's all. That's it.

And Mal? At least for now, he's just the person for the job.

Even if he does inspire some rather strong feelings I'd rather not examine too closely.

"Henrik?" Mal asks tentatively, making me realize I'd been standing in the kitchen doing nothing for the past minute or so after we finished cleaning up.

"Hm?"

"I'm going to go take a shower. Do you, uh, need anything?"

"No." I shake my head. I need some time alone to cool down. "I'll be in my study."

I walk away before Mal can reply, positive I'm making the right choice—the *smart* choice—but the soft "Okay" that follows me has me second-guessing my decision to distance myself.

Is that disappointment I hear or am I only imagining it?

Shaking my head, I shut the door tight, determined to regain control of my emotions.

Chapter 7
MAL

I've spent the last hour walking around Henrik's penthouse like a specter. That's what I feel like, anyway. Some sort of being haunting his place while he's at work for the day.

Technically, this is work for me, too, seeing as I'm being paid to simply exist for this man. But it sure doesn't feel like I'm doing anything worth half a million dollars. Especially since we haven't even fucked yet.

What's up with that?

I take in the vibrant modern art in front of me. It's all big, slashing purples and blues, cut in with some green and gold that feels almost ethereal in the otherwise-stormy color palette. The one next to it is similar, but the green and gold take up more space, like the colors leapt from the canvas beside it, growing and expanding.

The picture on the opposite wall is much bigger, about four times the size, sitting above the electric fireplace. It's...breathtaking. I don't have any other words to describe it. There are a myriad of colors coming together in a way that manages to look both chaotic and serene.

It makes me wonder if, at some point, Henrik was able to see these. I could probably look him up on social media or Google his name and find out, but that feels like an invasion of privacy. And in all honesty, it doesn't matter. I'm not here to dig into Henrik's past. I'm here to help him in the present.

For whatever reason, Henrik wants me here. Or, at least, he wants *someone*. I just happen to be the current choice. I don't need to question that. The men who've hired me all have their own reasons, none of which I've judged. And one thing I've learned is that if these men want to talk about themselves, they will. And if they don't? Well, then that usually means they're looking for a good time, not deep conversation.

Henrik is an unusual case, I'll admit to that. Living in his home, we're bound to run into each other with enough frequency that conversation is a given. That doesn't mean that Henrik wants to delve into his own issues, though. So far, he hasn't. I don't think I'm here for that sort of therapy.

But he's also not simply treating me like a plaything. So where does that leave us? I suppose time will tell.

A lot of time in which I have nothing else to do. I mean, seriously, what do I *do* without three jobs to keep me busy? I already temporarily shut down my camming profile. I won't be working any other jobs for Genevieve while I'm stationed here. And Jerome agreed to give me an extended leave of absence after asking me a good half dozen times if I was *really* okay. I appreciate that he cares, but it only made it harder to lie. I ended up telling him it was a personal family situation I had to take care of—which, now that I think about it, was only half a lie since I am paying for my mother's care—but I could tell he was dubious. I don't blame him. I was cagey as all get-out.

So now what? I just exist here and stare at the pretty walls all day? I need to find something to occupy my time.

I know it's only been a couple days, but I thought the fact that I'd be making nearly two grand each dawn to dusk would lessen my anxiety. So far, that's not the case.

Yoga, that'll help.

As I'm grabbing my mat from the guest bedroom, my phone pings.

Alex: Hey Curls. How's your sugga pop?

Alex follows his text with three lollipop emojis, a tongue, and an eggplant.

I shake my head, grinning as I type out my reply.

Me: So far, a gentleman.

Alex: Does that mean you haven't had a single lick?!

Me: You're ridiculous, and no.

Alex: Is the man blind? What's the holdup?

I cringe. Oops, I may have forgotten to mention that part. Not that *that's* why he hasn't cashed in on the benefits of our arrangement. Honestly, I have no clue why that is.

Alex: I have to get on set, but you're going to tell me all about it later. You are coming to Sublime, right? Or do you have to ask your daddy first?

Me: I'll be there.

Alex shoots me a thumbs up.

I don't have to ask, do I? Crap, maybe I should.

Shaking my head, I carry my yoga mat into the living room, rolling it out on an open space between the couch and dining area. I start with a few breathing exercises before I open into child's pose, following that up with downward-facing dog.

Running through the routine is second nature now, and it often helps me deal with excess stress. That's why I got into yoga in the first place: as a way to center myself when my thoughts were running every which way. I barely have to think about it now. Plank is next, and then four-limbed staff pose. Cobra. Tree. I focus on my body. On my breathing and the gentle stretch of my muscles. On keeping my balance. Everything else falls away, at least for a little while.

I'm in triangle pose when the elevator opens across the penthouse, breaking my concentration. Henrik steps through the door, setting his cane on the table in the entryway before toeing off his shoes and placing them on the mat. When he stands upright, he pauses, head swiveling my way. I'm barely making any noise, and yet somehow, he senses me here.

"I'm behind the couch," I tell him.

He walks toward me slowly, head canted, those brilliant green eyes of his inquisitive. "What are you doing on the floor?"

I sit back down, moving into a twist. "Yoga."

His head tilts even further as he stands in front of me, his hands propped casually on his hips.

"You're home early," I note, realizing it's not even four o'clock.

"Mm. Do you do this often?" he asks, ignoring my comment about the time.

I shrug. "Few times a week, usually."

He moves closer as I shift into bridge pose, and I watch in amusement as he toes the edge of the yoga mat and then squats down next to me. He reaches out along the mat like he's searching for me before halting his movement. "Will it mess you up if I touch you?"

My God, please.

I clear my throat. "No."

He inches his fingers closer, and when he encounters air, since my ass and back are raised off the mat for bridge, I bite my lip. His brow furrows, and I chuckle.

"Up."

Henrik looks confused, but he lifts his hand slowly, until finally he hits skin. Or, well, yoga pants. He stops still, that little furrow in his brow making a reappearance as his fingers brush over my ass cheek. My body responds instantly, heart rate and *other* things kicking right up. But it's the twin spots of color blooming on Henrik's cheeks when he realizes exactly where his hand is that hold my attention. It's the first time I've seen him have a reaction to me, and my flapping heart tries to take flight right out of my chest.

"Is this your ass?" he asks, deadpan.

"Yes," I say, a grin stretching across my face.

He raises a brow before dragging his fingers around to my hip, his touch no longer tentative. My breath catches as he traces the angle of my body, trailing those digits up the side of my leg to my raised knees and then back down, all the way to where my shoulder meets the floor. My hamstrings start quivering as he returns to his point of origin. I try to breathe evenly, but it's no use.

"You're shaking," he notes.

"Yeah. Uh, I've been holding this pose for a while." Longer than I usually would, but I didn't want to move a muscle if it meant Henrik's fingers might leave my body. I want him to keep touching me. To explore like he did that first night I was here. I want to see what else those fingers can do, where they might travel. I want him to light me up. And, maybe most of all, I want to find out exactly what would make that rigid professionalism of his scatter to pieces.

I simply *want*.

And based on the bulge I can see straining the front of Henrik's slacks, it seems he wants me, too.

So when is he going to take me?

He hums, fingers moving gently over my hip bone. "What's next?"

"Corpse," I mutter, watching those digits wander.

"Don't let me stop you."

With an exhale, I drop down to the floor, extending my legs out in front of me and lying completely flat. Henrik's hand never leaves my body; his fingers follow me down, a constant pressure on my hip. And even though I'm supposed to be relaxing in this final pose, my body tenses under the wake of those wandering digits.

Henrik runs his palm down my leg, from thigh to ankle and then back up again. He's so close to the erection straining the front of my yoga pants, and as he passes up over my hip, I can tell he's noticed it. He stalls, a little smirk on his face as he brushes up the V of my groin, the fabric stretched taut to accommodate my swelling dick. I curse lightly as he passes by, skimming up my stomach.

I want him to touch me, *really* touch me, but this isn't my show, is it? Can I even ask for that?

Henrik makes a sound low in his throat, a hum but rougher, as the pads of his fingers reach the top of my tank top. He traces along my exposed collarbones lightly, which are rising and falling with my rapid inhalations. I can't seem to slow down my breathing, but this is a sort of breathlessness I welcome.

He trails lower again before, suddenly, his touch is gone. *No, no, no.*

I exhale harshly and groan. "I didn't take you for a tease."

The words slip out mindlessly, but before I can take them back, Henrik wings up an eyebrow and stands.

"Is that what I am?" he asks, turning to walk away before I can protest. "I have a call to make. I'll be in my study."

Shit.

"Henrik."

He stops, turning back to look toward me.

I can't believe I'm going to ask this, but I'd rather feel ridiculous than break a rule. "Can I, uh, go out tonight?"

He looks at me incredulously. "Did you finish your homework?"

It takes my brain a second to catch up, but then I'm breaking into a grin. "Didn't realize you're such a smartass, too," I quip.

He crosses his arms, facing me fully, and he would cut an imposing figure if it weren't for the quirk at the side of his mouth. "I'm not your dad, Mal."

"I know."

"I'm not your daddy either," he adds, staring in my direction like he wants to make sure I get it.

"No, you're just a guy paying me for sex. Which we haven't had," I point out. Honestly, I don't know why I'm pushing it. I get paid one way or another, and yet I'm positive sex with Henrik wouldn't feel like a chore. Quite the opposite, in fact.

He watches me for a moment before skirting the topic. "What are you doing tonight?"

I release my breath. "Going out with friends. We frequent a club called Sublime on Friday nights."

His jaw clenches, real strain lining his features this time, same as it did last night at dinner, and the sudden shift in his demeanor takes me by surprise. "Be safe," he says tersely before turning on his heel. "And don't forget to put the damn yoga mat away when you're done."

I watch Henrik's retreating form, my mouth open.

What the fuck was that? What did I say that had him switching from fun and almost flirty to...angry dad mode?

Jesus, I really need to figure this guy out.

"Mali-boo!"

I roll my eyes, barely catching Alex as he sprawls onto my lap. We're in the VIP lounge at Sublime, where a hodgepodge of Elite 8 cast and crew hang out at the end of each week. There's plenty of us here tonight, like usual, amidst the dim lights and blaring music of the club. Servers in booty shorts and not much else walk around the crowd, both up here on the balcony and down below, and men, women, and enbies flood the dancefloor, moving their bodies to the endless beat.

I *was* enjoying a couch all to myself while I nursed a Sprite. Now, I'm enjoying a lapful of my friend.

"You're looking extra sparkly tonight, babe," I note.

Alex beams. "Sequins." He plucks at the hem of his cropped shirt before shifting off my lap and stretching like a cat.

One of the new servers does a double-take, bumping into the table in front of him as Alex arches and reveals the smooth expanse of his slim stomach. I snort as the man rights himself, taking one last look before heading off with his drink tray.

"You're trouble," I mutter.

"No, *you're* in trouble, Curls. You still haven't told me what's going on with your mystery beau." Alex sits upright and crosses his legs in front of himself to stare me down.

I shrug because I honestly don't know *what's* going on there.

"He's probably just being nice," I muse. "Taking it slow."

"What, like breaking you in? You're not a horse," Alex replies, wrinkling his nose.

"Not everyone needs to have sex every day, you know," I point out.

Alex shudders. "Perish the thought."

I roll my eyes. Alex is a serious horndog.

"At least give me *something*," he whines.

"He's...beyond," I say around a sigh.

"Really?" Alex asks, perking up. "Isn't he like, sixty or something?"

I laugh, shaking my head. "No. Forty-two and stupid gorgeous. Broad. Fit, but not like gym-muscly, you know?"

"Not like Dixon," Alex says.

"Right," I agree. Nothing against Dixon. Henrik is just... "He's kinda distinguished, but in a sexy way?"

Alex nods, pursing his lips. "All right, I see what you're saying. Sexy older dude, James Bond suit-type, still has game, wants you to call him Daddy."

"No," I say around a laugh. "He really doesn't. He's made that clear."

Alex pouts. "Fine. Boring, but fine. Well," he says, clasping my knee and squeezing, "if sugar beau isn't taking the bait yet, you know what you need to do, right?"

"Oh god," I groan.

Alex nods. "You need to amp it up a notch. A little 'oops, I dropped my towel' action. Or maybe the classic 'look how sheer this shirt is—you can see my nipples.'"

"That's a classic?" I ask, shaking my head to hide my grin. I don't bother to point out that neither of those tactics would be effective on Henrik.

"Totally. Works like a charm."

"Where do you get these things? You know what, no, never mind. Don't tell me. It'll ruin the mystery. And don't worry about it, Alex. I'm sure he'll cash in on the benefits of our arrangement at some point." I sure hope so.

Alex's ideas may not work, but it does have me wondering what I could do to encourage Henrik to take advantage of my services. I'm not used to men being so polite and distant.

"Fine," Alex says, interrupting my thoughts. "You better promise to dish when it happens, though."

"You're weirdly invested in me getting boned, Alex."

He just grins at me. "It's a passion of mine."

I roll my eyes for the millionth time and stand up, holding out my hand. "Come on, small fry. Let's dance."

Alex jumps up, taking my hand and practically dragging me toward the dance floor. We join the throng of bodies on the main level, getting lost under the strobing lights and pulsing beat of the club. And for at least a little while, I tell all those anxious thoughts whirling through my head to eff right off.

For the first time in a long time, I don't have to worry about money. And it didn't hit me earlier, when I was in Henrik's house perusing his art and wondering what I was going to do with my days, but it's hitting me now.

I don't *have* to do anything.

I don't have to hustle. I don't have to race just to break even. I don't have to worry about where I'm staying or what I'm eating.

For once, I can take a break.

I can simply *be*.

And isn't that a relief?

Chapter 8

Henrik

I'm wearing a hole through the hardwood floors when the elevator whooshes open. *Finally.*

I know I'm being irrational, but Mal has been gone for hours. And ever since I listened to him leave from the confines of my cracked bedroom door like a creepy fucking stalker, I've been on edge. I wanted him back here, and that's not like me. I've never had a problem with my companions coming and going as they please.

Maybe I'm still reeling after Mal's confession about the bruises around his neck. Maybe I'm worried he'll be taken advantage of again.

Maybe whatever instincts I've been warring with that have been pulling me toward this man have finally stretched taut.

Tight enough to snap.

Mal comes padding softly into the penthouse, stopping, I presume, when he catches sight of me at the opening to the hallway.

"Henrik?"

I stride forward, halting a few paces shy of where Mal should be because I don't want to actually bowl into the man. He seems to read my intent, however, and closes the distance between us. As soon as he touches my arm, I inhale a sharp breath.

That was a mistake.

Trailing my hand up Mal's arm to orient myself, I grip the back of his neck and tug him in close. Mal gasps as I lean forward and run my nose along the side of his head. He smells like sweat and a dizzying array of different colognes, barely a trace of his coconut scent remaining.

My spine stiffens as I retract my head.

"Why do you smell like other men?" I ask tersely.

"I was dancing," Mal says tentatively, his breath fanning along my collarbone in short bursts.

"Just dancing?" I ask, the words slipping out past gritted teeth. *Fuck*, I need to get control of myself.

Mal gasps again. "I..."

When Mal doesn't go on, I run my hands up into his hair, curling my fingers around the soft strands. I lean in close, lips above his ear. "Tell me, Mal. Did you break my rules?"

His chest heaves against me, but Mal doesn't move an inch. "No. Of course not," he says breathlessly.

I hum at that, this ridiculous territorial side of me mollified by his admission. It's not like I should care about Mal going out to a club. I never cared about Denny hanging out with his friends. But the fact that Mal smells like a hundred different guys, not his usual coconut scent, and not *me*, has me grinding my molars together so hard it's making my jaw ache.

"I didn't do anything except dance," he adds, seeming to take my silence as disbelief. "I wouldn't. I don't want them anyways."

"And what do you want?" I ask, nuzzling into his soft hair as my hand travels down Mal's body, landing on his hip. I can't decide if I'm trying to pull him closer or getting ready to push him away. I feel way too unhinged right now. I wouldn't hurt Mal; I was deadly serious about that. But the way I'm feeling right this instant is so far out of my controlled little box I can't even find the walls.

"Isn't it obvious?" Mal asks quietly as he presses forward, his erect cock grinding against the inside of my hip.

My breath catches. "Say it."

"I want *you*."

A groan rips from my throat, and my fingers spasm against Mal's body. I wasn't lying when I told Mal I'd be able to tell if he wasn't being truthful with me. I've always been adept at sensing that sort of thing, even before I went blind. It's a skill that has helped me in business and in life. I don't need to see to detect the minute shifts someone makes with their body when they lie, or hear how their breathing changes.

And Mal isn't lying. I might not be his first choice in the grand scheme of things. He didn't pick me, after all. But right now, in this moment, he wants me, and that's all I need.

I tuck my face against the smooth column of his neck and breathe deeply. Once again, I'm disappointed by the unfamiliar scent of him. "*Fuck*."

Mal's pulse thunders under my lips, but he leans more of his weight forward, pressing his erection against my hip shamelessly.

With a near growl, I pull back.

"Come on," I say, finding Mal's hand and tugging. My other hand skims the wall as I lead us toward my bedroom. "There isn't enough room for this in the hallway."

Mal's breath hitches, but he follows me without complaint, his palm tucked against my own.

"Is there anything you don't like? Any limits you have?" I ask on our way toward the bed.

"Not really," he replies.

"No?" I raise an eyebrow. "You're giving me carte blanche?"

"It's what you paid for."

I hum, letting Mal go once we bump into the bed. He scrambles upwards as I work on the buttons of my shirt.

"Can I see you?" he asks.

I huff. Right.

Backtracking, I flick the lights on. The shadows that make up the remainder of my vision become marginally brighter, like the sun rising behind a heavy cover of clouds. But it's all still gray.

Mal's breathing stutters as I pace back to the bed, shirt open now.

"What is it?" I ask.

"You...you look hungry."

Hungry? Possessed is more like it. At least, that's how I feel with the near-compulsory urge I have to claim this man, even temporarily.

I imagine what Mal looks like right now, spread atop my bed, his long limbs draped gracefully across the duvet. His head is probably thrown back against my pillow, long blonde hair spiraling around him like a halo.

I need my hands on him. Mouth, too.

I drop my pants with no finesse whatsoever, leaving them puddled on the floor as I stretch forward, checking Mal's position before I hike myself onto the bed.

"*Jesus*," he says softly.

"What?"

A leg, that's where I am. I roam upwards until I find Mal's waistband. I flick the button, pull down the zipper.

"You're..."

"What, Mal?" I ask again, tugging his pants free. *Goddamn it, I need him naked now.*

He pants, squirming a little. "You're really fucking sexy, Henrik."

I pause, pleased beyond measure at the sincerity in his tone.

"Lean up," I say, pulling Mal's shirt up his torso. He does, allowing me to divest him of the last of his clothing, underwear withstanding.

I run my hands over his skin as I straddle his body, not actually putting too much of my weight on him because I know I'm a bit stockier than he is. But I need the closeness. Knowing he's between my legs, under my body, soothes the restless beast inside.

Mal's hands drag up my thighs, his touch soft and warm. "I don't know what you want from me," he says softly.

"Mm." I slip lower, and Mal's clothed erection presses against my stomach as I bring my lips to his sternum, kissing the smooth skin there. "I haven't decided yet."

And that's the problem. I want Mal every which way. I want to fuck him into this mattress. Into the couch. Against the kitchen island. I want my dick in his mouth. I want *his* dick in my mouth. I want my tongue buried so far up his body that he's out of his mind with pleasure, forgetting all those boys he was dancing with. I want him to desire only *my* hands on his body. I want him to come to *me* when he's hot and horny.

I want him to know that, for now, he's mine. And I want him to goddamn smell like it.

I pull back and flip Mal onto his stomach. He lets out a soft yip of surprise that turns into a mewl when I drag my hands up his back, not stopping until I'm draped over him with my lips at the back of his ear and my cock nestled against his ass.

I brush his hair back. "You drive me goddamn wild, you know that?"

Mal lets out a strangled laugh. "No, I didn't. Not until I came home and you all but pissed on me."

I growl against the shell of his ear, nipping the lobe lightly before dropping my mouth lower to suck a kiss against the sensitive skin of his neck. Mal squirms under the pressure, his ass rubbing against my crotch.

I like the idea of marking him.

"I don't want them touching you," I grit out once I've released his flesh. Mal pants as I drag my lips lower, sucking small kisses against the side of his neck.

"I get it now," he breathes out. "The exclusivity thing. You're a territorial motherfucker."

I huff, trailing my hands over Mal's body, getting a better feel for his shape, trying to find the spots that make him squirm. "That a problem?"

It sounds as if Mal turns his head, presumably following my descent down his body. He has dimples on either side of his spine, right above the waistband of his briefs. I press my fingers into the grooves before snagging Mal's underwear and dragging them down.

"No. Not a problem," he says, voice a little strained. "Unless you actually piss on me."

I raise a brow, shucking his briefs away to deal with later. "I thought you said you didn't have limits."

Mal laughs. "You know, contrary to what everyone thinks, I'm not into watersports." His voice breaks into a whine when I drag my stubbled lips along the smooth expanse of his ass cheeks.

"Common misconception, is it?" I mumble, preoccupied by the firm globes under my fingers. *Fuck*, he has a nice ass. A definite weakness of mine.

Mal huffs another laugh. "You could say that."

I'm barely following the conversation as is—all of the blood in my body concentrated in my dick and my hands otherwise occupied with Mal's generous behind—but when I bury my face between his cheeks, all remaining rational thought flees my brain. His smell is strong here, heady, and it's all him, undiluted by the asshats from the club. I breathe it in, humming low in my throat before I lick a broad stripe across his asshole.

Mal jumps, a noise of surprise leaving his lips before he presses back against my face, meeting me eagerly. I span my hands across his hips, feeling the quiver in his body as I hold him still enough to take what I want. And what I want is for Mal's sole focus to be on me. I *need* it.

I run circles around his rim with my tongue, loosening him, listening to his whimpers and exhalations as my hands roam whatever skin I can reach, avoiding his cock for now. Mal rides back on my face, and when my tongue slips within the heat of his body, he groans out, body arching.

"Jesus, Henrik. Most guys don't bother with the detour before they fuck me," he says, voice half breath.

I make a sound of displeasure at that. I don't like the idea of Mal never being savored. I *especially* don't like the idea of other men fucking him, period.

"You're not a one-and-done, Mal. I'm damn well going to enjoy you whenever I please," I grumble before spearing my tongue back inside his body.

"Yeah, okay. Mhm," he says, squirming.

"Grab the lube," I tell him, pulling back. "Nightstand drawer."

Mal twists away from me for a moment, and when he comes back, he slaps the bottle down near my hand. I flick it open, leaning forward to give Mal one more long lick before I coat my fingers and slide two inside his body. He moans happily, shifting so his ass is high in the air. I pump my fingers as my other hand roams downwards, cupping Mal's smooth balls and tugging gently.

"You did say you were bare," I comment, remembering Mal's rambling during our interview of sorts.

"For work," he replies, pressing back to take my fingers further into his body. I add a third.

I idly wonder if Genevieve requires it, or if it's simply a preference of the clients Mal sees. *Saw.*

"You don't have to do that here. If you don't want to," I tell him, twisting my fingers around, spreading them.

Mal doesn't answer me, but he does whimper.

"Something you want to say?" I ask, sliding my hand up the velvety surface of his cock and finding a healthy dose of precum slicking his crown. I rub it over the surface before dragging my palm back down, pumping him lightly.

He blows out a breath. "Just wondering when you're going to fuck me."

"Is that what you want?" I ask, twisting my fingers further, finding Mal's prostate and pressing firmly as his dick jumps in my grip.

He whines. "You *are* a tease."

His goading makes me grin, and Mal's breath catches somewhere underneath me. I remove my fingers and give Mal's thigh a little slap.

"Turn over," I tell him. "And grab a condom."

Mal scampers away from my hands, grabbing a wrapper from the drawer and slapping it into my open palm. He lies on his back, sliding down the duvet until his legs drape over my shoulders.

I raise an eyebrow as I roll the condom down my dick. Cheeky fucker.

"You're smiling," he notes.

"Just thinking about where I'm going to be buried in ten seconds," I tell him flatly.

Mal chuckles, allowing me to bend his legs forward as I scoot into position. And I want to tell him to stop being such a smartass, except I kind of like it. There's something inherently charming about this man, and as much as his presence coils something in me tightly, like a snake ready to strike, now that he's within my grasp, I feel settled. That angry edge I had before is long gone, leaving only a strong and steady desire for this man.

"Hen."

"Hmm?" I ask, notching myself against his entrance.

"Will you fuck me already?"

I can feel my grin overtaking my face, stretching my cheeks tight as I shake my head. "My pleasure," I say, surging forward.

Chapter 9
MAL

God, yes.

I make what can only be described as a keen as Henrik pushes into my body. I know I've only been waiting for this for a couple of days, but it's felt like a lifetime.

Who knew all it'd take to unleash Henrik was letting some other men rub their scent all over me? Alex would get a kick out of that.

"The fuck is that little smirk for?" Henrik asks, the fingers of one hand resting against my cheek as he rails into me hard enough that my breath leaves me in a whoosh.

Ungh.

What was I thinking about? Oh, right.

"Thinking about my friend," I reply between breaths.

Henrik makes a sound low in his throat, all gravelly and displeased, and it makes my blood freaking sing. Then he wraps his fist around my cock, tugging in time to his thrusts, and I nearly swallow my tongue.

"Still thinking about your friend?" he grits out.

"*Shit.* What friend?"

I inhale sharply when Henrik angles his hips to tease my prostate, pumping shallowly over the spot.

"Mm," he hums, sounding victorious.

I tighten my legs over Henrik's shoulders, holding on for the ride as he toys with me, alternating those teasing pegs with vicious pumps of his hips. His hands roam over my body like he's a cartographer, mapping me out—up my chest, the backs of his fingers along my jaw, a few pumps of my cock, up my leg as he presses in closer, over my lips—and I can't keep up. It feels like he's everywhere.

And the way he's looking at me? Even though I know he doesn't see me the same way I see him, his eyes roam just like his hands, like he's picturing me below him.

I completely lose my voice as I watch Henrik. And when he drops in close to my body, practically folding me in half to nuzzle the side of his face against my own, I lose my breath, too.

He grabs my legs, pulling them down around his waist as his balls slap my ass. He doesn't say anything else for a while, and neither do I, but each deep rumble or punched-out groan greets my ears like a lover, soft and filthy sweet.

Sometimes his fingers dig into the meat of my thighs. Other times they cradle the top of my head. And all the while, Henrik keeps fucking me like he's going to damn well take his time and enjoy, just like he said he would.

I try every trick I learned from my career in porn to stave off my orgasm, but it's no use. I'm about to come, whether or not I want to.

"Henrik, I'm gonna come," I breathe out. "Can I?"

He lifts his head, looking at me with such incredulity that I laugh. His hand returns to my cock, tugging as he opens his mouth, but I cut him off.

"I know, I know. You're not my daddy," I say, gasping out at the last word as lightning shoots down my spine. "*Ohgod.*"

I groan as my orgasm hits, my legs squeezing around Henrik as I unload between our bodies. My cum hits my abs and chest, and Henrik pumps me through my release, his hand warm and solid, just like his dick inside of me.

Henrik's jaw clenches tight as my body clasps him like a glove, and as soon as my orgasm abates, he sits back.

"Can I come on you?" he asks, hands around my thighs.

"Yeah," I say, nodding as I refill my lungs.

Henrik pulls out of my body, stripping away the condom in a second flat and then bracing over top of me. He strokes himself a handful of times as I watch, boneless and captivated by the sight of him. And then he's coming, his breath leaving him in a rush as he adds to the mess across my skin.

When he's done, he slumps, chest expanding with his ragged breaths, hands on the bedspread to either side of me. His brow is slightly sweaty, and his hair is hanging over his forehead, and it's endearing to see him so disheveled.

But then he sits back and runs one hand up my stomach, my chest, and over my neck, rubbing our cum into my skin, and the word *endearing* flies right out the window.

Ho-ly shit.

"Is that better, you caveman?" I ask, a little smirk overtaking my face as I watch his expression turn smug and satisfied.

He doesn't even look contrite. "Much."

I shake my head, but I'm grinning. The man is filthy, and I'm on board.

He levers off my body, dropping down beside me, and I turn so I can take him in. He really is beautiful, even in profile. His lips are parted softly, and he's looking up at the ceiling, blinking slowly. His hands are folded over his chest, the hair there threaded through with the smallest amount of silver, just like on his head. He's broader than me, and although he's not covered in chiseled muscle, he's still fit. And honestly, I appreciate it all the more. It makes him feel real, more human.

"You're staring at me again," he says.

"Busted."

He doesn't say anything for a moment, just continues blinking up at the ceiling.

"There are fresh towels in the bathroom closet."

My head reels back. Wow. All right, yeah. I'm being dismissed.

"Right," I say, rolling off the bed. I gather my clothes off the floor, as well as his, placing them in the chair beside the bed so he doesn't trip over them, and then I take my leave, glancing back one more time before I'm out the door.

Rule number four. I sleep in the guest bedroom. No exceptions.

I should have expected it, but the easy dismissal feels like a slap all the same. I forgot what we were for a minute. Henrik made me feel like more. Cherished, almost. Warm. Even as he was rubbing his scent into my skin. I know I don't have the right to complain about being tossed out after sex because I did agree to this, but it still stings.

I should be used to it by now. Men only wanting me for one thing.

So why do I feel so goddamn bereft? And cold.

Literally. I'm shivering as I swing by my room, dropping my clothes into the hamper. My skin prickles as if I've been doused in ice. And then, all of a sudden, my vision swims.

Shit. Not now. *No, no, no.*

I reach out, steadying myself against the side of the bed as my pulse hammers and images flash through my head unbidden. My mother's disapproving stare. Callused hands grabbing me, dragging me. Water. So much water.

I drop my ass to the floor, lungs squeezing tight and cutting off my airflow as blood rushes through my ears like the roaring of the tide, too overwhelming for me to even attempt to stop it. I tuck my legs into my body and drop my head forward as I start to drown.

"Mal? I just wanted to check—" The voice is warbled, distant, and I glance up through my blurry vision in time to see Henrik step into the room. He stalls for a moment before rushing forward. "What's wrong?"

I shake my head, wishing I could get my voice to cooperate, but I can't make a sound. I can't even *breathe.* I close my eyes tight.

Henrik's weight drops down next to me, and he scoots forward until he bumps into my body. His hands run over me like he's trying to find the source of my pain.

Too bad it's in my own head.

"Your breathing," he says, voice tight, sounding far away. His hands bracket my neck as I drop my head back against the bed. "Do you have asthma?"

I shake my head *no*, but I can't respond. I can barely hear the sound of Henrik's voice through the onslaught of memories rushing through my mind. The old, decrepit cabins. The judgmental voices. The numbness. The *fear.*

No.

Sound. Focus on sound.

I hear it again—Henrik's voice. I'm in his penthouse.

He says something else then curses, leaning back like he's thinking about walking away, so I grab the first thing I can reach.

Touch. Henrik's wrist. I hold it tight. Safe. I'm in the present.

What else?

Smell. I inhale shakily through my nose, and Henrik's scent hits me. Musky from sex, but also warm like fall spices, with a hint of his sweet cologne.

"Mal," he says, thumbs brushing over my jaw. "I don't know what to do." It sounds like he's underwater, too.

I force a small amount of air into my lungs and hold it, counting to four before I let it out. "Stay," I croak, repeating the breathing.

Henrik leans forward, his stubble brushing against the side of my face, and I latch onto the sensation. He wraps his legs around my body and tugs me into the cocoon of his arms, enveloping me in more of his scent. I breathe him in with each forced lungful of air, and with each reminder of where I am, of who I'm with, my pulse slowly comes down. My burning lungs reinflate. And minutes later, the rushing in my ears and the blurriness of my vision abates.

"Mal," Henrik whispers against my ear.

"'S'okay," I say, utterly wrung out. I'm sore all over, yet my limbs feel like noodles. It's only when I look down at myself that I remember I'm naked, and I try to extract myself from Henrik, embarrassed he had to find me this way. But he holds on tight, and quickly, I give up the fight.

"What happened?" he asks.

Shit. I really hope he doesn't kick me out over this.

I rub my hands over my goosebump-riddled arms. "I have panic attacks."

He tenses slightly, but then his muscles smooth back out. "How often?"

I blow out a puff of air. "Couple times a week?" On a good week.

He makes a choked sound. "Did I do something to cause it?" he asks, voice pained. "Was I too rough or..."

I shake my head, huffing a laugh despite the circumstances. "You weren't too rough, Henrik. They just happen."

I can tell he wants to ask me more questions, but after a moment, he draws back. "Come on. Let's take a shower."

"You don't have to—"

"Come on," he repeats, standing up and holding out his hand.

Henrik tugs me off the ground, and, on shaky legs, I follow after him to the bathroom across the hall. He lets go of my hand to start the shower heating, and then he disappears, coming back a minute later with a glass of water. My throat feels tight as I accept it, swallowing down the cool liquid.

I let Henrik maneuver me under the spray. Normally, my ass would be on the floor, but Henrik keeps a hold of me, and his strength helps my exhausted body stay upright. I wash myself quickly with Henrik's aid, and then he shuts off the water, ushering me into a warm, fluffy robe.

He grabs a towel for my hair, squeezing out the excess moisture, and then another for himself, drying his body perfunctorily before wrapping it around his waist. Henrik leads me back to the guest bedroom, all but manhandling me into bed, and I don't complain or try to stop him. Honestly, it feels nice, having someone help do the little things that usually feel as arduous as scaling mountains after my anxiety spikes.

Henrik, much to my surprise, turns out the light and climbs in next to me. He wraps my robe-clad body in his arms, and without a single thought, I fall asleep inside the comforting cloud he's created for me.

When I wake, Henrik is gone, and the spot next to me is cold. It's not surprising, but I pull the toasty comforter over my head and go back to sleep, not ready to face the day.

My room is bright when Henrik tentatively rouses me some time later, his voice gentle as his fingers card through my hair. I blink him into focus. He's sitting on the edge of the bed, dressed and looking professional even on the weekend. He replaced his usual button-down with a light cream sweater, but it's much fancier than anything I own. I'm glad Henrik can't see how much of a bum I look like next to him.

His lips twitch into a sedate smile when I stir, but his brows are furrowed. *Crap.* He wants to talk about it.

"Can I have tea first?" I ask, my voice sounding rough like I haven't spoken in weeks.

He cocks his head at me curiously. "Tea? Not coffee?"

I shake my head, scrubbing my hand over my face and wishing it were a little dimmer in here. It feels like I have a hangover. "I don't drink coffee."

He hums. "I have Earl Grey. Will that work?"

"Actually, I brought some of my own," I tell him. "I'll grab it."

I make to sit up, but Henrik presses me flat against the bed. My skin flashes hot at the reminder of him pressing me into *his* bed last night, but I brush it off. Not the time.

"Tell me where it is. I can make it," he says.

"Uh, there's a tin on the dresser."

He stands up and paces across the room, running his hand over the dresser top slowly until he finds the little metal box. He carries it back to me gingerly, holding it out. I flip open the top, pull out my favorite calming lemon flavor, and hold out the packet to him. He snatches it without a word and walks toward the door.

"Henrik?" I say, halting him.

He turns his head.

"Would you mind lowering the lights?" I've come to appreciate how dim he keeps the rest of his home. The bright light in the guest room feels almost unnatural.

He raises a brow and lowers the dimmer. "Better?"

"Mhm, thank you."

Henrik nods before walking out the door, and I breathe a sigh of relief.

He doesn't seem upset, so maybe he's not giving me the boot after all. But I can't imagine Henrik is happy to learn what an anxious mess I am. I'll explain to him that it's not his job to help me through my panic attacks. He shouldn't have to worry about taking time out of his day to do that. I've been managing on my own just fine for years. I can keep managing.

Although I have to admit it was really nice to have someone there to take care of me for once.

With another sigh, I melt back into the bed, wishing I could magically make all of my problems disappear.

Chapter 10

Henrik

Mal's tea smells like lemon. It's not terrible.

I make up a second cup with my own blend while his is steeping, and then I take the two steaming mugs into the guest room on a small tray. Mal is still lying in bed, and even though his uneven breathing tells me he's awake, he's not moving.

I make sure the top of the nightstand is clear before I set the tray down. Mal shifts on the bed, and I resist the urge to reach for him, just to confirm he's here and well.

Mal picks up his tea and blows on it before taking a small sip.

"Thank you," he says softly.

I nod, retaking my spot on the edge of the bed. "Can you tell me what happened?"

Mal sighs. "I did."

"Right, but could you tell me *why* it happened?"

Mal said I didn't do anything to trigger his attack, but I'm not convinced he was telling the truth. And if I don't know what I did wrong, I can't prevent it from happening again. And *Christ*, I don't want that to happen again. It was terrifying, and I wasn't even the person it was happening to.

Mal said he goes through that multiple times a week? I can't even imagine.

My chest clenches, and I breathe out, taking a sip of my tea to calm my nerves.

Mal taps his fingernail lightly against the side of his own cup before answering. "I don't like talking about it."

"I think you need to," I say, trying not to make it sound like an order, even though I want to demand he explain everything so I can fix it. "At least so I know what to do, or what *not* to do."

"You don't have to do anything," Mal says. I make a sound of disagreement, but he powers on. "No, really. I've been dealing with this for a very long time, Henrik. It's not *fun*, but I can handle it. I'll try not to let it happen around you, but if it does, just ignore it."

I scoff in incredulity. "Ignore it? Bloody hell, Mal. I'm not going to ignore that!"

Mal inhales shakily, and I rub my hand over my face. My vision dances with specks of light, and I take a deep breath, making sure not to yell this time when I open my mouth.

"I'm not going to ignore it. I want to be able to help."

"Why? I'm not your responsibility," he says, a tinge of frustration lacing his voice.

"I disagree."

"I—"

"Mal, you are not a doll. I'm not going to place you in the corner to look pretty and take you out only when I want to play with you." I can no longer resist my urge to reach for him, and I set my tea aside so I can follow the wrinkled sheets to where he's lying. My robe is still wrapped around his body, and I trail my fingers up the soft fibers until I reach his hair. The strands feel like an absolute mess from being slept on wet, and I sift through them, trying to clear the tangles. "I know I'm paying for you to be here, but that does not make you an object. You're still a human with very real emotions. And while I can't promise to be a warm and cuddly shoulder for you to lie on, I can promise not to dismiss your feelings."

Mal exhales a little shakily before he sets his cup back on the tray. He doesn't pull out of my grasp, and I'm glad for it.

"I don't talk about this stuff," he says. "The only person who knows is my psychiatrist, and I haven't seen her in ages. Even my friends don't know."

"Why?" I ask gently, rubbing my thumb over his cheekbone.

He falls silent, and I can sense his body ratcheting tighter, like his mind has gone to a dark place he's doing his best to avoid.

My instinct is to distract him, so I say the first thing that pops into my head. "I still remember the day I lost the final piece of my vision."

Mal shifts slightly, exhaling shakily. "Oh?"

I nod, carding my fingers through his hair again, playing with the strands. "It had been going for a long, long time. And then one morning, I woke up, and that last little cloudy window of shape and color near the center was gone." I huff out a breath, remembering it vividly. It's funny how a memory can be of the absence of something. Just a murky darkness and the sounds and smells of my alarm.

"When was that?" Mal asks when I fall silent. His thumb is tracing shapes over my thigh, and it feels nice. It helps me focus instead of getting lost to those bleak memories.

"Two years ago."

"Oh, wow," he practically whispers.

"I didn't handle it well, but I called Benji, and he helped me through it," I say, a fond little smile curling my lips as I remember the way he was equal parts tender and no-nonsense. "It's better now."

I don't go into the fact that I can still feel it sometimes, clawing at the edges. That sensation of being unanchored in an endless expanse of space. So far, men like Mal have kept me from feeling unmoored.

"I'm really sorry," Mal says. "I can't imagine what it must be like."

I shrug. For the most part, my blindness is something I'm accustomed to. I've had a lot of time to acclimate. And I have a strong suspicion Mal understands panic far more acutely than I ever will.

"I don't want you to feel sorry for me, Mal," I reply. "I didn't tell you for your sympathy."

He squeezes my knee, almost like a reflex. "No, I know. And for the record, I don't pity you, Henrik. I'm sorry that happened to you, but... You're pretty magnificent the way you are."

My lips quirk. "Magnificent?"

"Oh, fudge off," he says, shoving my shoulder lightly.

I chuckle as Mal resettles against his pillows, the somber mood lifting somewhat. Mal picks up his tea again, and I let my fingers fall from his hair, realizing there's no reason for me to be soothing him like a child any longer.

Or was I soothing myself?

"Would you come up here?" Mal asks, patting the bed beside him. "I feel like I'm talking to my...teacher."

"You were going to say 'dad,' weren't you?" I mutter, not all that disappointed to have a reason to hop up fully onto Mal's bed. I lie on my back beside him, and this time, it's Mal's fingers dropping to my head, sifting through the strands lightly. *Mm.*

He doesn't reply to my teasing comment, but after a minute, he speaks softly, his tone flat like he's reciting verses. "I've had panic attacks since I was sixteen. My psychiatrist gave me tips for working through them."

He's been dealing with this for eleven years? The thought makes my esophagus burn.

"You said it's been a while since you've seen your doctor?" I ask when he doesn't say anything more.

"Yeah."

"Why's that?" I keep my focus on the ceiling, hoping Mal will open up if he doesn't feel *watched*. His fingers stall for a moment before he continues stroking my hair.

"Couldn't afford it anymore," he says simply.

I hum. "You can now."

He doesn't respond to that, and I wonder what else there is that I'm missing.

"Did something happen to make the panic attacks start?" I ask as gently as possible. Mal's fingers tense again, and it feels like he shakes his head.

"Can't..." It's all he says, the one word tortured.

"Okay," I reply with a nod. "That's okay. Can I ask—do you take medication?"

I know I'm being invasive, but I want to understand what I'm getting into with Mal. Not so I can pull out of our arrangement, but so I can make sure I know what he needs. That I'm doing everything I can for him while he's here. I may not dote on these boys—men—but I'm not heartless. I don't want Mal to suffer.

"I did have meds, but..."

He couldn't afford them.

I can feel Mal retreating, so I let it go for now, changing topics. "Would you like pancakes?" I ask him.

His fidgety movements stall. "Seriously?"

I huff a laugh. "Seriously. Why?"

"Yeah, I'd really like some pancakes," he says. I can hear the smile in his voice.

I lift myself upright, and Mal's fingers leave my hair. I have the strangest urge to lean over and give him a kiss, but I catch myself at the last moment and scoot hastily off the bed.

Leaving Mal to get ready in his room, I bring his empty mug and my nearly full one back to the kitchen before pulling out ingredients for pancakes. While I stir the batter together, my head remains wrapped up in the man down the hall.

Despite attachment being something I ardently avoid when it comes to these men that pass through my life, I can't deny I want to know more about Mal. I want to understand his past, learn who Mal is in the present, and shield him from whatever is causing him harm. And that's not like me.

I don't understand these urges, this desire to make things better, but I do know my curiosity toward the man is treading onto dangerous ground.

Mal is my escort. My paid company. I need to remember that.

Mal comes padding into the kitchen before long, right as I'm ladling out the last of the pancake batter onto the griddle. He makes a noise of appreciation.

"Do you ever burn yourself?" he asks curiously as he takes a seat at the island across from me.

I huff, my lips twitching. "Yes, of course."

"Does Benji kiss your boo-boos better?"

I pause on my way to the sink, shaking my head. "And you think I'm a smartass."

Mal laughs softly, and a smile curls my lips as I rinse out the bowl and place it in the dishwasher. I'm glad to hear him sounding lighter. "Blueberries or strawberries?" I ask.

"Both?"

I nod, grabbing the bowls of pre-washed fruit from the fridge and then flipping the final two pancakes. Mal makes a curious noise.

"What is it?"

"How do you know when to flip them?" he asks.

"A lot of practice," I reply. "I ate many a burnt pancake before I got the timing right."

Mal chuckles. "Open up," he says.

I cock my head. "What?"

"Open your mouth."

I frown. "You realize how strange of a request that is, right?"

"Come on. Trust me," Mal persists. My heart gives a strange little flutter at his words, but I brush the sensation off. "It's just a berry. It's not like I'm going to stick my dick in your mouth. I'd have to be on the counter for that."

Despite the recent reminder to myself to remain rational when it comes to my newest houseguest, a growl works its way out of my throat before I can stop it, and I turn off the burner and am rounding the corner of the island without a moment's hesitation. Mal is at the first stool, and he swivels as I approach, whimpering lightly when I crowd him against the countertop.

"Is that supposed to be a threat?" I ask, the need to be *closer, closer, closer* overwhelming in its intensity. Frankly, I don't know how I'm ever going to shove these urges back into a box now that I've had a taste of this man before me.

Mal whimpers again, and it goes straight to my cock. "Is it not?"

"Mm. Having your dick in my mouth? No, that is something I would rather enjoy."

"Oh," Mal says lightly, his breathing picking up into rapid little inhalations. He shifts against me, spreading his legs and allowing me to close the distance between us. I drop my face to his neck, breathing deeply. He smells like coconut again, and it makes my chest rumble in appreciation.

I'm placing a kiss against his thrumming pulse when my phone goes off in my back pocket. My sister's ringtone. I ignore it for once, spearing my fingers through Mal's hair and lifting his head back so I can nip along his jaw. Mal's hands roam up my back, clasping over my shoulders like he wants me to stay exactly where I am.

And I have no plans otherwise, but when my phone rings again, I groan. Dropping my forehead to Mal's shoulder, I retrieve the device and answer the call, holding my hand over the microphone.

With frustration lacing my veins, I take a reluctant step back. "Go ahead and eat," I tell Mal, my voice sharper than intended. Walking away, I put the phone to my ear to find out what it is my parents have been needling my sister about this time.

It better be worth the interruption.

Chapter 11

Mal

Henrik strides down the hall before I have a chance to register the cold he left behind. My cock is painfully hard in my jeans, and my pulse is still strumming away in anticipation, but I have no choice other than to let him go.

"What is it?" he snaps. A moment later, he sighs loudly and says, "I'm sorry, dove. It's not your fault." And then he closes the door, leaving the rest of his conversation cut off from my unintentionally prying ears.

Dove? Who's dove?

My cock deflates, but I remind myself I have no reason to be jealous over Henrik's use of an endearment toward someone else. As he so vehemently expressed to me, our exclusivity goes both ways. And I trust, at the very least, he's not lying to me about that.

So whoever this dove is, it's not a current lover.

That thought appeases my irrational disquiet somewhat, but I'm still left feeling off-kilter. Whatever that phone call was about, it burst the intimate little bubble Henrik and I had been in all morning.

I mean, for cripes' sake, the man made pancakes after we had a *moment*. I don't talk about my life with anyone. Not my friends, my coworkers. I barely even scratched the surface with my psychiatrist before I couldn't afford our sessions any longer. And yet, somehow, Henrik, after having known me for only a couple days, made me feel safe enough to at least share a little.

And now he's gone. I'm hesitant to eat without him, but after waiting for a few minutes, I make myself a plate and sit alone at the big pine table. Admittedly, the pancakes and fresh fruit are delicious. But they would have been better with some company. I remind myself that I'm here for Henrik, not the other way around, so there's no reason to be upset. It's not his job to keep me entertained. I'm not here to play househusband.

I'm here for sex, simple as that.

Half an hour later, Henrik still hasn't come out of his office. With a reluctant sigh, I open the contacts app on my phone, finger hovering over the number for my psychiatrist. Henrik was right about one thing. I should set up an appointment now that I have the funds to do so. I can get back on my meds, stock up on fast-acting benzos for when the panic attacks are bad, and hopefully get back to some semblance of balance.

It's just that the idea of spending money on myself when I have so much debt to pay off doesn't sit well. There are more urgent matters I should take care of first. With a flick of my thumb, I switch over to my banking app to check my current balance. And that's when I see something that has my eyes bugging out of my head. Five somethings, to be more precise.

"What the..."

I fling myself off my chair, almost sending it to the floor in my haste. Hurrying past Henrik's closed office door, I round the corner into the guest room, making a beeline for the small desk in the corner of the room. The contract Benji prepared for me only a few days prior is still sitting on top, and I swipe it off the surface, flipping to page two. My mouth hangs open.

Under the section titled "Advance," it clearly states I'm to be given a week's worth of pay upfront in order to take care of any necessary immediate costs.

That's five digits' worth of cash that's available in my checking account right this instant.

I plunk to the floor, my shaky legs unable to keep me upright.

I've never, *never* had that kind of money. And the only explanation I can come up with as to how I missed this in the first place is because I was too busy ogling Henrik to read the fine print.

I knew I'd be making a boatload of cash with this job. It's the reason I accepted it. Or, at least, the main reason. But somehow, I wasn't prepared for what that would actually look like.

And what it looks like is over $10,000.

I rub my mouth, realizing I could, right now, pay off one or two of my many credit cards if I wanted to. This could put my life back on track. This is what I wanted. Something miraculous to help me claw out of my hole.

This is a good thing. A *great* thing. I should be relieved. I should be thrilled.

But I'm freaking out.

Scrambling up on jelly legs, I grab my things, order a rideshare, and hoof it back down the hall. Henrik's door is still closed, and for a moment, I debate knocking to let him know I'm leaving. But in the end, I don't want to disturb him, so I pass by without a word.

Maybe I'm being a coward.

Right before I enter the elevator, I remember the mess in the kitchen, so I swing that way, quickly putting away the left-over food and loading the dishes into the washer. And then I'm out the door and on the sidewalk in front of this ridiculously swanky building, wearing my bright orange Converse and a worn tee, shivering slightly as my ride pulls to a stop in front of me. Without conscious thought, I give the driver the address of the one place guaranteed to help me relax.

Keith looks up in surprise when I step through the doors of the cat shelter twenty minutes later. "Mal. I wasn't expecting you today."

"Hey, Keith," I reply a little shakily. It's only ten in the morning, but I already feel like I've been through the wringer. I'm drained from my panic attack yesterday, yet I'm jittering out of my skin, flight mode kicking in hard as I try to make sense of the new circumstances I find myself in. "I hope you don't mind me stopping by."

"Of course not! More the merrier, you know that," the older man says, coming out from behind the front desk and appraising me in that fatherly way he has about him. "You look tired."

I huff. "Thanks."

"Well, get on back there. That's what you're here for, right?"

I nod, grateful Keith is giving me an easy out. I give his shoulder a pat on my way past, and when I step into the cat room and a chorus of soft mews greets my ears, my body deflates like a balloon.

"Hey, everyone," I say quietly as I sink cross-legged onto the ground. All at once, I'm swarmed in the most wonderful attack. Four cats climb onto my lap and over my legs, another two attempt to claw up my arms, and several others stand nearby, affecting aloofness while they wait their turn. I let out a deep breath, passing my hands over the different textures of fur in front of me, feeling the resounding purrs in my palms and deep within my soul.

"It's been a week," I tell my avid listeners, flinching when one unintentionally snags me with a nail. I pick it out of my jeans and give the cat a scratch. "A couple days ago, I had less than a hundred dollars to my name. And now…" I blow out another breath. "Now, I have so much I barely know what to do with it."

Well, that's not entirely true. I know exactly where it will go. Toward my debts, to pay off my mother's next care bill, maybe a little for my mental health. In a handful of weeks, I could have *everything* paid off. I could be even. I could get ahead. I could…

I shut down that line of thinking fast because there's every chance I won't make it that far. It's not a given. Henrik could end my employment any time he sees fit, which means I need to be smart. I can't blow the entire wad of cash at once on the assumption I'll be getting more.

My gut sinks, and I realize my behavior today isn't likely to endear me to my host. Henrik said I wasn't a prisoner, and I know he meant that, but I can already sense his need for order. And I get that. I understand needing things to be a certain way.

Because feeling out of control is frightening.

And that means I should have given him the courtesy of a goodbye. I shouldn't have left without a word after he so kindly helped take care of me last night and this morning.

"Crap," I mutter, grabbing my phone from my pocket, incidentally disrupting a couple cats in the process. Henrik answers on the second ring.

"Mal?"

"Uh, hey."

"Why are you calling?" he asks. I can hear the sound of a door in the background, like maybe he's only now emerging from his office to find me gone.

"I wanted to let you know I left for a little while, but I'll be back soon."

There's a pause, and I wait to hear whether or not he'll be upset with me. But he doesn't sound upset. "I see. Is everything all right?"

"Of course," I say out of habit. "Be home soon."

I cringe. Not *my* home.

"Mal," he says.

"Yeah?"

"Thank you for letting me know."

I exhale. "Sure. Yeah. Okay, bye."

I hang up before I can make more of a fool of myself and pet the cat trying to weasel onto my shoulder. I feel marginally better knowing Henrik isn't displeased with me, but it doesn't stop the lowkey buzz at the back of my mind. The worried thoughts circling like vultures, wings buffeting me to remind me of their constant presence.

I shake off the feeling as best as I can, focusing on the sweet creatures in front of me.

"It'll be okay," I say to no one in particular.

I try to believe it.

After another twenty minutes or so of cat snuggles, I extract myself from my pile of purring admirers and start cleaning up. I've been coming to Catty Commotions for nearly four years, ever since I moved to Las Vegas from my temporary home in Salt Lake City and started working at Elite 8 Studios. Usually, I volunteer on Wednesdays, but every once in a while, when my anxiety is high, I'll stop by for an extra visit. It always helps, coming here. I'd adopt a cat or twelve of my own if I could. If I had a stable place to live.

But until then, this'll do.

Keith pops in as I'm finishing up the litter pans. He crosses his arms and gives me a patient stare. I've always felt like Keith knows more about me than he lets on. For instance, I'm fairly certain he knows I work in porn, but he's never said so directly, I'm guessing out of courtesy more than anything else.

And I think he understands why I come here. That the cats help me more than I could ever help them. But he's never once made me feel insecure about it.

He's the closest thing I've ever had to a father figure, if I'm being honest. But I've never told him that, either.

"Making sure I stay on task?" I ask, popping my head out of a cat enclosure.

Keith snorts. "Not worried about that."

"Worried about me, then?" I ask, only half joking.

He shrugs. "I know you do all right. But if you're here on the weekend, there's a reason for it."

Yep, perceptive.

I wipe my hands on my jeans, watching as one of the younger cats, barely a year old, swipes at a hanging ball inside the cat tower she's lounging in. She keeps herself entertained, as cats so often do, and I idly wonder what it'd be like to have such a simple outlook on life. To play and eat and sleep. To not be bogged down by everything we humans get caught up in.

"I like it here," I say, to which Keith nods.

"Don't suppose you'd wanna talk about it?" he asks.

I shake my head.

"All right. Well, we've got a new batch of kittens next door that need feeding in"—he checks his watch—"five minutes."

"I can handle that," I say quickly.

Keith chuckles. "Knew you would."

Keith heads back to the front of the building as I finish up in the cat room, making sure to give Stella, one of the older and more crotchety residents here at the shelter, a few extra pats before I go. I wash my hands once I leave the adult cats, and then I head into the kitten room down the hall. My chest squeezes as dozens of tiny whimpering mewls ring out like an uncoordinated choir.

"Oh," I breathe out, dropping to my knees to look inside one of the penned-in enclosures. Six tiny kittens lie inside this one, spread out on soft blankets. Their sparsely furred bodies wobble as they move about, barely old enough to do anything other than accept food and leave a mess on the blankets in return. Their eyes are still an indistinguishable blueish-gray, squinted against the lights like they haven't acclimated to a world outside their mother's belly, and small color-coded collars hang around their necks as a way to tell the little similarly colored bundles apart.

I find the tub of liquid meal Keith already made up in the fridge and grab a handful of open-tip syringes. Instructions are taped to the side of the enclosure, per usual, and I make sure to read them twice before drawing up the correct amounts. Picking up a kitten at random, the one with the pink collar, I smile, holding it in my palm as I bring the food to its mouth. The kitten instinctively tries to draw liquid from the tip, and I press a little out through the syringe.

It never ceases to amaze me the level of trust that occurs in such a rudimentary interaction. The kitten has no choice but to rely on me or whoever comes in here to provide care in its mother's stead, and I don't take that job of caretaker lightly. It means a lot to me, being able to do something as simple as feed another creature. For me, it's almost no effort. But for this kitten, it's a literal lifesaving event. If we weren't here to take care of it, where would it end up?

There's so much in life that's uncontrollable. So much that comes our way that we can't predict. Maybe that we can't even overcome. But this...this is something I can do to make an impact. However small it may seem, to this one kitten, it's more.

Maybe I'm just sentimental when it comes to my furry friends. Or maybe I wish we all had that: someone to look out for us. Someone to help us survive. Help us *thrive*.

Someone who cared enough to try.

"But that's not how life works, is it?" I ask the little pink-collared kitten. "Knights in shining armor don't really exist."

Chapter 12

HENRIK

It's mid-afternoon when Mal steps tentatively into the penthouse. I don't rush him, but it's a near thing.

I've been tense ever since he called hours ago. I hadn't even realized he left until my phone rang and Mal's soft voice came over the line, unfamiliar sounds in the background of the call. My heart had beat like mad, and I chastised it. I shouldn't be so concerned over Mal's whereabouts. That certainly has never been an issue before.

And yet, with Mal, someone I've known for mere days, all I wanted to know as his soft breathing filled the other end of the line was why he left. Where he was. If he was okay.

It must be because of last night. The guilt remaining that something I did caused his panic attack. The lingering concern over his wellbeing. I'm simply worried, as any person would be.

Right?

"Henrik?" Mal asks softly, padding up to where I'm standing in the kitchen. He touches my arm lightly, as if to announce his presence, and I wrinkle my nose.

"Why do you smell like animals?"

"Oh." His hand falls away. "I can go shower."

"Wait," I say, reaching out and snagging his shirt. Mal stops moving, and I take a step closer. "That wasn't a criticism."

"Oh, okay. I was at a cat shelter," he says tentatively.

"A cat shelter," I repeat, feeling around Mal's torso. I'd like to say I'm only checking him over, making sure he's whole, but I'm not entirely sure I can convince even myself of that. The truth is he's warm and solid under my palm, and I like the reassurance that he's here. That, for the time being, he's mine. That he's not stepping away, and, if anything, is leaning forward into my touch.

"Yeah," he says, swallowing audibly. "Um, I guess I like cats?"

I huff through my nose. "You sure about that?"

I can imagine him rolling his eyes. "Yes, I like cats," he says in a more determined tone. "I usually volunteer once a week at an animal shelter downtown. Is that a problem?"

My eyebrows pop up in surprise. "No, not a problem," I say, slipping my fingers down Mal's nicely defined obliques. His breath hitches, and one of his hands lands on the outside of my shoulder. "I didn't expect you to be a cat person."

"Why's that?" he asks, his fingers dimpling into my arm as I run my nails over his abs.

I can't stop touching him. It's preposterous. He's like this shiny new toy I don't want to be apart from. I want to keep him out of the box, in my hands. I know I told him he's not a doll, but I do want to play with him. Over and over. I want to take Benji's advice and bend him over the kitchen island. I want him in my bed. In my arms. I want to be wrapped up in him while we fall aslee—

I take a step back.

What the hell?

As my fingers fall away, Mal makes a displeased little sound I do my best to ignore.

"No reason," I answer, throat tight. "You probably want that shower."

"Oh," Mal says simply, feet shuffling a bit.

I internally curse as he turns away and takes a few steps. "Mal."

He stops. "Yeah?"

"Earlier. Did I do something to upset you? Is that why you left?" I can't believe I'm even asking. I shouldn't care this much.

Mal is quiet for a moment. "I saw my bank balance."

I wait for more, but there is none. "And?"

"I wasn't expecting it," he says, yet I'm still not comprehending what he means.

Did he not receive his advance? I'll have to call Benji and have him—

"I have never, *ever*, had money like that," Mal says softly. "I know to you, it's not much. But to me, it's..."

He doesn't finish his thought, and I take a step closer. "It's what?"

"Terrifying."

With that, he walks away, leaving me alone in the kitchen, fighting not to follow.

"Boss."

"Hm?"

Benji nudges me subtly, and I realize Diane is wrapping up her summation of last month's earnings. I sit a little taller in my seat, and Benjamin snickers quietly.

I force myself to pay closer attention until the meeting with the charitable board wraps up a few minutes later, and then I stay put as everyone else files out of the conference room. The weight of my PA's gaze burns a hole in the side of my head as we wait. Once everyone has gone, I grab my cane, and Benji follows me down the hall to my office, slipping inside before shutting the heavy wooden door.

"What?" I grit out.

"Where was your head?" he asks lightly, trailing after me as I walk to my desk. I drop into my heavily upholstered seat and fold my cane, storing it inside the drawer on the top right. "I don't think I've ever seen you nearly nod off during a meeting before."

"I wasn't nodding off," I mutter brusquely.

"Oh? Pray tell, then, what *were* you doing?"

I sigh, rubbing the bridge of my nose.

"Oh," Benji says.

"Oh what?"

He makes a sound like a little chuckle hidden away behind closed lips. "I get it."

"Get to the point, Benjamin. What do you get?"

He lets out a long sigh. "You have no flair for dramatics. You were thinking about *him*."

I do my best to appear unaffected, even as my muscles lock tight. "Him who?"

"My God, boss. The jig is up. I know you better than that. You *know* I know you better than that. So spill. What's the deal with the new boy?"

"He's not a boy," I grumble.

Benji lets out a surprised hum of sorts. "He's in his twenties. You're in your forties, and I'm...well, fabulously unageing. But to us, he's a boy."

"He's twenty-seven, and he's..."

"What?" Benji asks, placing his hand on my desk. The scent of his cologne, expensive and woodsy, with a hint of apricot, wafts close. "You barely know the kid. He's the next in what we both know is a long line of distractions—"

Benji stops when I make a sound low in my throat, and even though I try to mask my slip, crossing my ankle at the knee and leaning back in my chair, I know I've been caught. *Damn it.*

"My God, Henrik. Do you actually care for this one?"

"No," I snap. Of course not. "Like you said, I barely know him."

Benji is quiet for a moment, and I power my computer on, hoping he'll get the hint and head off. He doesn't.

"Is the sex that good?" he finally asks.

"Benjamin," I bark, turning his way.

My smartass PA chuckles, stepping back out of reach—a wise decision. "I'm zipping my lips."

"I didn't think you were capable of such a thing," I mutter, slipping in the Bluetooth earbud that's synced to my computer so I can get to work.

"Then you do know me well," he says. He's partway to the door when he stops, his loafers squeaking as he turns around. "And like I said, I know you, Henrik. And I've never seen you like this. I don't know why this one is different, but I suggest you don't fuck it up."

"What's that supposed to mean?" I ask in irritation.

"It means," he says, papers crinkling like he's shifting his workload in his hands, "that you're always waiting for people to disappoint you. And I suggest you don't. Because if you expect Mal to disappoint you, too, then eventually, he will. You'll find a way to lump him in with the rest."

With that, Benji walks out the door. It thuds closed in his wake, leaving me to ponder the validity of his words.

I scoff, dismissing Benjamin's accusation that I look for the worst in people. And certainly dismissing the notion that Mal is somehow different from the rest. That *I* see him differently.

That I care for him.

Because I don't. Sure, I'm curious about what's going on in his life, why he's struggling, but any decent human being would be. And I admit I feel protective over him, but it's probably lust gone wild. It'll pass.

Like Benjamin said, Mal is just one in a long line of meaningless boys—men. There's no reason to entertain the idea of getting close. No reason to expect anything would be different this time around.

By the time I get home, I've mostly convinced myself Benji is full of shit. I'm positive the only reason I was reacting so strongly to Mal the other day—the only reason he was stuck on my mind today—was because of his panic attack. Because, like I said, I was concerned, as anyone would be. There's a big difference between concern and *like*.

Although wasn't I feeling unhinged before then?

"Henrik?"

I almost jump. "Hm?"

Mal's voice sounds like it's coming from the kitchen. And, now that I think about it, I can smell something cooking, something herbaceous and fresh. "You were just standing there for a moment. Is something wrong?"

I step into the foyer, toeing off my shoes and sliding them onto the mat before following the source of the smell. "No, I'm fine." Apparently still distracted, though. "Are you cooking?"

"Yeah," he says, reaching for me when I stop a few feet away. He lets his fingers sit on my arm like he's giving me the chance to orient myself to his position, and I appreciate it more than he knows. "I hope you don't mind."

"I don't mind," I admit, stepping closer and subtly inhaling Mal's own scent as his hair tickles my cheek. Mal pulls a short breath between his lips, making me wonder if I wasn't so subtle after all. "What are you making?"

It's been a long time since anyone other than Benjamin or his husband have cooked for me. I don't exactly have a large circle of friends. And seeing as I've avoided my family of late, that leaves me with my own company.

And, of course, the escorts. But none have put in the effort to cook before. Not until Mal.

Not that that means a thing.

"It's a Mediterranean orzo dish with olives, tomatoes, feta... What are you doing?"

I pull my face out of the crook of Mal's neck and draw back a step. *Shit*. Motherfucking shit.

Mal doesn't let me go far. His hand clamps around my forearm as he continues tampering with the meal on the stove. "It's fine," he says, sounding amused. "You're very tactile, aren't you?"

I grunt, neither agreeing nor disagreeing, but really damn pissed off at my own behavior. The truth is I'm not normally so...clingy. There's just something about Mal that draws me in like a magnet.

Goddamn it. Maybe Benji is right. Maybe I do like Mal more than the others.

It doesn't matter, though. That's the honest truth. At the end of the day, I'm paying him to be here. Nothing lasting could ever come from such a situation. I wouldn't be able to trust it.

And I'm not looking for lasting. All I need is *for now*.

"Smells good," I say, focusing on much safer topics.

"Thanks," he says, rubbing my arm before his touch disappears. "Do you want wine?"

"If you're opening a bottle, sure."

"I don't drink much," he says, stepping around me to open the cabinet. "But I'd have a small glass. Your wine is better than the crap I usually have."

He chuckles a little, but his admission surprises me. Considering he mentioned frequenting that club he went to on Friday, Sublime, I assumed he was the partying type.

"You don't drink?" I ask, mentally combing back over our prior interactions. He had a couple glasses of wine his first night here, didn't he?

"Not much," he clarifies.

"Why not? You're young."

He chuckles again, tapping my hip as he passes by. I follow him over to the table, taking a seat. "I'm twenty-seven. Not *that* young."

I raise a brow. "So what would that make me?"

Mal chokes on his laugh. "You're not old." The wine cork pops free, and then there's the sound of gentle pouring. "Glass is on your two," he says, using the positioning of the hour hand on an analog clock to guide me.

"Thank you. But you didn't answer my question," I point out, finding my wine and taking a sip. "Sauvignon Blanc?"

"I guess? I figured white would go well with the pasta, and I liked the flower on the label."

I chuckle. It's a good thing I only keep my favorites in stock. Mal won't be able to choose wrong any which way, even without knowing wine.

My houseguest takes a seat and picks up his fork. "I never have more than one drink," he finally says. His voice is soft yet sure, and it's easy to tell there are a lot of unspoken words rattling around beside what *was* said.

But what I find curious is that Mal could've easily begged me off. He could have said that he simply didn't like drinking or passed the subject by. Instead, he chose a very specific way to give me information without giving me the full story.

And as he sits there, still not eating, waiting like he expects for me to push, I wonder... "Do you want me to ask why that is?"

It's a good ten seconds before he says, "I would be okay with that."

My heart kicks in...surprise? Bewilderment? Hope?

I set down my wine glass. "Why do you never have more than one drink, Mal?"

He blows out a breath, as if he doesn't want to talk about this when it's clear he needs to. "It makes my anxiety worse."

I let that roll around in my head for a moment. "What else?"

"What do you mean?"

"What else makes your anxiety worse?" I ask.

He doesn't answer right away, so I slide my chair closer to the corner of the table and hook my foot around his ankle. He lets me tug him a bit closer.

"Alcohol, caffeine, too much sugar, anything that makes me feel out of control... My life," he says simply.

My heart clenches at the raw emotion in his words. At how desperate he sounds to escape whatever worries are chasing him down.

How he sounds beat up. Tired.

And as Mal finally digs into his food, his foot hooked around mine, I wonder if his problems are much grander than he's let on.

Chapter 13

MAL

Henrik went silent after my admission. I can't blame him. I spewed my feelings at him like something a boyfriend would do. Presumably. Again, no experience.

But that's not the type of company Henrik is paying for. He's probably trying to figure out how to politely move us on to a new topic or tell me off.

I'm about two seconds away from apologizing when he finally speaks up.

"What makes it better?"

"Huh?" I ask in surprise.

Henrik repeats himself without an ounce of frustration in his tone. In fact, there's a little furrow in his brow—now that I'm looking at him, instead of staring at my own plate out of embarrassment—that looks a lot like concern. "What lessens your anxiety?"

"Oh." I clear my throat and take a small sip of wine. It does taste quite nice. "Tea, I guess. Yoga. Meds, when I had them. Cats," I admit, a little bit unable to believe I'm even telling him any of this. But he did ask.

And what's the harm? If anything, it feels safe confiding in him. Henrik is only going to be in my life for a short while, and he's distanced from every thing and person I know. This arrangement—this man—is temporary. Safe.

Henrik nods, taking a couple more bites of his food. His foot is still anchored around my ankle, a comforting weight. A life raft amidst the chaos.

I shake off my thoughts. He's just being nice. I shouldn't look for meaning where there is none.

Although, now that I think about it, I'm a little baffled as to why all of his escorts before now didn't last long. Henrik hasn't been the least bit difficult to live with. He's been more caring than I expected, he hasn't made any unreasonable demands, and he's beyond nice to look at. He's been a little aloof at times, sure, but I can't blame him. I am a stranger in his space. And the sex, my God. Even though I've only had the privilege once thus far, it was memorable, to say the least.

So what's the catch?

I look over at him, watching as he eats. The way his strong brow is creased slightly, as if he's mulling something over. How his lips curve against the edge of his wine glass, and the way his throat works as he swallows. How he licks his finger occasionally after using it as a guide, his tongue red and broad, yet gentle against the digit. I remember how it felt on me. Over my skin. Pressed insistently against my asshole.

My throat catches, and Henrik stills, raising a brow.

"Wrong pipe," I mutter.

His lips twitch, but he doesn't comment. Instead, he shifts the weight of his foot against my ankle, as if reminding me he's still there. A soothing gesture, at most. Except I'm already keyed up, and the stroke of his body against mine, even a touch so innocent, is enough to have me swelling in the confines of my jeans. Henrik stills again, as if he can tell something is wrong. I don't know how he's so damn perceptive.

"Mal."

I whoosh out a breath, not realizing I'd been holding it. "Hm?"

"Are you all right? You seem tense."

"Fine," I croak out, clearing my throat and taking a sip of water.

Henrik purses his lips. "I can't help if you don't tell me what's wrong," he says, as if it's that simple. As if he's here to carry my burden, if only I wish it.

I blink heavily, shaking my head. "I'm fine, really. It's not what you think. I'm just, uh..."

Horny.

I should be able to say that, for Pete's sake. I'm a god-damn porn star who escorts and cams on the side. I'm perfectly comfortable with nudity, and I can flirt with the best of them. I don't get *shy* when it comes to sex.

And yet, something about this man has shifted my equilibrium.

In his presence, I've blurted things I don't tell anyone. I let him witness my panic attack and even begged him to *stay*, to help me through it. And I haven't even attempted to hold up my typical mask of happy-go-lucky calm.

He leaves me *flustered*, longing for something I don't even have a name for and blushing as he reaches forward, clasping his deft fingers around my wrist.

"Your heart is racing," he notes, stroking his thumb over my pulse point. "Am I making you nervous?"

"Yes," I admit.

Henrik draws his hand back as if I'd slapped him, and I internally curse, reaching forward before he's too far gone. I grab on, and he stalls, perched halfway forward in his seat.

"Why?" he asks.

Why *does* he make me nervous? "I don't know."

His brows draw in, green eyes dark, as he seems to ponder that, searching for clues. "I don't mean to make you uncomfortable, Mal. If I've overstepped, tell me. Or, if you need to make other arrangements," he says, the words grating slightly on the way out, "I can call to have your things delivered."

It takes me a moment to parse through his meaning, but once I do, an incredulous laugh escapes. Like I'd want to leave. "You don't make me uncomfortable in that way, Hen. You make me *want*. And I don't know what to do with that. I'm not used to..." To what? "Shacking up with someone I have sex with."

His grip tightens against mine. "You've never lived with a boyfriend?"

"Never *had* a boyfriend."

Henrik looks startled at that, but only for a fleeting moment. He politely schools his features, and in the back of my mind, I register the fact that not once has Henrik's foot detangled from my own. It lends me strength.

"Don't get me wrong," I say, "I have plenty of sex. *Lots* of sex." Henrik's grip tightens in mine again. "But it's always the job, you know? It's not for me." I cringe when I realize how that sounds to a current client. It *shouldn't* be about me. I'm here to provide a service, and I'm happy to do so.

I open my mouth to backtrack, but Henrik's dark gaze has me clamping my lips shut.

"When you say it's not for you..." he says slowly. *Crap.* "Are you telling me you've never had sex for personal pleasure?"

It's silent as Henrik waits for me to answer, and I don't know what to say. "I get pleasure from it," I finally settle on.

Henrik's jaw tics, and for a brief moment, I'm convinced I've officially put my foot in my mouth. That he's about to give me the boot. Rule five. Sex only when I'm willing. Did I just make it sound like I didn't enjoy our time together? That I didn't want it enough?

But no, now that the dust of my words has settled, Henrik's gaze is less murderous and more...heated. Or, maybe, a mixture of the two. He looks the same as he did that night I came home smelling like the club. Like sweat and other men.

"But you *want?*" he asks, tone carefully flat as he repeats the words I realize I let slip.

I swallow roughly, nodding, belatedly remembering I need to use my words. Ungluing my tongue from the roof of my mouth, I say, "Yes."

"Right now?"

I nod again. "Yes."

Henrik slides his foot up my leg, and I jolt. He doesn't stop until his arch is cupping my groin, and I let out a low, appreciative moan as he applies pressure to my rapidly swelling dick. I spread my thighs to give him better access.

He sits forward, leg bent under the table. "And what is it you want?"

"Anything," I breathe out, a tremor racing through me as Henrik's foot rubs slowly over my erection. *Anything that involves your body touching mine.*

In an instant, Henrik's foot disappears, and I practically whine. But then the man himself is rounding the corner of the table, stopping in front of me and scraping my chair across the floor until I'm facing him. I expect him to haul me up, maybe drag me to his room, but he doesn't. He stoops over me, bending his face to the side of my head and then reaching down to palm my swollen erection. My hips hitch up into his grasp, seeking more. More pressure, more friction, more Henrik.

He squeezes me as he runs his nose above my ear, his other hand holding steady on the arm of the chair. I imagine it creaking under the pressure of his grip. "You're allowed to tell me when you want to be taken care of, Mal," he says, squeezing me again for emphasis.

"Am I?" I ask.

Henrik rubs over the denim trapping my cock. Teasing me. Torturing me.

It's a beautiful torment.

"Yes," he answers near my ear, his autumn scent all-encompassing. "I want to be the one to take care of you."

"*God*," I moan a little breathily, enjoying the sound of that way too much. "Everything about you turns me on."

He hums at my admission. "I like that."

I huff a laugh. "Well, sure. What gay man wouldn't want to know he's making another man hard?"

"I'm bi," he says simply, sinking to his knees as I struggle to find breath. Henrik lowers my zipper slowly, pulling my shirt out of the way with his other hand and letting his fingers skim the skin of my abdomen. My stomach clenches under the soft touch.

"Oh," I manage.

He chuckles, gaze lifting a moment, green eyes piercing. A hunter on the prowl. A lock of hair has fallen over his forehead, and the slight dishevelment makes him seem wild.

When his broad hand slips inside my briefs, skin against skin, I inhale sharply. He pulls me free, stroking my shaft slowly until I'm sure I'll combust, convinced I'll burst apart into a thousand tiny embers and sear his gorgeous hardwood floors in a radiant burst of pleasure.

But all too soon, his touch disappears.

"No," I practically whimper.

Henrik arches an eyebrow, a slow, lethal grin taking over his face. "Up," he says, tugging the sides of my pants.

My breath leaves me in a relieved rush as I realize he's only trying to remove my pants. I lift my hips eagerly, and Henrik tugs down my clothing in quick, jerky movements, tossing the articles aside once they've cleared my feet. He shifts forward, unapologetically spreading my legs to accommodate his bulk, and I slide to the edge of the chair cushion, fleetingly hoping we don't make a mess of the black upholstery.

Henrik seems entirely unconcerned with the state of his chair as his palms glide over my thighs, thumbs digging into the skin as if he can't help himself from being at least a little rough. I noticed that the other night, too. That he was on the edge of losing control, as if trying to hold back whatever it was clambering to break through.

But I've caught glimpses of it. The beast within. The animal lurking behind that wild glint in his eyes, desperate to be uninhibited and free. Something within him that's tired of being locked up. That's restless and yearning for a taste of something real.

I wonder what it would take to break that cage wide open.

Henrik hovers over me, as if in stasis, his fingers indenting into my flesh. My dick strains toward the lips poised only inches above my crown.

"Henrik, would you please put your mouth on me?" I all but beg.

Those seem to be the magic words.

He grins, as if ever so pleased, and slowly lowers his face to my crotch. I inhale sharply as Henrik detours to the base of my dick, his tongue coming out to play. He swipes it across my skin, leaving wet stripes that feel cool in the open air. One hand moves to my shaft, angling me to Henrik's satisfaction, as he teases and tastes me.

I squirm, enjoying the sensation, and yet... In the back of my mind, I can't help but wonder why Henrik seems so content to prolong the foreplay. It was the same last time. Doesn't he want to get to the main act? Most men do. They want to fuck and be done. Or they want me to give them a show. Most don't *linger* the way Henrik does.

"Mal," the man says, grabbing my leg and hoisting it over his shoulder.

I snap back to attention and grip the armrests tightly as Henrik's tongue laves lower. With a groan, my body turns to jelly.

"That's right," Henrik murmurs against my skin. He tugs my ass to the very edge of the chair until I'm hanging half off of it, Henrik's broad shoulders the only thing keeping me from slipping to the ground. Then he ducks his head again and...

"*Oh*," I breathe out, plunking my head against the chair back as Henrik swirls his tongue over my opening slowly, again and again, as if he has all the time in the world. I briefly worry I should be doing more to pleasure *him*. That's what I'm here for, after all. But Henrik's insistent tongue stops teasing and *pushes*, breaching me, and all remaining coherent thoughts scatter like the wind.

I moan, the sound broken and reedy, as the smooth, wet surface of his tongue slides in and out of me, working further each time. I wish it could reach deeper. I wish he could truly fuck me with it. The surface is slick enough lube wouldn't be a necessity. I wish he could reach my prostate and flick that clever tongue against me until I was crying out his name, clamping tight and shooting across my abdomen.

The fantasy is vivid in my mind, and for a moment, it almost feels real, but then I realize it's two of Henrik's fingers sliding inside of me, wet and wonderfully deep as his tongue drags around my rim once more. I pant, squirming as those fingers find their intended target, rubbing over that sweetest of spots as Henrik's arm comes around my lifted leg, hand touching my stomach and fingers sliding under my shirt. He seems to anchor himself there, fingers splayed wide, clutching my abdomen as it heaves underneath his palm, as my breaths come shorter and shorter, as heat and electricity spread out from every point he's touching me.

"Hen," I groan, my dick twitching as he removes his fingers to make room for his tongue, pushing it as deeply as it will go.

I can't take it any longer. I grab my erection, stroking as Henrik pushes his fingers back into me, reaching and rubbing and pressing just so. His tongue never strays far, gliding around my rim, occasionally sliding alongside his digits, soft and wet. I cry out as I hover on top of that precipice, my body coiling tight as it fights the inevitable, wanting desperately to come and yet never wanting the torture to be over. But Henrik pushes his fingers deep, flicks his tongue once more, and I'm done for.

A hoarse shout leaves my lips as I grab Henrik's hair and come. My erection swells, and I spill over my fist onto my shirt, my ass clamping tight against Henrik's digits as he guides me through my release. He rubs firmly and then gently, pressing his lips against the inside of my quaking thigh as he slows. His eyes are shut, head tucked against me, but the tension is smoothed from his face. And, if I'm not mistaken, there's a small smile gracing his lips.

But it doesn't linger. Henrik places a final kiss against my thigh and gently extracts his fingers. He lets my leg lower to the ground outside his shoulder, and then he pushes himself from the ground, his erection tenting his slacks. I reach for him, but Henrik holds out his hand.

"Give me your shirt."

"My shirt?" I ask in confusion, looking down at the soiled mess.

Henrik raises a brow, hand held waiting, and I strip the tee over my head, placing it in his palm. Much to my fascination, Henrik unzips his pants with one hand, pulls out his erection, tucks my shirt over his crown, and then begins to stroke himself. I watch with wide eyes as he stands there chasing his own pleasure, stance wide and confident, hair disheveled, forest gaze dark. I feel like both a peasant and a king in his presence, ragged and wrung out, sprawled in my makeshift throne. Being watched. Coveted.

It takes maybe seven seconds before Henrik stiffens, unloading into my shirt with a grunt and an exhale. He shivers, balls up the garment, and hands it to me without a word. Then he tucks himself away. After a moment of silence in which Henrik's face runs through a myriad of emotions, he turns toward the table and starts to clear our dishes.

I watch, boneless and perplexed, as he goes about our evening as if *that* never happened. As if we just finished a nice dinner together, sans orgasmic finale.

After swatting away my pang of disappointment—what, did I think we were going to cuddle?—I grab my discarded jeans and briefs from the floor and tug them into place. I wipe my thoroughly used shirt over my stomach, catching the remainder of the mess I left behind, and then I disappear down the hall, dropping my tee into the laundry and washing my hands.

By the time I make it back to the kitchen, Henrik has a placid expression on his face, and the dishes have been taken care of.

I stand near the edge of the island, worrying the granite corner with my thumb and forefinger. "Thank you," I finally say.

Henrik's brow lifts. "I have a meeting tomorrow evening. I likely won't be home until late."

"Oh," I reply, taken aback by the abrupt subject change. "Yeah, okay. Thanks for the heads up."

He hums, walking past me but stalling at the last second. "Night, Mal."

"Night," I mumble, watching his retreating form, wishing I understood the dials in charge of Henrik's hot and cold settings.

And yet, at the same time, wishing I didn't care quite so much.

Chapter 14

Henrik

As George drones on about the new construction company he's hired to complete the build of our most recent workspace, I tap my fingers idly against the outside of my thigh. I can't get Mal off my mind, which is completely unprofessional of me. It's been a problem for four days now.

Well, maybe that's not true. If I'm honest with myself, it started before then. Quite possibly the moment he first walked into my penthouse.

But despite knowing I should be focused on what my head of property development is saying via conference call, my mind is stuck mentally cycling through the noises Mal made earlier this week when I brought him off in the dining room. The way he sank into it in total abandon. How his flesh felt under my fingertips. How velvety and warm he was inside. How tight. The way he grabbed my head when he came, fingers digging against my scalp as if he couldn't help himself. As if he was coming *alive*.

I shiver again, reliving the memory that's been stuck on repeat in my head for days.

We haven't had sex again. I've been keeping my distance.

I'd like to say that's because I've been busy with work. And while that's a partial truth, it's an incomplete one. The real reason is one I've been doing my best to avoid acknowledging.

"Hold up," I say, having caught a snippet of George's conversation about the estimated project completion. "Six weeks? It was supposed to be finished in two."

"Right," George says slowly, his voice slightly tinny over the phone. "But the new company is smaller. They don't have the same manpower available, so it's going to take longer to finish construction."

My mind turns over this unfortunate development. Part of me wants to demand George find a different construction company, a bigger one, but any further delay would end in the same result. And we have people, new entrepreneurs, waiting on this location. "Marissa?"

"I'll handle it," she pipes up over the line, sharp as ever and on the ball. "We'll delay the ribbon-cutting, and we can spread the new folks out across our other locations for a month until the new business incubator is ready."

I nod, satisfied with that solution.

"Carry on," I tell George.

He finishes updating us on the new timeline, and as the meeting comes to a close, I keep my head in the game and off thoughts of my newest houseguest. As soon as the call disconnects, Gloria appears with a cup of tea, her clacking heels announcing her presence.

"You're a lifesaver," I tell my administrative assistant.

She pats my arm in a motherly way. "Benjamin dropped off your transcripts," she says, setting said documents onto the corner of my desk. I reach over and find a small stack of embossed paper there.

Although I frequently use my braille display or speech software for work, Benjamin prints certain documents for me, such as budgets or other materials I need to comb through several times. It's easier to have the complete picture at my fingertips, versus having to scroll back and forth to find the information I need. And after working for me for so many years, Benjamin knows exactly which documents to prepare specially. He's always one step ahead.

He doesn't work out of the office or attend every meeting here at headquarters—only high-stakes ones for which I require more detailed notes—but he has full access to my files and zips in and out as needed, like a squirrel on speed. Always moving. Always making my life easier.

Gloria has been a trusted employee for the past decade, and she makes sure the office runs well like a well-oiled machine. But Benjamin...well, Benji ensures *I* can run like a well-oiled machine.

"And where is my personal assistant?" I ask Gloria, reclining in my seat.

"Off saving the world, I presume," she says lightly, straightening something on my desk before taking a step back. "Anything else I can do for you?"

"No, thank you, Gloria. The tea will suffice." It's just in time, too. I can feel the beginnings of a headache brewing.

Gloria makes a noise of affirmation before heading from my office. I sip my tea, check my schedule for the remainder of the day, and settle in to work, determined to outpace certain intrusive thoughts running circles in my head.

Specifically, thoughts of an enticing young man who's managed to beguile me without even trying.

Despite my best efforts to focus on work, I find myself home before eight o'clock for the first time all week. In fact, I'm home by five, thanks to the pressure in my head that did not abate, and in fact, only worsened as the day went on. I'm banking on grabbing my migraine meds and making a swift retreat to bed, but when I step through the elevator doors, that plan gets waylaid. Hearing a soft pant and the swish of clothes, I come to a standstill just inside the foyer to listen.

"Behind the couch," Mal says with a soft chuckle.

"Yoga again?" I ask, removing my shoes and setting my cane aside. I strip off my suit jacket as I step into the living room and place it over the back of a chair. Mal shifts again, grunting slightly.

"Yeah."

"Everything all right?" I ask in concern, toeing his mat and lowering myself beside him. My fingers ache to reach forward, to confirm he's safe and sound. To feel for myself after days of denying the urge. But I resist, keeping my hands to myself.

"Sure," he says, the word sounding like a shrug.

"Except you're feeling anxious?" I guess. He did say yoga helped.

Mal blows out a breath, not answering at first, and then a waft of air hits me, like he plopped to the ground. "Yeah, guess so."

I can't hold back any longer. I reach forward, finding a knee, and trace my fingers over the material of his skintight pants. *Fuck*, he probably looks delectable, all lean lines, muscles on display. "Did I disrupt you?"

"I don't mind your disruptions," he says, laughing lightly. He shifts, bringing himself closer, and I trail my fingers up until I find bare skin above his waistband. I could touch him for hours without getting bored. "Wasn't sure I'd see you again this week."

I nearly wince. His tone wasn't accusatory, but tendrils of shame snake up my chest nevertheless, constricting tightly. I'd been trying—successfully—to insert some distance between us. To give myself time to snap out of whatever bewitchment Mal has me under where all I want to do is touch him again. To taste him and hear him fall apart. To make him feel *good* and appreciated.

But that isn't what this is. I would never treat Mal—or any of my escorts—with less respect than any person deserves. But my interactions with the men living in my house have always been a little perfunctory. Scratching an itch. Enjoying a moment of passion. And then, when they inevitably can't stick to the simple rules I set out in order to keep my sanctuary intact, I let them go.

I have never so feverishly wanted to crawl inside another person and set up camp before.

The way Mal responded to even a little bit of attention showered his way was both intoxicating and disheartening. To hear Mal say he doesn't have sex for *his* pleasure... It made me determined to give him something he deserved. To make him the focal point.

What I didn't expect was for that brief interaction to make my blood sing in a way it's never done before. To make me feel powerful. Important. At least to one person for a momentary snapshot in time.

And that's what scared me.

So how did I react? I purposefully ignored the man for four days. I avoided him at all costs.

I thought the time away would lessen my desire, help me see my tinted goggles for what they were. Four days did nothing. Touching Mal again now, my fingers ache to roam. To never part from his smooth, soft skin.

"I'm sorry I wasn't here," I say.

Mal makes a curious sound in the back of his throat. "I understand."

He doesn't. Not truly. He thinks I was busy at work: an excuse. The guilt threatens to eat me alive. I shake my head, regretting it as the tattoo inside my head swells.

"What do you do all day?" Mal asks, his hand coming to rest near my leg, fingers plucking idly at the fabric of my suit pants.

"Mm? Oh, investments," I answer, swallowing as spots dance across the hazy gray of my vision.

"Like a banker?" he asks.

I huff a laugh. "Not quite. My company invests in startups. Entrepreneurs, small businesses, sometimes well-established businesses looking to branch out into new lanes."

"And they pay you back and then some?"

I shrug. "Essentially."

"Like a banker."

My lip twitches into a smile. "Smartass."

Mal prods my thigh. "You must do well."

No denying that. "Yes."

I wait for Mal to ask about my finances. To find out exactly how well off I am, assuming he hasn't looked it up already. Chances are he has.

But he doesn't. "Are you all right?" he asks instead, smoothing his palm over my leg and squeezing. "You look a little green."

I grimace as my head throbs. "Actually, no. Migraine. Excuse me."

Mal hums in sympathy as I push myself carefully off the ground. I make my way slowly to the kitchen and open the cabinet with my meds. Running my fingers over the braille labels, I find the correct bottle and pluck it from the shelf.

Mal comes up beside me, his touch ghosting over my sleeve. "Anything I can do?"

I shake my head, wincing again, as I drop two pills into my palm. "No. I just need to go lie down."

"Okay," he says softly, rubbing my back as I fill up a glass of water and chase down my medication.

Mal doesn't protest as I head down the hall to my bedroom, my fingers tracing the wall for balance, and for a brief moment, I'm hit with a pang of disappointment. Did I want him to follow me?

I shake off the notion. I'm in no condition to fool around, and with sex off the table, what reason would there possibly be for Mal to join me? Certainly I don't need him to...what, comfort me? Definitely not.

I never wanted Denny or any of the others around when my migraines flared. I don't need Mal, either.

I don't bother to strip out of the rest of my clothes before I fall into bed, my face hitting the blessedly cool pillow with a soft *whoosh*. The lights are off and the shades drawn, so it's as dark as it gets, my vision black as the night sky. And with the door shut, no sound filters in to disturb me. Not that Mal makes much sound anyways. He's generally as quiet as a mouse.

So it should be easy to fall asleep. Conditions are just right. And yet, I can't find any respite from the pressure inside my skull. I groan in discomfort when, suddenly, a damp cloth covers my forehead. Startled, I draw back.

"Sorry," Mal says ever so quietly.

"I didn't hear you come in," I reply. Probably due to the throbbing inside my head.

"I assumed you heard me. My bad."

Mal nudges my head lightly until I lay it back on the pillow, and then he settles the damp cloth over my forehead once more. I sigh, my muscles relaxing marginally. It does feel rather nice.

Mal lies down beside me, and the next moment, an unfamiliar scent tickles my nose. Something herbal.

"What's that?" I ask as Mal's thumbs press against my temples over the cloth.

"Chamomile," he replies, his voice whisper-soft. "I put some essential oil on my wrists. It's supposed to help with relaxation and sleep."

I hum, my eyes drifting shut of their own accord as Mal massages my temples lightly. He's close, his damp hair tickling my chin. He must've taken a quick shower, but with the chamomile so near my face, his coconut scent is masked. Shame.

It is pleasant, though. Reminds me vaguely of my tea breaks, although the smell doesn't quite match my preferred Earl Gray.

"Aren't you going out tonight?" I ask, not exactly *wanting* him to leave, but realizing it is, after all, Friday. Club night.

"Not tonight," Mal says softly.

I hum.

"Do you want to get out of these clothes?" Mal asks.

I quirk a smile. "How forward of you."

Mal snorts lightly, his fingers leaving my head and reappearing against the top of my shirt. He carefully maneuvers the buttons free, each movement slow and precise, as if not to disturb me. It's...sweet, really.

When he gets to the bottom, he tugs the material free from my pants, and then he keeps going, unzipping my slacks efficiently and without a hint of tease. Despite my rather horrible migraine—admittedly a little better now—and Mal's professional bedside manner, my cock takes interest, swelling slightly. Mal doesn't comment, although he does make a little sound in the back of his throat like he's pleased.

Without my clothes, my body cools. That is, until Mal presses himself gently against my side, one leg thrown over my own and his hands raised to once again massage my temples. I sigh in relief, the sensation wholly welcome and, quite honestly, helping greatly. All of it. Mal's soothing touch, the cool cloth, the smell of the oil, the feel of him tucked up against me so innocently and yet intimately.

It's scary how much I could get used to this. Having someone care for me of their own volition. *Allowing* someone to care. Someone like Mal, who slotted seamlessly into my world from day one. Who makes me smile, and who, thus far, has yet to disappoint me.

With Mal at my side, doctoring me with gentle hands and his comforting presence, it's all too easy to forget the truth of why he's here. It's easy to forget about the money and the contract. The fact that I'm his client. And that's not something I can allow myself.

Even so, I can't stop my brain from wandering down a rabbit hole, wondering what could have been if Mal and I had met under different circumstances. Would he have wanted me? Would he have given me a second glance? Would I have heard the warm cadence of his voice and been drawn to him all the same?

Why am I even asking these questions? It's pointless. I'm not looking for a relationship. And it's a moot point, anyhow. This reality is the only one we know.

Mal is here because I'm paying him to be. *I can't get attached*, I remind myself. Although the notion is fleeting, unable to grasp hold as Mal soothes me into sleep.

When I wake, my side is cold, and Mal is gone. And, for the first time in a long time, I wish my bed weren't so empty.

Chapter 15

MAL

"Hey, Mal. What's up?"

I glance down the hall, but Henrik's door is still closed. It's the first time I've been awake before him. I can't say I blame the man for sleeping in. Not after his whopper of a migraine last night.

"I was hoping you could give me some advice," I tell Niko quietly, keeping my voice down so I don't wake Henrik.

Niko hums through the call. "Of course. I was just about to grab some lunch. Wanna join me?"

I open my mouth to decline, so used to passing up opportunities that cost extra cash, but then I realize I can easily afford a simple lunch right now. "Yeah, that'd be great. Where at?"

"I'll text you the place."

I tell Niko "Okay," and twenty seconds later, an address pops up on my phone.

I could call the car service Henrik employs to bring me to meet Niko, but it sounds much too indulgent. Instead, I order an Uber, and within fifteen minutes, I'm walking through the door of a little hole-in-the-wall restaurant with a neon, taco-shaped sign.

Niko is already there when I arrive, and he waves to me from a table. Shaking my head, I walk over.

"This place reminds me of my high-school cafeteria," I say, plopping down across from him at the school-style table with pedestal stools.

Niko chuckles. "Yeah, Dixon was skeptical the first time I brought him here, too, but they have the best tacos. You'll see."

"Did you order already?" I ask.

"Yeah. I got enough for you, too. Hope that's okay? Extra shrimp."

It takes me a second to realize he's messing with me, but once I do, I reach across the table and shove him lightly. "Oh, eff off."

He laughs, grinning widely. "Love you, too, buddy."

I shake my head. "How's work?"

Niko crosses his arms on top of the table, leaning casually against its surface. "Good. Jerome hired on a new guy—Cas. He was hitting the flirt pretty hard, but I shut that down, letting him know I was with Dixon. You should've seen Dixon's face when I told him about it."

I chuckle. It's all too easy to picture Dixon's massive arms crossed over his chest, a scowl lining his displeased face. "I can imagine. What happened?"

"Cas stopped flirting. No harm done. He actually seems like a pretty nice guy. Just a little clueless, like a lost puppy looking for its owner."

"And Dixon?" I ask.

Niko waves his hand in the air. "Psht, Dixon knows there's nothing to be jealous of. That grump is the only guy for me."

I smile a little wistfully, shaking my head. "You two are goals."

Personally, I don't know how they do the *no jealousy* thing. Still working in porn, fucking other guys for the job even as they're dating.

A server stops by at that moment, dropping off a large circular tray of tacos.

"Thanks," Niko and I say in tandem.

When the server walks away, Niko hands me a plate off the tray. "Enjoy."

"You're going to let me pay half, right?" I ask, loading some of the tacos onto my plate.

"If you want to, then of course," Niko replies.

"Thanks," I mumble, glad he's not going to try to convince me to take his charity. "I sure can afford it now."

Niko chews his bite, nodding, before saying, "Right. Is that what you wanted to ask me about?"

I hold my finger up for a second, finishing my own mouthful of taco. Damn, that really is tasty. "Is that chorizo?" I ask.

Niko laughs. "Yeah. Good, huh?"

"Uh-huh." I finish it off in two more bites. "Okay, so I was wondering—what's the best way to pay off my credit cards?"

Months ago, Niko helped me consolidate some of my debt, moving money around a bit so I didn't have as many high-interest loans and cards I was paying off. Even though the guy is working in the adult entertainment industry now, he used to hold some job in finance that I don't entirely understand. He has a degree in money something-or-other, so he knows what he's talking about.

And I appreciate his willingness to help me. I didn't even know some of the options that he helped navigate me through *were* options.

Niko nods, wiping his mouth with a napkin before he answers my question. "Well, continue making the minimum payments we planned out. But, if you have additional payments you can make, start with the highest-interest cards."

"Okay. So... What if I could pay a couple off completely? Should I do that? Or should I spread it around?"

Niko tilts his head, eyebrows raising slightly. "If you can pay off the higher-interest balances, do that. The new job's going well, I take it?"

I huff a laugh. "I guess you could say that. I'm a little freaked out," I admit, something I never would have done before. Even the fact that I'm sitting here with Niko now feels like a big deal. Last-month Mal would've been determined to figure it out on his own, not wanting to burden his friends.

But now... I don't know.

I think back to last night and how fulfilled I felt helping Henrik work through his migraine. The absolute wash of gentle euphoria I experienced when his eyes finally closed and he sank into a restful sleep.

I've never had the opportunity to take care of someone that way before. Not any humans, at least. The cats are another story. But when it comes to people? I've always kept my distance.

Never really trusted anyone.

But *these* people—Niko, Alex, Dixon—they've shown me the veracity of their friendship. And maybe, finally, I'm ready to accept that they're here to stay.

Feeling the sense of accomplishment I did last night helping Henrik... Well, if that's how my friends have felt helping me out, I can understand why they've been fighting so hard. *For* me. I get why they do it.

And I feel guilty that I ever tried to brush their concern away.

"Niko," I say gently, looking up at the man. His warm brown eyes crease slightly, and his hair slips around his shoulder as he tilts his head. "I wanted to say thank you."

"What for?" he asks.

I swallow a little roughly, taking a sip of the water Niko set aside for me before I arrived. "That day in Dixon's kitchen." Niko's eyes soften as he remembers the moment I'm talking about. A few months back, when I was at a low point right before I got evicted, he tried to get through to me. To tell me that whatever it was I was going through, I had friends to help. "You told me I wasn't alone. And I didn't hear it at the time, not really. But I hear you now. So thank you."

"Mal," he says softly, reaching across the table to clasp my arm. I intercept him with my hand, however, squeezing gently. He squeezes back. "You know we're here for you."

"Yes," I say, nodding, because I do. Now, I do.

"Good. And you're welcome, but you don't need to thank me. I'm glad to see you looking so..."

"So what?" I ask.

"Happy," he says at last. "There's a little light in your eye that wasn't there before."

I nod, throat still tight. I'm not 100 percent better, not even close. Money won't solve all my problems. Neither will that man back in the penthouse, asleep in his luxurious Egyptian cotton sheets.

But it feels like, at the very least, my burden isn't quite so heavy.

"Things are good," I confirm.

"But you said you're still freaking out?" he asks, allowing me to reclaim my hand. I fidget with my napkin, folding it in half a few times.

"Yeah, because I have all this money all of a sudden, and it's..."

"Scary?" he guesses.

"Yes! Because it's not going to last."

And I'm afraid of what happens once it's gone. Will I be right back where I started? I don't want to get attached to this feeling if it's going to be snatched away again. I *can't* get used to resting on my laurels.

Niko nods. "Let's look at your finances and set out a new plan. We can do it as often as you want, okay? Anytime you want to reassess based on where your bank balance is, just let me know. We'll draw up a new plan."

"Really?" I ask, shoulders dropping. "Are you sure?"

"Absolutely. C'mon, show me what you got."

When I get back to Henrik's penthouse, I'm feeling lighter than I have in a long time. There's a big smile plastered on my face as I step through the threshold of his entryway, and when I spot Henrik himself sitting on a stool at the island in the kitchen, my smile only widens.

He's nursing a cup of tea, his head resting gently against his palm, but it swings upright when I step into the entryway.

"Mal?" he asks softly. He's wearing a soft cotton tee and gray sweatpants, and I about lose my tongue seeing him in something so unusually casual. And so...

I clear my throat. Really, though? Gray sweatpants? Might as well spray the man in catnip.

"Hey," I finally reply, walking up to him after taking off my shoes. "I brought you some food. How're you feeling?"

His eyebrows raise slightly in surprise. "Better today. Just a mild headache. You brought food?"

"Yeah. Did you get my message?"

The last time Benji was here, he showed me how to use the braille label maker. And since I didn't want to text Henrik to let him know I was going out, afraid it would wake him, I printed out a short message and left it on the handle of the teapot, figuring it would be the quickest way for him to know I was gone when he woke.

Looks like I was right. The label is now sitting on the island countertop beside him.

"I got it," he says, his fingers tracing over the letters once more. A small smile quirks his lips.

"Good," I reply, pulling out a stool next to him, making sure it doesn't scrape against the wood floor loudly. "I have tacos."

"Yeah?"

"Yeah," I say around a chuckle as Henrik scents the air. "Smell good?"

"Mhm. I need to take a piss first, though," he says, sliding off the stool.

"All right," I reply in amusement, watching Henrik's cotton-swathed ass as he walks away. "Damn. Yeah, all right."

No, Henrik and his money can't solve all my problems, but I sure am glad I'm here. That man is...

I sigh. He's divine. But he's not *mine*, and I need to remember that.

I grab a plate and get the tacos ready, but when Henrik's voice calls my name from down the hall, I stop to listen.

"Yeah?" I call back.

"Do you see a box of new razors out there? Benjamin said he dropped some off, but they're not in here."

I peek around the counters, spotting a bag beside the fridge. Sure enough, the razors are inside. Grabbing them, I trot down the hall, coming up short when I walk into Henrik's room and find the man shirtless, seated on a stool in front of the sink in his en suite.

His broad torso looks golden under the soft glow of overhead lights, the smattering of hair across his chest inviting. Just a hint of silver, same as on his head. The gentle dips of his abdomen lead down to the waistband of those damn gray sweatpants, and I'm almost positive I can make out the outline of his soft cock. *Is he going commando?* Good Lord.

Not yours.

"Mal?"

"Uh, yeah. Razors," I say, stepping forward and handing Henrik the bag.

He pulls out the contents, swiftly attaching the head of a razor to its handle and then spreading shaving cream across the lower portion of his face. I watch as he wets the razor and begins shaving away his stubble, his movements slow and sure.

"Staring again?" he asks.

I step all the way into the bathroom and lean against the wall beside him. "You're very good at that," I note, having a strong suspicion Henrik won't take offense to the comment.

"I've had a lot of practice," he replies, and I think back to him telling me he only lost the remainder of his sight a couple years ago.

"Is there anything you can't do?" I ask in earnest, almost backtracking when Henrik's eyebrow flies up.

But his lips twitch, and he shakes his head. "Plenty. You already know most of it. Benjamin labels my food and clothes.

My driver, Charles, escorts me around town. There are many things I'm limited in." He waves his hand toward the toilet, and it takes me a second to notice the device attached. There's one in the guest bathroom, too, but I never thought much about it.

"Oh," I say in realization.

"Oh," Henrik confirms, laughing once. "I can't exactly see when I wipe my ass. That's where the bidet comes in."

"Huh," I answer, biting my tongue to stop myself from asking more questions. Admittedly, I'm infinitely curious about this man and his life.

Henrik washes off his face, the foamy suds swirling down the drain as he drags his hand overtop his chin and cheeks, checking, I presume, for missed spots. "Not running?" he asks.

"What do you mean?" I reply, dragging my eyes away from his smooth skin.

He grabs a towel and pats himself dry, and then he swivels on the low stool. I try not to let my eyes drop to his crotch, I really do, but damn. "I just told you about my toilet habits. I figured that may have scared you off."

I laugh, kicking off from the wall and stepping forward. "Henrik, if I were afraid of the intimate details of backdoor plumbing, I wouldn't have lasted a day in my profession."

Henrik huffs a breath out of his nose. "Fair enough."

"I'm not running," I make sure to add, stepping close and trailing my fingers through Henrik's dark brown hair. He leans his head back, face tilted up toward me, eyes closed. His chin bumps into my abdomen, and Henrik's eyes open, so endlessly green. So bright.

And then his stomach rumbles, and I laugh.

"C'mon. Tacos."

"Tacos," Henrik repeats, dropping his head and pressing his closed lips against my stomach. I freeze, as does Henrik. But then he leans back, displacing my hands from his hair. "Feed me, Mal. I'm wasting away."

Henrik grabs his shirt and walks off. Chuckling, and more than a little flushed, I follow.

Chapter 16
HENRIK

"What is it this time?" I ask.

Alma makes a soft, affronted sound. "Can't I call my brother without motive?"

"You can," I say, not believing for one minute my sister called without reason. "So what is it you wanted to *chat* about?"

Alma is silent for a moment, and I laugh.

"Fine," she says. "Mom has ringed me twice because you still haven't returned her call."

I sigh, sitting down on the edge of the couch. "It slipped my mind."

"Really? The more likely explanation is that you're simply giving her and Dad the slip."

Not an unreasonable guess.

"It truly did slip my mind this time," I tell her.

She hums. "Why's that? Extra busy at work?"

When I don't immediately answer, my mind snagged on the real reason I'm so preoccupied—mainly a certain young man with coconut hair and a vibrant laugh—Alma pounces.

"If it's not work, what *is* it? Are you seeing someone, brother dearest?" she teases, although real curiosity is evident in her tone.

I'm about to tell her it's nothing like that—because it's *not*, and there's no reason to feed her nosiness—but at that moment, the elevator softly dings, and the door whooshes open. I turn my face that way on instinct.

"It's not, uh..." I falter.

Mal pads across the foyer, pausing for a moment before heading into the kitchen, likely having seen the phone propped against my ear and deciding to give me privacy. I listen to him moving about. There's a crinkling, like that of a plastic bag, and then he opens and closes the refrigerator door.

Alma gasps lightly. "Are they there with you right now?" She sounds equal parts incredulous and excited.

I turn my head. "Alma, I have to go."

"No, no, no," she says, but I end the call anyway. She'll forgive me.

"Mal?" I call out.

"No," he says in a voice not quite his own. "I'm here to steal all your things."

I raise an eyebrow, standing up and heading toward the kitchen. "If Delroy let a burglar up, I'll have to have words with the man."

Mal chuckles. "Please don't sack Delroy. He's incredibly nice."

"Is he?" I ask as I step around the island, even though I know that, yes, Delroy is perfectly well-mannered. I reach for where Mal's shirt should be, but instead of fabric, something cold and wet is shoved at my hand. I nearly drop it in my surprise. "What is this?"

"A green smoothie," Mal replies.

I frown, taking a sniff of the drink. Is that what Mal was out doing on his walk? Buying smoothies?

"It's healthy," he says. "It has a bunch of fruits and spinach and antioxidants, I think?"

"You think," I repeat.

"Well, that's what the girl at the shop said," he replies, pushing the drink a little closer to my chest. The outside is dripping in condensation, and I exchange hands to wipe the moisture off onto my pants.

"Are you hinting, Mal?" I ask flatly.

"Hinting?" he asks in confusion.

"That I need to be on a diet?"

He barks a laugh. "God no, Henrik. Your body is *fine*. More than fine."

My lips twitch up at that, chest singing in smug satisfaction. Despite my wariness, I try a sip of the smoothie. It's not that I'm an unadventurous eater, or that I avoid healthy foods—quite the opposite, in fact—but this smells...well, it smells like grass. And, as expected, when the thick concoction coats my tongue, it's bitter and bland, but I do my best not to showcase my displeasure.

Mal woke in a great mood this morning, practically bouncing around the penthouse. I think it was the first time I'd witnessed him so animated. So...innocent, almost. Even though it's an unusually chilly day in early March, he wanted to go out and get some fresh air.

Far be it from me to discourage him from doing anything that puts that sort of lightness in his step. It's not that Mal is an outwardly depressing person, but he does carry a wariness about him, as if there's a rain cloud above his head, and he's expecting it to unleash at any moment and soak him to the bone.

So to hear the excitement in his tone as he rambled on about going out for a walk and exploring the neighborhood was a welcome change. I might even have joined him if it weren't for the pressing call from a board member I received.

But now he's back, gifting me a smoothie, and I'll happily swallow down a little grass-like unpleasantness if it means I get to hear more of that joy in Mal's voice. At least the tacos yesterday were delicious.

When the straw leaves my mouth, I hum, trying to sound appreciative.

"Good?" he asks. I can hear him taking a sip of his own smoothie, and then he coughs. "Oh. Yeah, no. That's bad."

My lips twitch again, and I have to hold back my laughter as Mal snatches the drink from my hand.

"Hold up, I'll make something better." He tosses the drinks in the trash and opens the refrigerator.

"Mal, you don't need to—"

"I want to," he says, cutting me off. "You still had a headache most of yesterday. Don't tell me that you didn't. And I thought a fresh drink might be nice, but, well, that was crap. I'll try again. You have lots of berries in here."

"Mal, you don't need to doctor me. I'm fine," I say gently, sitting down. "You realize I've been an adult for a very long time, yes?"

"Well, so?" he counters. "Doesn't mean you don't deserve someone to take care of you sometimes."

My chest clenches, and I try to brush off the sensation, not liking how Mal makes me feel such...*hope*. It's dangerous, that feeling. Wanting *more*.

I clear my throat. "Are you petitioning for role of Daddy?"

Mal barks out a laugh.

God, I love that sound.

Fuck.

"No, that role is already filled," he says.

"I'm not your—"

"I'm *kidding*, yeesh," he cuts in, closing the fridge door and stepping close. "Take it easy, Dad."

I growl, making a grab for Mal, but he skirts back a step, laughing loudly.

"Henrik, I know you're not my daddy. I do. But honestly, I don't know..."

He stops talking, and I frown. "You don't know what?"

Mal steps close again, his leg brushing my knee. I reach up and find the hem of his shirt, tugging him a little closer and then slipping my fingers up until I find skin. Smooth, inviting.

"What is it?" I ask again.

He blows out a breath. "You're paying me an exorbitant amount to be here, but I don't feel like I'm doing enough to earn my keep. We've only had sex twice. You don't seem to want me to cook or clean for you—"

"You're not my *maid*."

"—and you work long days at your office doing whatever non-banker things you do. When you are here, I want to make sure I'm doing what I can for you. I want to make sure you're happy. With me."

My heart hammers, and I breathe evenly through the ache, reminding myself of the intent behind Mal's words. He wants me to be happy because this is his *job*. And he doesn't want to lose it.

That's it. Nothing more.

Despite the honesty in his tone.

"You're doing everything I've asked of you, Mal," I say steadily.

"Okay." The one word sounds tentative, and Mal inhales like he's about to say more, but then his phone rings, distracting him away from the conversation. He makes a quiet sound of discomfort before stepping back, and my fingers slip from his skin.

"Excuse me," he says, walking away.

I frown in the direction of his departure, curious, despite myself, when he closes the door to his room. Whatever the call is about seems to require privacy.

I force myself to give Mal his time alone and focus on other things, namely scrolling through and listening to a few business emails before the work week starts up again in the morning. Anything to get my mind off the man in the guest room. But when I hear a sharp *"Fuck,"* I'm on my feet and heading down the hall without a moment's hesitation.

"Mal?" I call out, knocking on his door lightly. He doesn't answer, and my worry ramps. I knock again.

"Yeah," he says, voice muffled and a little croaky. "Come in."

I ease open the door, and the first thing I hear is the harshness of Mal's breaths.

"Damn it. Are you okay?" I ask in alarm, stepping slowly forward. I assume Mal is on the bed and nearly slump in relief when I find him there as expected, my fingers connecting with a forearm.

"Yeah," he says, following it up quickly with, "no."

He grabs my hand and pulls it upwards, placing it against his neck and holding it there with both palms as his breath shudders in and out.

"Are you having a panic attack?" I ask, climbing onto my knees atop the bed so I can get closer. Mal is sitting against the headboard, but he seems to be splayed out somewhat diagonally across the bed, as if he landed there and just stayed put.

"No," he says softly, voice slightly hitched, as he shakes his head. "I'm just... I think I broke my phone."

"What?" I ask, confused about the non sequitur.

"I threw my phone, and I think the screen cracked."

"Okay," I hedge. "That's not a problem. We can get you a new one."

Mal hiccups. "I don't care about the phone, not really."

I hum in somewhat confused acknowledgement, settling in next to him. I don't remove my hand from his neck where he's holding it, but I sit down fully, pulling my legs up in front of me. Mal's pulse threads rapid fire under my fingers. "What was the call about, Mal?"

"My mom."

"Your mom?" I ask. He hasn't mentioned her before. "Is she okay?"

"No," he says almost harshly. "She's not. She has dementia."

My throat catches. "I'm sorry, Mal."

He shakes his head rapidly. "She's not a good person, Henrik. She's not."

"What...what do you mean?" I ask, trying to keep my voice calm.

He's quiet for a long moment, and I start to wonder whether or not he's going to answer me.

"Mal?" I prompt gently.

"She thought being gay was a choice," he finally spits. "And she made me pay for it. She made me pay for that choice, and then she held it over my head like a cleaver."

What?

"Mal, I—"

"I can't talk about it, Henrik," he rushes out, as if he's reached his limit. As if whatever dam temporarily burst, hurling those words forth like a necessary pressure release, locked back up tight. "I can't."

The visceral emotion is those two words chafes at me, body and soul, but I nod, doing my best to soothe him, running my thumb over his neck and whispering, "Okay, okay." But then a drop of moisture hits my wrist, and another, and when I register it's Mal's tears I'm feeling against my skin, I lose my own battle to stay strong. "Oh, Mal," I croak.

I tug him in, and he doesn't put up a fight. He falls against my chest, crying silently as I hold him in my arms. As something inside me cracks wide open, gaping and raw. I've never in my life heard someone make so little noise while they wept—as if they're accustomed to hiding their pain—and if it weren't for the wet spot dampening my shirt, I might not have believed it.

It absolutely breaks my heart.

All of it. I don't even know what's wrong, but whatever isn't *right*, whatever this is, it tears at me viciously.

"What can I do?" I ask, my fingers drifting shakily through Mal's hair, one palm rubbing circles across his back. I can't stop touching. Comforting.

Clinging.

"You already do too much," he says against my chest, his voice a whisper.

I squeeze him tighter, swallowing roughly against the ball of ragged glass lodged deep in my throat.

"You asked what would make me happy," I say, the words rasping on the way out. "Allowing me to help would make me happy, Mal. You being honest with me would make me happy. So please, let me ask again. What can I do?"

Mal inhales deeply before blowing out a slow breath, the air cooling my damp shirt. He shifts away from me, and although I'm remiss to let him go, I drop my hands as he resituates on the bed.

"Would you do the crossword with me?" he asks, a complete 180 from what I thought he might say.

"The crossword?" I say tentatively.

"Yeah," he replies, shuffling around on the sheets, his voice hoarse. "I like to do it on my phone sometimes. It clears my head." He pauses. "Crap, my phone…"

"Here," I say, pulling mine out of my pocket and handing it over.

Mal's fingers brush mine as he takes the device. "Are you sure?"

"Positive," I say. "Yeah, let's do the crossword."

Anything that will help. Anything to take away Mal's pain, at least for a little while.

Mal taps lightly away on my phone, not commenting as I feel out his position. He's leaning against the headboard again, and his legs are spread out straight in front of him. I sit at the top of the bed next to him, planting myself shoulder to shoulder. But as soon as I'm settled, Mal shifts downward, laying his head on my lap with a sigh.

"This okay?" he asks softly.

I smile a little tremulously, that wide-open space inside of me pulsing with something uncertain and warm. "Of course."

Mal hums lightly when I run my fingers over his hair, and suddenly, I think I understand why he likes cats so much. It's such an errant thought I almost laugh. But sitting here with the man, petting him almost, is just as comforting to me as I expect it is to him.

I never want to stop.

"Ready?" Mal asks.

I clear the notion of felines from my head as I run my thumb over Mal's brow, glad that the tension there is smoothed away. A little moisture lingers beside his eye, however, so I wipe it away, chest tight. "As I'll ever be."

He hums almost contentedly, shifting slightly before resettling. "Before you leap. Four letters."

My motions still, and I huff out a breath, shaking my head at the timely clue. "Look."

It's advice I should heed—*look before you leap*—despite the literal interpretation being something I'm incapable of. Because I *am* capable of weighing costs. It's something I do every day for my job.

And the cost of allowing myself to inch closer to this man, to take comfort in the way Mal is resting in my lap like it's the safest place to be, like he trusts me, is high.

Whatever this is—whatever shaky, baby-fawn emotion is trying to gain legs inside my chest—can't last. This isn't *real*. Mal isn't mine to keep. He's not mine to soothe and tend to. Not mine to love.

I know that. I'm well aware I can't allow myself to fall into the fantasy with Mal because without the paycheck tethering him here, the illusion would slip apart with the snap of a finger.

And yet, I can't bring myself to regret a single thing as Mal leans against my legs, one of his hands tracing my calf as my fingers thread through his hair. I can't bring myself to call a halt as he reads clue after clue aloud, his voice gaining strength with each word.

I can't distance myself. I can't stop, even though I know I should.

I don't *want* to stop.

And that crack inside me tears a little wider.

Chapter 17
Mal

"Well, well, well."

I pause mid-stride at the accusatory tone that greets my ears, and the door to the break room practically slaps my ass as it closes behind me.

Alex swings his feet to the floor, hazel eyes bright. "Lookie here, boys," he says with a flourish, standing up and sauntering my way in all his tiny glory. I take one more peek around, but the break room here at Elite 8 Studios is empty save the two of us. "Look what the cat finally dragged in."

"Alex," I say, huffing out a laugh. "It's only been a couple weeks."

Alex's shoulders sag, that blaze in his eyes lessening as he gives me a tiny shove. "I *know*, but where have you been, Curly Fry? You've skipped out on Sublime night twice in a row now. *Twice*. I was starting to get worried."

I shrug, slipping past Alex to grab a tea. I unscrew the cap before I can think better of it. Seeing as I don't technically work here at the moment, I probably shouldn't be taking advantage of the complimentary refreshments.

But as I ponder that, tea poised in my hand, Alex says, "Oh, go ahead. Jerome won't give a damn. Why are you here, boo? Are you done with your sugga pop?"

I roll my eyes and take a sip of my drink before heading for a table. Alex tags along. "No, I just wanted to visit. Like you said, I haven't seen you guys in a while."

Well, I saw Niko a little over a week ago, but I haven't stopped by Elite 8 since I started my new gig at Henrik's. That was twenty days ago now.

"And why *is* that?" Alex asks, raising a brow.

"I guess I got caught up in...things."

Not a lie, but a flimsy excuse at best. The truth is time got away from me. It really has felt like a different world up in Henrik's ivory tower. It's been all too easy to coast along, enjoying the cushy perks of being a sugar baby-slash-escort and not having to worry about everything else for a while.

Well, maybe that's an exaggeration. I've still worried plenty. About my finances. My mental health. And, of course, the past keeps calling—quite literally.

But at least I've had Henrik to help calm me. That's been...nice. More than nice. Spending time with him. Enjoying the feel of his fingers carding through my hair and letting myself be grounded by the soothing touch. Listening to the low near-grumble of his voice as he fills in the crossword with me at the end of the day.

I've never been in a relationship, but I imagine this is what one might feel like. Living together, eating together, taking care of one another. Enjoying the quiet moments.

I probably shouldn't get attached to the feeling, but for now, I'm choosing to live in the fairytale. I'm embracing the luxury of my arrangement with Henrik. The luxury of the man himself.

I'll deal with the harshness of reality when the time comes.

"Malibu. Earth to my best bud," Alex says, his waving hand brushing my nose.

"Sorry," I mumble, not even bothering to comment on Alex's best bud claim. I'm pretty sure every friend of Alex's is his best bud. The man is more of a people person than I'll ever be.

"I asked what could possibly be more important than spending time with your favorite coworkers, but I get it now," he says, nodding his head with pursed lips. "The guy must have a magic dick."

"Alex," I say, shaking my head with a smile. More like magic hands.

And it's not just the way Henrik touches me during sex. At least the two times we've had it. Don't get me wrong—his hands truly do work magic when they're mapping all over my bare skin, taking me apart, making me wild with pleasure.

But it's more than that. It's the way Henrik can't seem to help but touch me whenever he's around, which has been more lately, as if something shifted that night he held me after Great Oak called—when I all but broke down.

Over the past week, Henrik has been home in time to cook dinner every night, not staying late at the office once. And instead of retreating to his own solitude inside his study, he's sat with me on the couch, talking or doing the crossword, always connected in some way.

I don't know what inspired the change, compared to the week prior when I almost wondered if he was avoiding me, but I'm not complaining.

"Are you denying it?" Alex asks of his magic dick claim, drawing my mind to the present. When I don't answer—because, well, even though we only had anal once, his dick *was* divine—Alex titters. "Exactly. No worries, boo. I get it. If there's one valid excuse for blowing off your friends, it's magic dick."

"I'm sorry," I say, twisting the tea cap between my fingers, feeling guilty that I haven't been as good of a friend to Alex and the others as they've been to me.

"Hey, none of that," he says, reaching forward and squeezing my arm. "It wasn't a criticism. I'm just glad to see you, Curls. You've been okay?"

I think about all the extra times I've stopped into Catty Commotions—not because of my anxiety, but because my time has been free without three jobs to hustle to—and I smile.

"Yeah, I'm okay."

He nods slowly. "You know, if you ever want to talk—"

"Well, well, well," Dixon interrupts, narrowing his eyes as he walks through the door. He comes to stop before Alex and me and crosses his arms.

Dixon presents a tough-looking exterior, but I've known the guy for long enough to recognize his grumpy act for what it is. It's his way of appearing aloof and detached, even as he cares, because Heaven forbid somebody cares back. I get that.

Alex snorts. "That's what I said."

Dixon raises a brow, grabbing a seat at our table and plopping down. "Was about ready to send out a search party."

I shake my head, a little smile on my lips. "You're both being ridiculous. I've been texting," I remind them, pulling out my new phone as evidence. "Look, here's our most recent thread from last night."

Alex swipes my phone, nodding as he goes through our conversation. A wicked grin spreads across his face. "Yeah, speaking of magic dick. You should've seen the curve on that guy."

"I know," I reply blandly, grabbing my phone to read from the screen. "You told us. And I quote, 'It felt like he was mining for my kidney,' eggplant emoji, peach emoji, water emoji, screaming ghost emoji? End quote."

Alex cackles. "So true."

"And as I told *you*"—I waggle my phone before setting it aside—"that was way more information than I needed to know about your conquests, babe."

He scoffs, ignoring me. "In all fairness, it could've been your captor replying to our texts," Alex points out.

I huff a laugh. "I've been perfectly *fine*. I can leave the penthouse anytime I want." Alex opens his mouth, but I cut in. "No permission slip needed."

Alex snickers. "That'd be teacher, not Daddy."

"My God, he's neither."

"Whatever you say, sugar boo." Without preamble, Alex starts singing the chorus to "Sugar, We're Goin' Down," and I groan, dropping my forehead against the table.

"This again?" I mumble.

"Can we meet this guy?" Dixon interjects, all business.

I look over at him, recognizing the slant of his mouth as worry. I've seen plenty of it these past few months.

Dixon noticed before anyone else that something was wrong in my life. I still don't know how he picked up on it when he did, seeing as I kept a tight lid on my problems, but he was the first person to try and lend a hand when I was spiraling. When the bills became too much, the eviction was hanging over my head, and my emotions were all over the place, bleeding into my work life in particular. When I let a guy choke me for money. When I tried to get drunk enough to forget.

I can't help but wonder what would have happened if I'd accepted his help earlier. Or Alex and Niko's. If I hadn't let it get to the point where my landlord kicked me to the curb, hardly any possessions to my name because I'd sold them all for a little cash.

Cash that was never enough to cover the debt I started accruing when my mom became too unstable to care for herself. When I signed the agreement with Great Oak Home Living to pay for her palliative care back in my home state. When the woman who disapproved of me enough to have me dragged off and *converted*—an endeavor that, as far as she knew, was successful—managed to shove one last final *fuck you* in my face with her parting years.

It seems cruel that her dementia has allowed her to forget, when I'll never be able to.

That woman killed off the boy I once was. That young, innocent kid who was optimistic about life. The one who, with a single chaste kiss against the brick wall at school, suddenly believed in magic. I was *sixteen* then, but I can still remember my schoolmate's face and his lacrosse number—fourteen. I can recall that soaring feeling inside as I thought, *"I'm gay."*

And I can recall, with perfect clarity, my mother's face as she sent me off to *camp*.

I couldn't even tell her it was for nothing. When I got home, I couldn't say a word because I didn't dare do a thing that might land me back in that place. From that day forward, I became a different person. I started hiding.

And I never really stopped.

I realize, as my mind returns to the present, that I'm clutching the tea cap so tightly in my fist that the rough edges are cutting into my skin. I loosen my grip, but the damage is done. Little pinpricks lie in a circle, bright red amidst my flesh. I try to take a deep breath, to soothe my tight throat, but I can't pull in enough oxygen, and my pulse is racing like a greyhound around a track.

"Mal?" Alex asks in concern, reaching for my arm.

I push out of my seat, my chair wobbling precariously before it drops back on all fours. I manage a quick "Excuse me" before rushing from the break room. No one stops me in the hall, and for that, I'm grateful.

I've only had a handful of panic attacks at work over the years, but each time, I've been able to get out of sight before they escalated. I head for my usual hideaway now, a shower stall in the locker room.

Emil, another performer, is changing when I push into the room, but apart from a brief "Hey," he doesn't question me as I breeze past. I walk straight into the furthest shower stall and pull the curtain tight, backing up until I hit the hard-tiled wall. Bracing my hands on my knees, I try to catch my breath, try to call the panic back before it gets too far, but no matter how hard I focus, no matter how many times I try to reason that it's in my head, that it'll be fine, I can't slow my heart. I can't quiet the voice telling me to *flee*. Telling me it's *not* okay. Telling me the fear is valid. Real.

I sink to my butt, my legs unwilling to hold me up any longer, and shove the shower on, praying the pretense will cover me for however long I need. The water cascades to the floor next to me, the edge of the stream soaking my pant leg, but it barely registers. Instead, it's the thumping, erratic beat of my own pulse inside my head, the grip in my chest that feels as if a burning fist is squeezing my heart tight, the way I can't get my lungs to cooperate and take a full breath no matter how hard I try.

It's that memory of my mother's angry frown when the men from church hauled me into that big white van. How disappointed she was—disappointed in me. Not worried. Not concerned. And certainly not surprised. Only furious. Because of who I was. Because of *what* I was. Gay.

It's the flashes of cold and the lectures on sin. The old church camp. The embarrassment and the confusion of wondering *why?* Why would they do this? Why would *she* do this?

I vaguely register hands pulling my hair back from my face, soothing over the cheek not tucked against the denim at my knee. The sound of the water shutting off, of murky, muddled voices talking back and forth. Of someone pressed against my side, hugging me tight, whispering soft words against my ear, running fingers over my back.

"It's okay. You're okay," they say. And, "Breathe. Everything will be okay."

They feel warm.

Safe.

And I try. I try to breathe.

"Can't," I gasp out, the sound barely a croak.

"You can," they urge, petting, soothing, a kiss on my hair. "It will pass. This will pass. You're okay, Curls. We've got you. You know that, right? We've got you. We will always have you."

Alex wipes my face as I hiccup a sob.

"There," he says. "Just like that. Again."

I pull in another shuddering breath, my lungs on fire, my chest squeezed tight, my head aching. I catch sight of two sets of legs standing outside the shower stall, distorted in my vision, but I block it all out as I focus on counting *one, two, three, four*. Breath out *two, three, four*.

"Good," Alex murmurs, slipping the hair tie off my wrist. He pulls my hair back behind my head and secures it, a litany of soothing words trailing from his lips as he rubs over the back of my neck. Goosebumps pop up over my skin now that the shock has worn off.

I'm soaked and shaking.

Dixon squats down next to me. "Mal," he says gently, squeezing my knee.

"I know," I manage. I have a lot of explaining to do.

"How can we help?" he asks, his usually stern features creased into worry. "What can we do?"

I no longer feel like escaping my own skin, and my breathing has returned mostly to normal, but the ache inside my chest lingers, like a burn. And I'm dropping fast as the adrenaline vacates my system.

"I have clothes in my locker," I say.

Dixon nods, standing up and disappearing around the corner. Alex rubs my arm, encouraging me to stand, helping me along the way. I realize the other set of legs belongs to Emil, who's standing off to the side with that same expression of concern Dixon was wearing a moment ago. I give him a wan smile that I'm sure falls flat as Alex and I step out of the shower stall.

Dixon returns with a set of clothes, and I thank him, starting to tug off my own without bothering to find privacy. These men have seen me in all manner of dress and undress. We've been more intimate than most friends. A little nudity now means nothing.

Alex helps with my pants when I wobble, and then Dixon hands me the dry clothing one item at a time. Once I'm dressed, we make our way to the benches by mutual unspoken agreement. Even Emil plops down with us. Alex hands me a granola bar—likely from the break room—and I accept it gratefully, the crinkle of the wrapper stark in the otherwise silent room.

No one speaks until I've taken a bite.

"Relatively speaking, are you okay, boo?" Alex asks, his hazel eyes locked intently on mine.

I should beg him off. I should say I'm fine and it's no big deal and he shouldn't worry.

But I can't. I can't do it anymore. I'm so tired of lying to these men. It's deep in my bones, that fatigue. I'm tired of pretending like everything is okay when it's not.

I've spent the last few weeks away from Malibu. Away from that guy I imitate who's easygoing, who wears a smile like a shield. The casual surfer-dude who eats clean and practices yoga for aesthetics, not out of necessity.

It's been less than a month, but in that time, I haven't had to act like someone I'm not. And now that I'm faced with the decision of whether or not to pick that mantle back up, I realize it's not a decision at all. I'm done with it. Done being Malibu.

Maybe it wasn't a matter of digging myself out of the dirt. Maybe it was simply deciding to stand.

"Right now, yes. I'm okay," I answer.

Alex picks up on the *but* I left floating in the air. "In general, you're not?"

"No, not really," I admit easily. Much easier than I thought this conversation would go. The words practically took a running leap out of my mouth.

"What's going on?" Alex asks gently as Dixon hands me a bottle of water. I accept it gratefully, drinking some of the cold liquid.

"I have panic disorder."

Alex makes a surprised sound in the back of his throat. Dixon and Emil watch me carefully. Not in a judgmental way, just like they're unsure how to take the news. Understandable.

"How long has that been going on, Curls?" Alex asks.

I shrug. "Over ten years?"

Alex makes another little shocked sound.

Emil is next to ask me a question. "Are you on any SSRIs or benzodiazepines?"

I huff a laugh. I'd forgotten Emil is a psych major. He probably knows more about this stuff than I do.

"Zoloft was working for a while, but I couldn't afford to keep taking it," I say, that shamed pinch curling around me as it so often does whenever the topic of money—or my previous lack thereof—is brought up.

Emil doesn't bat an eye, but I keep talking, the words spilling free like a loose ball of yarn now that the end has been unraveled.

"I started seeing a therapist when I was twenty. Bounced through a couple. It was while I was seeing the second one that I was diagnosed with panic disorder. When I moved to Vegas, I found a psychiatrist I really liked. I was doing therapy with her, but it's been over a year since I had an appointment. I ran out of meds eight months ago, and the panic attacks have gotten worse, like they were in the beginning. I do my best, but..."

"Without a proper support system, it's been difficult to cope," Emil fills in gently.

I nod, glad he understands. I don't *want* to feel like this. I don't want my anxiety to rule my life, but sometimes it's impossible to stop the tide. To fight the undertow. It sweeps me along without a life raft there to buoy me.

I can barely remember those brief couple years where I felt more balanced—after I moved to Vegas and started working here, when I had regular appointments and was taking my meds. For a time, I was okay. I could see my past mindset from the outside and recognize how much my everyday outlook was skewed. How much my anxiety truly affected my thoughts and judgment. How, once that excessive, unending worry was taken away, I just...was. My brain was quiet.

It was peaceful.

Until it wasn't.

Dixon squeezes my knee. "Mal, let's get you home. You look beat."

I nod, the motion making my head feel like it's about to topple off my shoulders. My limbs feel sluggish, too, the tiredness finally catching up to me.

Alex grabs my wet clothes off the floor, carrying them in his arms and soaking his own shirt, but I'm too tired to tell him not to bother. Dixon walks next to me to the door, as if he's ready to grab my arm should I stumble. I'd laugh at the absurdity of it if I were capable.

Emil walks out of the locker room with us, but as we reach the parking lot, he pauses. "Mal?"

"Hm?" I ask, turning his way.

He pushes his glasses up his nose, blinking a few times. The guy sure does have that shy nerd thing down pat, which is likely why Jerome gave him the moniker Felix. But it works for him. Fans love his authenticity. "It seems like you're aware of what resources are available to you, but, uh...if you need help with that, please let me know."

I nod. "Thanks, Emil. I appreciate it."

With a returning nod of his own, Emil splits off towards his own vehicle, and Dixon leads Alex and me to his car.

As Dixon drives us toward the penthouse, Alex strokes my arm. I'm half-asleep in the back of the car when he speaks up. "I'm sorry. I wish I'd known you were dealing with this."

I open my eyes, locking onto Alex's concerned gaze. For all his cutesy bluster, Alex is a soft soul. He's a good friend, and I haven't been one to him.

"It's not your fault, Blondie. I hid it from everyone."

He frowns. "Why?"

I think that over, having an idea of the answer but unsure of how to voice it.

"I needed to be someone else," I tell him. "And I wished for it so badly, it became true."

Chapter 18

HENRIK

When I step inside my home, I'm brought up short. Someone is laughing, and it's not Mal.

The voices quiet, and then Mal calls out. "Henrik?"

I resume taking off my suit jacket and shoes, eternally grateful as I step forward that the guests' footwear aren't lying haphazardly on the floor. "We have company?"

After another stressful day at work, I was hoping for a quiet evening at home with Mal. It appears my plans have been thwarted.

Mal steps close—easily identifiable by scent alone if I weren't also accustomed to the cadence of his walk—and brushes his hand down my arm. "Sorry," he says softly, not quiet enough to avoid reaching the visitors' ears, but gently like he means it. "I should've called to let you know. I didn't realize how late it'd gotten."

I shake my head, brushing off my earlier disappointment in the wake of Mal's sincere, concerned words. "You're free to have guests whenever you please," I remind him. "Care to introduce me?"

"Of course," he says, taking my hand and tugging me forward. I hide my surprise, not anticipating Mal would have been so comfortable being familiar with me in front of his friends. I can't say I mind one bit. "Henrik, these are my friends Dixon and Alex. Guys, this is Henrik."

"The sugar daddy," one of the men says, his voice light and teasing.

"That's Alex," Mal fills in for me, dropping my palm. I can practically hear the eye roll in his tone.

I reach forward, and, as expected, Alex fills in the distance to shake my hand. His palm is smaller than Mal's. I don't bother to correct his *sugar daddy* assessment because it's not exactly wrong. But I do make sure he knows, "He doesn't call me Daddy."

"No?" Alex asks, releasing our shake. "Are you looking for a firm hand of your own, then? 'Cause I'm available."

Alex laughs, and by the way he stumbles back suddenly, I get the sense Mal shoved him. "Back off, you horndog. Be polite."

"Don't know the word," Alex mumbles.

"Nice to meet you," the other man, Dixon, says. His voice is deeper, and when he clasps my hand, it's larger, too. I remember Mal letting slip that Dixon was upset about the client who choked him. I have a feeling Dixon and I will get along just fine. "Sorry about the children."

"You're like, four years older than me, Dixie-poo," Alex says.

"Five," he corrects, letting go of my hand.

"And how many years older are you than Mal, Henrik?" Alex asks sweetly. I get the impression he's a well-intentioned shit-stirrer. He and Benji would get along swimmingly.

"Doesn't matter," Mal answers for me, guiding me to the left toward the two-seater chair as his friends settle on the couch. "You sure it's okay that they're here?" he asks me again.

"Yes, Mal," I reply, running my fingers up his arm to his neck. His hair is pulled away from his face today, I notice, and I miss the feel of the strands against the back of my hand. "It's more than okay. I'll leave you be so you can enjoy your time with your friends."

He latches onto my wrist, holding me against his neck. "You don't have to do that. Stay. Please?"

"You're sure?"

He nods.

"All right," I say, more than a little pleased Mal *wants* me to stay. He drops his hold and takes a step back, and I turn toward his friends. "Would anyone care for a drink? Water, wine? Unless Mal has already taken care of it, of course."

Mal snorts. "No, I've been a bad host."

Alex snickers, saying something about Mal "needing a spanking," but then he clearly states, "I'd love a glass of wine. One for Dixie, too."

"Just a tea for me, but I can get it," Mal says, walking toward the kitchen.

Tea.

I follow with a frown. "Everything okay?"

Mal lets out a slow breath, and when we get to the kitchen, he steps close, speaking softly. His friends aren't entirely out of earshot, but seeing as they're talking amongst themselves, I doubt they'd overhear. "Alex and Dixon found me having a panic attack today. I wasn't at my best."

I frown again, not liking the implication that Mal is to blame for his panic attacks, as if he'd been better, he could have prevented it. But I do appreciate that he's telling me, offering up the information willingly as if he trusts me.

Grabbing a hold of Mal's hips, I run my thumbs along the defined V of his abdomen, and his breath hitches. "I'm sorry you had a bad day," I tell him.

He lets out a quiet sigh. "It's better now."

I smile, probably reading more into his words than intended, but I can't help but hope part of that reason is *me*. "But you still want some tea," I say, running my thumbs in soothing circles over his skin.

"Yes," he replies, sighing again. "And you need to stop that or my friends are going to get a show."

I chuckle, taking a step back. "I'll get the wine."

Mal prepares his tea as I pour glasses of a nice Sangiovese. He grabs one of the glasses, along with his drink, and I carry the others. In the living room, Mal takes one from my hand to pass to his friend. Then, much to my continued surprise, he pushes me into the two-seater and claims the spot next to me, one of his legs thrown over my own, as if settling at my side was a given. As if it's the most natural thing in the world.

The scariest part is it's not scary at all. My mind quiets as I take a sip of my red wine, my other hand resting against Mal's thigh. His tropical scent washes over me, and I relax into the cushy seat, all those warning bells telling me to stay away long gone, cracked and crumbled into dust.

"Well, isn't this cozy," Alex says after a moment.

Mal sighs. "I'm flipping him off," he informs me.

I snort, but I can't help but agree with Alex. This sure is cozy.

"So, Henrik," Alex says, voice mischievous. "Tell us all about yourself."

"So the new suit is in the labeled bag in my closet. Forest green, you said, to *match my eyes*. And you'll pick something up for Mal?"

Benji doesn't respond, and I frown, nudging the spot where he should be standing a foot away from me. He jumps when I prod his side.

"Shit," he mutters at a whisper, clearing his throat. "What was that for?"

I cant my head. "You didn't respond. What's going on?"

He's silent for a moment. "Does he do this often?"

Understanding dawns, and I hold back a growl. I don't like the idea of Benjamin checking out my Mal. No, not *my* Mal. Just Mal.

"Yes," I bite out. Mal's yoga habit has never bothered me before, but he's never done it with an ogling audience, either. Well, apart from me, but that's different. "He enjoys it."

It also calms him, but I don't go into that with Benji.

My personal assistant blows out a breath.

"What?" I snap.

"I'm sorry," he says around a laugh, not sounding it one bit. "It's just... Damn, that boy is flexible."

I grit my teeth.

"And shirtless," Benji adds. "Very shirtless."

"And right there," I remind him.

"He's wearing his headphones," Benji says, brushing me off. "And not much else. I mean, damn Henrik. Damn."

"You said that already."

"Let me paint you a visual—"

"*Benjamin.*"

"It's early evening. Golden light streams through the window, lighting the slab on which Apollo stands. Or, well, bends. His tousled blonde hair is tied behind his head, a few wisps escaping to frame his chiseled face. Rough stubble, pouty lips, oceanic eyes as fresh as the sweat dripping down his back—"

"Benjamin," I warn.

"Please, I'm just getting to the best part. *Downward dog*," he stresses. "Ass high, *high*, in the air, firm buttocks swathed in nary but the thinnest cloth ever to have been woven up in Heaven or here down on Earth. We mere mortals exist only to bear witness to such miraculous sights. Thigh muscles taut, glutes glutastically firm, arms…existing, I'm sure, if I were able to drag my eyes that far, upper body bent to the floor like—"

"*Enough*," I bite out, a muscle in my jaw popping. I don't like Benjamin looking at Mal. I don't like him *objectifying* him, even though, realistically, I know Benji's intent is harmless. I just don't *like* it.

Benjamin chuckles darkly, the wicked, wicked man. "I should go," he says.

"Yes, you should. Send my love to your *husband*."

"My husband would love this," he says wistfully.

I give him a half-hearted shove. "Don't forget a suit for Mal."

"Of course," Benjamin replies, all business once more. "I'll have it here mid-week."

I nod, blowing out a breath as Benjamin packs his things.

"Leaving?" Mal asks, presumably having caught sight of Benji's departure.

"For now. If you need someone to spot you through the rest of your workout, I'm sure Henrik would be up to the task."

I bite my tongue, but Mal chuckles. "Yeah, he's an expert at that."

Benji guffaws, no doubt sending me a mischievous grin. "I'm sure he is. Bye, lovebirds."

"I have no clue why I pay you," I mumble.

"Because I'm the best," Benji calls right before the elevator doors whoosh closed.

"What'd I miss?" Mal asks.

"Nothing important," I tell him, heading right over to his mat. He startles as I crouch down and feel him out none too gently. "Do the thing you were doing." I find the sweat Benjamin was talking about, a hint of it along his back. "Please," I add belatedly.

"Which thing?" Mal asks, inhaling sharply when I find his half-hard bulge and squeeze.

"Benjamin called it downward dog."

Mal chuckles a little breathily, amused, or maybe surprised, and then he switches position. I follow him with my palms, skating them over his body and groaning at what I find. Benjamin was right. His thigh muscles are stretched taut, straightened and firm under my hands. Warm even through the material of his thin yoga pants. His ass is high in the air, plump and indescribably lush beneath my fingertips. And he's bent down like...

"*Fuck*," I hiss, my cock throbbing, painfully hard within my trousers.

Mal moves from his pose, ignoring my sounds of displeasure and shoving me gently. "C'mon, sit back. I want to taste you."

Well, shit.

Am I supposed to say no to that?

I let Mal push and guide me to the floor until I'm leaned back against the couch. His hands scramble at my waistband as soon as I'm seated.

"I've wanted to do this for a long time," he says.

I open my mouth to question him, to ask how long exactly, but my teeth clack shut as Mal lowers himself between my bent knees and sucks me, without warning, into the heat of his warm, welcoming mouth.

I kick out my leg, one hand grasping at the smooth hardwood beneath me and the other wrapping in Mal's hair, as he steals the breath from my lungs. His lips wrap around me like a glove, sinking deeper and deeper, until I'm tucked entirely inside the snug expanse of his mouth and throat.

Fuck, he can deepthroat.

My eyes roll up, and I offer a brief prayer to a god I don't believe in.

"Mal," I croak out, my fingers flexing in his hair, holding on as I fall apart.

Mal hums around me before drawing back, suckling my crown while he catches his breath, and I trace one hand inward, feeling the way his mouth curves around me, a perfect "o." He turns his head, releasing my dick and nipping my finger lightly, and I laugh.

My laughter dies as he sinks down my length once more, working me deep inside his throat. "*Fuck*," I gasp out. I chant his name—*MalMalMal*—over and over again, my hips driving up of their own accord. He doesn't seem to mind. In fact, he stills, letting me punch into his mouth in shallow thrusts. When I feel the evidence of tears streaking down one of his cheeks, I try to pull back, but Mal follows me down, working me with renewed vigor. I curse, tightening my grip in his hair as my balls draw up tight.

"So good," I all but whisper, to myself or him, I'm not sure.

Mal tightens his lips around me, cheeks hollowed, the pressure demanding release. And with a punched-out groan, I give it, emptying down the back of Mal's throat in dizzying bursts of pleasure. His tongue teases me as I come down from my high, like a soothing embrace, and then he sits back.

I'm panting, still trying to catch my breath, but I lean forward, finding the tent in Mal's yoga pants. "Lie back," I tell him, palming his hard length.

He does, lying down across the yoga mat as I brace myself over his body, hand slipping under the stretchy material at his hips. He gasps as my palm encounters the smooth flesh of his erection, and when I start to stroke, he moans, a happy hum of a sound. I bend my neck, running my day-old stubble across his smooth pec and taking a nipple into my mouth with a suck and flick of my tongue. Mal's back arches with the assault, and my chest hums.

"Hen," he gasps softly, sinking his fingers into my hair.

He's the only person who's ever dared call me such, and I should discourage the familiar endearment. I shouldn't thrill every time the syllable reaches my ears. But I stay silent, letting the nickname worm itself deep inside me in search of a home.

I trace my lips to Mal's other nipple, wondering idly if it's dusky pink or perhaps brown, but as his hips start meeting the strokes of my hand, I refocus my efforts, certain he's close. I don't need to see Mal to know that much. The sounds he's making, all breathy and hurried, the way his fingers have tightened in my hair in anticipation, how his dick has started swelling in my fist, it tells the story just fine.

Mal groans long and low as he comes, his hips jerking when I give his nipple a tug. Once he becomes too sensitive, he pushes my head away, but I don't go far, wrung out still after my own orgasm. Simply needing a minute to recoup, I slump down next to Mal, one hand resting on his softened dick, my chin near his shoulder. He blows out a breath, and when he next speaks, it sounds as if he's turned to look at me, his voice right near the top of my head.

"I'm going to need to do laundry."

I bark out a laugh, and Mal's shoulder shakes with his own chuckle.

"Seriously," he says. "Did you have to make me come inside my pants?"

"I didn't hear you complaining," I point out, squeezing his satisfied dick for emphasis.

He snorts. "Hardly. Are you going to hold that all night, though? 'Cause if so, maybe we could move to somewhere more comfortable."

I huff a breath through my nose, letting Mal's dick go. He chuckles as I push myself up, and I nearly jolt when Mal's warm fingers tuck me back into my pants, patting my crotch once I'm zipped up. I catch a quick whiff of his coconut shampoo, and then Mal's presence disappears.

"We should clean up," he says, sounding as if he's rolling up his yoga mat.

He's right, but I can't resist. "Whatever you say, Daddy."

Mal's laughter follows me down the hall, and there's a grin on my face I don't even try to hide. When I get back to the living room, having washed, I find Mal sprawled across the couch, wearing soft sleep pants and a tee. He doesn't protest as I sit next to him, lifting his head onto my lap.

"Crossword?" he asks.

I smile. "Mhm."

Mal's smooth voice lulls me as he starts to read the clues, and I lean my head back against the couch, closing my eyes, occasionally offering up an answer. Who would have thought I'd get such enjoyment out of something as simple as this? Sitting with another person, spending time doing a daily puzzle.

Somehow, with Mal, everything is different.

I know this isn't wise. I know I shouldn't allow my happiness to become wrapped up in another person, one I barely even know. I told myself long ago I wouldn't let that happen, that I wouldn't depend on another person in that way.

But despite knowing this make believe happily ever after is all Mal and I could ever have, I also know I'm done fighting the draw. It's useless. His presence has been tugging at me ever since that first night I heard his slightly insecure voice. He's been urging me, unknowingly, off the unattainable cliff I'd perched myself upon.

And I've already tumbled down. Leapt, more like. I think I took that ill-advised jump the moment Mal rested his head on my lap much like this over a week ago. When I caressed the tears from his face and felt like, for a brief moment, someone's *everything*.

I didn't care then—and I don't care now—that it's not real. I don't care that the Henrik of a month ago would have scoffed and told me I'm being foolish. That I need to remind myself of my priorities.

Because Mal is something...special. The word doesn't even do him justice, as overused as it is. He's softness. That sinking feeling when your muscles let go and relax into a warm bath at the end of the night. He's fresh air and a tropical breeze. The brushing of a palm bough against your skin, both gentle and exhilarating. He's a spark, vibrant and fleeting but capable of great destruction.

He very well might be the end of me.

But if we only have a few months to burn, might as well make the blaze touch the sky.

Chapter 19
MAL

"Shit, he's going to kill me. On a scale of one to ten, how bad is this?"

The kittens, of course, don't respond. Which is good. I have enough problems on my plate without adding delusions to the mix.

The one with gray fur mewls pitifully, and I pick it up, petting along its spindly spine. Its black-furred companion is quiet inside the dirty, cardboard box I found them in. Honestly, it was pure luck I discovered them at all, left alone as they were in an alley behind the homeopathic store a few blocks away. I only meant to pick up some more essential oils. Instead, I picked up a pair of bedraggled kittens.

Henrik really is going to kill me.

Cats weren't against the rules specifically, but tidiness is a big deal. And cats aren't exactly...compliant. They'll need a litter box, toys, food and water dishes.

Not that they'll *stay*, of course. I just need to keep them here for a night. In the morning, once Catty Commotions opens, I can take them there.

Even though Little Gray is staring up at me like I'm the best thing in the world, the little bundle purring loudly in my palm. My heart clenches, and I pick up its brother or sister, making sure to give the black-furred kitten the same attention. Just because that one is quiet, that doesn't mean he or she doesn't want some cuddles, too.

"I'm sure it'll be fine. It's just for a night."

"What's for a night?"

I startle, looking over at Henrik in the doorway of the guest room. He's still dressed in the suit he wore to work this morning, the pinstripe gray making him look sexy in that clean-cut way he has about him. The slight hint of silver in his hair adds to the overall appeal. His face is shaved, but a hint of shadow graces his jawline, and even though, as I watch, his lips turn down into a frown, I can't help the bolt of lust that hits me square in the gut.

Why do I always want this man?

"Mal?" Henrik asks, taking a tentative step inside the room. "What is that sound?"

Oh, God. I look down at the kittens in my arms. "About that..."

Henrik straightens, eyes wide. "That's a cat."

"Two cats. Kittens, technically."

"Mal—"

"I *know*. I'm sorry," I tell him, standing up with the pair held close to my chest. "I found them outside, and I couldn't just leave them there without food or shelter. They're so skinny, Hen. They haven't been taken care of, and someone clearly abandoned them. I'll bring them to the shelter in the morning, I promise. I just...I couldn't leave them all alone."

Henrik frowns again, but then his face smooths out. He takes another step forward, and shuffling the kittens around, I reach out, brushing his forearm and drawing him near. Henrik follows my arm to the kittens, his hands looking massive as he gingerly runs them over the raggedy bundles of fur.

"They're skin and bones," he says.

"Yeah."

Little Gray rubs eagerly against Henrik's hand, and his face pinches. "We don't have any food for them."

"Well, no, but—"

Henrik reaches into his pocket, and I gape as he voice-directs his phone to call his personal assistant, his free hand suspended over the kittens as they use him like their own personal scratching post. "Benjamin, we need cat food. Yes, cat food." He holds the phone away from his face. "What kind of cat food?"

"Um." My heart thrashes around wildly inside my ribcage. "They're old enough for solid food. Anything made for kittens would be fine."

Henrik nods. "Solid food for kittens. Yes. And bowls. Litter pan?" he asks me. I mumble an affirmative. "Litter, too. Mhm. Oh shut up, Benjamin. Yes, grab a couple toys." He sighs. "You and Gary can have a good laugh about this later, after you've delivered the necessary essentials." With that, he hangs up. "Such a smartass," he grumbles, sliding his phone into his pocket. "Benjamin should be here within the hour. Will they be okay until then?"

I open my mouth to say *of course*, but nothing comes out. Instead, with my insides fizzing, I lurch forward, my fingers threading through the short strands at the back of Henrik's head as I clasp our mouths together.

I kiss him without thought, without restraint, just wanting—*needing*—to show him my appreciation. Needing him to understand how much it means to me that he didn't bat an eye at the inconvenience to his home, instead jumping straight into problem-solving mode. Into caretaker mode.

Needing him to understand how light he makes me feel. Like in his presence, I could simply float away, untethered from all the worries that root me to the ground.

Needing him to know how *happy* he makes me. How free.

And for a moment, I am. I'm gliding in an endless plane of sparkling white, my heart in my throat, my toes barely touching the ground.

And then Henrik makes a surprised sound, going rigid against me, and I realize my mistake.

Henrik has never, not once, kissed me. And like a cold slap in the face, I remember why.

Because I'm his escort. His *sugar baby*. I'm here for sex, not intimacy. Not whatever *this* is.

I draw back, utterly humiliated, about to apologize or brush off my actions or—I don't know—offer to pack my things.

But Henrik says, "Mal," and then he's the one pressing forward and slotting our mouths together in a gently rolling bang.

His lips, this time, are soft and yielding, and he kisses me back like he means it. Like he wants to inhale me. My pulse trips, tumbling before racing ahead, urging me closer to this man who makes me fall apart, who holds me together with the simplest touch of his hands. One rests tensely against the small of my back, and the other wraps in my hair as Henrik inhales sharply, breaking the connection between our lips for a moment before surging forward again, coaxing me open.

I'm not proud of the whimper that breaks free, but Henrik swallows it down, asking for more, demanding it. He'd be pressed against my body if it weren't for the two kittens in my arm, I'm sure of it. As is, we're both angled not to squish the felines, and I wish I could set them down and get closer, climb into this man who owns my breath, but I can't bear to pull back for even a moment.

And Henrik seems to feel the same. He backs me up until I hit the bed, and ever so gently, he plucks the kittens from my hold, placing them on the comforter. "Will they be okay?" he asks, barely shifting from my mouth long enough to get the words out. I nod against him, falling backwards as Henrik climbs over me, hands and knees on either side of my body.

The kittens wander the bed, one batting at my hair. But I focus on Henrik, who glides carefully down to his elbows, bringing his body against mine. We both groan as we fit together from chest to groin, but Henrik leans to the side as soon as I try to wriggle my leg free. I wrap it around his hip instead, driving up against him, bringing us closer. His mouth never leaves mine, his tongue relentlessly tangling with my own, and even with one of the kittens hopping atop his back, Henrik never wavers.

Why haven't we kissed before?

Why haven't we done this a million times? It's the best thing ever. It's joyful and wicked and sensual all in one. It's—

Henrik's ringtone pierces the air, and with a muttered curse, he draws back. We're both breathing heavily, suspended a half foot apart, and even though I know Henrik can't see me, it feels like he can. It's in the way he's focused on me. How he doesn't move for the longest moment, his cheeks flushed and his brown hair in disarray.

I want that. I want it to be true, what I'm seeing on his face. I want to believe he truly sees *me*.

He stalls, inching forward as if he wants to continue exploring my esophagus, but then his phone begins ringing a second time, and he pulls it from his pocket, bracing himself awkwardly, as if he aborted sitting up all the way. Realizing why—one cat is still dangling from his back—I laugh and help to pluck it free. Henrik's mouth tips into a smile as he plants himself beside me, having patted the bed first to make sure it was clear.

"Hello?" he asks briskly, brushing his hair off his forehead. I watch the way his chest rises and falls, mirroring my own, and eye the neglected bulge inside his suit pants. *Me, too, buddy. Me, too.* "I...I don't know. Does it matter?" He huffs. "Go with the grain-free. If it's more expensive, it must be better." I smile, chest warm. "Yes. That's fine. Bye."

Henrik blows out a breath, and when he turns my way, I reach over, tangling our hands together atop the mattress. He gives me a responding squeeze.

"He'll be here soon," Henrik says needlessly.

"Okay," I answer with a nod. After a moment, I let Henrik's hand go and push myself off the bed. My body is still tingling, still firing, but I shake it off. "I should give them a bath."

Henrik looks perplexed. "I thought cats hated water."

Chuckling, I pluck Little Gray off the comforter. "Some do, but they're filthy." I pause, eyes trailing over Henrik's suit. "You could give me a hand."

His brow wings up. I expect him to laugh, to beg me off, but he holds his hand out instead. "If I get covered in scratches, I'm blaming you."

I smile widely, handing the kitten over and grabbing the other. "I'll kiss them better."

Henrik hums, his lips curling in a smile. "I'll hold you to that."

"Oh, Henrik. Kittens? This is precious."

I pause in the hallway, seeing only Henrik's side as he talks to Benji. He's shed his suit jacket, and the sleeves of his shirt are rolled up to his elbows. His pants are spotted with moisture and covered in cat hair, but he doesn't seem to mind.

I have to admit, the Henrik I've seen a side of tonight is worlds away from the man I thought he was when we first met. I never would've envisioned that neat and tidy businessman helping to bathe two rowdy kittens without a single complaint. Maybe even enjoying it.

And yet, despite the fact that the pair of felines were not tolerant of the water, as Henrik correctly predicted, he patiently helped me clean them off: holding them while I lathered and smiling when the little bundles calmed.

"Get it out of your system," Henrik says to his friend, sighing as Benji chuckles at his expense.

The man arrived ten minutes prior, laden down with cat supplies. Way more than needed for a single night, but I couldn't bring myself to tell Henrik it was overkill. Not when he so readily came to the rescue.

Now the two kittens have a litter pan, food, water, and toys set up in the guest room, where I'll confine them for the night so they don't get into trouble in Henrik's penthouse. Henrik doesn't seem to mind them racing around in the meantime, getting their after-bath zoomies out, hopping all over the furniture and skidding past Henrik's bare feet.

Benji clicks his tongue. "Buying a guy a new wardrobe is one thing. Letting him bring home cats?" He whistles softly.

I know I should alert the men to my presence, but my feet feel rooted to the floor.

"They will only be here for the night," Henrik says, voice tight.

"So you say," Benji replies. "But you're different with this one, Henrik. He must be great in the sa—"

"*Benjamin.* That is quite enough," Henrik barks as my pulse thrums wildly.

"Henrik, you know I was joking."

"You should get back to your husband. I've hogged enough of your time tonight," Henrik says, tone still clipped.

Benji sighs, speaking softly. "I was only teasing, Henrik. You know that. I like the kid. But clearly, I hit a nerve." He reaches forward, squeezing Henrik's arm. Henrik barely moves. "I didn't mean to offend. Have fun with your cats. And your Mal."

Henrik stays standing in the same spot as Benji leaves, but the kittens zoom past me down the hall when the elevator door opens. Once it closes, Henrik lets out a sigh, and I step from the hallway. He turns his head, and I stride right up.

I don't know if what Benji said is true—if Henrik really is different around me. I don't dare assume he cares for me beyond the bounds of our arrangement. That's much too dangerous a game.

But I do know, tonight, Henrik has shown me the depth of his kindness. And when Benji's teasing words were aimed my way, Henrik shut it down immediately. He came to my defense when he didn't have to. Maybe that's just who Henrik is. Or maybe that means something.

Whatever the reason, I don't want to question my desire for this man any longer. Something about Henrik calls to me. Maybe it's his calming presence, his sense of order that feeds my own need for control. The way he's like a pillar of strength, steady and strong. Maybe it's the way his careful demeanor slips apart when we're together. How his verdant eyes light up before they darken. How he seems to crave being near. How he can't stop *touching, touching, touching.*

Maybe I simply crave more of that exhilarating mouth of his.

Whatever the reason, I don't care. I want Henrik. I want this man.

Henrik hums curiously when I approach and pull him around to face me, a sound that pitches low when my lips greet his. There's no hesitation this time as Henrik meets me move for move, his hands in my hair as mine clutch against his shoulder blades. He sucks my lower lip after I nip his, and his tongue greets mine like a long-lost lover.

I don't know who moves first—if I pull or he pushes—but Henrik guides me down the hall with lips locked. We breach his doorway, and I slap my hand against the wall, flicking on the light. Henrik keeps backing me up until my legs hit his bed, much as they did to my own earlier this evening, and then he's on top of me as if the past hour's interruptions never happened.

He tugs at my shirt, and it slips over my head, blocking mouths for two seconds too long. He scrambles to undo my jeans next, and I pull frantically at the buttons of his shirt. Henrik growls low as my zipper gets stuck, and when it finally gives, he tugs my pants swiftly down my thighs.

I practically whine as Henrik's lips leave mine, but then he's hovering over my crotch, tearing my jeans the rest of the way off and lowering his face against the cotton of my briefs. My whine turns into a moan when he kisses my erection through the fabric, and I bunch his bedspread in my hands, my hips rising to meet his mouth, silently begging him to remove the barrier between skin. He takes his time, though, planting slightly parted lips against every inch of my covered cock, worshiping me, it seems, even as my blood begins to boil. His hands roam over my exposed torso, fingers flitting over the dips and swells of my abdomen, blunt nails grazing the grooves of my hips.

I moan low, needing more, never wanting it to stop. "*Hen.*"

Henrik looks up at me, and my breath hitches. *There.* That feral glint in his eye. That wildness. That's what I want. What I long for.

Knowing he's coming unhinged.

Desperately wishing it's because of *me*.

"I know, Mal," he says, finally, finally tugging my underwear down, his lips moving lower. "I know."

Chapter 20

HENRIK

Mal groans, his hips moving restlessly under me, and my chest sings. The way he so eagerly responds to my touch is a heady aphrodisiac.

I lave my tongue up the length of his erection, playing with his crown, flicking the slit. Mal curses, so I do it again and again before pulling back.

"Turn over," I tell him, backing up enough to give him room to maneuver. Mal doesn't question me; he simply rolls onto his stomach, rustling the sheets below him. I take a moment to divest myself of my clothes, and then I slide my hands up his legs, finding his ass hitched high in the air.

"You adore my ass," he says simply.

"Yes," I readily confess, mapping the taut globes with my hands. The way they swell out slightly from his hips, round and just firm enough, but not without give. I dig my fingers into the flesh, imagining the way the cheeks would indent around the digits, blanching and then blooming red.

"I like that you adore my ass," he replies, jumping a little when I lean close and scrape my barely there stubble against his skin. "*God.*"

I kiss the spot I abraded, admitting, "I want to fuck you."

It's been weeks since that first time, and I haven't gone there again. Maybe I thought it would help me maintain some distance from my tempting houseguest. Maybe I was afraid of how good it would feel.

Maybe—*definitely*—I'm past caring.

"Yes, fuck me," Mal responds instantly, hips wiggling.

I chuckle, slipping away to grab the lube and a condom. When I return, Mal is in the same position I left him. I allow myself a few strokes of my own erection, biting my lip against the pleasure, before I drizzle lube onto my fingers. Kneeling abreast Mal's hip, I roam my hand along his back as the other slides over his pucker, massaging the flesh. Mal shifts slightly, resituating himself, and I ease a slicked finger in, my palm resting above his asshole.

"Fuck, yes," Mal says, pressing back against me. "More."

I oblige, circling my finger around before retreating and sliding two in side by side, curling the digits and rubbing his inner walls. Loosening him. Imagining what it will feel like when he's caressing my dick instead of my fingers. I let my other hand trail over his back and into his hair, the tresses unbound and falling over the pillow and his face. I brush them aside, running my fingers through the strands. Mal reaches back, his hand connecting with my thigh. He digs in, turning his face into the pillow as I press another finger in alongside the others. He's tight and warm, and he bears down against me, sucking my digits in with ease.

I groan, my impatience to get inside that snug heat getting the better of me.

Mal slaps my thigh impatiently. "Go on," he says, as if he can hear my internal thoughts.

I pull my fingers free and skirt behind him, wrapping my dick and adding more lube before I position myself, notching against Mal's entrance like we're two pieces of a puzzle, waiting to be snapped together.

"*Hen*," Mal groans. "What are you waiting for?"

What *am* I waiting for?

When I finally sink into Mal's body, he punches out a sigh, driving back until his ass cheeks are flush against my crotch. I grab on tight, fingers spanning his hips, as I roll against him again and again. I can all-too-clearly picture the way my cock would look disappearing between his cheeks, and I slide one of my hands to his entrance, feeling how he welcomes me in. How much he's stretched to accommodate me.

"*Fuck*," I hiss.

"This is so much better than porn," Mal moans.

I concur. Not that I've watched porn in quite some time, but a real body has nothing on fiction. You can't touch a video. Can't taste.

And fuck, do I want to taste.

I slip out of Mal's body despite his protesting whine. "Turn over," I tell him.

"I feel like a record," he mumbles, his leg hair brushing against mine as he rolls onto his back. I chuckle.

You can't laugh with a video, either.

I ready myself against Mal's body again, but he touches my wrist. "Wait, you turn over. On your back."

I raise an eyebrow, but considering Mal so rarely asks for anything, I readily oblige, trading places and lying flat on the bed. Mal straddles me, his legs snug against my hips, and then he sinks down, taking me inside his body in one fluid motion.

We both groan, and Mal starts to ride me. *Fuck*, it's so good, but I wanted...

"Come here," I tell him, reaching.

Mal grabs my hand, leaning forward as he slides it to the side of his head, and then he's kissing me like I wanted. I tighten my grip in his hair—*God, I love all that hair*—and do my best to map the inside of Mal's mouth. He tastes like lemon and smells like coconut, and I can't get enough. Even the underlying hint of wet cat hanging on one or both of our bodies doesn't do a damn thing to detract from the lust coursing through me as Mal's body dances over mine. As he uses me the way he pleases. As he moans into my mouth, grinding over me again and again.

As he spills, sudden and sharp, between our bodies, gasping in obvious surprise and squeezing me so damn tight I see stars. I punch up into his body, seeking my own release, but Mal has other plans. He lifts himself swiftly, shucking off my condom and stroking me with a firm grip.

"Come all over my face," he says, the simple words and his fervent motions sending me over the edge in an instant.

I swell in his fist, and Mal pumps me through it, working every last aftershock from my body until I'm wrung dry, only softening his grip once I've spent. Then he grabs my hand, places my palm against his cheek, and rubs my seed into his skin.

Groaning, positive I've died and gone to Heaven, I continue the work Mal started, letting my fingers drift over his face, finding my release and dragging it across his cheekbones, over his chin, along his lips. Marking him. Making him mine.

"*Fuck*," I breathe out at last, leaving my thumb pressed against Mal's plump lower lip.

"Had a feeling you'd like that, you barbarian," he says, almost fondly.

I chuckle, my eyes closing as my body goes lax. "You've no idea."

Mal tugs my hand down, keeping it in his as he leans forward and kisses me softly, gently, my taste on his lips. My eyes flutter open, and for the briefest of moments, it's like I can see him suspended above me. An angel of riotous golden hair, blue eyes deep like the ocean. The bow of his lips. The planes of his face. The flush on his cheeks.

For a moment, my imagination brings him to life.

But the truth is that it doesn't matter to me what Mal looks like. Curiosity aside, it never has.

What matters is the way he's cupping my face like I'm precious to him. The way his mouth ghosts over mine once more, whisper soft, the intimacy of it profound in the wake of our coupling. The way he pours his emotions into the air between us, crackling like electricity, so close I can touch.

What matters is the way my heart ga-thumps when he sighs, a hair's breadth away from my lips. How I know, somehow, against all reason and despite the unfathomable odds, I've fallen for a man who was never destined to stay mine. Who wandered into my life under the strangest of circumstances, through pure happenstance, and who has yet to leave.

And I don't want him to leave. Six months doesn't sound like nearly enough time. And when's the last time I thought that? Never.

But how could this possibly work? Our relationship is based on a business transaction. There's every chance that, to Mal, that's all this is. That's all this could ever be.

Do I ask him now and risk breaking off our arrangement? Or do I wait, keeping him for longer and yet risking much more than my bank account?

Mal sits up before I've finished contemplating my conundrum, his body leaving mine as my mind continues to race. He sighs again, sounding as if he's stretching.

I call back my thoughts and rub against the long expanse of his naked back. "Everything all right? Are you sore?"

He huffs a laugh. "No, I'm good. Definitely need a shower, though."

I nod my assent, wondering if I should ask him to join me in my en suite. But Mal stands up before I have a chance, displacing my wandering fingers.

"And don't worry," he says. "I'll make sure the cats didn't make a mess, and I'll keep them in the guest room tonight."

"Mal," I say before he's reached the door, grasping for something to keep him with me for longer. "They can stay here for a while. The cats, I mean. Uh..." I scratch the side of my head. "They'd probably be more comfortable, right? In a home, instead of at the shelter. At least until we can make sure they're healthy."

Mal is quiet for a couple seconds. "Are you sure?" he asks softly, coming closer to the bed.

I barely manage to keep myself from reaching for him. "Why not? It's no trouble."

Mal's weight leans against the mattress, and then his hand brushes my cheek lightly. "Thank you, Henrik," he says, his lips greeting mine softly once again. I chase after him, wanting more, but Mal pulls back. "Night."

"Night," I reply a little numbly.

As Mal leaves my room, closing the door behind him, I know I've broken my own code. I've done the one thing I promised myself I would never do.

I let someone in.

And now that it's done, I fear there's no turning back.

"Come on, Little Gray. Hold still."

I chuckle. "Little Gray?"

"I didn't know what else to call it, and since it has gray fur, it's Little Gray," Mal explains.

It's a rarity for Mal to be awake this early, before I've left for work, but with the cats causing a ruckus in his room, he was up at the crack of dawn, same as me.

"And the other one?" I ask, smiling into my morning cup of tea.

"The other one has black fur."

"You should give them real names," I point out.

Mal makes an "mm" sound. "I don't want to get attached."

I'm tempted to tell him we can just keep the cats. They're so small, and even though they have a lot of energy, they don't seem to be destructive. So long as we keep plenty of toys around, I'm sure it wouldn't be an issue.

But then I realize where my mind has gone, assuming Mal and the cats would stay here with me. I shake off my thoughts, not ready to get my hopes up.

"Boy," Mal finally declares. Little Gray scampers away as soon as Mal sets him down, and I hand over the black one, who'd been lounging across my arm without a care in the world. It doesn't seem to put up as much of a struggle, seeing as five seconds later, Mal says, "Another boy."

"At least they can't make more kittens."

Mal chuckles, and my phone dings, alerting me of the time. I finish my tea, place my empty mug in the dishwasher, and wash my hands.

"Time to go?" Mal asks.

I nod, wishing I didn't have to leave him today. *How quickly the tide has turned.* At least tomorrow is Saturday.

"Shit," I say in surprise, "I forgot to tell you about the benefit."

"Benefit?"

"Yes," I reply with a groan. Not because I don't want to go—I always look forward to this event—but because I haven't given Mal any notice. "It's tomorrow night. My company presents this year's best and brightest from our incubators, matching investors with up-and-coming business ventures. Win-win all around."

"I'm sorry," he says, laughing. "Did you just say 'incubators?' Like for chickens?"

I chuckle, finding Mal on a stool at the island and stepping in close. He places his hands loosely on my hips, and I reach up, feeling the smile at the corner of his mouth. "No, not for chickens. We have several business incubators scattered across the city. They provide resources for startups."

"Oh," he says. "So a little less like a banker."

I chuckle again, leaning close to kiss Mal in a way that has nothing to do with sex. He doesn't seem to mind, kissing me back just as sweetly.

When I draw back, I ask, "Will you come with me?"

"To the benefit?" he asks, voice going a little high.

"Of course."

Mal's fingers flex against my hips.

"What's wrong?" I ask, stomach sinking. Maybe Mal doesn't want to be seen with me. Although, as an escort, isn't that part of the job?

I banish the word *job* from my mind immediately, hating the sound of it.

"Aren't you worried someone might recognize me?" he asks.

I startle, realizing I hadn't even contemplated that. I've never brought one of my companions to an event before. Never wanted to before now. "Because of your job?"

How likely would it be that a previous escort client would be at the benefit?

"Well, yeah. It's not like I'm a fan favorite, not like Silver," he says. I have no clue who he's talking about, but he goes on. "But sometimes people recognize me."

I think it over for a moment, but in the end, I shrug. Anyone who had hired Mal as an escort would be discreet about their dealings. Even if we do come across a prior client, I don't see it being an issue. Outing me would be outing themselves.

"It's fine. I can't imagine it would cause a problem."

"If you're sure," he says slowly, seeming concerned.

"I'm sure," I say, squeezing the back of his neck.

"Okay," Mal says, leaning forward. I read his intent and meet him in the middle, our lips brushing once more. Now that the seal has broken, it's like we can't stop. I want to attach my lips to Mal, to produce more and more of those addictive, breathy little moans that decorate the air between us every time my mouth is linked with his.

Rather reluctantly, I let the back of Mal's head go. "I really do have to leave," I say, stepping back. "Have a good day with the cats."

Mal huffs a laugh. "Have a good day at work, honey."

His tone is clearly teasing, but I don't hate it. In fact, I like the sound of that *honey* more than I should. It makes me feel warm and cozy, and even as I head off to work, the phantom of Mal's words stay with me like a physical touch.

I can't deny it anymore. I've developed feelings for my escort. *Real* feelings.

I'm officially fucked.

Chapter 21

MAL

"Does this look all right?"

Henrik raises an eyebrow my way, and I curse.

"Crap, I'm sorry," I say sincerely.

He looks nonplussed, stepping forward and proceeding to run his hands all over me, from my shoulders, down my lapels, to my hips. He brushes over the suit jacket fabric at my waist, as if wiping away nonexistent wrinkles, and then he steps back, hand on his chin as he nods.

"Hot."

I laugh, even as my face flushes from embarrassment. "Sorry," I mumble again.

Henrik shakes his head. "Benjamin said the color would suit you."

"It does look nice," I admit. The stylish gray suit Benji dropped off not only fits perfectly, but the steely tones make my eyes pop, even more so since my hair is pulled out of the way in a bun behind my head. A simple white shirt completes my look, a piece of clothing that likely cost more than my entire personal wardrobe.

I try not to focus on the cost. Technically, I could have afforded the outfit I'm wearing tonight by myself now that my bank balance is sitting at a ridiculously high sum I never imagined I'd see. But Henrik made it clear this was his treat. And after a brief internal debate, I sucked up my pride and thanked him.

I am, after all, his sugar baby. His escort. I'm not his boyfriend or significant other. More like arm candy. And if Henrik needs to make that distinction clear by paying for the transaction of our night, I can respect that.

Even as it stings.

After fidgeting with my cufflinks for the tenth time, I turn to Henrik, who's patiently waiting for me. "The paisley looks nice," I say.

Henrik straightens. "What?"

"I didn't think they still made suits in that print."

I keep my lips pressed tightly together as Henrik frowns, feeling down his lapels as if he can detect the pattern there. But then his face clears.

"You're fucking with me," he states plainly.

"Busted," I admit, laughing as Henrik strides forward. He finds my arm and tugs me into his body. Our chests collide as Henrik frames my jaw in his hands, angling up my face. His lips are pursed, and he shakes his head, but then his mouth twists into the tiniest of smirks before smooth lips meet my own.

I go lax, absolutely melting as Henrik kisses me senseless, the onslaught feeling like the most welcome sort of payback. I don't even care that this blurs that whole escort-client line I was reminding myself of moments ago. Because when Henrik's lips are against mine, when he nuzzles into that space against my neck like he's trying to inhale my scent, when he rubs me raw with his short stubble, as if trying to leave his own mark behind on my skin, I simply float away. All those worries about money or what happens next or what this means stay behind on the cold hard ground, unable to reach me.

"Hen," I groan, angling my head as he sucks against the skin of my neck. My fingers spasm into the fabric at his back, and I force my hands to relax, smoothing out any wrinkles. "We need to stop. You're gonna leave a mark."

"Don't want to stop," he grumbles, releasing my flesh and nuzzling his nose under my ear.

Fuck. He's so goddamn tactile. I love it.

"We can pick this up later," I force out. *Before I come in my $4,000 pants.*

Henrik sighs, his breath fanning over my skin. He doesn't move for the longest time, and the position feels a lot like an embrace.

My heart skips frantically.

Finally, Henrik steps back, smoothing his hair into place. I help him out, enjoying the feel of the thick strands between my fingers.

"C'mon," I say, giving him a little tug. Henrik follows after me as I head out of the guest room. "We should let the kittens free."

I had shut them in the bathroom while Henrik and I were getting ready, not wanting fur all over the bottom of our pants. But as soon as I open the door, the kittens spring right against our legs anyway.

I sigh. "So much for that."

"It's fine," Henrik says, always careful to step gently when the kittens are around. "I'll have Benjamin grab a lint roller."

I huff a laugh as I follow him toward the front of the penthouse. Henrik slips his wallet into his pants and grabs his cane, and I realize it's the first time I'll see him use it. The first time I'll be out of this building with him, in fact. As his date.

My smile slips as my brain so helpfully reminds me it's only a date for appearance's sake. This *thing* between Henrik and me isn't real. Yes, the past month has thrown us together in a way that makes the intimacy we share feel authentic. As if we truly are two lovers building on something good. Building a relationship.

But sex doesn't equal partnership. And living with Henrik doesn't make me someone important to him. It's only escalated my feelings for the man I see more frequently than any other person in my life at the moment.

But this will end. Whether some day soon or five months down the road, this will be over. I won't be living here anymore, and Henrik will go back to being someone I never see. As if this didn't happen at all. As if I was never here.

I can't get used to being pampered and fawned over and having someone treat me like I...what, matter? Like they care? *Christ.*

"Mal?" Henrik steps close, palm skating up my chest and resting against my neck. "Are you okay? Your breathing is labored."

I force myself to relax. To count and focus on slowing my heart rate. After a moment, I nod, although my throat still feels tight and my chest is squeezed in an angry fist. "Fine."

Henrik frowns. "Is this too much? We don't have to go."

"What?" I say before shaking my head. "No, it's fine. I was just in my head."

Henrik hums, his other hand coming up to smooth over my cheek. My breath rattles a little shakily as he leans close, his lips ghosting over my own. "When we get home, I'm going to help you relax."

"Is that so?" I reply, laughing when Henrik bumps his nose against mine in an approximation of the type of kisses I'd see the girls and boys doing in school, when everything was simple and I was still a naive little kid who believed in tender happy-ever-afters.

I'm not sure what I believe in now, but I'm certainly not that kid anymore.

Henrik nods, drawing back, his green eyes bright and mischievous. "Mhm. I'll lay you out on my bed, run my hands all over you until you're boneless and unwound—"

"Mm."

"—and then I'll swallow your cock until you're moaning my name," he says, leaning close, his lips brushing my ear. "And after you come down my throat, I'll paint your asscheeks and start the process all over again."

I swallow roughly, my cock throbbing at the promise he's giving. "Yeah. That sounds...fine."

Henrik chuckles, stepping back and pressing the button to open the elevator doors. "Come on, Mal," he says lightly when my feet stay rooted to the marble floor.

Shaking my head, I follow Henrik into the mirrored elevator. "Yes, Daddy," I mumble, laughing when Henrik pulls me close and play growls. He wiggles his fingers against my ribs, and I gasp, flailing in his grip. "I take it back! Good God, I take it back."

Henrik stops tickling me, but he doesn't let go, and as I catch his reflection in the glass wall, seeing a small smile on his lips as he holds me tucked against his body, a hopeful little bird takes flight behind my ribs, battering to be let loose.

For one eternal moment in this tower of gleaming white, I forget about my worries, I forget about my past, and I simply breathe. It's not so hard to do with Henrik's arms holding me tight, keeping me from shattering.

When Henrik and I step out of his fancy-ass black limousine, Benji just behind, I freeze. There's an actual red carpet and photographers ahead, already snapping pictures in our direction, the flashes blinding. Quickly, I paste on my most practiced smile, weaving my arm through Henrik's.

He already coached me on how to guide him, so I do my best to ignore the photographers and walk us forward, stopping several steps behind the short line at the door. People call for Henrik's attention, but apart from turning his head and offering a close-lipped smile, he doesn't react or answer questions. I follow his cue, heart thumping wildly as we move slowly forward.

There are steps up to the entrance, and even though Henrik's cane alerts him to their presence, I still lean close to let him know there are two. At the top of the stairs, Henrik gives his name, and the attendant nods before letting the three of us through the doors, welcoming Henrik profusely and smiling wide.

Henrik told me a little about tonight's benefit, but I didn't understand how integral Henrik himself was to the proceedings until Benji explained it on the way over—how involved Henrik is in his business ventures and the success, specifically, of the incubators. Henrik shook his head as Benji sang his praises, clearly not keen on being complimented, and yet, seeing the number of heads that turn as Henrik makes his way into the ballroom, I'm starting to realize exactly how big of a deal he is. This is *his* company that he started from the ground up when he was in his twenties—before he was my age. He's made a name for himself in the Las Vegas business world, and until tonight, I didn't understand the scope of that.

I didn't understand exactly how many lives he's changed, but seeing all the young entrepreneurs in attendance tonight, their gazes bright as they talk amongst themselves, I realize Henrik does more than shove money in people's pockets. He makes dreams come true.

Maybe, to him, it is about cash. About success. But to these people, it's their future. And after Benji told me avidly about the incentives for ventures designed for or by people with disabilities, I can't help but feel like it's about more than money to Henrik, too.

As we clear the crowd at the door, Henrik takes off his sunglasses—which he explained are more for the flashing lights than anything—and stows them inside his jacket. I love that he's not afraid to go head-to-head with people without the barrier. That he's unconcerned with what others may think of his eyes that wander a little differently around a room than most. He wouldn't call it bravery; I know that. But I still wonder if he realizes how strong he is.

"Come on," Benji says, stepping up to my side, his voice cutting across the din of the room. "Let's get drinks."

I nod, and the three of us navigate toward the bar. Henrik gets stopped multiple times on the way there, and he makes polite, quick conversation, introducing me each time as his "companion, Mal." But Benji helps herd us forward, clearly a pro at polite, efficient goodbyes, and before too long, we reach the side of the ballroom where servers in black tie are pouring drinks.

"Red for you, I assume, Henrik. What'll you have, Mal?" Benji asks, stepping up in line.

"Red is fine," I say.

Benji nods and turns forward as Henrik leans in close, speaking quietly. "Are you sure drinking is a good idea?"

"It's fine," I say, refraining from adding a "dad" to the end of my sentence, knowing how that ended last time, less than an hour ago. "I know my limits."

Henrik nods, and I appreciate that he doesn't push it. A minute later, Benji has our wine, and the three of us wade back into the throng of people. Henrik is clearly popular, even though his demeanor is not the friendliest. Don't get me wrong; he's perfectly polite. But he's all business, very brusque and formal. It reminds me of the night I met him, and it makes me realize how much has changed since then. How *different* Henrik is with me now.

I try not to let the thought warm me, but warm me it does, all the way to the tips of my toes.

I get a few inquisitive questions thrown my way—*what do you do, how did you and Henrik meet*—and I answer them vaguely each time. Henrik never gave me explicit instructions on what to say, but I can easily assume he doesn't want people knowing I'm his escort. So I tell them I'm in between jobs at the moment and that we were introduced by a mutual acquaintance—both true—and that seems to be boring enough to dissuade further interrogation.

Benji comes and goes as we mingle, presumably handling some things behind the scenes. When Henrik finishes his glass of wine, Benji brings him a second, but I refrain from drinking any more. Servers bounce around the room periodically with hors d'oeuvres on their trays, and one—a tall, dark-haired man—eyes me for a prolonged moment as he passes by. I can't help but wonder if he recognizes me as Malibu.

A niggle of worry settles in my gut, but Henrik was firm that he didn't care. I admit I was surprised, considering how territorial he got that one time I came home from the club, but maybe he doesn't care that people have seen me naked and engaged in all manners of activity, so long as he can claim me now.

I shouldn't like that—the idea of him claiming me—but I do. I like the way he's always touching me, whether affectionately or with dirtier intent, like when he rubs his cum into my skin. How, even now, standing here, his hand sits at the small of my back as if proclaiming *this one is mine*.

It might not be real, but right now, it's real enough.

The server moves on, and I try my best to listen to the conversation Henrik is having about the advantages of mutual shares vs ETFs, but admittedly, I'm glad when a murmur goes around that dinner is about to be served. Henrik says a polite goodbye, and Benji reappears like magic, leading us to our seats near center stage. Fancy cream tablecloths cover the round table, atop which sits pristine place settings and crystal glasses. A low flower arrangement sprawls in the middle, and in front of the chair Benji leads me to is a little place card that reads "Mal Jones."

I almost bark an incredulous laugh, seeing my shortened stage name butted up against my real one, as if my two worlds are colliding, mashed together and printed in gleaming gold. Once again, I feel like an imposter. Like I'm gliding along in a world I don't belong to, and it's only a matter of time until the people around me realize I'm a fraud.

But then Henrik takes a seat next to me, reaching over and placing his hand on my thigh like a tether, and I breathe out, relaxing.

Dinner is an elaborate affair, dish after dish of exquisitely prepared food. Henrik seems concerned when plates of Tuscan butter shrimp are set in front of us, and I'm shocked he remembered my dislike for shellfish, but I assure him it's all right. There's plenty else to eat.

After dessert is served—a chocolate mousse I would gladly give up a day's pay for—a woman in an impeccable crimson gown appears on stage, approaching the microphone. A hush falls over the crowd.

"Welcome, everyone, to the twelfth annual Larsen Co. Meet and Greet. We're so happy you could attend." There's a smattering of applause, and the woman waits as the sound dies down, a genuine smile on her face. "I'm Arshpreet Bakshi, Larsen Co.'s head of public relations. It's my pleasure to tell you about tonight's event, as well as share a presentation about the promising young entrepreneurs we've gathered here today and what their bright minds have come up with. We have a wonderful assortment of soon-to-be flourishing businesses that you, our esteemed guests, will have the opportunity to invest in. Their success is your success, and I'm thrilled to present these exciting new ventures to you."

There's another smattering of applause, and Arshpreet waits a beat before leaning into the microphone again. "But first, I'd like to welcome up to the stage the man who's made all this possible. The man who's responsible for bringing us together tonight, who's invested billions into the entrepreneurial success of Las Vegas. Please give a warm welcome to our host, Henrik Larsen."

Arshpreet steps back, clapping along with the rest of the room as Henrik leans close to me, his mouth right beside my ear as he speaks over the noise. "Is Benjamin beside you?"

I startle at the question. "Oh, no. He stepped away before dessert came out."

Henrik nods, looking nonplussed. "Would you be so kind as to escort me to the stage?"

My heart gives a great, big, painful *thump*. "Me?"

Henrik nods again, standing up and holding out his palm. Time seems to stall as I look at it, the clapping hands around me narrowing into a slow cacophony of noise. *Slap, slap, slap.* Smiling faces look on as my blood races quickly—much too quickly—through my body, my heart aching with the force of it. Yet I stand up, legs both stiff and wobbly, and take Henrik's hand into my own, clammy one.

The noise of the crowd diminishes as my ears start to ring, as my pulse rises loudly inside my head, the whooshing of it overtaking everything else. The short walk to the stage feels like a mile, step after step with Henrik beside me. We ascend the stairs, Henrik's arm laced through mine, my other hand on his forearm, squeezing in time with each step up. The trip to the podium seems to last a lifetime, no sound reaching me apart from the snuff of my own breath, sawing raggedly in and out through my nose and my mind. I swear I can smell rotted wood.

Arshpreet steps aside, and Henrik takes her place, feeling along the podium as I pace back, wanting to run, wanting to *flee*, but unable to leave Henrik alone on stage. I brace my legs, willing my body to cooperate, to last for just a little while, as Henrik smiles and leans into the mic.

I don't hear a word of what he says. For a minute, I focus on the faces around the room, the people smiling, nodding, flushed with drink and a merry time, until I can't make them out anymore. Until it's all a blinky gray blur, my vision wobbling precariously as I struggle to get breath into my lungs. *A couple more minutes. A couple more.*

I focus on my breathing, on the in and out, counting, imagining my lungs inflating inside my ribcage. I stare at the back of Henrik's head. The dark brown hair, threaded through with the occasional silver, combed neatly atop his head. I imagine I'm drowning, wishing the thought away as soon as it surfaces, but it's too late. I feel suspended in water, floating, floating away, even as my body protests, screaming its displeasure. Even as I beg to reach the surface.

Henrik's hand bumps into mine, seemingly out of nowhere, and I latch onto it, leading us off the stage, praying it's the right thing to do and that I'm not dragging him off in the middle of his speech. My foot falters on the last stair, and Henrik is the one to help me regain my balance, lending his weight under my palm. I intend to head back to the table, but my vision narrows on an open door off to the left, and I bank that way, past a couple tables, skirting the crowd, and Henrik keeps pace beside me.

I don't stop moving until I've rounded the corner into the hall and then another into a deserted corridor. It's there, in a recessed corner in front of a lit-up bronze statue, that I finally allow my legs to crumple.

For several long minutes, I can't control the images that course through my mind. My mother's disapproving face, her frown severe. The white van I was dragged into. The sight of the camp as we pulled off the road. *Summer Blessings.* I can feel the hands of the men hauling me toward a cabin. The rough wood of the floorboards in the musty, old church beneath my bare feet. The chill of the water, enveloping me again and again, blocking out the light and pooling around my ears and nose.

I'm cold. So damn *cold*.

The voices surrounding me, the condemnation trying to wriggle inside my ears. Other boys, one after another, up on stage. Crying. Scared. Dripping wet. I know how they feel. I want it to stop. I want this to end. I want to go *home*.

I'm freezing, shivering, a bone-deep chill settling into my body and mind. But then warm, soft hands lift my face, and the gentle press of smooth lips linger over my closed eyelids. A soothing voice, a hand rubbing rhythmically over my back and then over my heart.

It feels like a lifeline, that touch, and I lean into it, chasing more.

A relieved exhale. "That's it, that's it."

Henrik.

As soon as I recognize the source of the comfort through my fractured, muddled thoughts, breathing becomes easier. I pour all my focus into it. Onto Henrik. I focus on the feel of his hands and the cadence of his voice. On the way his suit swooshes slightly as he shifts. On the smell of autumn that hangs around his person, like crisp leaves and cranberries. On his lips as they press repeatedly over the skin of my cheek. My ear. The corner of my lip.

"I've got you, Mal. I won't let go."

I'm here, I remember. *It's now.*

Another kiss.

"The car is ready." A different voice. Benji.

"Okay." Henrik. "Give us another minute. He's coming around."

Gentle caresses, soft kisses against my hair.

"Mal."

I nod, unable to speak. My chest is still tight. My heart pounding like a brittle, used drum.

"Can you stand?"

Another nod. I think so.

Henrik pulls me upright, and I slump against his frame. His palm soothes over my back, his lips at my temple.

"So tired of this," I whisper, a croak. I turn my face against Henrik's shoulder. "Hate it. Don't want to be like this anymore, Hen."

Henrik swallows roughly, his hands spasming against my back. "I know, Mal," he says, voice ragged. "I hate it, too." He inhales audibly, his hand drifting over my hair. "Come on. Let's get you home."

I'm too worn out, too depleted to point out it's Henrik's home, not mine. I simply nod, and with heavy limbs and an even heavier heart, I accept the hand he's offering.

Chapter 22

Henrik

I've never in my life been more afraid than when Mal lay curled on the floor, his chest drawn tight as he wheezed, sucking in harsh puffs of air like a fish out of water.

I felt helpless. Utterly clueless as to how to help. Remembering the things Mal told me before seemed useless in the face of him *not breathing*. No amount of yoga or lemon tea was going to help.

But I also remembered him asking me to stay, so that's what I did. I held him as best as I could. I told him I was there, hoping he could hear me. I tried to lead him back from wherever he was. Tried to comfort him.

I felt like a failure.

But then, slowly, Mal regained some sense of cognizance. His breathing deepened, as infinitesimal as it was, and his hand flexed against my arm as I kissed his cheek. So I did it again and again, anywhere I could reach.

But that whimper—that *whimper*—as I told him I wouldn't let go nearly did me in.

We're back at the penthouse now, and Mal is fast asleep in his bed. I haven't been able to leave him. I haven't been able to sleep, either. The two kittens and I have been jockeying for position closest to Mal, and now they're resting atop his stomach and chest, one on either side of the arm I have thrown across his middle.

I can't let go.

I wish I understood what happened tonight. I could sense something was off as soon as Mal led me onstage. But it was as he stood behind me, barely breathing, that it clicked and I realized he was having a panic attack. I wish I'd figured it out sooner. I wish I'd been able to lead him somewhere safe. Instead, I'd wrapped up my speech in a few succinct sentences, and then it was Mal leading us away to safety.

And still, I'd never felt so frightened.

I tighten my hold on the man in front of me, tucking my face against his neck and breathing in the coconut scent I've become accustomed to. The scent I *thirst* for.

Whatever happened to Mal, whatever is still happening to him, I don't think it's a problem I can throw money at. But what else can I offer?

"Okay?"

"Mhm."

"You sure?" I ask.

Mal sighs. "Yes. You can stop hovering."

"I'm not hovering," I argue by rote.

"Your leg is literally pinning me to the couch, and your hand is down my shirt. This," he says, reaching over my stomach to tap the coffee table, "is the third cup of tea you've forced down my throat tonight. And the last time I went to the bathroom, you followed me."

"That doesn't mean—"

"You took a day off work," he continues, "and then you've come home by three every day since. Which is four days in a row now. You're *hovering*, Henrik. I'm fine. It's been nearly a week."

I rub my hand over Mal's pec, enjoying the sensation of his skin against my palm. There's a light dusting of hair there now that Mal has stopped waxing.

"And now you're petting me so I stop arguing," he says.

"I'm not—" I sigh. "I'm sorry. I was worried."

"I know," he says lightly, laying his head against my shoulder. I'm spread out on my back on the deep couch, and Mal is between me and the cushions, sprawled halfway over me because, admittedly, I pulled him there.

I groan, realizing he's right. I'm babying him. Mal is a grown man, yet I'm treating him like...

Oh, God. I'm treating him like he's fragile. Watching his every move like he might trip and break. Just like how my parents treat me.

"You're having a moment, aren't you?" Mal observes.

"Yes," I admit.

I'm realizing when you care about someone—and *fuck*, yes, I care about this man deeply—it's hard to let go. It's hard to stand by and watch as they, theoretically, wade into danger.

"I made an appointment with my psychiatrist," Mal says quietly, making my heart skip.

When nothing else is forthcoming, I hedge, "That's good, isn't it?"

He nods against my chest, and I continue running my fingertips over his skin.

"Getting back on my meds should help," he says.

"And then what?" I ask.

"And then..." He exhales against me, tucking his arm around my middle. "Paying off my debt should be a stress reliever. It's a surface problem, but it's easier than tackling the internal."

Hearing Mal talk about money, the confirmation of what I am to him, has me tensing. But I try to force my muscles to relax. I fully plan on having a conversation with Mal about *us*, and soon. But I didn't want to throw it at him on the heels of his major panic attack last week. Although Mal has been back into his usual routine—yoga here and there, visiting the cat shelter, doing the crossword on his phone with me before bed—he's been a little more subdued. As if whatever he experienced is rolling over still, or simply hasn't sloughed off as Mal has moved forward. It hurts witnessing him at 80 percent. Mal has been nothing but *good* and pure, and I wish he didn't have that cloud hanging over his head.

"You have a lot of debt?" I ask gently.

He nods against me again, his hair brushing my chin. "Accumulated in the last couple years. It drained my savings, so I had to put a bunch of stuff on cards. Important stuff, like food and withdrawing loans for rent. It wasn't because of frivolous purchases. I wasn't buying a bunch of crap."

"Mal," I say softly, stroking his chest. "It's okay. I wouldn't judge you either way."

He exhales, the tension leaching from his body. "I'm paying for my mom's care. That's what started it all. It's so damn expensive, and I couldn't keep up."

"Your mom?" I ask with surprise. "Because of her dementia?"

He makes an "mm" sound.

I haven't gleaned any additional information about Mal's mother after that phone call weeks ago, but it was obvious Mal and his mom didn't have a healthy relationship. So why is he paying for her care?

"I thought—"

"I don't want to talk about her, Hen," he says, sadly this time. Not angrily. Just like he's defeated.

I hate it.

"Do you have any other family?" I ask, continuing to run my fingers over Mal's chest.

He shakes his head against my shoulder. "No."

I open my mouth to ask more questions, but the elevator descends, and Mal tilts his head. "Expecting company?" he asks.

I nod idly, my thoughts still stuck on Mal, wondering what happened between him and his mother. He said she made him *pay* for being gay. How? What did she do?

"Benjamin is stopping by with a new teapot," I reply at last.

Mal huffs. "Your teapot was fine."

"The whistle was broken," I point out.

"Still worked. You didn't need to have Benji bring a new one by on a Friday evening."

I shrug, the movement jostling him some. "He's used to it."

"You're spoiled," Mal says, turning his head and kissing my chin.

I smile. "I won't deny it."

Mal chuckles, the start of a word dying on his lips as the elevator dings open and several voices tumble over one another all at once. I freeze, as does Mal, and when the newcomers' conversation abruptly halts, I realize they've caught wind of us.

Mal is already sitting upright, detangling our bodies, when a familiar voice calls out, "Well, isn't this a surprise?"

"Dove?" I ask in alarm, swinging my legs to the floor. I stand up in a hurry, running my hands down my clothes to make sure everything is in place, as my sister Alma's gentle laughter washes over me.

"And Mom and Dad," she says, stepping closer.

"What are you all doing here?" I ask, meeting them halfway. Mal stays near the couch behind me.

"We came for a visit, and Delroy was kind enough to let us up," my mother replies, stepping forward and touching my arm. I'm unsurprised my doorman recognized my family—the man has a penchant for faces—but a heads up would have been nice. An actual burglar would have been less of a shock.

I give my mom a short hug, our customary greeting, before my father sweeps in.

"Sorry to barge in," he says quietly, patting my back. "Your mom was on a mission and wouldn't be dissuaded."

I huff as he steps back. I'm sure he didn't try hard to stop her. My parents are, and have always been, determined to stick their nose into my life. *Except*, I realize with a cringe, *I kind of get it now*.

"Who's this?" Alma asks, her voice sugar-sweet and tinged with an edge of mischief. I have no doubt she's put two and two together, deducing Mal is the one who was distracting me last we spoke.

I reach back, and Mal steps into my touch, coming to stand beside me. He hasn't said a word since my family barged in. Not that I can blame him. I'm just as surprised as he must be. I'm sure he never expected to meet these people.

"This is Mal. Mal, this is my sister, Alma, my mother, Sigrid, and my father, Diederik."

"Nice to meet you, Mal," my mother says warmly, if not with a bit of confusion. "And how do you know Henrik?"

There's a beat of silence, and then Alma clicks her tongue. "For God's sake, Mother. We saw them when we walked in."

"I didn't want to assume," my mother replies quietly. "You're dating?"

There's another beat of silence in which my mind races, realizing not once did I consider having to explain my escorts to my family. As far as they know, I haven't dated anyone in a very long time.

"Yeah," Mal replies, saving the day. "I'm his boyfriend."

Alma makes a pleased little sound, and my father says, "Huh. I didn't know you were into men."

And then there's that.

"Oh, for gosh sake, Diederik," my mother hisses, sounding as if she's slapped her husband's chest.

"What?" my father replies. "I didn't."

Because as far as my family was aware, I was straight. I hadn't bothered mentioning my more recent, late-life attraction to the same gender. It didn't seem pertinent when I wasn't dating anyone. All the escorts I hired have been men, but I wasn't about to share that particular piece of information with my family.

I don't care for dishonesty, but there's no world in which my parents *needed* to know the truth about the men I've paid to keep me company. For all intents and purposes, the fallacy Mal provided fits the bill just fine. He's not truly my boyfriend—despite my own desires—but for the time being, he is with me. And now's as good a time as any to come out.

"Yes, I'm attracted to men," I reply, running my fingers over the small of Mal's back. "And women. Or whomever."

"That's lovely, dear," my mother replies as Alma covers her laugh.

"Yes, very nice," my father pitches in.

Alma steps forward, wrapping her arm around me. "I never got my hug," she says softly. "And congratulations, you wanker. We have a lot of catching up to do."

I hum, hugging her tightly with one arm. "I suppose we do." Stepping back, I add to the group, "Well, come in. Not that you needed an invitation."

Alma laughs, and my parents detour into the kitchen. It smells like they brought dinner.

Mal pulls me off to the side of the room furthest away from everyone, near the fireplace I never use. "Was that okay? Calling you my boyfriend? I didn't know what to do."

"Of course," I tell him, squeezing his arm. "They would've realized pretty quickly that you're living here. It was the smartest thing to say."

"Yeah, okay."

"Don't worry," I say, tugging Mal close. He doesn't protest, leaning against my chest as I sink my face into his hair. "It'll be fine. If they get too nosy, I'll redirect them."

Mal nods. "You came out," he says softly.

I hum. "I did."

"I didn't know you *weren't* out with your family. I assumed, after you brought me as your date to the benefit, everyone in your life knew."

"I hadn't gotten around to telling them yet," I admit. "I hate to say it, but it didn't feel important at the time. I wasn't looking for a relationship, so it simply didn't come up these past few years." I shrug, only belatedly realizing my wording implied my desire to avoid a relationship was past tense.

"They were really cool about it," Mal says, his voice almost wistful. And a little strained. I understand why. Even though I don't have the whole story, I know Mal's mother was not the same.

"I knew they'd be supportive," I agree gently. "Alma came out when she was in high school."

"Proud lesbian," my sister pipes up, having wandered closer. "Although, Mal, you are quite pretty. Love the hair."

"Really, Alma? Must you compliment my partner?" I grouse.

She only laughs. "My, my. That word looks good on you."

I open my mouth to retort when the sound of skittering nails comes flying down the hall. The kittens race past us, one meowing loudly—likely Little Gray—as my mother makes an exclamation of joy from the kitchen.

"Oh, my goodness! Look at these two. When did you get *kittens*, Henrik?" my mother calls out.

"Yes, Henrik," Alma says sweetly. "Kittens? My, oh my, we *do* have a lot to talk about, don't we, brother dearest?"

Looks like I have some explaining to do.

Chapter 23

MAL

I spent ten minutes on pins and needles before I concluded what, instinctually, I knew immediately: that Henrik's family is nothing like my own.

My initial worry vanished quickly, yet I can't deny I'm still feeling tense. I don't know how to act around these people. I'm worried I'll let something slip.

"Here," Henrik says, handing me a cup of tea. A quick whiff confirms it's lemon.

"Thank you," I say, warmed by the gesture.

Henrik smiles lightly before heading back into the kitchen. I watch him for a moment, noting the ease with which he navigates the space around his parents. I didn't even know he had family, and now I'm getting a crash course.

"You like this one?" Alma asks from beside me.

I follow her gaze to the colorful canvas on the wall, just a few inches to the right of where Henrik was standing in my line of sight. I don't bother correcting Alma that I was staring at her brother, not the art on the wall.

"Yeah, I do. But I like the one above the fireplace best," I tell her, turning to the canvas in question.

She hums and follows suit, taking a dainty sip of her wine.

Henrik's sister screams sophistication in her wrinkle-free white sheath dress, with her brown hair pulled back in some sort of complicated twist. Yet there's a playfulness about her demeanor and an openness to her expression that warmed me to her on sight.

It doesn't hurt knowing this is the mysterious *dove*. Any hint of jealousy I'd been harboring prior dispersed like a puff of fresh air.

I had no right to be jealous about Henrik in the first place. He's not *mine*. And yet...

I rub my finger along the mug between my palms, the ceramic warm like the man who gave it to me. The thought brings a smile to my face.

"Because it's brighter?" Alma asks, tilting her head as she appraises the canvas.

I refocus on the art in front of us. It's the piece that looks like a chaotic mess, slashes of every color imaginable strewn across the canvas. Some swirling, some blotches. It's riotous, but it's beautiful.

"Because it's realistic," I say.

"How so?" she asks, turning her attention toward me.

"All the colors," I reply, waving my hand slightly. "They run together. There are strands of bright, pops of hope, but there's also darkness. And one isn't *more* than the other. They just are, existing in the same space. And I think...I think that's how life really is. Chaotic, messy, good, and bad. We can try to apply some rhyme and reason to it all, but in the end, life is unordered. And that's as lovely as it is terrifying."

Alma hums, and when I look over at her, I'm struck for a moment by her resemblance to her brother. Same dark hair, same green eyes—their father's eyes—and the same little smirk in the corner of her mouth.

"Are you droning on about your art, dear sister?" Henrik asks from a few feet behind us.

I whirl from him to Alma in confusion. "*Your* art?"

Henrik rolls his eyes, taking a step closer. I hold out my hand, and he sidles up beside me, his arm winding around my waist. "You didn't tell him you painted these?"

"I'm afraid not," Alma says, hiding her amused smirk behind her glass of wine. "I was having a bit of fun."

Henrik tsks at her, shaking his head, before leaning close and planting a soft kiss beside my ear. My eyes flit to Alma on instinct, wondering what she'll think of the display, but I find her turned passively back to the wall, a small smile on her lips.

"My sister is a wonderful artist and a terrible human being. You'll have to excuse her," Henrik says.

Alma shakes her head, rolling her eyes in much the same way as her brother did moments before. "You're one to talk, Henrik. You've been keeping secrets."

She gives her brother a stare he can't see, but when her eyes swing my way, she winks, and I can tell she's not truly upset.

"Yes, well, we better get to the table. Dinner is ready," Henrik replies, giving me a little tug toward the dining room.

Alma follows us. "Avoiding the topic as usual, I see."

"I'm not avoiding," Henrik counters, holding out a chair for me. The casual chivalry makes my skin tingle. "I'm simply moving us along. I'm sure you're all starved after your long, unexpected journey."

"Subtle as a train," Alma says, sitting across from me. Sigrid is to my right with Diederik across from her. Henrik takes his customary seat at the head of the table.

"Runs in the family," Henrik mutters.

"Well, cheers, everyone," Sigrid says, holding up her glass of wine, prompting the rest of the family to hold theirs up in return. She gives me a warm smile before picking up her fork.

"So, son. How's business?" Diederik asks, cutting into his steak.

I eye my own plate, my mouth watering. I haven't had prime rib in a very long time, and certainly nothing of this standard. I barely manage to hold back a moan as I slip a piece into my mouth. It melts like butter.

Henrik's lips twitch, and I wonder if I didn't do as stellar of a job as I thought hiding my appreciation of my food. "Fine, Father. The new incubator is on track to open in a couple weeks."

"That's wonderful," Diederik replies, looking genuinely happy for his son. "That makes this how many?"

"Seven," Alma answers. "Have you visited Henrik's place of work, Mal?"

"Oh, no," I say, wiping my mouth. "Haven't had the chance." Not that it's been offered. Would a real boyfriend have seen his office already?

"How long have you two been dating?" Sigrid asks.

"Just over five weeks?" I ask Henrik.

He nods. "Five of the best weeks of my life."

Heat flushes up my neck. I know Henrik is laying it on thick for his parents, selling our boyfriends status, but it doesn't stop my pulse from taking off. It doesn't stop me from wishing those words were true. Wishing he felt like these past five weeks have meant something, too.

"And you're living together. Must be serious?" Sigrid says, her voice hopeful.

Henrik raises an eyebrow, and Diederik pats his wife's arm. "Don't pry, lovie. You know he doesn't like that."

"You know he can hear you," Henrik says.

"I'm his mother," Sigrid replies, poking at her potatoes. "I'm allowed to be curious."

A brief silence falls in which Henrik's family all turn their heads his way, as if bracing for his reaction, but when the elevator door opens, the tension breaks.

"Oh my! The whole fam is here," Benji says loudly, coming through the foyer with a box in his arms. There's a wide smile on his face as his eyes bounce around the room, brows rising in unspoken question when his gaze lands on me. I shrug slightly, as if to say *I didn't know*.

"Benjamin," Sigrid says warmly, standing up and rounding the table. To my surprise, she engulfs Benji, box and all, in her arms.

Benji chuckles. "Let me set down this teapot first, Sigrid, so I can give you a proper hug."

"Oh, of course," she says, stepping back. Diederik gets out of his chair, too, giving Benji a handshake and half-hug after his wife has finished her turn.

Alma stays seated, although she turns to look at Benji over the back of her chair. "Good to see you, Benjamin. How's Gary?"

"Oh, fabulous as ever. At home wondering why I'm delivering a late-night teapot instead of spooning him on the couch," Benji says, ignoring Henrik's huff. "But I told him the bonus would buy him a *new* couch, so he's content to wait."

"Thank you, Benjamin," Henrik mutters.

"Of course, boss. What's everyone doing in town?"

"Visiting Henrik," Diederik says.

"Checking on Henrik," Henrik replies under his breath.

"And seeing the city," Sigrid adds. "We booked a hotel room for the weekend. Thought we'd do some sightseeing tomorrow and Sunday. Would you care to join us, Henrik? You're welcome, as well, of course, Benjamin."

Benji waves his hand. "I appreciate it, Sigrid, but my husband and I have plans for the weekend."

"Quite all right," Sigrid says, turning to her son. "Henrik?"

"Perhaps. And only if Mal is welcome," he says pointedly.

Sigrid looks affronted. "Of *course*," she says vehemently. "I thought that was implied. My apologies. We'd love to have you come, Mal, dear."

"Oh, sure. Whatever Henrik wants to do," I mumble, unsure about whether or not he'd appreciate being roped into a weekend with his family. They seem incredibly nice—genuinely caring—but Henrik never mentioned them before, so I don't know how close they really are. And he's giving off some tense vibes I can't quite decipher.

Sigrid looks pleased, and Alma gives me a wink, whispering, "It'll be fun."

"Would you care to join us for dinner, Benjamin? There's plenty of food," Sigrid says.

Benji appraises the spread. "As delicious as this looks, I already ate."

"You're welcome to have a seat as we finish," Henrik offers.

Benji shrugs. "For a few minutes. Gary would likely throttle me if I didn't pester Diederik about his golf game."

As Benji and the others take seats at the big pine table, Diederik all-too-gladly launches into an in-depth play-by-play of his season. By the time I polish off my potatoes and dinner comes to a close, my stomach is comfortably full. At one point during the meal, Henrik's foot found my ankle, and it rests there still, his toes glancing over my skin in a way that makes me squirm. When I discreetly peek his way, there's a sedate little smile on his lips.

I don't know if he's trying to work me up or simply can't stop himself from being connected to me in some manner.

With dinner concluded, Alma sets the new teapot to boil. I watch, taken aback, as she grabs my mug of cold tea from the table, washes it out, and doctors me a new cup. She sets it in front of me before refilling the rest of the table's wine glasses.

I shouldn't be surprised, considering Henrik is the same way—keenly observant and courteous—but I appreciate it nonetheless. I'm not used to people noticing me in that way. Apart from Dixon, Alex, and Niko, I don't have acquaintances in my life who even bother to try. Well, there's Henrik, but that's temporary.

When I catch Alma's eye, mouthing a *thank you*, she simply winks and retakes her seat.

"So, Mal," Sigrid says. "That sure is a unique name. Is it short for something? Mallory, perhaps? Or Malcolm?"

"Oh, uh." My mind spins, trying to think over any potential ramifications of revealing the truth, but I sincerely doubt any of Henrik's family would know about my adult films. And, at this point, I'm confident Henrik wouldn't be upset over Benji finding out, assuming he doesn't already know. He shares nearly everything with his personal assistant and trusts Benji to keep his confidence. In the end, after only a second's hesitation, I admit, "It's short for Malibu."

"Is it?" Henrik asks, brows furrowing as he sets down his wine glass.

I turn to him in surprise, opening my mouth but saying nothing. Surely he knew as much from my file? A quick glance at Benji shows him just as confused, but his befuddled expression isn't aimed at me. It's aimed at Henrik.

"Um, yeah," I say, realizing Henrik must be playing dumb for his family's benefit. I can't fathom why, but I relax having come to that conclusion.

"Oh, your mother must've loved the city to name you after it," Sigrid assumes. I don't bother correcting her. "That's lovely."

I hum noncommittally. This time, when I glance Benji's way, he's watching me with a carefully neutral expression. Yet I'm more than certain now—he knows who I am. He wouldn't have been surprised at Henrik's feigned ignorance earlier otherwise. I wonder how long he's been aware. Perhaps Henrik told him.

Either way, I dismiss my concern, grateful when Alma moves the topic onto this weekend.

It's after ten at night when Henrik's family finally leaves, Benji having gone home an hour earlier. I enjoyed their company more than I thought I would, considering my initial nerves. And truth be told, I'm looking forward to spending more time with them this weekend. If nothing else, maybe I'll gain a little more insight into Henrik himself.

When the elevator shuts, ushering Henrik's family downstairs to the waiting town car, I grab the remaining glasses and bring them to the sink. Henrik glides up behind me at the counter, his hands smoothing around my hips to rest on my stomach.

He notches his chin over my shoulder. "Leave them," he says gently. "I'll take care of the dishes tomorrow."

"Okay," I acquiesce easily, leaning back against the comfort of Henrik's broad body. He turns his head, nuzzling into my neck as goosebumps race over my skin.

"Are you okay?" he asks gently, face in my hair.

I nod slightly, realizing it's true. "Yeah, I really am. I liked them."

"I'm glad," he says, his hands trailing lower. My breath hitches as his fingers slip under the hem of my shirt, teasing along my waistband. "I'm also glad they're gone."

"Yeah?" I ask, my cock filling as Henrik traces little circles against my skin.

"Mm. Come to bed with me?"

"You don't have to ask," I say, turning in Henrik's arms and catching his hands, slipping them behind me. Henrik takes my cue and slides them lower, over my ass.

"I do," he replies, running his lips over my jaw. "I don't own you, Mal."

I gasp lightly as he bites the side of my jaw, tempted to argue his point. Not because he's paying me, although that is true. But because I know, in a way, Henrik does own me. He has since the beginning. Since the moment I sat on his couch and told him my name, he's owned a part of me no one else has. He's seen me in a way no one else has. And even though I told myself I wouldn't let my heart get involved, it's much too late for that.

To Henrik, I may simply be his escort. And in less than five months' time, he'll send me on my way without another thought.

But maybe not. Maybe I could change his mind. Maybe I could show him what the possibility of *us* would look like. Maybe the story we told his family tonight wouldn't have to be a lie.

I'm tired of lies.

I want Henrik. I may not be able to have him, the real him outside the bounds of our contract, but I'm gaining the courage to try. Maybe that makes me foolhardy or naive. And perhaps I'll be crushed.

But I've come to realize I'm never *on* around Henrik. I never have to pretend. I don't know why that is, why he's different, but I'm not ready to let go of the freedom I've found with him.

He makes me feel safe. He makes me feel wanted. He makes me feel like I'm worth something.

Just me.

"Come on," I say, grabbing one of Henrik's hands from where it was wandering over my ass. "Bedroom."

Henrik follows me without a word. As I step into his room, turning on the light, he's beside me. As I unbutton his shirt, revealing his chest and stomach slowly, he waits. And once he's naked and I strip my own clothes off my body, Henrik's hands begin to wander. They slide over my skin, caressing, exploring, igniting.

And when Henrik lays me out on his bed, pushing my knees wide and swallowing my dick, it doesn't matter how we started. It doesn't matter that, when we're done here tonight, I'll retreat to the guest room like normal.

Escort. Porn star. Camboy. *Malibu.*

None of that matters. Because, for the first time in a long time, I feel like I'm finding a piece of myself in Henrik's arms.

The past falls away. The future lies ahead. And I'm desperate to write the story I deserve.

One that, hopefully, includes this man.

Chapter 24

Henrik

"Are you sure this is appropriate?"

"Of course," Mal says, brushing my arm and squeezing reassuringly. "I wouldn't have invited you if I thought it'd be a problem."

"But isn't there paperwork I have to fill out or an interview to complete or—"

"Henrik." Mal laughs. "It's just volunteering with cats. I'm sure Keith will have a form for you to sign, but you don't need to worry. He's always happy to have more help."

I blow out a breath. "Okay."

He rubs my arm again. "I'm not used to seeing you outside the house without a full, pressed suit."

"Yes, well," I say, smoothing my palm over my jean-clad thigh, "I didn't think that would be appropriate where we were going."

"Definitely not," he replies, laughing again. "Although I miss the gray sweats."

"Hm?"

"Nothing," he says. "Thank you for coming."

"Of course," I breathe out. "Happy to."

And I mean it. I want to know more about Mal. I want to be a part of the things that make him happy. I'm thrilled he invited me along in the first place.

We need to have a conversation. Soon. Once I can muster up the nerve.

"We're here," Charles says from up front.

I extend my cane, waiting as Charles rounds the Mercedes to open the door for me, ensuring a clear exit. Once on the curb, Mal takes my arm.

"I'll call when we're ready," I let my driver know.

"I'll be waiting, Mr. Larsen," Charles replies.

The car door shuts, and as Charles drives away, Mal leads me forward. A bell jingles overhead as we pass into the shelter, and immediately, the smells of cat dander and astringent cleaning agents assault my nose.

"Well hey there, Mal. I see you brought company today," a man says, his voice deep and gravelly. He steps closer, his gait slightly uneven, as if he has an injured leg.

"Hey, Keith," Mal replies, keeping his hand on my arm. "This is my friend, Henrik. He's here to volunteer with me today."

I try not to let the *friend* label get to me. I understand why Mal wouldn't want to disclose the nature of our relationship, even using the boyfriend ruse, out in the real world. It shouldn't hurt.

Shouldn't being the key word.

"All right," Keith says, his tone laced with curiosity. "Nice to meet you, Henrik."

I hold my hand out on autopilot, and Keith gives me a shake, his grip firm but not aggressively so.

"Likewise," I reply. "Mal has told me a lot about this place."

"Is that so?" Keith says. "Well, c'mon. Let's get you squared away."

Mal gives my arm a little squeeze, and I follow him over to a chair, which he all but plops me into.

"I'll read you the form, okay?" Mal asks.

I nod, lips twitching into a smile as Mal sidles up next to me, his leg pressed against mine as he goes over the volunteer waiver for Catty Commotions. When he's done, I sign where indicated.

"Looks like you two are ready to go," Keith says. "Mal, I assume you'll show Henrik the ropes?"

"Yep. We'll stick together," Mal replies.

Keith chuckles. "I'm sure you will. And those kittens of yours, they doing all right?"

"They're good," Mal says. "They'll probably be healthy enough to rehome soon."

I frown at that, but Keith is the first one to speak. "Heh. We'll see about that."

"Keith," Mal says quietly, almost a warning.

"Right, right," Keith replies. "Well, get on back there. Stella will be glad to see you."

"Stella?" I ask as Mal gives me a little tug. I follow him further into the building.

"The oldest resident. She's been here for years," Mal says, leading me around a corner. The noise is louder here, numerous cats meowing.

"That's sad," I note.

Mal hums. "It's the way it is. This is a cruelty-free shelter, though, so cats don't get put down just because no one wants them."

I frown again—not really having considered what happens to animals who don't find homes—but Mal makes a happy noise as a door swings open, and I'm distracted away from that unsettling thought. The chorus of mews intensifies inside the room, and Mal helps me navigate forward, chuckling slightly at whatever the cats are getting up to. I shuffle slowly, not wanting to step on any number of tiny toes attached to the felines brushing against my legs, and when Mal comes to a stop, I collapse my cane.

"Hello, beautifuls," Mal says lightly, greeting the room.

He sinks down and gives me a little tug, and, carefully, I follow him to the floor. As soon as my ass hits the ground, little paws start inching up my legs. I hold out my hands, letting the cats sniff and rub all over me, and Mal chuckles.

"I knew they'd love you," he says.

"Is that so?"

"Mhm. You're good with the kittens at ho—at your penthouse, too," Mal says.

"They still need names," I point out gently.

Mal makes a soft sound before clicking his tongue. "Come on, Stella girl. Come get your rubs out." He shifts slightly, pressing against my side from shoulder to hip, before grabbing my hand and pulling it over to the cat in his lap. "This is Stella."

I rub over her soft fur, feeling the rumble of her purr under my fingertips. "Why has no one adopted her?"

Mal shrugs, his shoulder jostling mine. "She's older. Maybe fourteen or so? It's hard to tell for sure. Most people want young cats or kittens."

"She seems sweet," I point out as Stella rubs her bristly whiskered cheek against the back of my hand.

"She is." Mal is quiet for a moment. Then he says, "Your family was shocked about the kittens."

I chuckle. "No doubt. I've never been an animal person."

"You seem like one to me," he says, his hand brushing mine over Stella.

"Maybe I just needed the right person to bring me around."

Mal is quiet for a moment, and I'm unsure how to take his silence, but then he says, "I really liked them. Your family."

I hum. "They liked you, too."

Wouldn't stop talking about him, in fact, even after their weekend visit was over. I had to listen to Alma wax poetic for a solid fifteen minutes the other day when she called.

"Did they really?" Mal asks a little tentatively.

I nod. "They adored you."

Like I do.

"They seem to really love you," he says quietly, and my heart clenches.

"Mal..." I shift my hand from Stella over to Mal's knee, squeezing gently, and he blows out a quiet breath. "Did you have anyone before?"

He understands what I'm asking. "No, it was always just me and my mom. And she never accepted me. Being gay, I mean."

He told me as much, of course, but the idea of Mal being so alone digs at me. I keep my hand on his knee as he pets Stella. "I'm sorry."

He shrugs, as if applying less weight to the matter makes it more palatable. "I haven't seen her in a very long time. And, hopefully, I won't ever have to again."

"Yet you pay for her care. Why?" I have to ask.

Mal sighs, his fingers continuing to stroke Stella's fur. "I don't know," he answers quietly. "I think I felt like if I didn't show her the minimum amount of respect she deserves as a human being, then I'd be no better than she was to me. I didn't want to be a monster."

"Mal." I turn my body, finding Mal's arm and trailing it to his neck, grasping there lightly, fingertips in his hair. "You could never be a monster. Never."

He lets out a shuddering breath I can hear as much as feel. "She was a *bad* person, Henrik. A bad person hiding behind her faith. And now...she barely remembers it. And I hate that, even though I feel guilty even thinking it. I hate that she gets to forget. I hate that she's still fucking with my life, and she doesn't even know it."

My throat is tight as I lean forward and sink my face against the side of Mal's head. He, of course, smells like coconut, and I wish it could comfort me this time, but the chasm in my gut remains, wide open and sore from the sheer *hurt* residing in each of Mal's words.

"Did she abuse you?" I ask.

He leans more of his weight against me, grabbing one of my hands and tugging it around his body like a life preserver. "My psychiatrist would say yes, but it never felt like that exactly. Not at the time. She never hit me."

"What'd she do?" I ask quietly.

"She...scared me. She made it clear I wasn't allowed to be gay. That it was a choice. A sin. And she held it over me like a threat, all the time. That if I wasn't a good, straight boy, she'd send me back to—" His words cut into a choked sort of sob, and I hold him tighter. "I can't, Henrik. I can't talk about it right now."

"All right," I say gently, kissing the side of Mal's head. I'm desperate to know what happened in Mal's past, but I won't push him. "All right."

"Thank you," he mumbles.

We're both quiet for a moment, the only sound keeping us company the gentle purring and occasional meow of the cats around us.

"Just so you know, Mal," I say cautiously, slowly, "you don't have to be okay around me. You don't have to hide your pain. You don't have to pretend."

"I know, Hen," he says softly. "I know that. It's what makes this so easy."

He sniffs as my heart beats roughly, a loud crescendo in my body and my mind. But then Mal shifts back slightly, dislodging my arms from around him.

"Let's talk more about your family," he says. "Your parents always accepted your sister?"

I nod, clearing my throat, as another furry head bounces against my hand. "They did. They've always been supportive in just about everything we do. I don't think I appreciated that as much as I could have."

"What do you mean?" he asks, his voice a little more even now. If the distraction helps, I'll talk all day.

"When I was nineteen, during my freshman year of college, I found out about my Retinitis Pigmentosa. I was staying up late, studying like mad for my finals week, and there was this almost blurry spot in my vision, or, like...this missing piece of info, off to the side. I figured it was fatigue, but it didn't go away, even after my exams were over."

I pause, petting another cat vying for my attention. "When I went to the doctor and received my diagnosis, my parents went supernova. They were determined to find out every single thing they could to help me. But I knew it was out of my control. I'd lose some or all of my vision over time, and there was nothing I could do to stop it."

"I can't blame them," Mal says softly.

"No, I can't either. Not now. But back then? I did. I just wanted to live my life, and I was determined not to let my impending blindness change the course I'd set out for myself. All they wanted was to coddle me, and I didn't take that well."

Mal's hand bumps into mine, and he steals it away from the cats, twining his fingers with my own.

"In the end, it took nearly twenty years for the disease to progress to full vision loss," I tell him. "My rods went first—my peripheral vision—and then my cones. And here we are."

"I think," Mal says slowly, twisting my hand, toying with the digits, "your parents are very proud of you."

My lips quirk into a smile. "Yeah, I think they are."

Mal gives my hand a squeeze before disentangling us. "I'm going to start cleaning up. You can stay here and act as a scratching post."

I chuckle lightly, spreading my legs out in front of me and jolting slightly when a wet nose brushes my cheek.

"I would've liked to see 'college Henrik,'" Mal says from across the room. "I bet you were hot, all buttoned-up and smart but rocking the mysterious stoic-guy vibes."

I quirk a brow. "Is that how you see me now? Except old?"

"You're not *old*," he says in exasperation, making me chuckle again.

"Did you go to college?" I ask.

"Mm. No." He starts scooping some litter. "I was just focused on getting out of Iowa."

"Iowa, that's where you're from?"

"Yeah. I worked a lot of entry-level jobs after high school. Food service, retail, telemarketing once. Trying to make enough to get by. To move on," he says, the last few words almost too quiet to hear.

"Well, I'm glad you ended up here," I say.

"Yeah?" he asks.

"Yeah."

He makes a pleased sound, and I can't help but wonder what Mal would be doing if he weren't so driven by money. If he wasn't in survival mode just to make ends meet.

"What would you do?" I ask, voicing my thought. "If you could pick. What's your dream job?"

Mal is quiet for a moment. "I don't know. I've never thought much about it. I guess, maybe, something like this."

That chasm inside me breaks open a little more, warm and aching.

If Mal could choose anything, he'd want this. Being among the animals that keep him calm. Caring for them. Helping them.

How could Mal possibly think himself capable of being a monster?

"Maybe someday, you could have that," I say softly.

"Maybe," he mutters, not sounding the least bit convinced.

I want to convince him. I want to tell him I'll help make his dreams come true. I want to tell him I'll care for him through good and bad. That I want him to stay. That I don't want him to be my escort any longer.

I desperately want to believe I have a chance with this beautiful, vibrant, hurt man.

But I'm terrified the moment I reveal the truth, I'll find myself more alone than ever before.

Chapter 25
MAL

"Come on, baby, give it to me!"

My eyes widen as Alex, bent over a fake bar top, takes a pounding from behind. Cas, the new performer Jerome hired, holds his hips tight, their bodies smacking together on each hard thrust. I close the set door quietly behind me, staying out of the way as the pair finish their scene.

When Alex texted me to meet him in Studio 3, I thought he wanted a quiet place to talk. I didn't think he'd be *in the middle* of filming.

Alex doesn't notice me, but Nathaniel, Jerome's right-hand man and the assistant producer here, does. He's overseeing the shoot, tablet in hand, customary argyle sweater in place, and when his head swings my way, I uptick my chin in greeting. He nods and goes back to work, keeping his eye on the screens broadcasting the camera angles.

It feels like ages since I was the one in Alex's shoes. Or Cas's, for that matter. I always held a versatile role here on set. It's only been a month and a half since I started staying at Henrik's, but it feels like longer. Categorically, life isn't that much different. But in a few significant ways, it is.

I palm the small pill bottle in my pocket, the evidence of one of those changes. I met with my psychiatrist, Delilah, this week. She squeezed my appointment in quickly and was ecstatic to see me, and I left her office with three additional therapy sessions in my phone's calendar and a new prescription for Zoloft.

Which means, as soon as I work up the courage to swallow one of the pills burning a hole inside my pocket, I'll be one step further on my journey toward better mental health.

I've been desperate for this. Needing it badly.

So why am I so afraid?

After a couple minutes of waiting in the wings, watching Alex—or rather *Tink* at the moment—and Cas go at it, I slink out of the room. I'll find my friend when he's done.

In the meantime, I head to the break room, saying hello to Raylin, our cosmetologist, as she passes by. Grabbing a cold, bottled tea, I take a seat and pull the pills from my pocket. I roll the pill bottle around in my hand, weighing it, wondering how something so light can relieve something so heavy inside of me.

Wondering why I'm hesitating.

"Mal? Hey."

Looking up, I find Dixon watching me curiously. The door swings shut behind him, and he walks over, taking a seat next to me. His bulky frame makes the couch groan slightly.

"Hey, Dixon."

"Everything okay?" he asks, his arm spreading out along the back of the couch.

"Yeah," I reply, holding up the bottle he clearly caught me appraising. "Anxiety meds."

He nods, pursing his lips. "Are they working?"

"Haven't taken any yet," I admit. "I just picked them up before coming here."

"Ah." Dixon kicks his foot up on the coffee table in front of us.

I've always loved this room. The plush couches, the snacks and drinks, the tastefully cropped stills of the performers, like a dirty version of family photographs on the wall. It feels like a home, in a way. Or, at least, the closest thing I've had to a home since moving to Las Vegas, Henrik's penthouse aside. My apartment before that never felt like mine, and Dixon's place was, well, Dixon's.

"When you and Niko finally got together, was it weird fucking other people?" I ask, curious about their boundaries. Dixon and Niko met here on set, but it took a couple months before they became boyfriends. Yet still, they have sex with other guys. It's part of the job.

Dixon's situation isn't my own. There's a good chance Henrik won't want more with me when all is said and done. But if he did, then what? Surely, I would continue to work. I wouldn't expect to live off Henrik's wealth. Would he even be okay with me coming back to work here? Would he still want me if I did?

"It wasn't weird," Dixon says, shaking his head. "I was worried I'd be jealous, but what we do here is different than what Niko and I do together. It's easy to separate the job from our relationship."

I nod. I'm not sure it'd be so easy for Henrik. He's definitely the possessive type. Should that bother me? Because it doesn't, apart from the fact that it leaves me concerned about job prospects.

Although I'm thinking as if Henrik is truly my boyfriend, when that's not the case. Chances are, it will never be an issue for us because in a few months' time, or even sooner, we'll be done.

I hope not. I hope I can convince Henrik to give us a shot. But would that mean giving up all the pieces from my life before? Would that even be an issue for me?

There's plenty I'd be glad to part with. All those demons from my past I've been running from. I became a new person because of them, first by necessity and then by choice. I left so many things back in Iowa when I moved forward, hopping from place to place, time and time again. I even adopted a new name, all too glad to slip into a life that wasn't mine. I did my best to leave my past behind me.

But in that time, I also gained. I gained friends here at Elite 8 Studios. Friends who still don't know my whole story. I gained a job that, although not my dream, has worked for me for many years. I gained a sense of belonging, and things were starting to look up. Until my mom's dementia.

Am I ready to say goodbye to this part of my life and move on once again?

I'm not sure what I see when I look forward—I've always been so focused on surviving the now—but thanks to Henrik, the path is smoothing out in front of me. There are meds in my hands. Therapy appointments on the books. Enough money in my bank account that I can no longer rationalize away paying off my credit card debt. And plenty of zeros left over to help with my mom's care for the foreseeable future. I could likely afford my own place now, assuming I'm still careful with my money. The balance won't last forever, but it will last a while.

But more than that, I have something that's been absent from my life for far too long.

I have hope.

The wheel isn't spinning. I'm on solid ground for the first time in a long time, and I can finally just...breathe.

"Dixon," I pipe up. "I know I thanked you before, but I need to do it again. I haven't been the best friend, but you were there for me when I really needed it. And I don't know what I would've done without your help."

"Mal," he says softly, squeezing my knee. "You don't need to thank me. I'm just glad you're doing okay. You are, right? Everything with Henrik, with your mom, it's going okay?"

I spin the bottle in my hand. "Henrik's been great. My mom—"

"There you are, Curls," Alex says, practically skipping into the room, freshly showered and slightly flushed.

I give the man a smile. "Heya, Blondie. So nice of you to invite me to a private viewing earlier."

Alex laughs, plopping down in a chair next to us and folding his legs up in front of him. "I thought we'd be done by then, I swear. I didn't see you stop by. Enjoy the show?" he asks, waggling his eyebrows.

"A-plus for enthusiasm."

Alex titters.

"Hey," I say, swallowing around the lump in my throat. "There's something I wanted to tell you guys."

Alex tilts his head. "What's that, boo?"

"Could we, uh, get Niko on the phone?" I ask.

Dixon's brow furrows, but he grabs his phone and calls his boyfriend.

I look from Alex's curious gaze to Dixon's soft, compassionate one. Both of these men, so very different, but who've been there for me for years. And when Niko's voice pipes over the speakerphone, I think about how he integrated so quickly into our little group, supporting me without asking anything in return.

I don't feel right lying to them anymore, even by omission. I want to give something back. Or maybe give something I should've offered up a long time ago.

I only pray they're not pissed at me.

"I'm not from California," I blurt, eyes pinging between Alex, Dixon, and the phone, afraid of missing a single reaction even as I dread what I'll see or hear. "I've never even been to the beach. I've never surfed. Never been in the ocean. I kind of hate the sand. I grew up in a perfectly ordinary landlocked suburb in Iowa. I didn't mean to lie, I swear. But this guy"—I wave my hand down my body for emphasis—"isn't me. I'm not Malibu."

"Mal," Alex says softly, leaning forward. "You're still you."

I shake my head vehemently, frustration making my voice tight. "That's the thing. I'm *not* this person you all think I am. And I'm sorry. I should've said something right away, but I never expected to last here. I thought I'd stay a short while and then move on to something else, like I'd been doing ever since I left home. But then *years* went by, and I ended up caring for you all way more than I expected, and then I was stuck. And I didn't want to say anything because I didn't want you all to hate me."

When I fall silent, waiting to hear what they'll say, my heart is hammering, and my hands are clammy.

But Dixon's voice is calm when he speaks from my right. "We could never hate you, Mal."

I look between him and Alex, both of my friends gazing at me with sympathy in their eyes. They look a little confused, which I get, but there's no anger there. No hurt, and something in me snaps. Because they *should* be hurt. They should be angry. They shouldn't be leaning forward like they're about to comfort me when that's the last thing I deserve.

"But I *lied* to you," I spit out, scooting forward to the edge of my seat. "Dixon, remember that one time we were talking about our crappy parents, and I let slip that my mom wanted me to go to conversion therapy? Well, that wasn't the whole truth. Not even close. She *succeeded.* She got men from our church to haul me away in the middle of the night and bring me to this run-down church camp who-knows-where. I was there for a *month* before they brought me home, a different person. And I wasn't the only one. There were other boys there, too. The youngest was only twelve."

Dixon looks at me with profound sadness in his gaze, but when he reaches for my knee again, I swat his hand away and turn to Alex, whose mouth is open behind his palm.

"All the times you've called me Malibu? All the times we've hung out and danced together? Every day I've sat by your side pretending to be someone I'm not? How can you be okay with that?" I run my hand through my hair harshly, my words coming faster now, my leg bouncing. "I'm not some cool, breezy person. I'm a mess. My anxiety, my panic disorder... I've been acting like I'm fine for so long when I'm not." I huff out a frustrated breath. "I didn't tell you guys about the escorting until recently. I was camming, too, for extra cash, did you know that? No, because I didn't say anything. And that one's *definitely* against the rules. I've been shoving every single one of my problems down deep where you couldn't see them. A friend wouldn't do that. A friend wouldn't hide. Wouldn't *lie.* And I've lied to you. All of you. You don't even know who I am."

"Mal," Niko pipes up.

"No, I'm not—"

"Enough," Alex says, cutting me off. He grabs my hair-raking hand and tugs it down between us. His grip on me is absolute, the fire in his eyes even more shocking. "I *do* know who you are, Curls. *We* do know." I shake my head, but Alex won't be deterred. "No, you listen up. You're the guy who puts on a brave face, even when times are tough. You're the guy who has a kind word for everyone he meets, who's good and gentle and more caring than most. You're the guy who would give any of us the shirt off his back, who's been hurt and doesn't know how to accept anything in return. You're our *friend*. Our brother." He squeezes my hand tightly. "It doesn't matter what your name is. That's never mattered. And it doesn't matter that there are some things you've kept close to the chest. We all have a past. What matters is *you*, Mal. Just you. And despite what you may think, we all know that guy, and we love him."

"Fuck," I breathe out, dropping my head. My heart is beating furiously, but it's not in panic. It's something I don't have a name for.

"He's right," Dixon says, his large palm smoothing over my back. "You're ours. And a couple little white lies don't change that fact."

I choke out an incredulous laugh. "I think it was more than that."

Dixon shrugs. "Like Alex said, it doesn't change who you are at your core. But Mal, you don't have to lie to us. I think I understand why you did," he says, frowning, "but we're here for you no matter what."

I shake my head. "You guys really mean that, huh?"

"100 percent," Niko says through Dixon's phone.

Alex nods, squeezing my hand again. There's a smile on his lips, even as moisture lingers in his eyes. "I'm excited to get to know the real you. Still our Mal, just...freer, I hope."

"I hope that, too," I say softly.

Alex clears his throat. "What do you want us to call you? What's your name?"

I huff a breath, shaking my head. "I think... I like Mal," I say. Not the guy I was long ago—the one my mom tried to break. And not the persona I fell into here. "Not Malibu. Just Mal."

Alex nods, smiling crookedly. "Mal it is. Still our Mal." He leans forward, wrapping me in his petite arms before I can protest, not that I would. "I'm so sorry about what happened to you," he whispers harshly. Sincerely. "But we're here for you now, okay? You're safe here. Please believe that."

I blow out a shaky breath, ready to accept that what he's saying is the truth. "I do."

"Good," Niko adds.

Alex sits back and wipes his eyes as Dixon squeezes my arm, nodding his head in agreement.

"Now," Alex says, turning his lips up and practically flooding the room in his natural sunshine. "What will it take to get your fabulous ass to join us this Friday at Sublime? You haven't been in forever. Is your daddy keeping too tight of a leash on you?"

I bark out a laugh, eternally grateful for Alex's ability to lighten any mood. "No," I reply, shaking my head. "Henrik has been...great."

"Oh," Alex says with a coy little smile. "Do tell."

I relax back against the couch, the remaining tension bleeding from my frame. "I thought he was going to be...I don't know, strict when I first met him. But he's actually very sweet."

I think back over all the affectionate touches. The way Henrik can't seem to help but attach himself to me when we're close. How patient he is, and the look on his face when I do something as simple as thank him for dinner. How his hesitancy from the early days is gone. How he seems to believe me when I tell him I want him.

"Oh, hun," Alex says, folding his hands under his chin. "You've gone and gotten attached to the sugar daddy, haven't you?"

"Maybe?" I hedge. Definitely.

Dixon chuckles. "I know that look. You're trying to convince yourself it's nothing. You don't want to get your hopes up."

"Well, can you blame me?" I ask. "I'm just his escort."

"You're not *just* anything, Mal. You're wonderful. He'd be lucky to have you," Niko says loudly through the phone.

"I'm afraid to go for it," I admit. "I'm afraid I'll get hurt."

"Well," Alex says, slipping close and squeezing himself onto the couch next to me. "If Henrik doesn't feel the same, we'll be here to help you find someone who will, okay? But I don't think you have anything to worry about."

"No?" I ask.

Alex shakes his head. "No way. That man was smitten. He couldn't keep his hands off you."

I scoff. "That doesn't necessarily mean anything," I point out, even though I was thinking otherwise not a moment before.

"Alex is right," Dixon says. "When we were there, it was like you were the center of his universe. He kept turning to you, aligning himself to you, following you wherever you went. I don't think it's just physical for him."

"Huh," I say, my chest tingling with hopeful little bubbles. "Maybe."

"Only one way to find out," Alex sing-songs. "You gotta confess to your sugga beau."

I sigh, hanging my head. "Could we not call him that?"

Alex starts singing the chorus to "I Can't Help Myself (Sugar Pie, Honey Bunch)," and I lose it, laughing loudly along with Dixon and Niko.

"You're ridiculous," I say once he's finished his short rendition of the song.

"Guilty as charged. Now, I need some fuel," Alex says. "Who's with me?"

"I could go for a bite," Dixon says.

I nod, smiling a little, knowing I can afford to treat myself once in a while now. "Me, too. But then I have somewhere to be this afternoon."

"Oh?" Alex says, standing up.

"Well." I huff a laugh, realizing I have one more secret to confess. "I volunteer at a cat shelter nearby."

Alex's face brightens. "Kitties? Can I come?" he asks, bouncing on his toes.

I chuckle. "If you want."

Keith is going to be thrilled. First Henrik, now some more recruits.

"Grumpy Bear," Alex says, looping his arm through Dixon's. "You have to come, too. Please, please, please."

Dixon sighs, but the corner of his mouth turns up infinitesimally. "Fine."

"Count me in," Niko says. "I'll meet you guys there. There's no way I'm missing my boyfriend surrounded by a pile of kittens."

Alex laughs as we head toward the door. "Yeah, this calls for photographic evidence."

Dixon groans as Alex tugs him forward.

"This is the best. Anything else you want to get off your chest, Mal? Perhaps a secret yacht we can visit tomorrow?" Alex asks lightly, determined to make sure I know he and the guys aren't upset with me. I appreciate it more than he could possibly understand. I didn't want to lose these guys. My real family.

"I'm afraid not," I say, shaking my head, following them out the door. "But I *did* get to ride in a limo recently."

Alex *ooohs*, demanding I tell the story. And as we set off together, stepping out into the Las Vegas sun, I pluck a little pill from the container in my pocket, feeling lighter than I have in quite some time.

Chapter 26
HENRIK

"That went well," Benjamin says on the elevator ride up to my penthouse.

I nod. "It did. We had a great turnout."

Benjamin and I spent the evening at the unveiling ceremony for the newest Larsen Co. incubator. Despite the construction delays, the location came together superbly, and now, the entrepreneurs of Las Vegas will have more resources to turn their visions into reality. It feels good, being able to provide that.

I'm especially looking forward to following the progress of a couple bright, new minds who have developed a portable real-time text-to-braille translator that's supposed to be an improvement on previous designs. I invested in that project myself.

"Now how much time do we have to relax before the next big thing?" Benjamin asks.

When I huff a breath through my nose, Benjamin laughs.

"Right," he says. "No rest for the wicked. And I *know* you've been wicked. Because you haven't told me what's going on with you and that snack of yours."

The elevator opens, and I sigh, setting my cane aside and taking off my shoes. Benjamin removes his own and follows me into the penthouse. He goes right for the refrigerator, presumably pulling out a bottle of the bubbly soda he keeps stocked just for himself.

For once, Benjamin doesn't push. He takes a seat at the island and waits for me to collect my thoughts. Out of all the people in my life, Benji and Alma are the only ones I share personal information with. I love my sister, but I don't know how to talk to her about this. Benji, on the other hand, would be the perfect confidant.

He's known about my escorts from the beginning—from that very first call I made to Genevieve, when I lost that final piece of my vision and the loneliness threatened to take me under. Benji has been with me through all of it. And yes, he's my personal assistant, but he's also my close friend.

When he and Gary got married, I was there. When Gary had an emergency appendectomy, I stayed in the hospital with Benji, providing moral support. All those times I needed an extra hand, Benji offered his, never once making me feel badly or like I was less than whole. We've known each other for years. We've been friends for years.

So yes, I could reveal to Benji how terrified I am to tell Mal how I feel, and I know he wouldn't judge me for it. He wouldn't make light, not about this. I could tell him that I've planned out a dinner for me and Mal next week. I already made the reservation. I'm going to sit across from the man who's invaded my home and my mind and my heart, dare I say it, and ask him to *stay*. I could tell all of this to Benji, and maybe he could help me feel more confident. Maybe he'd have a word of advice for me.

But before I get a chance to say anything, my hand brushes over a pile of papers on the kitchen table, and my attention is waylaid.

"What is all this?" I ask, running my fingers lightly over the clutter, careful not to disturb it much. Mal ran out quickly earlier—before I left for the unveiling ceremony—saying something about Keith needing his help at the shelter. He must have left these out in his rush.

Benji comes over, picking up one of the papers and reading under his breath. "Loan and credit card payoff confirmations. Huh. Looks like several different accounts. Tens of thousands of dollars' worth. For Adam. Oh," he says a little louder, "these are Mal's."

"Wait, what?" I ask in confusion.

Who is Adam? And why is Mal paying off his debts?

With a sinking gut, I clutch the edge of the table, my mind supplying the most reasonable explanation. Mal told me he doesn't have family other than his mother. So if this Adam isn't family, he must be something *else*. Someone important.

A boyfriend. A *real* boyfriend.

Why else would Mal throw tens of thousands of dollars at him?

But no, Mal told me he's never had a boyfriend. He wouldn't lie to me, would he?

"Why is Mal paying off someone else's credit cards?" I ask in trepidation, my tone uneven. Shaky.

Benji makes a sound of annoyance that catches me off guard. "I knew it. I was almost positive after that dinner with your family, but this clinches it. You never read Mal's file, did you?"

"What?" I ask, frustrated with the change of topic. "No, I forgot. Why does it matter?"

"Because," Benji says, clearly short with me, "Adam is Mal's real name."

I shake my head. "What are you talking about? He said it's Malibu."

Benjamin clicks his tongue. "Malibu is the name he goes by for his job."

"It's the name he uses for escorting?"

"No. Malibu is the name he goes by for his career in porn," he answers, shaking my foundation.

I plant my palms on the table, exhaling loudly. "His career in porn?"

No.

"Yes," Benji says in a clipped tone. "Which you would have known about had you read his file. Not that it should *matter*, by the way, but now you have that face going on like you don't want to believe me."

Because I don't.

"Mal works in porn?"

"He does. Or did. Before you hired him," Benji says.

Before I hired him. "Oh god."

I sink down into a chair, confusion, anger, and fear warring within me. Confusion because I truly don't understand what's going on right now. Anger at myself for forgetting something as basic as reading the file Genevieve sent over on the man staying in my home. Maybe I simply wanted to trust him. And fear that this changes everything.

"Explain," I say.

Benji pulls out a chair next to me, the feet of it scraping across the ground. He plops down, and a whiff of his expensive woodsy-apricot cologne puffs over me. "Mal's legal name is Adam Jones. Apart from working for Genevieve for the past half year or so, he's kept a career at Elite 8 Studios here in Las

Vegas for four plus years. They produce adult entertainment videos, and in them, Adam goes by the moniker Malibu."

My lungs squeeze tight, and I can barely breathe.

"What part are you having trouble with?" Benji asks me.

"All of it," I wheeze out, my heart beating too fast, my palms starting to shake.

"Jesus," Benjamin clips out.

"What are *you* upset about?" I ask, unable to keep the irritation out of my voice.

"You," he spits back. "As soon as I realized you hadn't read his file, I knew you were going to react like this. Because you *care* for him. You like that boy, and now you're being all pissy because your feelings are hurt. Mal doesn't deserve that."

"Mal lied to me," I grit out.

"He *didn't*," Benji says vehemently. "It's your fault you didn't learn the relevant facts. They were all there, waiting for you. Mal isn't responsible."

"He lied about his name," I point out, rubbing over the ache in my sternum.

"Not really," Benji shoots back. "He does go by the name Malibu."

I shake my head, squeezing my eyes shut tight. My heart won't stop pounding, and it's making me dizzy. "I can't believe this."

"You're overreacting," Benji says.

I push out of my chair, pacing to the window and setting my shaking palm on the glass.

"He's the same person," Benjamin says at my back.

Is he?

My fingers curl against the pane. Apparently, there's a hell of a lot about Mal—*Adam*—I don't know, and it's difficult seeing past the metaphorical red in my vision to sort through it.

"People can watch his videos?" I ask, voice raw.

I need the confirmation. Even though I don't want to hear it, I need to know the scope of what Benji is telling me.

"Of course," he says softly.

"Have you?"

He sighs. "Do you really want me to answer that?"

I shake my head rapidly. "*Fuck.*"

"He likes you, too, you know," Benjamin says.

I shake my head again. "Don't."

"He *does*. It shouldn't matter what's in the past. Don't let this wreck things, Henrik."

"How can I—" I cut myself off, not liking the direction my own thoughts are headed. I don't want this to fuck things up, but I can't even make sense of the things running through my head right now.

"You're angry," Benji states.

Am I angry? Yes, of course I am. It's not because Mal has been with other people or because he works in the sex industry. I always knew that was the case, and how could I possibly judge? I've been with a plethora of men and women, too. I can't condemn him for his past, nor for the occupations he chooses. *I* chose him for his occupation, at least at first. We wouldn't have met otherwise.

And I'm hurt. That's painfully obvious. Because even though Benjamin is right—that it's my own fault for not knowing this ahead of time—an irrational part of me insists Mal lied to me. Insists he should've made it clear.

But why would we have talked about his career in porn? Or have we, and I completely missed the signs?

And then there's the fact that I don't know how much else I don't know. I hate not having all the facts, all the figures. What else is in Mal's file? Does it matter?

Is he still the same person now that I know the truth? In theory, of course. But what scares me is wondering if I would have felt the same had I known all along. If I'd known Mal worked in porn, would I still have allowed myself to feel something more? That's a thought that unsettles the ground at my feet because I'd like to think my feelings aren't that fickle, but it's no secret I'm a possessive fucker, as Mal so aptly put it once.

Which brings me to what's needling me most. The simple fact of the matter.

That an indeterminate number of people have seen, and will see, Mal naked. They'll see him giving pleasure. See him taking it. Anytime they want, they can watch the man I love—because *fuck*, yes, I love Mal—in the most intimate of acts. They can see his lips. His cock. The curve of his shoulders. The dips in his abdomen. Whether or not his blue irises darken or sparkle when he falls apart.

They get a piece of him I can never have.

And *that* knowledge—that truth—is what jabs under my ribs like a hot poker, burning and sharp.

I'm angry, and I'm irrefutably jealous.

"This is unbelievable," I mutter, pacing away from the glass.

"Come on, Henrik," Benji practically pleads. "You need to think this through calmly. Work through the facts."

"I *am* working through the facts!" I spit. "The fact is Mal is a goddamn porn star, and I had no idea!"

"So?"

"*So?* Anyone can see him stripped down, Benjamin," I retort, pointing out the part of this I'm having trouble coping with. "Anyone can pull up his videos and watch him have sex. They can see the way his eyes transform in passion, watch the expression he makes when he comes. They know what he looks like at his most vulnerable. And that's something I have *never* seen," I say hotly, my own words coming out so choked, I have to clear my throat. "That is something I *will never* see. I will never see that, Ben."

"Oh, Henrik," he says softly.

"So yes, I'm goddamn angry that Mal—or *Adam*, as is apparently his name—is a porn star."

"Henrik," Benjamin says a little more seriously.

"No, I'm allowed to be upset, Benjamin. How can I trust him? What else don't I know? What else hasn't he told me?"

"Henrik."

"It's the money, isn't it?" I say, gesturing toward the table as my mind runs dark paths. Telling me everything was a lie. Telling me everything I thought I had with Mal was a show. "That's why he's doing this. I must pay better than porn. That's the only goddamn reason he's here. That's the only reason he wanted me."

"*Henrik.*"

"What?" I spit out.

It's only then I hear a faint sound in the foyer. A soft shuffling of shoes. A rough, shaky inhalation.

My heart flatlines.

"I thought you knew," that familiar voice says, ever so quietly. *Mal.* It's him, but it's not the same. He sounds gutted, like I scooped out his insides and deposited them on the floor. "I never meant to lie to you, Henrik."

He takes a couple steps before stopping, and part of me is screaming to say something. To apologize. To run forward. To *fix this*.

But the other part of me is frozen in shock. My anger, jealousy, fear all mixed into one, cementing me to the floor.

"For what it's worth," Mal says calmly, taking a deep breath, "I needed your money, but I never wanted it."

With that, the elevator doors close, and I'm left in silence so loud my ears ring with it.

"Oh, Henrik," Benjamin says quietly.

"I know," I breathe out.

"You fucked up."

"I *know*," I say, finally moving into action.

"He won't be there by the time you get down," Benjamin points out.

I groan in frustration, tugging at my hair. Then I pull out my phone, voice commanding to "Call Mal," but unsurprisingly, he doesn't answer.

"Fuck. *Fuck.*"

I drop to a crouch, feeling unsteady on the balls of my feet, my prior irritation dissolved in the face of my current panic. How much did he hear? What did I say? Goddamn it, I was just so angry. I don't remember half of what came out of my mouth.

"You can fix this," Benji says, walking up and squeezing my shoulder.

"How? What do I do?"

Benjamin sighs. "You tell him the truth, Henrik. All of it."

Chapter 27
MAL

I stare at the wall in Dixon's living room, wondering how everything could have fallen apart so quickly.

One minute, I was riding the elevator up to the penthouse, a smile on my face after my evening helping Keith welcome a new batch of kittens, and the next...

"Yes, I'm goddamn angry that Mal—or Adam, as is apparently his name—is a porn star."

I flinch when Dixon sets down a glass of decaffeinated iced tea on the coffee table. "Thanks," I mutter, making no move toward the drink and, instead, tucking my legs up in front of me.

Niko exchanges a worried look with Dixon.

"Do you want to tell us what happened?" Niko asks, rubbing his palm over my back gently.

"I think I lost my job," I say.

Dixon's eyebrows pop up. "Did something happen?"

I cringe. "Kinda? Apparently Henrik didn't realize I worked in porn."

Dixon makes a noise of displeasure at that, almost a growl. "And that was a problem for him?"

"Seems so," I say flatly.

"That seems pretty judgmental of someone who hired you as a sex worker," Niko notes.

I nod. "No, I know, but..."

"But what?" Niko asks. He grabs my legs and tugs them across his lap, rubbing my calves through my pants.

Niko and I have fucked on the job, but we've never been particularly physically affectionate. I think the man could tell I was retreating into myself, though, curling into a tight little ball where I could hold my issues all on my own. Make them as small as possible and hide them away from the world so they wouldn't feel as real.

I appreciate that he's not letting me hide.

"I'm not surprised that he's upset," I say. "He's very...possessive."

Dixon frowns. "That doesn't sound like a good thing."

"No, it's not bad. At least, it never felt like it. It was more like..." I try to put into words the way Henrik made me feel. How special. How safe. "It was like he wanted me all to himself. And before you say anything, let me finish." I give Dixon's pointed glower a look. "It was like he wanted to be the one to take care of me. And he let me take care of him, too, even though he's so guarded. He let me see the real Henrik. And he put me first, even when he didn't have to. I felt like more than an object to him."

I think about the time he made me pancakes. The week he spent nursing me back to health after the benefit. Visiting the cat shelter with me, and making sure I knew I didn't have to *pretend* with him.

"I've never had that, you guys," I say quietly. "I've never felt so...coveted. So the jealousy didn't bother me because I didn't want to share him, either. I didn't want to share that with anyone else. I just thought...I thought he knew about my job." I heave a shrug, exhaling harshly. "I guess I was wrong. I've never heard him so angry."

They're both quiet for a moment.

"It sounds like you still care for him, Mal," Niko says softly.

"Yeah," I reply sadly. "I really do."

"Did he say for sure it was over? Did he ask you to leave?" Niko asks.

I shake my head. "Not exactly. I ran."

Niko squeezes my calf. "Do you think, maybe, you should talk to the man blowing up your phone?"

I look down at the device, buzzing on the coffee table. It's the tenth or so time it's gone off tonight, in addition to a few unanswered phone calls. I'm too scared to pick up. Too scared to face the truth.

Because I'm not ready to say goodbye to Henrik.

"Eventually," I mutter.

Maybe, despite what I heard coming out of his mouth, it's not as bad as I think. Maybe I don't know the full picture. Maybe Henrik is calling to apologize.

Or maybe it's all wishful thinking.

"Jealousy is a problem in our line of work," Dixon points out, as if he can read my thoughts. As if he knows I'm running through the *what ifs*.

I nod, because that's the real crux, isn't it? If Henrik can't accept me—past, present, and all—then there's no future. Simple as that. If he can't *trust* me...

"How can I trust him?"

The buzzer goes off, and Dixon gets off the couch to check the door.

"Mal," Niko says gently, pulling my focus. "You can't avoid him forever. You should talk to him."

"Tomorrow," I say. "I'll call him back tomorrow."

After I've had time to work through my own thoughts. Once I figure out what to say. Once I prepare myself for the worst.

When Dixon comes back into the room, he's not alone. Alex trails in on his heels.

"Oh, boo," my pint-sized friend says, frowning at whatever he sees written across my face. He plops down next to me, squeezing me in his arms, and my breath shudders out of me. "Tell Mama all about it."

"Mal, I'd like to talk about the 'stage fright,' as you've called it."

I nod, fidgeting with the strings of my lightweight hoodie. Delilah waits patiently as I stall, my foot tapping against the soft, carpeted floor of her psychiatrist's office. It's nice in here. Cozy and warm. The colors are light and airy, and the couch I'm on is wide enough I could easily lie down and take a nap if I wanted to.

But Delilah wants to talk. That's what I'm here for, after all.

It's only our second appointment since I resumed my therapy sessions, but we dived right back in where we left off before. And even though I'm feeling raw this morning after my night spent sleeping fitfully, tossing and turning and resisting the urge to check my messages from Henrik, I know what we do here is good. It hurts, but it's helping.

"It's only happened twice," I finally say.

Delilah nods. She knows as much, seeing as I told her about the recent panic attack I had at Henrik's benefit. The first time was at an industry convention for Elite 8 Studios years ago, when I had to go on stage to accept an award. "And both times were particularly hard on you, you said."

I nod.

"So what is it about the stage?" she asks gently, her legs crossed in front of her. Delilah is about my age, maybe a few years older. I like that it feels like talking to a friend. Not someone older than me, who might not understand my way of life. Not someone motherly.

"Uh. Summer Blessings," I say, the words staccato.

"The abandoned church camp," Delilah fills in for me.

I nod. I wasn't able to tell her all the details before, but she knows the gist of what happened there. The so-called "conversion therapy camp" and the men from church who ran it. How my mom was the one who sent me there.

"There were a dozen of us. Kids, I mean. The camp was small, but there were some bunks, and that's where they kept us. And the church. It was this, uh, little building. Drab and brown. Musty. It was basically a log cabin."

I can still taste it in the back of my throat, the rotting wood from inside that old, decrepit church. It tickles at me now, but I take a deep breath, clearing my lungs.

Delilah gives me a nod of encouragement.

"Every day," I say, voice tight, "as part of the *program*, they brought us there. Dragged us, really." My pulse starts to hammer as I recall that terrible feeling of helplessness—of being too young, too weak, to fight what I knew was coming. But I focus on the present, rolling my hoodie strings between my fingers as I talk. "One by one, they would...uh, they would bring us up onto the pulpit. On stage." My voice cracks on the last word, and I clear my throat.

"Take your time," Delilah says softly.

I nod, bouncing my leg, trying to view it from the outside, as if it weren't happening to me. As if only remembering a dream. A bad one. "They would strip us down. Naked. It was cold. The, uh, church didn't have heat, and it was the middle of winter. So we were already freezing. But there was this, uh...this tub almost. Metal, big enough for a person. And it was filled with water. Cold water, like ice."

Delilah nods again, gently urging me to continue.

"They called it a rebirth." I exhale shakily, feeling as though I'm shrinking. Feeling like I'm that scared teenager again, confused, alone, *terrified*. Stuck in a nightmare that wouldn't end. "They'd dunk us in the water. Over and over again. Hold us under. To cleanse us, they said. To absolve us of our sins. It was frigid. I...I couldn't breathe. And the whole time...the whole time we were up there, they'd *lecture*. They'd read scripture about sin and make us do the same." I shake my head harshly, feeling, for the first time, a tinge of anger overriding my fear. "When it was our turn in the pews, watching, they'd make us recite those words about how we were *wrong*. Immoral. And when it was finally done, when they pulled us out of the water and we stood there on the pulpit, dripping wet, toes too numb to feel, they'd tell us it was okay...it was okay because we could still be saved." I look up at Delilah. "They weren't trying to help us. They wanted us to be ashamed."

"Yes, they did," she says, her tone soft but firm.

"They failed," I grit out, tugging at my hoodie strings roughly. "I'm not ashamed of my sexuality. I don't think I'm *wrong*."

"That's good," Delilah answers, her eyes wide open and kind. "That's really good, Mal."

"It didn't work," I go on, my body flushing hot. "It didn't even work, so why can't I forget it? Why do I still *feel* it, that numbness prickling at me sometimes? Why can't I let it go?

It was just water and words." *Just water and words*. "It wasn't like they beat us. They didn't do anything all that bad. They didn't..." I shake out my hands, trying to slough off the heavy feeling blanketing me. "It could have been so much worse."

"Mal," Delilah says calmly. "First, I want to thank you for sharing this with me. For trusting me." She pauses, and I nod. "Now, I'm going to say something you might not want to hear, but it's important that you do."

"Okay," I mumble.

"They assaulted you."

"No." I shake my head. "No. They didn't. They barely touched us. They didn't *hurt* us, not really. They didn't—"

"Hurt comes in many forms," she interjects softly. "*Trauma* comes in many forms. And even though they didn't leave lasting physical reminders, that doesn't mean what you experienced was any less scarring."

I shake my head again, but Delilah leans forward, catching my eye.

"You were abducted, Mal," she says, gently but insistently. "While you were a minor. You were held against your will for a month. And yes, you were assaulted. Not only that, but you were forced to pass that trauma from boy to boy with every *rebirth* that occurred up on that stage."

I swallow roughly.

"They made you participate because they were trying to break you down. They wanted you to believe the hateful rhetoric they were spewing was real. The water, the demoralizing—it was all psychological games as much as physical. They wanted you to take that part of yourself—your sexuality—and lock it up tight. They wanted you to associate it with pain. With weakness."

I nod slowly because what she's saying makes sense.

"But just because they didn't beat you or use electroshock therapy, that doesn't make your experience less valid. What those reckless, horrible men did to you and those boys—you relive it. Every time you have a panic attack, your body is right back in that church, scared and stress-reacting to the fear as if it's real. Because, in your mind, it is. You have PTSD, Mal."

I reel back, her words hitting me like a sucker punch. I blink, shaking my head rapidly because *no*. I can't have PTSD. That's for war veterans and people who've faced horrible, life-changing events. Not for boys who were dunked in water and told they were sinners. But Delilah goes on, holding her palm up as if asking me to hold tight.

"What you experienced by the hands of those men was very real trauma. An immeasurable violation. I know facing that—acknowledging it—is not easy, but I need you to hear my words right now because this is a really important step you've taken today, telling me about what happened at that camp. And facing this diagnosis head-on, not running from it, is going to help us—help *you*—move forward."

I swallow repeatedly, fidgeting with my hoodie strings. I want to deny her words, to contradict her. But Delilah knows what she's talking about. This is her field. Who am I to tell her she's wrong?

My thoughts run every which way, trying to view what happened to me with perspective, trying to imagine how I'd feel if it happened to someone I knew. Wondering what I would tell them. That it wasn't a big deal? That it shouldn't have hurt? Shouldn't still hurt?

I wouldn't be able to do that.

I grab the glass of water sitting in front of me and swallow it down in a handful of gulps. My foot bounces incessantly, and I look down at it, at the red Converse I wore today.

"I have PTSD?"

"Yes, you do," Delilah says softly. "The 'stage fright,' as you called it, is one of your strongest triggers. Your panic disorder has exacerbated the attacks, causing your mind and your body to get stuck, in a way, on a loop. Anxiety over having the attacks leads to more, as you well know. But you also have specific triggers that send you right back to when you were sixteen. And now that we understand that, now that we know the source of your trauma, we can work in a more targeted way on breaking your cycle."

"It could get better?" I ask, hope blooming inside my chest amidst the swirling chaos and doubt.

"It could. Your medications will help reduce your overall anxiety, which will lessen your panic attacks on the whole. But identifying and addressing your triggers and working through your past trauma is what, I hope, will have a greater effect moving forward. We can focus on those things now in our sessions."

I shake my head, but this time, it's more in astonishment than disbelief.

"I have PTSD," I say.

Delilah gives me a gentle, approving smile. "And now, together, we can figure out where to go from here."

When I get back to Dixon's, neither he nor Niko are there, and I'm grateful to have a few moments alone to process. After my session, I'm completely wrung out. Bone-tired and exhausted. I haven't had a chance to fully come to terms with what Delilah told me, but I'm working on it. I have a feeling that part may take a while.

Truth be told, all I want right now is to be back in Henrik's penthouse, snuggled up next to the man on the couch while I take a nap. I want to feel his hands running soothing circles over my body. I want his arms around me, holding me tight. Keeping me together.

But I might have lost all that.

"Yes, I'm goddamn angry that Mal—or Adam, as is apparently his name—is a porn star. How can I trust him? What else don't I know?"

My gut sinks as I remember the words Henrik all but yelled at Benji last night. How upset he was. How *betrayed* he sounded by the truth, even though it was never a secret to begin with.

But the more I mull it over—running the entire encounter through my head again and again—the more I wonder if there's...well, more to it. Because there was something else Henrik said. One thing that was unlike the others.

"It's the money, isn't it? That's the only goddamn reason he's here. That's the only reason he wanted me."

Why would Henrik have been so torn up, so *wounded* over the subject of money, unless he saw me as more than his escort? Of course a paid escort would only be there because it was their job.

If I was only a transaction, like all the rest, his words wouldn't have grated like glass on the way out.

He wouldn't have been in so much pain.

He wouldn't have *wanted* me to care beyond the promise of cash.

Right?

With shaking fingers, I pull my phone from my pocket and open the text thread to Henrik—the one I'd been avoiding. I scroll slowly past the many requests to call him, to text him, to let him know where I am, or at least let him know I'm safe. And with each "please" I read, my hope grows a little bit more. When I get to the most recent message, a smile spreads across my lips.

Henrik: The cats are doing all right. Little Gray spent the night in my bed. He missed you.

He didn't want me to worry. Niko's right. I need to talk to the man.

But before I can click Henrik's name on my phone, another call comes through. *Genevieve*.

"Hello?"

"Hello, Mal dear," the woman says, sounding much less peppy than the last time we spoke.

"What is it?" I ask as politely as I can manage.

"I'm afraid I was contacted by Mr. Larsen this morning to terminate your contract."

I inhale sharply, my butt hitting the floor as those hopeful little butterflies I was nurturing crumple right with me to the ground in a sad, pitiful heap. "Oh."

"The good news is he had the remainder of your pay forwarded to your account, despite not finishing out the full six months. The transaction should be visible as pending."

"I..." He paid the full amount of the contract? Why? As an apology for the things I heard? For some other reason?

"He also asked me to send along a message that he would really like to speak with you. What about, I'm unsure, but that seemed important to him," Genevieve says gently.

"Yeah, okay," I all but mumble, too caught up in the implications of Henrik officially canceling my employment yet paying me the remainder of the full half million we initially agreed upon. What does that mean? Why would he do that?

"Would you like me to reinstate your status as available for escort services?" my boss asks.

"I, uh... Can I think about it?"

"Of course," she says. "Why don't you give me a call once you've made a decision. I'm sure we could find you a new client quickly."

My gut tightens.

I don't want a new client. I want Henrik.

But Henrik doesn't want you.

"Thank you, Genevieve," I say, pulling myself out of my head long enough to finish our conversation.

"Of course, dear. Have a good day."

"You, too."

When the call disconnects, I quickly switch off my phone, the prospect of accepting any other calls today too much to handle. Leaning my head back against the couch cushion behind me, I close my eyes and stare up at the darkness behind my lids.

I think about Henrik. About the short month and a half we had. About what I *thought* was growing between us.

I think about Delilah. About my PTSD. About the monsters from my past I've been running from. The ones I never truly escaped.

I think about my mom. About her dementia and the fact that most of the time, she doesn't even remember her gay son. She doesn't remember the part she played.

And I think about myself. About the person I want to be. The person I've *become*. Someone who was finally starting to drop their walls and trust again. Who was letting people in instead of lying and hiding and feeling hopelessly adrift.

Someone who'd begun writing their own story.

So, I guess the question is—what do I want my next chapter to be?

Chapter 28

Henrik

I haven't regretted much in my life, but allowing my emotions to get the better of me and hurting that beautiful man who walked out my door is one of my biggest regrets.

I haven't heard from Mal since. It's been over two days.

"What's that?" Benjamin asks from beside me in the back of the Mercedes.

I'd been worrying a braille label between my fingertips—the message Mal left me the morning before he left. "*Butterfly and French. Six letters.*" Kisses. He was sending me kisses.

So simple. So goddamn sweet.

And what did I go and do? Blow up spectacularly. And Mal caught the shrapnel.

"It's a message from Mal," I finally answer.

Benjamin hums thoughtfully. "He leaves you braille messages? That's cute."

I don't bother correcting my PA that Mal *left* me messages before—past tense—because even though Mal isn't returning my calls, I refuse to believe it's over. I refuse to believe I can't fix this.

I just have to find the man first.

"We're here," Charles says, slowing the town car to a stop.

"Are you ready for this?" Benjamin asks.

I grip my cane tight. "Yes."

Over the weekend, Benjamin filled me in on everything I'd failed to learn from Mal's file. And despite trying, I realized I couldn't think of him as Adam because that man doesn't exist. Not to me. Adam may be his legal name, but Mal is the man who walked into my penthouse all those weeks ago and rearranged my entire world. He changed what I thought I wanted. What I thought I needed.

I wasn't looking for companionship beyond some vague figure to keep the loneliness at bay, but then I found Mal. And now, that vague figure has substance and form. Nothing else, no one else, will do.

I only want Mal.

It's the way he smells irresistibly like coconut, despite the fact that he told me he's never been to the ocean. It's how he feels under my fingers, warm and solid and true. It's the soft cadence of his voice and the tinkling laughter that lights me up inside. It's the feel of his lips under mine. The way I can taste my name, *Hen*, whispered into the air between us, like sweet honey and the loveliest tea.

It's how, without a doubt, I know I'm in love with him. That man who stepped tentatively into my life, whose confidence in me—in *us*—grew more and more over time. That man who showed me it's okay to lean on someone else every once in a while. He trusted me with his vulnerability, and he taught me how to do the same.

And I feel it, on a bone-deep level, when I slow down and sift through all that transpired between us. I feel the whisper of Mal's words, his touch, the way he always welcomed me with open arms and a soft heart. How transparent he was with me, how sincere.

I know that I didn't fall alone.

It was never about the money. It was never a game. As soon as I cut off my external reactions—namely, the jealousy and hurt—I recognized that. Mal wouldn't have been so upset by my words if he didn't care. His voice wouldn't have crumpled. He wouldn't have left if I was only a job to him. He would have stuck it out for the pay.

Whatever Mal and I built brick by brick over the last month and a half was real. And now...now I don't want to live a day without that. Without *him*.

I have to win him back.

But I can't do that with Mal as my escort. There's no way to move forward if he doesn't trust that my intentions are genuine and not contingent on the arrangement we made when we met.

Which is why I called Genevieve to cancel our contract. And it's why I'm currently sitting outside his last-known residence.

After a little digging on Benjamin's part, we learned the apartment Mal listed in his file belongs to his friend, Dixon. Or, as he's also known, Dix. Because not only is Dixon Mal's friend, but he's also his coworker at Elite 8 Studios. As is Alex, or Tink, the other man who I met at my penthouse.

How I missed that fact is beyond me. Perhaps I was too caught up in the comfort of Mal sprawled half on top of my lap to pay close enough attention. But after thinking back, I was able to recall a conversation about Dixon's boyfriend, Niko, dressing as a sailor for his scene. It makes sense in hindsight, the words that were spoken, but at the time, I didn't think anything of it.

It's beside the point now. I missed the signs. I fucked up. I hurt Mal. And I need to remedy my monumental error.

Benjamin opens my door, and together, we walk up to the front of Dixon's apartment building. Despite my conviction that tracking Mal down is the right thing to do—I can not let him continue thinking, for even one more day, that I meant those hurtful words I said—my hands are clammy, and I'm nervous about what happens next.

I'm afraid there's a chance I *can't* fix this.

But no, I refuse to go down that road. I spent enough time this weekend following dark paths. I need to focus on the bright point of light that refuses to let me give up. That refuses to accept that Mal was only one in a long line of people passing through my life.

I wipe my palm on my slacks and step forward.

"It's a nice area," Benjamin says, describing the scenery to me as he so often does. "There's a park a little ways down the street. The building is six stories tall, well-kept, with covered parking spaces."

I nod, stepping up when my cane finds a rise in the sidewalk. I stop when Benjamin does, my hand on his bicep acting as further guide. Benjamin presses the buzzer for Dixon's apartment, and I jolt. The silence is pressing as we wait, the only sound passing cars, the breeze drifting through some trees nearby, and my own blood rushing through my ears.

A minute goes by with no answer, and Benjamin tries again. Another buzz. Another minute of silence.

"Well, shit," he says succinctly.

I take a deep breath. I already called Catty Commotions, and unless Keith was lying to me, Mal wasn't there. I'd hoped we'd find him here at Dixon's because if he's not with the cats, and he's not at home, the next most likely alternative is...

"Let's try his place of employment," I force out, jaw tight, the words not wanting to leave my mouth.

I tamp down my surge of jealousy because I have no right. Regardless of how much the burn threatens to consume me.

Benjamin sighs, as if he can tell I'm struggling. He turns around and leads me back toward the car. "Can you handle this?"

"Of course," I reply a little tersely.

"You need to keep a calm head, Henrik. You can't barge in there demanding to see Malibu—"

"Mal," I correct.

"—and cart him away to your cave. He might not want to see you. He might be working."

"You think I don't know that?" I snap as I edge into the town car, the cool air inside the vehicle welcome against my overheated skin. I wait for Benjamin to join me and shut his door before continuing at a more level tone. "I *know* I fucked up, okay? I am perfectly aware. But it's only been a couple days. He still has funds." I made sure of it. "He wouldn't start up at Elite 8 again so soon, would he?"

I don't know who I'm trying to convince more—Benji or myself.

"You fired him, Henrik," Benjamin states in an unimpressed tone.

"I had to! I couldn't ask him out with that contract hanging over our heads. He has to know it's real. He has to know it has nothing to do with money or how we started. That I want him. Specifically him. Not just an escort. *Him*."

"We're going to try the studio, Charles," Benjamin says before sighing gently. The car sets into motion, and Benji shifts in his seat, presumably giving me his patented stare-down. "You should have waited."

"You already told me that," I grouse.

"And I'm telling you again. You should have waited to terminate your agreement until after you'd had a chance to talk to Mal."

I grunt, but Benjamin goes on, determined to make me hear him out, even though we've rehashed this argument a couple times already.

"I'm serious, Henrik. As far as Mal is aware, you severed ties. He likely thinks you don't want to see him anymore, which is exactly what I would assume in his situation. So why wouldn't he go back to the job he had before *you*?"

"Benjamin," I groan, rubbing the bridge of my nose. Is he right?

"You fucked up on so many levels, and I'm not afraid to tell you that. So if we go in there and Mal is otherwise occupied"—he pauses to let his words sink in, and I swallow uncomfortably—"you don't get to be upset about it."

I nod rigidly. "You're right."

"Damn straight."

We ride in silence for a minute.

"Be honest with me. Is it going to be a problem?" Benji asks.

I frown, pulling my head out of my own cycling thoughts. "What?"

"The porn," Benjamin states, clearly exasperated with me. "You're still tense about it, I can tell."

I wriggle my shoulders, trying to drop the tension from my body as best as I can. "It won't be a problem."

"Really?" he asks incredulously.

"Really. It doesn't matter. I won't let it," I say.

It was never the principle of the job that bothered me. I don't *like* thinking about the men Mal was with before me, but

I can't judge him for having sex, whether through his personal life or through his job.

It's the videos. I'm jealous over the goddamn videos.

"And what if he wants to keep his job?" Benjamin asks. I swallow roughly, my brain repelling the very idea. "Will that be a deal-breaker?"

"No," I answer immediately.

Do I want him sleeping with other men? Absolutely not. Even the thought of it makes me feel violent. I want to rip the hands off any man who'd dare touch my Mal, just as I wanted to hurt that man who put bruises around his neck.

But it's not my *choice*. I can ask Mal to stop, and I will. Politely. But if he wants to keep his job at Elite 8 Studios, I can't, and I won't, let that come between us.

I'll figure out a way to tamp down my jealousy. I'll talk to Mal about it, learn why he does it, understand his viewpoint. If it's money, I can offer that, and maybe that'd be enough for him to call it quits. If it's something else, well, then all I can do is keep an open mind.

Because I want Mal and everything that comes with him.

"We're here," Charles announces from the front of the vehicle.

"Thank you, Charles," I respond.

"Here we go again," Benjamin says before opening his door and stepping out of the car. Ten seconds later, he's at my side, and I accept the arm he holds out for me.

It's a short walk to the building, but when Benjamin stops and all I hear is a clunking sound, followed by his curse, my worry ratchets.

"What is it?"

"The door is locked," he says. "There's a keypad."

"Is there another door?" I ask.

"Not that I can see. Wait here, I'll check."

Benjamin leaves my side, and for a few minutes, I listen to the sound of cars driving past and my PA's retreating and advancing footsteps. My mind runs wild as I bide time.

If Mal isn't here, I'll try the cat shelter again. And then I'll wait at Dixon's apartment. He has to show at some point, right? I'll try calling again, and sending another text. Maybe I should be more explicit in my message. I might have to lay it all out on the line through the impersonality of a handheld device. I didn't want to do that. I wanted to talk to Mal in person so he could hear the conviction in my voice and see for himself how sorry I am. How much I mean it when I tell him how I feel.

But if Mal doesn't want to see me, that may not be an option.

"No other door," Benjamin confirms when he reaches my side. "I'll try calling their phone number."

"All right," I say with a nod, twisting my cane in my grip as I wait impatiently.

"Good morning," Benjamin says chipperly a moment later. "I have a bit of an odd request, but I'm here with my friend at your facility, and we were desperately hoping to be admitted entrance in order to speak with Malibu, who we know personally. My friend here fucked up royally, and he wants a chance to beg for forgiveness." There's a moment of silence. "Mhm. Yes. I absolutely understand. We'd just ask for a few minutes of your time to explain the situation. And if you conclude we're not welcome, we'll be on our way. Yes. Thank you so much, sir. Yes, we'll be waiting."

My breath expels from my lungs as Benjamin snaps his phone shut.

"You owe me so much for this shit," he mumbles.

"Whatever you want," I say sincerely, my heart beating hopefully now that I know there's a chance. Now that I know, in a few minutes, I could be in front of Mal again. I could have the chance to apologize.

"I want a boat," he says, and although I assume he's joking, I'll gladly get Benji a boat for the trouble he's gone through to help me get here.

A moment later, the door clicks, and Benji squeezes my arm. "Here we go."

Chapter 29

Mal

"What do you think is taking so long?" Alex asks, leaning back and crossing his legs. He swings one lightly.

Dixon shrugs, his attention on Niko, who's chatting with our coworker Teddy—a true teddy bear of a man—about a scene they're doing later today after our team meeting.

I still need to talk to Jerome. I haven't decided what I want to do about my job here. On one hand, I know I can't rely on the money in my bank account to last forever. It might not even last a year. Who knows what additional costs I could incur with my mother's living arrangements? What if she has sudden medical bills? What if she needs more round-the-clock care?

Realistically, I know I should go back to work. Not sit idly by while my funds dwindle.

But...

Henrik.

I'm not ready to write him off.

I've been rolling everything over in my mind all weekend, and there are too many factors that don't add up. I want to believe Henrik felt more for me—that he feels even a fraction of what I feel for him—and so many things support that hypothesis. Like the hurt behind his anger. His actions over the past month. The feeling in my gut that tells me not to give up.

But then I hear the way he said my name—*Adam*—as if I were a complete and utter stranger to him, and that icy shard pierces again, the same as it did that night. I could barely stand the disappointment I heard in his voice.

There's also the fact that Henrik terminated our contract. He kicked me to the curb. That should be a pretty clear indicator that the man is through with me.

Except...he keeps calling. Keeps texting. As if he's not done with me, either.

I know the only way forward is to talk to Henrik—that's a given—but I wasn't ready before. I needed time to figure out where I was at. Time to mentally tally what my priorities were and what I was willing to part with.

I have those answers now.

But until I sort everything out with Henrik, I don't think I can talk to Jerome about my position here, despite the fact that I'm at today's meeting. I can't ask for my job back until I *know*. Because if Henrik and I have a chance at repair, I won't break his number-one rule. Exclusivity.

I don't even want to—that's the rub. I don't want anyone else. I don't want to go back to porn or escorting or my webcam. I don't want to be treated as a commodity to be bought and sold.

Henrik made me feel like *more*. Like I was important. Despite his callous words the other night, he made me feel appreciated above my body's worth. I refuse to believe that was fake.

I know what desire is. What *base want* is—fulfilling a sexual urge without emotional attachments. I've been on the receiving end of that plenty in my line of work. And I know the difference between that and mechanical sex. Going through the motions.

Like I had been doing for years.

But I'd never, until Henrik, felt a third option. I'd never felt a true, intimate connection with another person that left me wanting more of them once the condom had been trashed. I'd never felt *loved*. I'd never loved.

Maybe I truly am naive. Maybe Henrik never felt that way, and he really has discarded me. Maybe he'll move on to a new escort, and I'll simply have to *move on*. I might not have a choice but to pick up and reassemble the pieces of my life as it was.

But I won't know for sure until I talk to him. Today. I'll make sure we speak today, as soon as this meeting is over.

Alex sighs from beside me, and when I look over his way, I catch him eyeing the bagels on the buffet table longingly. My lips twitch in amusement.

"If Jerome comes back and you're chewing, it'll be a dead giveaway," I point out.

Alex pouts. "Yeah. Well, he better hurry up. I haven't had a carb in *days*. And he left us all hanging." He fans his hand indistinctly around the room. "Doesn't he know it's not polite to edge your own employees—"

The door to Studio 1 opens, and Alex's irritated musings cut off, along with the buzzing chitchat of our coworkers. But it's not Jerome that steps through the door. It's Nathaniel, and at his heels are Benji...and *Henrik*.

My jaw about hits the floor.

"Oh, damn," Alex whispers, perking up and shooting me a sideways glance.

I barely pay him any mind, too enraptured by the sudden appearance of the very man I'd been thinking of a moment prior. The man I'd been gearing up to have a conversation with.

He's wearing a charcoal-colored suit that makes him look impeccably distinguished, his hair is combed neatly, and every piece of the man—from his Windsor-knotted tie to his brogue Oxford dress shoes—is exactly as I remember. But it's his eyes, red-rimmed and worried, that have me leaning forward, nearly catapulting from my seat in order to race into his arms and offer comfort. I want to wipe that miserable expression off his face. Yet I hold back, unsure if that attention would actually be welcome. Unsure of so many things.

Licking my lips, I grip the edge of my chair tight. "Henrik?"

Immediately, his head turns my way—as does nearly every head in the room—and the wary pinch of his eyes smooths out into immense relief. The tension in his frame drops as he exhales deeply, and he relinquishes his hold on Benji's arm, taking a single small step forward. His cane is collapsed, held in his hand, so he doesn't go any further.

Instinct is urging me to go to him, but I stay put.

"Mal," Henrik says tentatively.

The room remains politely quiet, but from the confused faces around me, I can tell no one knows what to think of the mystery man. Only Alex, Dixon, and Niko know who he is to me.

"What are you doing here?" I ask, voice trembling.

Henrik twists his cane in his grip, a nervous gesture. "I had to see you."

His words sound pained, and my eyes flick to Niko, who gives me an encouraging smile.

Eyes back on Henrik, I ask, "You did?"

My fingers strain with tension as I white-knuckle the metal folding chair beneath my thighs, my emotions warring. Part of me wants to launch myself at him already. To feel his soothing hands running along my back, twisting in my hair, cupping my neck and my cheeks.

And the other part of me... The other part is waiting for the cleaver to drop, sure Henrik is only here to sever ties in person.

But he wouldn't do that, would he? Apart from the glimpse of the man I witnessed the other night, my Henrik was never cruel. Never mean for the sake of it. And even though I want to be angry for the things he said and for the way he said them, the truth is I'm not angry, and I never was.

I was only sad. Dejected.

Alex said I'm worth more than being treated carelessly, like a penny tossed into the gutter, and he's right. But I can't shake the feeling that there's a piece of the puzzle I'm missing. And I desperately wish that to be true.

It's why I never gave up hope. Not completely.

Henrik takes another miniscule step forward, and my fingers tighten painfully against my chair. "I did." He twists the cane again and clears his throat. "Before I begin, may I ask how many people are about to witness my groveling?"

My breath catches, and my heart kicks up a heavy beat inside my chest, unseating that hopeful flutter from its cage. It takes flight. "You're here to grovel?"

"Yes," he says plainly, verdant eyes set in determination.

"There are about thirty of us," Dixon pipes up, his arms crossed in front of his chest. It's clear he hasn't quite thawed to Henrik after this past weekend.

"And we're all on Mal's side," Niko adds, even though he sends me a wink and a thumbs up.

"Well, fuck," Henrik mutters.

At that, the room erupts into chuckles, the tension breaking. Even Benji's concerned face splits into a wry smile from his spot a few feet behind Henrik.

"Hey, Daddy Henrik," Alex calls out, earning a swat on the arm from Niko. Alex's grin tells me he's not the least bit sorry.

Henrik shakes his head slightly, but his only retort is responding, "Hello, Alex. Nice to hear you."

"Just so you know," Alex says, "I'm not afraid to punch a blind guy. Although I'd warn you first."

I gape as Henrik nods. "I'd deserve it."

Alex looks pleased with that answer, his leg swinging once more.

"What the hell is going on?" Bill, one of the cameramen, finally asks.

"I fucked up," Henrik says.

"Well, no shit," Marco, our boom operator, calls out. The room erupts into laughter, and Henrik's lip twists at the corner, the saddest little smirk I've ever seen.

"Henrik, you don't have to do this here," I interject. Because even though I want to hear what he has to say, I don't need him to do it in front of my coworkers.

But Henrik shakes his head. "No, I do," he replies, standing a little taller, his cane at his side. "You see, there's this guy, and I like him. A hell of a lot. But I never told him that."

My pulse thrums wildly, those butterfly wings flapping against my ribcage.

"He didn't know how I felt because I was coming to terms with it myself," Henrik says, shifting his weight from foot to foot. "And instead of owning up to my feelings like an adult, I hesitated."

"Why?" Dixon asks, earning a few nods from the others.

"Because I was scared," Henrik replies, causing my chest to squeeze tight. "I'd never felt that way about anyone before. In fact, I tried really damn hard not to feel that way about anyone before. But this guy..."

"Malibu," Marco calls out.

"Mal," Henrik confirms with a nod. "He's different."

I can't take it anymore. I push out of my seat and weave my way to Henrik on shaky legs. His head raises as I approach, and when I reach out, my fingertips brushing Henrik's arm, he latches on like a reflex. The first touch is sweet relief, electrifying. And the way Henrik's fingers curl around my bicep, the way he inhales sharply as he steps into my space, feels like coming home.

He doesn't tuck his face into my hair, but it looks like a near thing. Like he has to physically hold himself back those last few inches. His breath fans out slowly, and I wonder if my proximity is affecting him just as much as his is affecting me. I wonder if he feels the same sense of rightness, of relief, that I do.

"What you heard," Henrik says softly, no need to raise his voice now that I'm right in front of him, "what I said, was completely unacceptable. I *hate* that you caught those words coming from my mouth, but what I'm even more ashamed of is that I spoke them in the first place. When I found out you worked here"—he swallows harshly—"I was incredibly jealous."

"You were?" I ask quietly, even though it's much as I suspected.

I don't even have to peek backwards to know my coworkers are watching with rapt attention. I can't blame them. This is better than daytime drama.

"I was," he confirms with a sharp nod. "It's no excuse, but it caught me off guard. I was jealous, and I reacted poorly. I lashed out and said things I can never take back."

"What'd you say?" Dixon calls out, even though he well knows. He's not nearly as ready to forgive Henrik as I am.

Henrik answers him steadily, though the weight of his attention never strays from me. "I spoke poorly of Mal's job, which was judgmental and completely unfair of me. I implied he was only with me for my money, when I know that is not the truth." He does? "And I said I couldn't trust him. But I do. I absolutely do."

"I never tried to lie to you, Henrik," I say a little shakily.

"I *know*," he responds, his palm trailing down my arm to my hand. He threads our fingers together tentatively. "I know that. And now, when I comb back over some of the things you said in the past, I realize I simply failed to hear what you were saying."

"Does it bother you?" I ask, practically holding my breath as I wait for his response.

"I'm coming to terms with it," he replies, which is not exactly the answer I was hoping for, but an honest one. "And I will. Because Mal, I can't fathom the idea of this being the end." He shifts a little closer to me, his face beside my hair, his small inhale audible. "You've changed me. And I don't ever want to go back to that version of myself I was before. I don't want to go back to a time where I didn't have *you*."

"But," I say softly, my eyes flicking over my shoulder to Alex, who's clutching his chest. He gives me a wobbly smile. Facing forward, I all but whisper, "You had Genevieve end our contract."

Benji scoffs, and when my gaze trails to him over Henrik's shoulder, the man is rolling his eyes. But Henrik immediately pulls my attention back his way.

"I did," he says, speaking just as quietly. "Because when I ask you to accompany me on a date, I want you to know it's real. And that you have a choice."

My breath stutters, and when an *aww* sounds out from behind me, I realize it's time to move this conversation somewhere without an audience. I turn Henrik toward the door. "C'mon, let's go find some privacy."

Henrik nods, not protesting in the least as I lead him past Benji, who gives me a small smile. There's a whistle and some happy chatter as we go, and someone says something about "needing a daddy of their own," but no one seems to mind us slipping from the room.

We're almost to one of the private suites when Jerome's voice rings out, halting us. "Malibu."

Turning in place, I appraise my boss, who's looking at me with a highly arched brow.

"Everything all right here?" Jerome asks, pointedly eyeing Henrik.

"Yeah," I say, squeezing Henrik's hand encouragingly. "We just need a minute to talk."

Jerome nods stiffly—I appreciate his concern—and walks off. He heads toward the team meeting as I lead Henrik into the small room in front of us, over to a couch.

"There's a coffee table a foot in front of you," I let him know.

"Thank you," he mumbles, shuffling into a seat but only seeming to settle once I'm next to him. His hand flies to my thigh, more out of habit than anything else, and he stills, as if unsure the touch is welcome. But I plant my hand over his own, holding him to me, and he exhales.

"I'm still a little confused, Henrik," I admit. "I thought, when you canceled our agreement, that was it. And I didn't blame you. I ran off, and I wasn't returning your calls—"

"Mal," Henrik interrupts gently, running his hand up my arm to the side of my neck and holding tightly. Reassuringly. He rubs his thumb over my pulse point, and the simple caress calms my frayed nerves. "You did nothing wrong. I realize contacting Genevieve before I had a chance to talk to you in person was maybe not my brightest decision, but I wanted a fresh start and was running high on emotions, not thinking through each step logically. I didn't think about how you would view that termination. All I knew is that I wanted to make sure you understood my intentions when I finally had a chance to apologize. So let me make myself clear."

He scoots closer, his thigh bumping mine, his fingers toying with the ends of my hair.

"I'm *sorry*. I'm truly, immensely sorry. I never meant to hurt you, and I've kicked myself a hundred times over for it. If I had a do-over, that would be it. I'd go back in time and process my feelings internally before letting my words bounce off the wall brash and untethered. I wasn't lying before when I said I liked you. In fact..." He pauses, blowing out a single breath as if steeling himself. "The truth is I love you. I love you, Mal. And before I went and fucked things up, I was trying to figure out a way to tell you that."

"Oh," I say quietly, stunned, my mind running in tight circles with the same revolving thought. *He loves me?*

"I hope you'll give me the chance to earn your forgiveness," Henrik goes on before I have a chance to tell him I love him, too. That of course I do. How could I not? "Because I desperately want to take you on a proper date."

"Yes," I say without hesitation. Yes, I want to date this man. Properly. I've wanted that for a long time; I just didn't know if it was a possibility. It doesn't feel real, that I could be getting all those things I wanted. That, for once, something big and earth-shattering could be going *right* in my life.

"Yes?" Henrik asks in surprise. "Just like that?"

"Well, yeah," I say, attempting to smooth away the furrow in Henrik's brow with my thumb. "Hen, I'm not mad at you. Maybe I should be, but I'm not. I want to be with you, too."

"I..." Henrik flounders a bit before saying, vehemently, "You *should* be mad. Mal, I don't want to be the next guy leaving metaphorical bruises on your throat that you brush aside, thinking it doesn't matter. It *does*. What I said was not okay, and I don't want you to be okay with it. You don't deserve that kind of treatment. I don't want you to accept it, ever."

"Henrik," I say quietly, his words and the obvious way in which he cares warming me. "That situation and this one are so completely different, they're not even in the same universe."

"I disagree."

I shake my head. "That guy who paid for that? His intention was to hurt me. That was his goal, and he accomplished it. I let him, and he thanked me after. You never meant to hurt me," I stress. "And you regret it. Intention matters, and I know you're sorry. I can see that, and I can feel it. And I'm telling you I forgive you. So please, accept my forgiveness. You said you wanted a fresh start, but that's not what I want. I don't want to start over, Hen. I want to move forward. Move on because..."

When I hesitate, all my emotions trying to jump out of my mouth at the same time, Henrik prompts me gently. "Because what?"

"Because I missed you," I say with a sigh. "I missed you so much these past few days. And the cats," I add for good measure.

Henrik huffs a soft laugh, shaking his head slightly. "I'm not sure I deserve you, Mal."

"Too bad," I reply lightly, pulling Henrik to his feet. After the events of the past few days, I feel like I'm floating on air, my relief and happiness filling my insides like helium. Nothing could weigh me down. "No take-backsies. You owe me a date."

"Yeah?" he asks, lips quirking.

"Yes. So c'mon. I'm ready to go home."

Chapter 30

HENRIK

"Are you sure this is all right?"

Mal laughs softly. "For the tenth time, yes."

I frown as I bring the pasta to the table. "But I had reservations at—"

"Henrik, this is what I want, okay? I don't need fancy dinners. This is perfect for me. For *us*."

I let out a breath, setting the serving dish down and taking off my oven mitt. Mal grabs my hand, squeezing lightly and tugging me close. One of the kittens bumps into our joined hands, meowing lightly.

"I appreciate the thought. I really do," Mal goes on. "And if you want to go out sometimes, I'd have no problem with that. I'd enjoy that with you. But I like our nights eating in. And I missed this. Being here with you and the boys."

"Okay," I say with a nod, taking Mal at his word and accepting his preference for humble over hauteur. It's one of the things that immediately set him apart from the other escorts, after all. He never did ask for more.

But I do hope he lets me pamper him at least a little.

Mal squeezes my hand one more time and then lets go. The clank of silverware tells me he's dishing up his pasta, so I take a seat kitty-corner from him—our customary positions at the table. Like usual, I hook my ankle over Mal's, and he hums happily.

"Are you going to eat with the cats on your lap?" I ask when one meows again.

"Sure am," he says.

I shake my head, but there's a smile on my face as I fill up my plate. After I've had a couple bites, I broach the topic I know needs to be discussed further.

"I'd like to talk more about what happened," I say gently.

"We can do that," Mal replies.

I twirl some more pasta but leave it on my fork. "What I said—"

"You already apologized, Henrik. I'm not holding it against you," he cuts in, and although Mal has been in high spirits since our conversation at his workplace, I know I hurt him. And I know I need to do everything I can to make it right.

I'd apologize a hundred times more if it'd help. But I don't think that's what Mal needs. Like Benjamin said, he deserves the whole truth.

"I want to make sure I explain myself fully," I say. "Not for exoneration, but so you can understand why those words came out of my mouth in the first place."

"Okay," Mal replies, reaching over and squeezing my arm, and the fact that it's him comforting *me* makes me shake my head. He's too good.

"I said I was upset about you being a porn star. It's not because I judge your choices, but because I was—*am*—jealous of what other people get from you."

"You did say that, but what do you mean?" he asks gently. "I don't have a romantic emotional attachment to any of the men at my job."

I blow a breath through my nose, setting down my fork. "I'm not jealous of the ones you worked with. I'm jealous of everyone else out there. The fact that they can *see* you, Mal. I hate that they can watch you, that they know what you look like when you're most bare. I don't want them to have that privilege over me, and I recognize how archaic that is. I get it—I do. But I am protective of the things and people I care about, and that feeling is exacerbated tenfold with you."

"Oh, Henrik," Mal says. His chair screeches lightly across the floor, and then there's the sound of soft scampering on the ground as the kittens pad away. "You're going to want to scooch back because I'm coming in."

"What?" I ask, even as I do what he says and back up my chair.

The next second, Mal is in front of me, his hands clasping either side of my neck. I lift my face, hands reaching. Finding hips, I grasp him tightly.

"I have never in my life felt more seen than I do with you," he says clearly. My breath stutters. "So don't be jealous of them. They don't see me, not the real me. You do."

I drop my head forward, leaning against Mal's stomach. My arms circle his body, and I hold on tight.

"I've been alone most of my life, Mal," I say, my lips brushing the soft cotton of his shirt. "I wanted it that way. I have my family, of course, and they're great, despite their overprotectiveness." I huff. Pot meet kettle. "But it was a point of pride for me, my independence. I valued it, and I put it above nearly everything else to prove I could get by in this world as a blind man. To prove I wasn't at a disadvantage. I didn't realize the only person I was proving it to was myself."

Mal's fingers card through my hair lightly, and I pull back so he can see my face.

"The truth is I was lonely," I admit. "That day I woke up without that final percentage of my vision, I'd never felt so utterly alone. There was nothing. No spot of color or light. No one. And for the first time, I'd regretted pushing everyone away. Apart from Benji, of course. He's always been there for me, that pain in the ass. He's saved my hide more times than I can count. And he was there for me that day it went dark. And then there were others."

"The escorts," Mal fills in.

"Yes," I confirm. "But never, not once, did I feel about any of them the way I feel about you. The way I felt almost immediately. I knew you were different. And that scared me."

"And now?" he asks lightly, brushing my lower lip with his thumb. I kiss the pad.

"Now, the only thing that scares me is the thought of you walking out that door again."

"I'm not going anywhere," he says softly.

I nod, breathing deeply and expelling the air. "I know we have a lot to talk about. A lot to work out still. And God, Mal, I want to, *need* to, work that out with you. But would you please stay with me tonight? Because *fuck*, I missed you so much, too."

He dips down, his lips at my temple. "Like I said, I'm not going anywhere."

I nod again, letting Mal tug me to my feet. Dinner forgotten, we head back to my bedroom—*our* bedroom soon, I hope. Mal doesn't turn on the light as we climb atop the covers, each of us on our sides facing one another, and for the first time in days, that tight band around my chest loosens. Mal is here. He's with me. And I can breathe again.

"I, uh, talked to my psychiatrist," Mal says softly, his fingers skating over my shirt. Mine are in his hair. Always that hair. "She gave me a new diagnosis."

"She did?" I ask, surprised.

He nods. "I still have panic disorder, but I guess I also have, uh, PTSD?"

My hand stills. "Oh, Mal. Are you all right?"

He puffs a breath. "I think I will be."

I run my fingers through his tresses. "I'm so sorry I wasn't there."

He scoots a little closer, and I throw my leg over his, tangling us together.

"It's okay. You can't be there all the time."

"I wish I could," I admit.

"Mm, well. We'd probably have to be chained together for that to happen." I smile, not at all disliking the idea of that, and Mal laughs. "Should've figured you'd like that, you barbarian."

I shrug. "What can I say? I'm quite possessive over you."

"Yeah, you are," Mal says, although he doesn't sound particularly upset over that fact. "I wish I wouldn't have run."

"What do you mean?"

"That night. I left, and I wish I would've stayed to talk things through," he says.

"To be entirely honest, I wasn't in a good headspace that night. Maybe it worked out for the best that I had time to cool down. To realize what was real and what I was imagining," I admit. "But...I didn't like being away from you, so maybe not."

"How about next time—"

"I don't want there to be a next time, Mal," I cut in.

He smooths his hand over me, rubbing my side. "What I mean is next time we have a disagreement, let's stick together. Even if we need some time to work things out inside our own heads, let's do it side by side."

"Yeah," I agree, throat tight. "Side by side. I like that."

We're quiet for a moment amidst the comfort of once again being near. My hands wander gently over Mal. Feeling his shape. Reassuring myself that he's back, that he's real. Recommitting every piece of him to memory.

"I have a question," I say at last, knowing I need to address my jealousy, even though Mal told me I have nothing to be jealous over. His words soothed me, I'll admit. But they didn't answer one particular detail.

"Go ahead," Mal says, his finger toying with my chin.

I buck up my courage. "Will you be resuming your job at the porn studio?"

Mal's fingers stop their motion for a moment, but then he continues his lazy exploration of my face in the dark. "No, Henrik. I know how much exclusivity means to you."

I shake my head. "You're not under contract to me anymore, Mal."

Mal scoffs. "Maybe not, but I still know *you*, and I know you wouldn't be okay with it."

"But it's not my choice," I say, not liking the words but knowing they're the truth.

"You're telling me if I fucked other men, even for work, you'd be okay with it?" he asks incredulously.

"No, I'm not saying that," I admit. "I would have a very, very hard time with it. But if it's something you *need* to do, I think we should talk about it. If you're only quitting for me—"

"I am," he says immediately, making me scowl. But then he goes on. "I am quitting for you because porn was only ever a job to me. It was just money. You mean more to me than a job. But Henrik? I don't even want to do it anymore."

I breathe out in relief at that. "Are you sure?"

"Yeah, I'm sure. I've thought about it a lot this past weekend, and even sitting in that team meeting, I couldn't stop thinking about how I wanted to be done. Now that I know what real intimacy is, I don't want to simply go through the motions again."

"Oh, Mal," I say softly, brushing my fingers along the stubble at his jaw.

"I never felt bad doing it before. I really didn't," he says. "So don't feel sorry for me. I liked my career, but I'm ready to be done. I'll find something else."

"You don't need another job, not if you don't want one. I can support us."

He huffs. "I'm not going to live off your money, Henrik."

"Mal—"

"No, I'm not. I told you before, I never wanted it."

"And I believe you," I say, pushing up and rolling on top of Mal's body. He welcomes me instantly, settling on his back and bracketing his legs around my hips, holding tight. "But please let me help you where I can. I want to do that. If you *want* a job, I won't stop you. But you don't need one. I have a lot of fucking money, Mal."

He huffs out an amused laugh, and I smile.

"A lot," I go on. "And I can't think of a better use for it than making the man I love *happy*. I just want you to be happy."

Mal is silent for a moment, but his fingers trace my back lightly. I drop my face against the side of his head, inhaling deeply, letting his coconut scent infuse and settle me.

"I don't want to do porn," Mal says again, and I nod slightly, utterly relieved.

I would have accepted it; I wasn't lying about that. I would have hated it, but I would have accepted it. But I'm so grateful the only one holding the honor of touching this stunning man will be me.

"But...maybe I could do something with Keith at the shelter," he goes on.

"Yeah?" I ask, thinking that sounds just about perfect for Mal.

"Yeah. That would be nice. Volunteering more of my time there."

I smile against the side of his head, his hair tickling my face. "You're lovely, Mal."

His chest hitches under mine. "You really love me, don't you?"

And his voice is so hopeful, so vulnerable, my heart nearly bursts from my chest. I'd never understood that saying before, but I understand it now. The swelling. The feeling of rapid expansion, as if my heart has grown two sizes too big. Too big to be contained.

As if love is capable of reaching out and touching another.

"Yes," I say confidently. "I really, really do."

Mal inhales a shaky breath and then makes a sort of hitched "mm" sound. "Would you show me?"

He tightens his legs around my hips, arching up against me, and I understand exactly what he's asking, but it gives me pause. "We still have so much to discuss. So much air to clear. We don't need to rush anything."

"Hen," Mal says lightly, and there's that bursting again. That swelling inside my chest. How I'd missed that word. "I'm not worried about that. We have all the time in the world to talk. Right now, I want to feel you. Please."

"Anything you want, Mal." And I mean it.

Leaning up on my elbows, I drag my hands through Mal's hair. Our hips are pressed together already, and I rut against him gently, enjoying the little gasps and moans that leave his mouth.

As Mal hardens beneath me, I bring up something that's been on my mind ever since he let it slip. "You once said that the sex you'd been having wasn't about you. That it wasn't *for* you."

"It was never like that with you, Hen," he says, sliding his hands down my arms and holding my biceps through my dress shirt.

Although he sounds sincere, and that gives me more satisfaction than I can say, I forge on. "But what, specifically, do you want? What would you choose? What's your ultimate fantasy?"

Mal is quiet for a moment, his heels on my ass urging on my slow, grinding movements. He's fully hard now against the inside of my hip, and even though I wish all these clothes weren't between us, it can wait. Mal deserves my full focus.

"What I want," he finally says, his words measured, "is for you to hold me after."

My breath whooshes out of me, and I sink down, stuffing my face into Mal's hair to hide the sudden tears escaping from the corners of my eyes. "I will hold you tonight and every night after if you'll let me," I tell him, throat tight.

"I'd really like that," he replies softly, his hands rubbing up and down my back. "Would you kiss me, Henrik?"

I nod, wiping my eyes, and drawing back, I press my mouth to Mal's for the first time in days.

It's sunshine and waves and lemon tea rolled into one. It's the feeling you get at the end of the day when the suit and tie are gone and you can just *be* again. It's fizzing anticipation and the excitement of summer, of running in the street as a kid and riding your bike down to the corner store for dime candy.

It's pure and aching and right in a way that doesn't come along often. It's *home*.

I belong to this man, and for every day and every night that he'll have me, I'll make sure he knows he has somewhere to belong, too.

Chapter 31

MAL

Henrik is quiet as he undresses me. His movements are slow but steady. Intentional.

Each time an article of clothing is stripped away, his fingers and his mouth follow in its wake, caressing me. Branding me.

Worshiping me.

He teases me through the fabric of my briefs before they join the pile on the floor, and then his mouth descends, soothing over my flushed skin, his lips soft and sweet.

"Are you planning on torturing me tonight?" I ask lightly, humming when Henrik's tongue skips, featherlight, up the underside of my erection.

I can barely make out his features in the dark room, but it looks like he smiles.

"Can I ask you a question?" he says before popping his mouth over the tip of my dick and suckling gently, his tongue working the sensitive underside of my glans.

I drop my hands above my head, sinking into the sheets. "Mhm."

"Why the coconut shampoo?"

I bark a laugh as Henrik ghosts his tongue back down my erection. He draws one of my balls into his mouth, and I try to focus on the question.

"Uh, I guess I just thought it fit the whole Malibu thing. Why? You don't like it?"

He practically growls, the vibration wonderful against my sac. "I love it."

I grin, lifting my head to get a glimpse of Henrik as he works. "You're wearing too many clothes," I point out.

Henrik hums, wrapping his hand around my shaft as he tongues my perineum. "You want me to stop?"

"No? Yes. No."

Henrik chuckles, stroking me slowly. "You'll stay here, right? With me?"

I frown. "Of course. I thought we already covered that."

"No, I mean... Will you live here with me?" He lifts his head into my line of sight.

"Yeah," I say gently. "I already told you I wasn't going any-where."

"I know, but... I want to make sure you understand that it has nothing to do with our arrangement before. That I want you here as my partner."

"Oh, Henrik." I give his arm a little tug, and Henrik climbs up over my body. His suit pants and nice button-down are entirely too formal for the occasion, and I make a mental note to tell the man he should wear his sweats around the apartment more often. They did such lovely things for both of us. "Yes. I will live here with you as your partner. I'd like nothing more. Except maybe your mouth on mine."

Henrik nods before swooping down, his lips clashing against me wonderfully. I work on the buttons of his shirt as Henrik nips and licks and sucks at my mouth. Once he's finally free from his top, I flick open the button of his pants. Henrik leans up enough for me to tug the material down his hips, and then I use my feet to drag them the rest of the way as Henrik chuckles.

"You're very flexible," he says against my lips.

"Mm, I am. Know what else I can do?"

Henrik cocks his head, as if asking *what*, and I grab my ankles, pulling them up beside my head so that I'm practically folded in half.

"See for yourself," I say.

Henrik's eyebrows lift, and then he reaches forward, his palms flattening over the backs of my legs and dragging upwards. He groans once he reaches my ankles, and then he reverses course, hands coming to a stop on my ass. His thumb trails inwards, skimming along my crease. And then Henrik slides down the bed, replacing his thumb with his tongue.

I bite my own as Henrik laves over my exposed asshole, offered up as I am, and the moment he adds his talented fingers to the mix, I groan.

"Will you fuck me?" I ask, dropping my head back as Henrik does something I don't have a name for. Some sort of rubbing, twisting flick of his tongue.

"You want me to fuck you?"

"No, I was talking to the other man in this room," I retort.

This time, Henrik most definitely does growl, and I grin as he grabs my legs and tugs them down. He wraps them around his body and holds tight. "There's only you and me," he says roughly.

I nod fervently, even though he can't see it, and Henrik doesn't let go as he rolls us both to the side, reaching into the nightstand.

I know Henrik said he'd accept me working in porn if that was what I wanted to do, but it would have been hell on him. And I get it; I do. I understand the source of his jealousy because I feel the same. I don't want anyone other than me to touch him ever again. He's mine. And I'm his.

He would have done his best, of that I have no doubt. He would have found a way to live with it, but I would never want to put Henrik in that position. I would have chosen him over porn, regardless of my own desire to be done with that part of my life. I would have chosen him.

Maybe some people wouldn't agree with that. Dixon and Niko still have sex with other people. I can't imagine if Alex were to enter a relationship that he'd give up porn.

But for me, it's the right decision for so many reasons.

I'm happy with my choice. Because it's mine.

Henrik rolls us back into position, and I grab the condom from his hand. I open it as Henrik starts loosening me, first with one oiled finger, then with two. He takes his time, his hand tuning me like a maestro. Each touch expert. Each caress by design.

Once he's at three fingers and my muscles have given up the fight, resistance lending way to pleasure, I swat his arm, and Henrik pulls back.

"C'mere," I instruct.

Henrik knee-walks closer, and I slide the condom down his length, notching him against my entrance. My legs are still wrapped around his hips, my heels at the top of his ass, and I pull him forward, urging him on without words.

Henrik takes my cue, pressing inside my body with a barely muffled groan. He's thick and oh so hard, and that sensation of fullness lights me up. But more than that, it's this man I'm with. How one hand travels up my abdomen, landing splayed on my chest like a tether. How the other holds tight to my thigh, not allowing a millimeter of distance between us. How, even in the dark, I can see the look of absolute wonder on his face.

That's what makes this different. What makes Henrik different.

How do you put into words something as abstract as love? How do you define that swirling, chaotic mess of emotions? It's like the canvas above Henrik's fireplace. Beautiful. Terrifying. Unordered. And perfect.

There's no sense in trying to understand it. It's better simply appreciated for what it is.

"Kiss me," I mutter, too caught in sentiment to come up with more eloquent words.

Henrik obliges instantly, leaning forward and slanting our mouths together. His body rolls over mine, inside mine, the glide smooth and slow and shallow. The two of us riding a wave. No hurry, no artifice.

Just simple. Raw. Real.

It's exactly what I need.

"Mal," Henrik breathes out, the one word loaded.

"I know," I say softly.

He nods, kissing me again. And just when I start to relax, to slip into the current of Henrik's lovemaking—because what else could you possibly call this?—he slips one hand down between the tight press of our bodies, bypassing my dick. I'm curious for all of two seconds before I feel the unmistakable pressure of additional thickness stretching my rim.

I gasp out, arching slightly as Henrik's finger slips in alongside his dick. "Henrik."

"Too much?" he asks.

I shake my head rapidly, and then there's more. "*Ohgod.*"

"Good?" he checks.

"Good." I nod, the pressure of two added fingers a blooming ache that spreads throughout my body, cascading and sharp in the best way. Overwhelming. Too much and yet, with Henrik, never enough.

And suddenly, that slow lovemaking is like a tidal wave, rushing me out to sea, unstoppable.

"Gonna come, Hen," I groan.

He makes an unintelligible sound, fucking me a little harder, his free hand cradling the side of my head. I reach down, wrap my hand around my dick, and it's all over.

"Fuck," I gasp out, my body squeezing tight against Henrik's cock and his fingers as I spill between our bodies.

He slips his digits free as my insides milk him and plants his hand on the bed beside my waist. A punched-out groan leaves his chest as he grinds his way home, swelling inside me and finding his own bliss. I don't unwrap my legs even once he stills. I simply pull Henrik to me, reveling in the way he rubs his short stubble against my neck and breathes me in, as if my scent is air.

"I love you, too," I say once I've caught my breath.

Henrik freezes against me.

"I do. I'm not just saying that because your dick is still buried in my ass."

He laughs once, an almost choked sound. "Mal."

"I love you, okay? I knew it before, and it's why I never gave up hope, even though I was stubbornly refusing your calls."

Henrik breathes out, almost a sigh, and then he leans back. I let him go so he can safely secure the condom as he slips from my body, although I immediately mourn the loss. Henrik isn't gone long. He blankets my body once more, the pair of us sticky and naked but not minding one bit.

"I love you so much," he says at last, his voice hoarse. "And I'm so *sorry.*"

"Hen, stop. Please. We've gone round this plenty tonight. We can talk more in the morning. But, for now, I just want you to hold me like you promised, deal?"

"Deal," he says gently. "Can I ask something else?"

"You and your questions tonight," I tease, arranging my body into a more comfortable position under Henrik's bulk.

"The PTSD... Does it have to do with your mother?" he asks, the very question wary.

I let out a deep breath, and Henrik toys with the strands of my hair, stroking and twisting. "Yeah, in a way."

"Will you tell me more about that tomorrow? I'd like to understand."

I nod. "Yeah, I will."

I have a feeling it won't be as hard the second time around, having talked to Delilah so recently about it.

"And..."

"What is it?" I ask.

"Will you tell me about what that means? To have PTSD. What that means for you and how I can..."

"How you can help?" I fill in, understanding where Henrik is going and why he sounds so unsure, afraid he's overstepping.

"Yes. I want to help," he says simply. So sincerely.

"Yeah, Hen. We'll figure it out together, okay?"

He exhales, nodding against my shoulder.

"Now, will you let me go for a moment so I can let in the kittens?" I ask.

Henrik huffs a laugh, loosening his grip.

When I open the bedroom door, the pair of young felines are right there, staring up at me. I laugh as they sprint by, jumping onto Henrik's prone frame as if it's routine.

"Tell me the truth," I say, sliding back over the sheet and moving the little black kitten off Henrik's chest so I can be closer to my man. "Was it really only Little Gray you were sleeping with?"

Henrik sighs. "No. I commandeered the both of them, and we all slept in your bed because we missed you."

My chest clenches.

"And they need names," Henrik goes on. "Because if you think for one second these kittens are going to live anywhere else, you'd be sorely mistaken."

"They're here for the long haul, huh?" I say, my insides swooping and settling into a new order.

"Yes. I've gotten quite attached."

I grin against Henrik's shoulder, planting a kiss there before I say, "So have I."

So have I.

Chapter 32
HENRIK

"I hate this," Mal says, making me chuckle.

"Not a toes-in-the-sand kind of guy?" I respond, skimming my palm over Mal's arm until I find his hand. I interlace our fingers together on top of his beach towel, and Mal gives me a squeeze.

"Not in the least. It's *everywhere*. Pretty sure I have some in my ass crack, which doesn't even make sense. I've been sitting on a towel."

"You went in the water with Alma," I point out as the breeze cools the sweat on my skin. "It probably floated inside your trunks."

Mal scoffs. "Well, it can float right out next time. I'm going to have to wash every-damn-where." He snorts a laugh. "Reminds me of my last scene at Elite 8."

"Oh yeah?"

"Mhm." He twists my hand in his grip, running his fingers over my knuckles gently. "It was a lot like this."

My brows draw in. "Fucking on a beach?"

"Yeah, exactly," he says with a laugh. "I thought I was sealing my fate as Malibu that day, but instead I found you, and everything changed."

I smile at the wistfulness in his tone. "Six months."

It's been *six months* since this man walked into my life. Six wonderful, life-altering months.

"Half a year," Mal adds in agreement. "Just think, if I were still on contract, you'd be done with me right about now."

I scowl. "Cut it out. I don't even want to think about that."

Mal chuckles gently, swinging himself onto my towel and proceeding to rain sand down on my body. He leans close, blocking the sun from my face. "I'm not going anywhere."

"Good," I say, squeezing his hips. His suit is wet beneath my fingertips. "I can't..." I swallow. "I can't imagine you being gone. Six months wouldn't have been nearly enough time."

"And what *would* be enough?" he asks cheekily, leaning close enough that his hair brushes the sides of my face.

"Let's start with a lifetime."

I can practically hear the smile in Mal's voice when he says, "I like the sound of that." His lips press against mine chastely before he sits back, finagling his towel and plopping down right next to me, arm against arm. The sun shines over my face and body once more, hot enough that I'm grateful for the breeze, and the sound of children playing nearby drifts on the wind.

"Is Benjamin relaxing?" I ask.

Mal twists away for a moment before confirming, "Yep. Sitting in a chair next to Gary."

"Good. And my parents?"

"Under the giant umbrella still. Looks like your mom is reading a book. And I think your dad is asleep."

I snort. "Most likely. Alma?"

There's a pause before he answers, "Hm. Not sure. I don't see her at the moment."

I hum, thinking we'll probably need to reapply sunscreen soon if we're out here much longer.

It was my idea, vacationing at the beach for our half-year anniversary. We didn't go to Malibu—the city. Instead, we opted for San Diego. I brought my family along because, well, I'm trying to be better about accepting their well-intentioned presence in my life. I understand my parents a little better than I used to. The protectiveness. The need to *help*.

I didn't appreciate it when I was younger, when all I could see was the inevitable stripping of my independence. I wanted to cling to as much of my sense of self as humanly possible before some changes had to be made to accommodate my declining sight.

Now, I can see my reticence for what it was. And I think, possibly, it was easier to push them away than to let them see me change. It didn't matter in the end. They never cared about all that. They just wanted to be there for me. And now, I'm letting them.

Better late than never, I suppose.

Alma is still giving me shit about Mal. She's the only one to whom I told the truth about how Mal and I met, and, of course, she didn't judge. But she does like to tease me. Never Mal. She's made it perfectly clear that Mal is a precious gem who is never to be picked on. And, well, I appreciate that more than I can say.

Benjamin was glad I pulled my head out of my ass, and he reminds me every week how lucky I am. And how happy he is for me. And the four of us, Benji's husband Gary included, get together every once in a while for dinner. Often at my penthouse with me acting as chef, at Mal's behest. He seems to love my cooking, and I have no problem offering up my services if it makes him happy.

Mal has spent a lot more time at the cat shelter, another thing that makes him happy, and with my continued encouragement, he's been working with Keith on expanding Catty Commotions so they can house more adoptable pets. He has a hard time accepting money and is frugal as ever, but it seems easier for him to acquiesce if he's putting it to use elsewhere. And what better cause than the cats he so loves? He mentioned once that it'd be nice to open up another location, and I'm determined to help him bring that idea to fruition.

As for *our* cats, well...

"How do you think Stella is doing?" I ask. She's getting up in age, but the elderly feline integrated into our little family with ease. And Mal assured me she has plenty of good years left.

Mal huffs a breath from next to me. "Probably ignoring the boys like usual while Alex spoils her with tuna."

I smile. "Sounds about right."

"And L.G. is running amuck, likely batting all your ties off the rack," he says, referring to Little Gray, who has an *official* name now. As does his black-furred brother. "Whereas Clue is sleeping the day away on our bed. On *your* pillow, no doubt, because he loves you more than me."

I chuckle. "That's not true."

"It's definitely true," Mal defends. "That's okay, though. I get L.G. and Stella."

"Whatever makes you happy, Mal," I say with a smile.

"Oh really? So, if there was this cat that—"

"Mal, darling, let's go swimming again. I need to wash off this sand," Alma says, swooping in and unintentionally saving me from adopting another cat. Granted, if Mal wants a fourth cat, I know no convincing will be necessary. The man can have the world as far as I'm concerned.

"Yeah, okay," he says, sitting up, his arm practically peeling off my own in the sticky heat. "You'll be okay here, Hen?"

"Of course. You two go have fun."

Mal gives me a quick peck before heading off into the water with my sister, and not a mere moment later, another presence bears down next to me.

I adjust my sunglasses. "Benjamin."

"So how much longer do we need to spend out here relaxing?" my personal assistant asks.

I shake my head. "Not enjoying yourself on vacation?"

"I know it's been a while since you've seen me, Henrik, but this alabaster complexion does not go well with UV rays. If I'm not careful, I'll *tan*, and all my hard work will be ruined," he laments.

"We can head back to the hotel soon. I'm pretty sure Mal has had enough of the sand," I note.

"It looks like he's enjoying himself, though," Benji points out.

"Yeah?"

"Mhm. He and Alma are both grinning, standing about waist-deep in the water."

A smile tips my lips imagining Mal out in the waves. He may not enjoy the beach, but he'll always remind me of coconut drinks, a fresh breeze, and the gentle rustling of palm fronds. But I think that's more about the feeling he invokes in me than actual association to sand-laden locales.

He's simply...refreshing.

"Ben..." I ask slowly, almost not finishing my thought but powering through at the last moment. "What does he look like?"

"Mal?" Benjamin asks in surprise.

I nod. I've never asked him outright, and although Benji has commented on Mal's appearance from time to time, it wasn't anything I didn't already know. I don't know why I'm asking now, six months into our relationship. It's not like it matters. It never has.

But for some reason—maybe I simply want to add a few more brushstrokes to the image of the man who occupies my mind—I'm desperate to hear what Benjamin might tell me.

"You really want to know?" he asks.

"Please."

Benjamin is quiet for a moment, as if he's studying my boyfriend. "He's...beautiful, Henrik. Breathtaking. His hair is a hundred different shades of gold. His eyes are deep blue like the water, and they're kind and caring. They crinkle at the corners often, even though he doesn't have lines yet, the lucky bastard. His bone structure could land him in a magazine, and he's in his physical prime. Fit and nearly flawless. He's absolutely exquisite."

It's much as I'd imagined, but it's not what I wanted to know. I can't figure out how to explain that to Benji, how to voice what I'm looking for, but his palm against my arm halts my frustrated line of thought.

My friend leans closer, voice soft. "But the way he looks at you? Oh, Henrik," he sighs. "I'd give up every cent of my savings if it meant you could see that look in his eye. The way he lights up when you're in his sights. The naked adoration in his gaze. That boy loves you—I can guarantee it."

My pulse skips frantically. Erratically. Even as that space in my chest that's grown to accommodate my love for Mal fills with warmth.

I have to blink my eyes against the moisture accumulating, and when that doesn't work, I swipe it away. "I know," I say a little raggedly. "I know he loves me."

Benjamin hums. "Well, then. I think you already knew the answer to your question."

I nod. I guess I did.

"And you, old friend, are obsessed," Benji points out needlessly. "You fell head over ass in love when that boy walked into your life."

"Yes," I agree. Something about Mal was always different. I fought it at first, but not for long. I couldn't stay away.

"Who would have thought, huh?" Benji says. "You called for another escort, and instead, you got Mal. Love at first..."

I raise an eyebrow when Benjamin doesn't go on. "You were going to say 'sight,' weren't you?"

He sighs. "Yes, I was."

"It's all right, Ben. I can see you didn't mean it."

"Henrik," he groans.

"No, no, really. It's fine. Out of sight, out of mind."

"Okay, I'm going now. Shout if you need me." He stands up, brushing some sand over me, surely intentionally.

"See you later," I call out, chuckling when I hear his groan.

"Are you harassing your PA?" Mal asks, flopping down onto Benji's vacated spot.

I sit up, needing to switch positions, and Mal rolls until his head is on my thigh. The cool water running out of his hair feels nice against my skin.

"I never harass Benjamin," I reply.

"Mhm. Sure. I think his husband would say otherwise."

I hum. "All washed off?"

"Best as it's going to get before I can shower. Next time, let's go somewhere other than the beach. I really hate it here."

That has me laughing. "It's a deal. Next time, you pick the place."

"And when we get home—" He cuts off when his phone rings, and even though I love Mal's frequent and easy use of the word *home* these days, his silence has me worried.

"What is it?" I ask.

"Great Oak," he replies as the ringing ends. His mom's care facility. "They're going to call again. They always try twice before leaving a message."

"Mal," I say gently, running my thumb over his brow. "Would you let me take care of it?"

It's not the first time I've asked. Mal's continued connection with his mother does nothing but harm him. And I've offered to take over, to take the matter of her palliative care off his hands. But he hasn't been ready yet. And I can understand. That step is a big one. And even though I know Mal longs to be free from her metaphorical grasp, I can't rush him.

But much to my surprise, as soon as Mal's phone starts to ring a second time, he bumps it into my hand. "Please."

"Yes?" I ask, surprised and so very happy.

"Yeah. I'm done. Please take care of it, Hen."

I squeeze Mal's arm, taking the phone with my other hand and swiping up to accept the call. "Hello, this is Henrik Larsen speaking for Mr. Jones. I'd like to talk about removing Mr. Jones as Dorothy's acting agent, changing the point of contact immediately, and adjusting the method of payment on file."

The woman sounds surprised. "Oh. Um. Okay, yes. Mr. Jones will have to revoke his power of attorney and—"

"Yes," I interject, trailing my hand along Mal's arm, feeling the sun-warmed skin below my fingertips. "Adam is fully prepared to sign all necessary documents."

The woman in my ear discusses necessary steps to remove Mal as Dorothy's caretaker—steps I've already researched—but my attention is on the man beside me. The one leaning on me, trusting me.

Is it possible for love to grow? To stretch endlessly like the horizon?

I wouldn't be surprised. I've only fallen more for Mal each day. And now, knowing he's ready to move on? I'm so proud of him. So goddamn proud that he's making the choice to prioritize himself because I know, for Mal, that has never been easy. And I'm beyond honored that Mal is trusting me to take the weight from his shoulders. That he's confident enough in me—in us—to accept my help.

Mal still struggles. Of course he does. His yoga mat sees plenty of use, and he's not completely free from his panic and PTSD. But this, this is big. His mother has been a constant reminder of the pain Mal endured, *still* endures. But now, with that final string being cut, maybe he can find some peace.

I hope so. I would do anything for Mal. Anything to make his life a little brighter. A little easier, even though he's never asked for it. Anything to feel that smile on his face.

I've had a lot of successes in my life, a lot of accomplishments, but I never had someone to share it with.

Yet now...

I trail my hand to Mal's chest, drawing a heart with my fingertip. Along skin, over irrevocably strong spirit. Mal turns his head, and his whispered, "I love you, too," reaches my ears over the wind and the waves.

Now, I have someone I can share *everything* with.

Epilogue
MAL

One Month Later

"I think I'm in love," Alex says, practically swooning into the seat next to me inside Studio 1.

"Wait, really?" I ask. "With a man?"

He snorts, looking at his phone with near-literal heart eyes. "No, with this dick. Do you wanna see?"

"Alex," I groan, shoving my hand in the way before he can shove a dick in my face.

"I'm meeting him later today," he says.

"The dick?" I ask, thoroughly confused. "How?"

Alex's eyebrows wing up, and he tilts his head. "Grindr, boo. Has living with Henrik aged you?"

"Har har," I say with a roll of my eyes.

"Hey, Henrik," Alex calls out. My boyfriend turns his head, focusing his attention Alex's way. "What time is Mal's bridge tournament? I want to make sure my schedule is free."

Henrik purses his lips like he's thinking about it. Most of the time, I appreciate that he and Alex have such an easy, joking camaraderie. But, right now, I'm bemoaning the mind meld.

"Seven?" Henrik answers. "But don't get any big ideas in your head. He needs to be home by nine for bedtime."

Alex cackles next to me, and Henrik smiles, looking pleased with himself.

"Thanks, Daddy Henrik," Alex calls out.

I shove my friend's shoulder. "You're such trouble," I tell him, not for the first time.

"And you love me for it," he retorts. He's not wrong. "You love all of us, I know it. We're going to miss you, Mal."

I nod, looking around the studio here at Elite 8. At all the men—and one woman—gathered for my sendoff. The cast, the crew, the producers, and even some loved ones.

I knew months ago, the moment Henrik showed up here to beg me to come home, that I wouldn't be resuming my role as Malibu. It was never my dream, working here. It fit into my life for a long time, and I'm happy I had the experience. I'm glad to have met these people and that I had a safe place to land for a while. Elite 8 Studios kept me going when times were tough.

But now, I'm ready to move on officially.

I won't be far away, of course. Just a drive. And I have a feeling I'll be back here from time to time to visit. Not to mention, I know I'll see plenty of my boys—my brothers—outside these walls.

But even knowing that, it's bittersweet, putting this part of my life in the rearview. I couldn't be happier with where I'm going, with my life with Henrik, but my past played a part in me getting here. And if nothing else, I'm grateful for that.

"I *am* going to miss you all," I agree wholeheartedly.

"But you're happy," Alex fills in for me, his hazel eyes soft.

"So very happy," I sigh out.

My eyes seek out Henrik in the crowd, and I smile. He's nodding his head along to something Emil is saying.

"You're going to give me a toothache," Alex teases. "You and those moon eyes. And you're not the only one. One by one, my friends are getting picked off."

"And what about you?" I ask, turning back his way. "You used to date, but it's been a while."

Alex shrugs nonchalantly, but there's a sad little glimmer in his eyes. "Yeah, well, I guess I'm more of a realist these days. Happily ever after might not be in my cards."

"Why do you say that?" I ask, nudging him gently. "You have suitors lining up around the block."

Alex huffs. "Suitors... Sure, for a night. Men talk a big game, but no one actually wants a nympho boyfriend."

"Alex," I say softly.

He shakes his head. "No, it's the truth. I know who I am. I know what I *need*. And when it comes down to it, none of the men I've been with want my kind of extra for the long-term. It's *fine*. Don't go all gooey eyes on me, Curls."

I hold up my hands. "Fine, fine," I concede, knowing Alex doesn't want me cajoling him. I nudge him again, though. "Maybe that's the problem. Maybe no *one man* is enough."

Alex titters at that. "Now there's a thought."

"Hey, assholes, we're cutting the cake," Jerome, my former boss, calls out.

Everyone laughs and, as one, the crowd starts to filter into the center of the room, where a buffet table houses said cake.

The thing is massive and, of course, dick-shaped. Jerome holds a knife at the ready, and I wince, nearly reaching for my own junk in sympathy.

"Malibu, anything you'd like to say first?" Jerome asks, as is custom. Anytime someone leaves Elite 8 Studios, they give a goodbye speech. Usually, there's also a cast orgy. But I opted for cake.

I nod, stepping forward. Everyone watches me patiently as I collect my thoughts, and I take a moment to look around the room. At the lights overhead. The collection of props lined up neatly against one wall. The cameras and boom equipment set off to the side. And all the people within, most of whom I've known for years.

These people—they're my family.

"I'm not big on speeches," I say, "but I would like to say a few thank yous. First, to Jerome, for offering me a job here in the first place. That little business card you handed me all those years ago at that tiny diner in Salt Lake City meant more than you could know."

Jerome clears his throat, nodding tightly, and I smile. That's about as sentimental as the man gets.

"To Dix, Adonis, and Tink," I say, using their stage names out of deference to where we met. How we started. "Your friendship kept me afloat. You proved to me I wasn't alone, even when I felt it. Thank you for that. Truly."

Dixon smiles, Niko tips his head, and Alex swipes furiously at his eyes.

"And to everyone else—working with you was a pleasure. Thank you for accepting me with open arms. For always being kind. For giving me such a wonderful goodbye."

There are some smiles and more head nods at that.

"And, uh, I have one more thank you." I look over at the man I love, who's standing beside Dixon now. His arms are held clasped in front of him, and per usual, he's sporting an impeccable suit. A dark, teal-blue today, like the ocean. "Henrik." His eyebrows pop up in surprise. "I know we had an unusual start, but from the moment we met, you made me feel safe. You made me feel seen. Thank you. Thank you for seeing me." Henrik's gaze softens, and I clear my throat, clapping my hands together once. "And that's it. Thanks, everyone."

People call out their well-wishes, but when the noise quiets, before Jerome has a chance to cut the cake, Henrik speaks up. "I'd like to say something, as well, if that's all right."

Jerome raises an eyebrow, mimicking my own surprise, but he waves Henrik on. "By all means."

Henrik nods, and before I know what's happening, Dixon is walking him forward. They stop just a few paces in front of me, and I watch in confusion as Dixon pats Henrik's arm and then backs away. But as soon as Henrik drops to one knee, my eyes shoot wide in understanding. There's a collective gasp at once, and without hesitation, Henrik pulls a ring box from his pocket, holding the black velvet in his palm.

"Mal," he says softly.

"Yeah," I breathe out, my hands starting to shake.

Henrik orients himself to me, that bright green gaze of his making my breath hitch. "Mal, I remember the first time I heard your voice. It was so warm, and it settled over me like a cup of Earl Grey." I choke out a laugh, and Henrik smiles. "Every day that I get to wake up, hear your voice, and feel your hand clasped in mine is the best day of my life. You make me *happy*, Mal. You make me wild and happy."

I wipe the moisture from my eyes as my smile wobbles and shakes.

"I didn't know what I'd been missing until you came along," he says. "With you, I'm never alone. And I don't want to be alone again. Not if it means I'm without you. I have a clue for you. Are you ready?"

I inhale a breath, nodding, even though I'm puzzled. "Yeah, okay."

Henrik tilts his head gently, his gaze soft and open. "A grand proposition. Seven letters."

My breath whooshes out of me. "Marry me," I say, the words practically a sob.

Henrik grins, slow and steady, before popping open the box in his hands. "Would you marry me, Mal?"

I laugh, swiping at my eyes before dropping down in front of Henrik and touching his arm. He grabs a hold of me, his other hand presenting the ring, and I nod furiously. "Of course I'll marry you, Hen. I'm already yours."

He exhales in relief, swiping the ring from within the box and holding it out as the room erupts in applause and a few wolf-whistles. I give Henrik my hand, and he eases the brushed platinum band onto my finger. There's a ribbon of emerald running through the center all the way around, and it glimmers under the lights of Studio 1.

"If you don't like the ring," he says a little shakily, "we can get something else. But you said it's your favorite color."

It is now. It's the color of Henrik's eyes.

"It's perfect, Hen," I say, running my finger over the smooth metal. "I love it. I love *you*."

"I love you, too, Mal," he says vehemently, not letting go of my hand, even though the ring is in place.

"I know," I reply around a laugh. "Fuck, I know."

Suddenly, Alex collides into my side, his arms wrapping around me like a vise. I laugh harder, so damn giddy I could float away.

"Congratulations, boo," he whispers into my ear, shaking me. "You deserve it. Your knight in shining armor."

I huff a laugh, shaking my head as Alex smacks a kiss against my cheek.

I'd wished for that once. A knight to cart me off.

And although, yes, Henrik did sweep me off my feet in a way, falling for him was never about being saved. It wasn't about grand gestures or money or slaying the monsters from my past. It was something—many somethings—more unassuming, more modest, than that.

It's the gentle way he cares for me each and every day. It's how he gets me tea when I'm upset, or holds me close when the panic attacks threaten to overwhelm me. It's supporting me through the little wins and all the days that feel like losses, and how he lets me do the same for him.

I don't bother correcting Alex, but Henrik's not my knight. He's something better.

Because he's real.

It takes what feels like a lifetime for my party to wrap up. I field a million congratulations, pats on the back, and kind words. The cake is cut and passed around. And before I go, I make sure to embrace each and every person who helped me along in my journey.

It's nearly midnight by the time Henrik and I walk toward the exit of Elite 8 Studios, hand in hand. I pause one last time in the entrance hall, facing the sign that welcomed me so many years ago. The large neon letters run nearly floor to ceiling, yellow and bright, and I trace the curve of the number eight, offering a final farewell. Saying goodbye. To this place.

To Malibu.

Knowing I'm well and truly ready to leave parts of my past behind.

Henrik squeezes my hand, his grip comforting and warm. "Ready, fiancé?"

Turning, I take a deep breath, catching a whiff of cranberry and leaves.

"Yeah," I reply, my heart full, my steps light. "Let's go home."

The End

About the Author

Information about Emmy Sanders and her complete list of works can be found on her website. Subscribe to her newsletter, join her Facebook reader group, Emmy's Enclave, and connect via email or social media:

www.emmysanders.com

Find online:
www.facebook.com/emmysandersmm
www.instagram.com/emmysandersmm

www.ingramcontent.com/pod-product-compliance
Lightning Source LLC
Chambersburg PA
CBHW070611300726
48975CB00006B/1781